Advance Praise for Second Acts

•

"Tim W. Brown has created an absolutely fascinating — and truly American — character with Listening Rabbit, the transvestite ("two-spirit") healer and guide. *Second Acts* draws equally upon history and imagining, and the result is a brilliant book that Mark Twain might've written had he shared a brain with Jack Finney for a while." — Sharon Mesmer, author of *In Ordinary Time* and *The Virgin Formica*

•

"Half-magical, half-farcical, *Second Acts* is full of vitality and humor, a modern update of Mark Twain's Connecticut Yankee in *King Arthur's Court*. A sly commentary upon the American past and present, *Second Acts* is also a ribald trip through the nineteenth-century frontier, told by modern-day Americans who take back with them not only their technological apparatus, their know-how and their weak morals, but also enough money to pave their streets with gold. It is a view of an America in which Chicago is named not for stinking onions but for hemp, in which New York's water supply is saved by a transvestite Native American's assault upon speculator Jay Gould, and in which a married couple re-ignites their love by traveling 175 years into the past. *Second Acts* is a sparkling gem of a book, one that inspires both contemplation and more than a few belly laughs."–Greg Downs, author of *Spit Baths*(2006 Flannery O'Connor Award winner)

•

"Really clicking, *Second Acts*, is a picaresque, sci-fi/western, such as Verne or Welles might have penned it, but with tongue planted firmly in cheek. Tim W. Brown's tale of a husband's search for his fugitive wife takes readers on a whirlwind tour of America, circa 1830. In subverting history Brown's tale celebrates it, with a scholar's eye for authentic details and at a pacing so swift the pages give off a nice breeze."–Peter Selgin, author of *Life Goes to the Movies* and *Drowning Lessons* (2008 Flannery O'Connor Award winner)

•

"With *Second Acts* Tim W. Brown may well have written his masterpiece. In this surprising, satisfying novel, he channels Twain, both by updating *A Connecticut Yankee in King Arthur's Court* and through *Bunny*, Brown's most vivid character to date and an homage to Jim in *Huckleberry Finn* – and yet the end result is not at all derivative, but unexpectedly personal and unique. Brown's clever construction, arch humor and unforgiving candor are on hand as ever, but they're leavened this time by a goodly dose of heart, as he steers the protagonist and two other likable characters toward a *renaissance* of their own. Funny, engaging, relatable and even educational, it's a great read."–Paul McComas, author of *Planet of the Dates* and *Unplugged*

Second Acts

By Tim W. Brown

5/3/11

To Bill & Laura:

All, too, second acts in American lives!

—Tim Br

Arlington, Virginia

Published by Gival Press, an imprint of Gival Press, LLC.
For information please write:
Gival Press, LLC, P. O. Box 3812, Arlington, VA 22203.
Website: www.givalpress.com
Email: givalpress@yahoo.com
First edition ISBN-13: 978-1-928589-51-8
Library of Congress Control Number: 2010933400
Format and design by Ken Schellenberg.
Artwork for bookcover by Photolibrary.
Photo of Tim W. Brown by Liz Keifer.

Chapter One

It was a typical spring day in the metropolis of Chicago — that is to say, forty-four degrees and raining — when I arrived home from work on April 25, 2015. The tiny apartment was empty, unusual for six-thirty in the evening, when my wife, Rachel, having gotten home from her job minutes before, would normally be heating food in the microwave oven (a miraculous invention that cooks meals in mere seconds without fire). I concluded that Rachel had to work late again. The Physics Department at the University of Chicago was closing in on a breakthrough discovery, the details of which she wouldn't divulge, and her duties as Department Secretary had no doubt detained her.

Instead of skinless chicken and rice pilaf or lean beef and new potatoes, a note written in her typical, purple ink greeted me on the dining room table. My response after reading it, uttered aloud to no one save myself — but infused with strong feeling nevertheless for reasons the reader shall soon see — summed up a predicament I had not foreseen:

"My wife goddamn left me!"

I re-read the note and let the news sink in. I wadded up the paper into a tight ball and threw it into the trash can.

"My goddamn wife left me!" I shouted. That quickly, my mind leaped from the adverbial to the adjectival.

The sentiment of damning one's wife deepened as the night wore on and the circumstances of her leave-taking tossed me in their wake. First, I telephoned Rachel's parents to learn if they had any news regarding their daughter's abrupt departure (in 2015 all persons had telephones), for her note did not spell out any reasons. I was certain that they knew why she had done this to me, because, maddeningly, Rachel discussed every aspect of our marriage with them, ranging from the financial to the reproductive.

A recorded message advised me that they were unavailable and messages were being taken at a telephone number in the 868 area code, which I recognized as that of the Caribbean island they frequented, which experienced unreliable telephone service. I knew better than to try to reach them there.

Next, I attempted to phone my father in San Diego, California, with whom I did not speak very often — he had his sailboat and a new wife to occupy him — to report this major disturbance in my life back in Chicago. He, likewise, was not at home to take my call. I settled for keeping myself company. I opened the first of many bottles of beer I would drink that night and turned on the television (a device similar to a stereoscope but with moving pictures). Upon tuning into the news channel (the television equivalent of a daily newspaper), I quickly found out to where Rachel had disappeared.

The calm face appearing on the television screen announced that a physics professor at the University of Chicago, Bruce Bilson, plus Rachel Levy — please note the use of her maiden name — had successfully traveled into the past.

A spokeswoman for the University explained that Bilson had solved the right equation and perfected the necessary technology for time travel. Scientists were hailing his accomplishment as larger than when Americans landed on the moon in 1969. The storyline that emerged depicted Bilson as a hero on par with Christopher Columbus. Rachel was portrayed as the second incarnation of Eve. Bilson's associate, Barry Stompke, was also considered important in that he possessed the secret of time travel, but news coverage placed him in a supporting role under Bilson, the primary hero in the yet-unfolding scientific drama.

Planning to speak with Stompke, I set out for the University of Chicago, taking a series of omnibuses from the North Side of the city to the South Side, where the campus is located. I had to know the details of Rachel's leave-taking and to be assured that she was all right, and not the victim of bad science, a murderous plot, or some publicity hoax, because I was having trouble believing the whole time-travel phenomenon.

It was a scene of pandemonium at the Physics Department offices in the cluster of buildings on Ellis Avenue comprising the school's Research Institutes. Hundreds of students, journalists, and curiosity seekers clamored underneath umbrellas outside the plain limestone edifice for additional information about the momentous event. I knew that I would have trouble obtaining entrance, despite faculty and staff members' familiarity with my face as Rachel's spouse. On any other day I could have waltzed right in, despite the presence of sensitive military and civilian secrets. But not today.

I was aware of an alternative way into the inner sanctum of the Department where I might possibly encounter Stompke. Given his issues with hyperactive eye-blinking, I doubted I would find him amidst the crowd. From what I remembered of him, he was extremely self-conscious about this tic and enormously reluctant to engage the public. I left the mob behind me and entered the building to the south across 57th Street. Here I anticipated finding Stompke, in either a classroom or a laboratory.

I passed through the glass doors without incident. I peeked inside every unlocked room and found each one empty, despite the proximity of final examinations in two weeks, when one would expect the lecturing, tutoring, and experimenting to be at their most intense. Apparently, everyone was out celebrating the Department's triumph, either across the way at the Physics Office or at one of the surrounding neighborhood's watering holes.

After I had searched all four floors, I prepared to admit defeat, abandon my hunt, and try to push through the throng back at the Research Institutes.

But lo, whom did I hear but a group of physicists and graduate students squirreled away holding an intimate party in a break room on the top floor. I entered the tiny room, in the process stepping on several feet and toes. Bottles of champagne cooled in ice cubes piled high in the sink. The persons surrounding me drank the bubbly beverage out of glass beakers. Everyone was chattering nervously; nobody seemed at all bothered by my presence. I pushed my way through the gathering, peering into faces until, along the back wall, I found the one I sought. Looking positively aphasic, Stompke sat on a counter hugging his knees. Beside him an empty beaker was turned on its side and threatened to roll off the counter.

I hated to interrupt Stompke's drunken reverie; in his near-catatonic state his eyes, relaxed for once, blinked at appropriate intervals with normal force. I expected my presence to fluster him, and I had little doubt that his uncontrolled blinking would re-commence when I addressed him.

"We need to talk," I said, enunciating each syllable as calmly as I could.

His blurry eyes gradually focused on the agitated individual confronting him, and, sure enough, his eyelids mashed together three or four times, signaling his unwelcome return to sobriety and the resumption of the involuntary reflex that plagued him. Trapped and resigned to his fate, Stompke motioned me to follow him to discuss my grievances against him and the University's Physics Department in private. We trod between the oblivious celebrants, headed down the hall, and entered a closet that smelled strongly of ammonia, alcohol, and Stompke's fear. Prefatory to speaking, he blinked violently several times, Morse code for how uncomfortable he felt.

"I know why you're here. You're Rachel's husband. She said you might pay me a visit."

"So were you the one that flipped the switch that sent my wife packing to the past?"

"In a manner of speaking. It involves a lot more intelligence to send somebody into the past than the ability to flip a switch." Stompke couldn't resist inserting a University of Chicago reference into our conversation. All people connected to the school did it, even Rachel. They could not go more than two minutes without reminding you of their brilliance and the implication that mortals of ordinary intellect couldn't possibly understand their lofty thought processes. It was a nervy tact to take with a husband angry at you for your co-starring role in his wife's disappearance.

"I came looking for you after hearing your name on TV. You're second-in-command around here, right? Under Bilson?"

"First-in-command presently. Bilson's gone to the past." He smiled smugly.

"Can you bring them back, Mr. First-In-Command?"

"It's a one-way trip, I'm afraid. You can't come back from 1833 because the technology won't have been invented yet."

"That's where they went, 1833?"

"Actually, 'when' is more the operative word. As for 'where,' we estimate they're within two degrees of the spot they launched from."

"Why 1833?"

"Today's technology can only get you back so far in time. The accelerator as configured at present produces only enough energy to go back about a hundred and seventy-five years. That number will increase as the technology evolves." He referred to a high-powered machine used to study atoms and molecules.

"Are you sure she made it? Is Rachel safe?"

"We didn't find any burned carcasses in the accelerator like we did cats in our early experiments."

I grabbed hold of his shirt collar and glared into his eyes, which started blinking so fiercely that his head lurched each time. "I mean it! You've got to tell me. Is she all right?"

"I'd say at T-plus-seven hours (seven hours after their departure, that is) they're in what is now the western suburbs of Chicago, looking for a place to sleep."

Looking for a place to sleep *together*, she and Bilson. I hadn't yet pondered that wrinkle. I let go of Stompke.

"In effect, you've made my wife disappear. She's dead to me and her family."

"Dead? No. In a new time thread? Possibly." He blinked seven or eight times with much less force, almost nonchalantly. "Rachel may have left you ignorant of her intentions, but she consulted extensively with her parents about the experiment. She had their complete support."

Probably to flatter their own vanity rather than out of any concern over their daughter, I thought. At the country club they could now boast to their tennis partners and golf foursomes about birthing the first woman to travel in time, which would trump other members' heart-surgeon and investment-banker offspring.

A ball of emotions turned inside my stomach as if wrapped on a spit — love, hate, jealousy, resentment, guilt, insult, injury, sadness, and hurt roasted together, basting in my stomach juices. I had to act in order to put an end to this cooking, which threatened to burn down the whole bleeding house.

"Send me back in time, too. Let's go, right now, tonight."

Stompke smirked. "I'm afraid that's not possible. There are preparations to make that take at least a day. A lot of calculations need to be made based on your body mass, the weight of your cargo, variables like that. Besides, I'm not in any condition to drive fifty miles to Fermilab, let alone operate the accelerator."

"Tomorrow then. You get your act together, I'll get mine together..."

"Impossible. You're not an authorized user. There are permissions to get. A committee made up of University and Government people is supposed to approve any passengers."

"You owe me. You're the one that flipped the switch that sent my wife into the past. That's worth a lawsuit at the very least. At worst ... you don't want to see what I'll do in the worst-case scenario."

This time Stompke did not correct my choice of words. Between eye blinks he studied me to evaluate my potential to do him harm. In an effort to enhance the threat I posed, I took a step forward and stared at him like a lion contemplating lunch. Incapable of prevailing in a stare-down with me, he capitulated — whether owing to fear of my kicks and punches or pity for my plight it was not yet clear, nor ultimately did it matter.

"Okay, okay. I'll try to do something. Meet me in my office tomorrow morning at ten o'clock. That should give me sufficient time to recover from my hangover."

"I appreciate it."

"I hope you do. I'm already supposed to fill out a mountain of paperwork for the Nuclear Regulatory Commission, the Environmental Protection Agency, the Pentagon, and every other Government entity. Now I'll have to spend extra time explaining you."

"A small price to pay for the fame you're about to enjoy."

Stompke's eyes stopped blinking for a moment, allowing him to contemplate his imminent celebrity. The blinking returned as he recovered from his daydream and considered the risks and responsibilities of the present moment.

"You're about to become famous, too. Unless you have second thoughts and decide not to go. Believe me, I would totally understand."

"I won't chicken out. Don't you."

Thus, for a host of conflicting reasons, from salvaging my honor to seeking vengeance, I would defy common sense, contrary advice, and science as it was taught up until then to attempt to win back my wife.

Later, at home, I still could not reach my father to inform him of my decision. There was no need to contact my mother, who had died of breast cancer when I was nineteen. I decided to write a long letter to him, laying out my reasons and apologizing for exiting this world so abruptly. I also expressed my regret for the journalistic hordes he should expect to be camped out on his lawn, which I knew he cared for so lovingly, awaiting the scoop on his son, the second man ever to travel through time. I signed it "Your son, Dan," and I sealed it in an envelope, which I addressed, stamped, and dropped in a mailbox on the morrow.

Into the wee hours of morning, I thought hard about Rachel and where we had gone wrong. Her separation from me could easily have been predicted the night we met, in a bar, where we had run into each other during a musical performance by a Jamaican sextet, for we were as opposite as people could be. She was Jewish, I was not. She had attended Northwestern University, I had gone to Northeastern Illinois University, a vastly inferior school. Her life revolved around shopping and calling on friends; my life revolved around tinkering with computers (inventions resembling typewriters that perform rapid math calculations). Her parents lived nearby and were constantly present; my surviving parent lived in California and was uninvolved in our lives.

However, there was one thing that we both had in common: we were addicted to adrenaline rushing through our circulatory systems.

Exerting ourselves in the marriage bed raised our pulse, respiration, and hormones generally, not exclusively adrenaline, though that was also in much abundance during our interludes. Rachel is a supremely gifted practitioner of the sensual arts — she is frank in expressing her desires and fluent when seeing to their execution. Moreover, she has the loveliest female parts I have ever seen in person or in drawings and photographs. Perfectly symmetrical, as if chiseled by Michelangelo or Leonardo, Rachel's womanhood should be on exhibit in a museum, where its transcendent beauty would inspire all who gazed upon it to weep with joy. Laying claim to it again was reason enough to follow Rachel into the past.

We each also craved in addition to sex the speeding heartbeat and heightened awareness produced by cocaine (powdered coca leaf inhaled like snuff). But we discovered, too late — for it took our trips to the past to confirm the lesson — that living and striving merely to raise our adrenaline levels, no matter how enjoyably the time was spent, was not a sufficient foundation for a successful marriage. There must also be a community of shared interests. After spending a few harmonious years together, we reached our late twenties, laboring in underpaid and undervalued jobs, and we began to diverge from our pleasure-seeking path in life, which did not suit us anymore. Indeed, we largely gave it up — although I suspect Rachel continued to sniff cocaine in secret, I had not consumed the seductive crystalline powder since 2011. We also made love far less often, for even this activity had become habitual and therefore tiresome.

Yet while I was mired in a go-nowhere network administrator job connecting wires between computers, Rachel's job had begun looking up. The recent top-secret project demanding so much of her time of late took her to Canada, England,

and Switzerland. Somewhere during this interval, she locked onto Bilson, and he responded in kind by inserting his key into her latch. I'll admit that my eyes roved, too, as I gazed upon strange women on the elevated train or smelled the hair of a female colleague as we huddled over a broken computer device. The difference being Rachel had acted on her impulses, regaining that adrenaline charge she craved, while I labored away suffering adrenaline withdrawal and alienated from just about everyone and everything.

The next morning I switched on the television. Media coverage of the event continued, only now, as the news had sunk in, discussion drilled down to the level of Bilson's family, Rachel's parents, and, unhappily, me. My honor and Rachel's reputation became the sport of monologuing television talk show hosts and bloviating newspaper pundits. Two hosts of a morning program that took a lighthearted tone toward the news said this:

"How 'bout that guy whose wife not only left him for another man, but she ran away to the past, too?"

"Whoa! Things look pretty bleak in his bed at present!" (If he only knew how keenly I felt Rachel's sudden conjugal absence!)

"Ha ha ha! I hear she didn't even divorce him first! Just up and left him yesterday while he was at work!"

"Poor guy! Imagine what's going through his head this morning!"

"Rejection City!"

I fervently hoped during the course of the day to keep contacts with the mass media, most especially with dunces like these two gentleman, at a minimum. I did not relish the thought of my name being spread and my face publicized across the nation. In the modern world the fourth estate firmly believed that its manifest destiny lay in embarrassing hapless folks like me from coast to coast. Plus I worried that I might be tricked by a clever reporter into revealing my plan to fly the temporal coop. Once I was gone they would have my explicit permission to ransack my life's record. But on the eve of my departure I wanted no one to step in and try to dissuade me from my intent.

When I entered his office, Stompke was looking out the window at a gargoyle jutting from the building across the street. "I've made an appointment for you with an M.D. friend at the U. of C. Medical Center," he said, continuing to face the window. I had rather gotten used to Stompke's blinking; not looking at me was a fresh barrier he had thrown into our conversation. "He will give you a stress test, test your blood, and give you a battery of shots against diseases like tetanus, small pox, and tuberculosis. Your appointment is in about fifteen minutes. If you leave now, you should just about make it. Come back when you're through, and I'll instruct you further in what we have to do."

"This doctor, he's a real doctor, not a med student?"

"Oh, he's a real doctor. He's pledged to keep your visit confidential."

Wondering what sort of pledge this doctor had taken, I walked across campus to the Health Sciences building, where I found Dr. Brnjzrk waiting, stiffly saluting me with dripping hypodermic needle raised. His formal posture, taciturn demeanor, and Eastern European accent lent him the air of a mysterious Austro-Hungarian spy. Very efficiently he dispatched me, inoculating me in the shoulder, bicep, and buttocks. I imagined his steely blue eyes above his high Slavic cheekbones just as easily overseeing my execution by poison or political torture.

Back at the Research Institutes Stompke waved me into his office, whereupon we discussed the next phase of the day's pre-launch activities. "How much cash can you put your hands on today?" he bluntly asked. "You need to convert it to gold. In 1833 gold's the only legal tender merchants will accept from a stranger like yourself."

"How much do I need?"

"Even if you have only a couple of thousand dollars saved, it can add up to tens of thousands in 1833 money. This is the only government project in history where less money invested actually buys you more. Inflation is a good thing as far as this project is concerned. We're reversing a lot of things with this project, not just time."

"How much did Rachel take with her?" If the amount approximated what I knew was deposited in our bank accounts, then I was in trouble. I hoped that Rachel wasn't so malicious as to leave her husband bereft and clean out his bank account, too.

"Bilson and Rachel between them took about a half-million in 1833 dollars. Her parents put up her portion. With a measly few thousand in gold, you'll never have to work a single day of your life in your new century. Remember those gentlemen planters like Washington and Jefferson? That's how you'll be — a man of leisure."

"With plenty of time on my hands to search for Bilson and Rachel."

"Indubitably. Now go to your bank and empty your checking and/or savings account. Take the cash to the Bank of South Africa NV and change your cash into Krugerrands."

"Krugerrands?"

"It's a type of gold coin issued by South Africa...."

"I know what Krugerrands are. How can I spend Krugerrands in 1833?"

"There weren't the same monetary standards at the time. Everybody used Spanish or English or locally minted coins. Stores and banks will see that your coins are solid gold. They'll take your gold any day over all the other miscellaneous coins that are in circulation."

"You've got every angle figured out haven't you?" My mind boggled over the width and breadth of the conspiracy that had sent my wife to the past.

"We've done it twice already. Look, we just want to make your journey safe and life in your new century as comfortable as possible. Bilson got advice on this project from historians and anthropologists on how to best survive in the primitive conditions of the early 1800s. It boils down to three things: protection against disease, spending money, and clean water. Now go."

I rode the Illinois Central electric train downtown, where my bank was located. Rafael, the young teller, informed me that I had nearly thirteen thousand dollars at my disposal, thanks to the timely automatic deposit of both Rachel's and my paychecks at midnight. I instructed Rafael to withdraw all the money and cut a check made out to the order of "Bank of South Africa NV." He seemed genuinely disappointed that I was closing my account, as if the bank had somehow failed me in its mission. I thanked him for his concern and walked my check down La Salle Street to the Bank of South Africa.

Here I presented my check to the officer in charge, a humorless middle-aged man with a boxy suit and square head, and I requested my Krugerrands. My request occasioned all sorts of whispering in the Afrikaans language among this individual, security personnel, and two vice presidents. Finally, after much chattering and nodding and shaking of heads, he asked me to wait while my gold was gathered together. A half-hour later I was summoned into a conference room where a satchel lay on a conference table. It veritably bulged with the gold equivalent of my life's savings.

"You're certain, sir, that you wish to leave the bank with this amount of specie?"

"Yes, thanks, that's all I'll be needing."

"Cash would be more easily concealed. And lighter. There are almost four kilograms of gold here. I strongly recommend..."

Seeing their point I said, "Tell you what. I'll run down the street to Macy's and get a shopping bag. I'll be right back." And so I did: I jogged to the department store and retrieved a paper bag from the coin-operated machine by the door, and I returned to the Bank of South Africa. I informed my hosts that I intended to minimize my contact with the public by taking a taxi instead of a train back to Hyde Park, and they needn't worry about my safety.

I returned a third time to Stompke's office toting eight pounds of gold coins. I arrived around lunchtime and found Stompke feasting on chocolate-covered peanuts, which he washed down with big gulps of Diet Coke (a fizzy, cola nut-flavored drink popular among the weight-conscious).

"How much money do we have to work with?" asked Stompke.

"That's a rather personal question," I replied.

"Nothing personal. I have a conversion chart here." He burrowed under a stack of papers to locate the magic document. "If you allow me to look it up, I can tell you about how much you should expect when you deposit it in a bank.

Speaking of banks, make sure you deal with state or federally chartered banks. Apparently there were a lot of fly-by-night operations in 1833."

"Thirteen thousand dollars."

Stompke stared between blinks at his conversion chart. "Three hundred thousand. Not bad. That'll give you ample purchasing power. Provided you reach civilization before a bear eats you or an Indian scalps you, you'll be set for life."

"Really?" I was beginning to like what I was hearing.

"Do you have a retirement plan? A 401K plan? With more notice we could've cashed those in like Bilson did and added to your total."

It increasingly struck me how premeditated Bilson and Rachel's disappearing act was. I felt foolish over how I had missed the telltale signs of their impending perfidy. There must have been some warnings regarding her love affair with Bilson, cannon shots fired across my bow, but I was too obtuse to recognize them. "Why Rachel?" I demanded to know.

"Because she was, um, convenient?" His voice raised an octave in pitch on this last word, still nervous perhaps that I could yet lash out and belt him. I encouraged the reaction by rising up and shouting, "What?"

"The project team..."

"I.e., you and Bilson."

"The project team decided it would be good to include a female on the mission. It was politically correct, plus it would be advantageous to send a helpmate with Bilson. It was really quite logical: Rachel worked in the department, she and Bilson were, uh, having an affair, so off they went."

"Into the wild blue yonder, I know. Did the project team take into account that I might have something to say about the whole plan?"

"That was supposed to be handled between Rachel and you."

"Well, she never brought up the subject, and now here I am."

"Our statistician pegged the odds at four to five that you'd show up. However, nobody foresaw you as a time pilot. That's our little name here for time travelers like yourself."

"My motivations for taking this trip ought to be clear. Why did *you* agree to sign onto this cockamamie plan?"

"It does two things, one bad and one good. On the bad side, you're an unauthorized user of the technology, and if I send you into the past, it means I'm likely subject to prosecution under a bunch of acts, laws, and statutes in a multitude of jurisdictions. On the good side of things, I'll be untouchable. I'll have accomplished time travel on my own. I'll have shaken off Bilson's influence. I'll be my own man and a free agent. I can transfer to Stanford or MIT — and get a properly endowed physics chair."

"You keep using the word 'technology' like 'time travel technology.' There's a time machine, right?"

"We don't call it that. It trivializes what we do. There's no Dr. Who phone booth or H.G. Wells plumbing project. It's more a process than a single piece of machinery."

"Just how does one travel through time?"

"You know Fermilab, out in Batavia? We use a combination of high energy levels and powerful electromagnets that open a wormhole, which, in essence, is a miniature black hole. You and your capsule will pass through the wormhole to the year 1833 in what will seem to you a trip of short duration."

When I flashed him a dumb, uncomprehending look, Stompke stood up and erased a collection of mathematical formulae scrawled on a blackboard. He drew a circle. Then he drew a straight line from one side of the circle to another. "This circle represents curved space-time. This straight line represents the path you will take through a wormhole. Notice the shortcut. It was really a simple engineering problem once the theoretical hurdles were surmounted."

"Can you go forward in time, too? What if I blew off my plan to re-take my wife and shot instead into the future?" The prospect tantalized.

"Theoretically, yes. But we felt more confident about solving the issues going into the past, which has already happened. It allows us to train and prepare for what we know as opposed to what we don't know.

"One concern I do have that we haven't talked about yet: you haven't undergone the proper training. Do you have any survival skills?"

"You mean like eating bugs and berries and stuff?"

"Er, yes. The landing zone is in the middle of frontier territory. Where Fermilab stands today, only a few scattered white families lived in 1833." Stompke directed my attention to an Illinois map pinned to the back of his office door. He referred me to a thick blue line connecting Batavia, Illinois, to downtown Chicago. "This is roughly the route you must take."

"And how do I get there?" I imagined a kindly settler in a straw hat, carrying a rifle and smoking a pipe, to serve as my guide.

Stompke let out peals of laughter, quickly dashed by his infernal blinking. "You walk there, naturally. Do you know how to use a compass? Can you ford a stream?"

"I was in the Boy Scouts. I used to go camping when I was in college."

"That's good experience to have. Bilson and Rachel both had no experience with camping, so we held training retreats out in Starved Rock State Park. They learned how to pitch a tent, navigate by compass, rappel."

Retreats. Rachel had gone on these two or three times earlier in the spring. She said the University required her to go in order to build confidence and become a better communicator. They were supposed to have played games where they conquered their fears by climbing a rope upside down across a river. Instead, they were playing games of an entirely different sort.

"I have a tent still. And a compass."

"No need. I've packed your gear — tent, dehydrated food, canteen, all very high-tech in a super lightweight roll that weighs only twelve kilograms. Your best bet," he said, turning to the map, "is to contact civilization here," pointing to Chicago. "Bilson planned to take a boat from Chicago to Buffalo and set up shop in western New York. It's where our anthropologists claimed he'd find the most opportunity and the fewest questions asked. You're advised to follow their trail. But beware. Transportation will be spotty. You may have to wait long periods between boats and stagecoaches. Do you know how to paddle a canoe?"

"I got a canoeing merit badge in Boy Scouts."

"Good. For this mission practical skills are better to have than intellectual skills." I felt a little stung by the University of Chicago reference, then I realized, "I am going into the past and you are not. So, yes, practical knowledge *is* better than intellectual knowledge, you pompous ass!"

"Oops! It's only about four hours until your departure," he said, consulting the watch worn on the underside of his wrist. Stompke informed me that it was time to drive to Fermilab. He grabbed a knapsack, and we exited the building. When we crossed Ellis Avenue, a sidelong glance at the downtown Chicago skyline swinging into view alerted me to the fact that it would be the last time I would have the opportunity to gaze upon this impressive sight. We climbed into and took off in a brown University-owned automobile (horseless carriage), heading toward the far western suburbs of Chicago. As we reached cruising speed on the East-West Tollway, I asked, "Does anybody else know you're sending me back in time?"

Smiling mischievously, Stompke answered my question without speaking a word. Then his smile was shattered by a torrent of eye blinks. When his eyelids settled down, he said, "You know, between you and me, I wouldn't be too broken up if you caught up with Bilson and became a major inconvenience in his life."

"Why is that? He left you in charge of things. You're here to reap what he sowed."

"WE sowed," he yelled. "Bilson may have directed the project, but I did about ninety-nine percent of the actual work — the calculations and formulas, plus the hardware, which I put into place with my own hands. Bilson stole credit for the project — it's more glamorous to ride in the spaceship than work behind the scenes. Everybody remembers the names of the astronauts — Alan Shepherd, John Glenn, Neil Armstrong, Buzz Aldrin, Jim Lovell, even Sally Ride. But nobody remembers the nerds sitting behind the computer screens at the Houston control center."

(Stompke referred here to the era of outer-space flight, which began in the 1950s, when rockets similar to Chinese fireworks carried men and women as far away as the moon, only these rockets did not explode at their apex, at least not often. A "nerd" was a socially maladjusted individual.)

I got to thinking about how fate had dealt me a hand similar to Stompke's. I would be famous for fifteen minutes, yes, but how many people in the long haul would remember the second man to travel through time? Everybody will remember Bilson, the first, and Rachel, the first woman. Everybody in 2015 knows that Neil Armstrong and Edwin "Buzz" Aldrin were the first men to land on the moon. Does anybody recall the names of the astronauts who made the second manned flight to the moon?

"Oh, I intend to give him grief," I declared, refocusing on the topic at hand.

"There isn't some enemy of yours who's going to show up and want to follow you back in time seeking revenge on *you*, I hope."

"Nope, there shouldn't be. I've got a clean conscience."

"Good. That's a success factor. We scientists try to remain morally neutral, but with you hot on their trail, I'm happy, at least in regards to Bilson, that they're in store for some real problems."

"It sounds like you're a believer in karma. That's not a very scientific attitude."

"What goes around comes around. Matter is neither created nor destroyed. For every action there is an equal and opposite reaction." Yes, Stompke was a hopeless geek with a weight problem and a severe blinking condition. But he and I were closer in type than I wanted to think. We were both in our thirties under the thumbs of managers a little older than we, who daily reminded us of our inferior places in the world. Through our brief relationship together we would finally become our own men.

After an hour's drive on the toll road, we entered the grounds surrounding Fermilab. We passed an incongruous sight: a herd of bison grazing above the twenty-some-mile particle accelerator underground, as if to foreshadow what I could expect to see on my journey.

"The equivalent of the miner's canary. It's supposed to symbolize that wildlife and nuclear energy can peacefully co-exist," commented Stompke, anticipating my question as to why there were bison here. Nuclear energy, based on the agitation of atoms, was a potentially explosive proposition in 2015, like steamship boilers were before they had been perfected.

We entered a tall concrete building and were ushered straight through the main security checkpoint owing to Stompke's position as Project Director — inherited or not, he clearly was in charge and made everyone we met snap to attention. We rode an elevator many levels below ground, exiting into a vast man-made cavern filled to bursting with giant machinery. There were derricks, storage tanks, pipes, valves, levers, switches, dials, cables, pulleys, and generators manufacturing every kind of power — kinetic, steam, vacuum, magnetic, electric, and nuclear. The air crackled and hummed. A curious smell of sterile hospital blended with dank basement invaded the nostrils.

"We're going to be using the straight accelerator tonight," said Stompke to the driver of a golf cart (a buggy that lazy modern golfers ride on between swings). We rode some distance through a tunnel to another vast room containing a fifty-yard-long metal tube of such wide diameter that I could stand inside it. Lining the interior were magnets, Stompke explained, that directed unbelievably strong magnetic fields inside the tube. The electromagnetic forces were so strong that a miniature black hole was pried open, just enough to let a long cylindrical object pass through it. Whatever entered the black hole exited the other side at another point in space-time. In my case this would be the future site of Fermilab on or about July 12 in the year 1833.

At one end of the tube was erected a platform on top of which lay a kayak-shaped capsule. About nine feet long, it was made of fiberglass (a twenty-first-century construction material popular for making small boats).

"There's your portal to the past," said Stompke, pointing to the immense contraption. "How far you move down the track determines how far back in time you go. For 1833 you go about six feet inside, find that rip in space-time, then CHOOM! You're gone."

"You said that there wasn't a time machine. There were processes."

"And so there are. You might as well say the whole universe is a time machine."

I had no idea what he was talking about; I had simply to trust that he knew what he was doing.

"From here on out, we're going to have to operate very discreetly. Nobody is expecting me to send anyone back tonight. Here, take this," he said, handing me his knapsack to juggle with my bag of gold. "That's your tent, food, and sleeping bag. A compass is inside this zipper pocket. Here," he pointed, "hang out inside this room. It's Bilson's old office. There's a refrigerator" — an electrified ice box — "next to the desk. I don't advise eating any food, but you could have a soft drink or something." He opened the door into and flipped on the lights inside a modestly furnished office with a steel desk and blackboards covered in physics formulae, ubiquitous among this crowd. "I'm going into the control room to perform a few final calculations, and then we should be set. Stay out of trouble for, like, fifteen minutes. I'll be back."

I reached straight for the refrigerator door handle, pulled, and looked inside at its chilly contents. I found a bottle of beer, opened it, and guzzled about half. Regardless of how addicted I was to adrenaline, a little too much was pouring into my bloodstream right then, making me intensely nervous and afraid, similar, I'm speculating, to the condemned man awaiting execution. I wondered, "What if Stompke wishes to rid himself of me, his main problem in life at present, by going the expedient route of incinerating me rather than engaging in the harder task of sending me back in time?" Moreover, even without any malign intent on Stompke's part, the almost ritualistic attention paid to the details of my departure indicated a real possibility that something could go horribly wrong with the largely unproven technology.

"Are you sure you're ready for this? You're white as a ghost." Stompke had opened the door to the office to retrieve me.

I am certain I looked petrified. My nerve endings jangled like after a night spent ingesting cocaine. I was all but overdosing on adrenaline. "I'll be okay," I replied, not too convincingly. Indeed, I was on the verge of hyperventilating.

"Take one of these," commanded Stompke, handing over an apothecary bottle that rattled with pills. "Dr. Brnjzrk said to give you one so you don't crap yourself or have a nervous breakdown during your trip."

"Crap myself?"

"It might be a bumpy, stressful ride. We really don't know for sure. The only people who can tell us are Bilson and Rachel, and they're in 1833 now. Better safe and sedated than sorry with soiled pants."

"I see your point."

I popped the pill into my mouth and washed it down with the last of the beer. Stompke scooped up the parcels being mailed with me and led me to the time-sailing kayak. He opened the hatch at one end and inserted all the worldly goods I would need when I was reborn in another world.

I climbed into the center hatch, gave Stompke a thumbs-up sign, and lay along the bottom of the vessel. Stompke looked in on me and bade me good-bye, saying, "Enjoy the ride." Then he closed the hatch, leaving me in total darkness.

Outside my container, which immediately transformed into a casket in my imagination, I heard the sound of dynamos revving up. The noise rose in volume and pitch. The kayak levitated, and then it began to ride feet first into the magnetic tube. Outside, as Stompke had earlier shown me, a telescoping rod nudged me forward. I flashed on those cremation ceremonies I had seen on television wherein a casket slowly was drawn on a track into a blazing furnace. "This is it!" I thought, "I'm gonna burn up like those cats Stompke spoke of. Like maybe Rachel and Bilson burned up." Then I figured it didn't matter; my world was in such an uproar that I frankly didn't care if I lived or died. Either way, I needed to prepare myself for this life ending, whereupon I'd be delivered into either an unfamiliar primitive culture or the unsolvable mystery of death.

As I passed within the tube's walls, sounds outside of my vessel became muffled; thereupon a new set of sounds took over. First, an electric fan or oxygen supply turned on, blowing fresh cool air onto my face and chest. Next, a curious set of noises familiar to a twenty-first-century denizen emerged: an extended series of squealing tire sounds, like someone had edited together a bunch of automobile chase scenes from television. (Modern conveyances rolled on rubber wheels that loudly screeched when turned abruptly at high speeds.) These sounds were accompanied by all manner of shaking, jerking, and tumbling movements of the space kayak. It appeared that Stompke's contraption had started altering time, and I had begun traveling backwards through it.

Things become sketchy at this juncture, due to the sedative and the disorienting effects of my ride. Judging by the intense light seeping into my capsule through the sliver of space surrounding the entry hatch above, I was passing through a field of pure white light that suggested the white light described by people who have undergone near-death experiences. I wondered at the time whether death was simply a journey to another time. Suddenly, re-incarnation seemed plausible to me. Only the birth canal from which I now emerged took the form of a wormhole, not a mother's womb.

I cannot be sure how long my trip took — a hundred and seventy-some years, but how long in my perception? Eventually, my capsule came to a rest. Outside I heard nothing but silence. After a few minutes I determined it was safe to exit. I opened the hatch and poked my head out. I found myself in the midst of a dense forest. I climbed out, retrieved my survival supplies and gold, and used the dead brush from a fallen tree to camouflage the kayak, taking seriously Stompke's advice concerning nineteenth-century minds happening upon a vessel constructed of an unfamiliar material containing advanced electronics equipment.

Chapter Two

August 13, 1833

Oh. Thank. God. At long last I have somebody to talk to, even if it's only this stupid diary.

Bruce has taken the buggy to town, leaving me alone for the first time in this farmhouse that's three miles from anything, which I begged him not to buy, I wanted a place in town, but he bought it anyway. "For the privacy." Trapping me here with him 24/7. And here I thought living with Dan Connor was oppressive.

GOD, I WISH I HAD A LINE OF COKE RIGHT NOW!!!

Sorry, diary, I had to get that out of my system.

Actually, talking to you gives me the same illicit thrill as doing coke. I'm stealing time to write a diary while Bruce is away. Try and forbid me from keeping a diary because you're paranoid it'll fall into the wrong hands!

Just like the old days with Dan. He'd go out to the Walgreen's or the Jewel or something. As soon as the front door clicked shut, I was clawing through my underwear drawer looking for my stash. I'd lay out a line on my dresser and enjoy a quick buzz without Dan all in my face about it.

Like I said before, Bruce tried to forbid me from keeping a diary.

He's like, "It could fall into the wrong hands."

I'm like, "Whose hands?"

"We don't want people finding out where or when we're from. It'll create serious hassles. Our origins have to remain a secret."

I love you, Bruce, but I've got to talk to someone.

In reality I said, "Okay."

The ride sure was a kick, wasn't it? Like being shot out of a cosmic cannon. Better than the second night of my honeymoon when Dan made me orgasm eight times. Better than any coke I've ever done. Even that pinkish Peruvian flake that Sarah Feldman gave Dan and me for our second wedding anniversary.

I felt SO horny at the end of our trip. Bruce explained that our hormone levels built up while we traveled. It was like we hadn't been laid in a hundred and seventy-five years. Soon after landing we fucked three times in a row right there on the ground next to our space ship on a tinselly fireproof blanket.

After that everything went downhill. A period where we wandered together in the wilderness for about five days until we found Chicago. In our new time zone, Chicago is not the Second City, it's like the four-thousandth.

We stayed in a hotel there, the Sauganash, that I'd give maybe one star. Less than one star, half a star. God, the awful violin playing the proprietor did! Made a street musician playing scratchy show tunes on Michigan Avenue look like Itzhak Perlman.

The boat rides on the Great Lakes were a bore. When I was thirteen I rode with Rebecca Goldman's family on their sailboat all the way to Mackinac Island and back in the most tedious week of my life.

All we did was play checkers and cards with her parents looking on, when we'd rather have been hanging out at Old Orchard Mall smoking cigarettes and meeting boys from other junior highs.

Our trip to Fredonia reminded me of that, only much MUCH longer. And scarier, with a bunch of rowdy drunken crewmembers falling in the water and nearly drowning five times a day.

Can you believe the captain gave his crew free access to whiskey? Like with anything free — I've seen it a million times at work as the vultures descend on doughnuts left after meetings — they overindulged, endangering everyone on the ship.

I confess I drank it, too. Three or four healthy shots every day. I was jonesing pretty bad, having left my coke home and seeing zero chance ahead of getting any. Probably hasn't even been discovered and smuggled up from South America yet.

Bruce criticized me for drinking all day, but I was good and lubricated by nighttime, when there was nothing to do on the boat but fuck in our dark cabin. Believe me, he wasn't complaining then.

I can complain — some. Both Bruce and Dan have plenty in regard to meat. But Dan's got more in the motion department. Once the initial, naughty excitement of an affair has worn off, and you're attached for life as Bruce and I now were, motion is all there is that's left.

You hear about men who calculate baseball statistics and football odds in their heads so they last longer during sex. I believe that Bruce calculates numbers simply for the sake of calculating numbers — with the same abstract, detached results.

Buffalo was almost as crappy as Chicago. Hookers and homeless people everywhere. Or maybe they weren't homeless. It's just that everybody looks that way in pre-Civil War days, because they work all day and sleep all night in the same outfit for two weeks in a row.

The Eagle Tavern in Buffalo, really a hotel but they call it a tavern, wasn't too bad, actually. Reminded me of a middling small hotel in an artsy town like Galena, Illinois or Mineral Point, Wisconsin.

But the guys who ran the place, the Rathbun brothers, they creeped me out. In their antiquated suits they looked like characters out of a Frankenstein movie. They owned half of Buffalo we were told, but even they looked homeless!

No one can blame the Rathbun brothers for talking Bruce into his cockamamie scheme that's brought us to Fredonia. I would've listened to them and bought real estate.

But NO, he wants to invest our money — note the word "our"; I told him he couldn't use any of mine — and drill for oil. Said the geographic surveys the team did showed there was lots of oil underground here.

So what does this mean for little old Rachel? Long lonely days bored out of my fucking skull in a broken down farmhouse, while Bruce is in town or further away in Buffalo drumming up investors.

He's probably generating thousands. In his former life Bruce was a whiz at fundraising — grants, endowments, corporate sponsorships, you name it. Bruce could talk the cheapest CEO of the most cheapskate corporation in America out of a few hundred thousand.

Get this: In 2009 he discovered a black hole in a far corner of the Milky Way, and he named it "Motorola" in honor of his chief benefactor.

There's a house that's maybe a mile away. Otherwise we're surrounded by farm fields with a shit smell constantly wafting overhead from all of the pigs or cows or whatever.

The wifey who lives there is a domestic goddess. I discovered this one day when she invited me over for a visit. She makes all her own candles, clothes, soap, pies, bread and canned vegetables, plus she cooks three humungous meals a day for her husband, seven children and the farm help.

Without a microwave. Or a decent gas stove. In between all that, she's constantly knitting, quilting or doing needlepoint. She looked at me like I was pathetic when I confessed I couldn't do a single one of these things.

I knew in the abstract that 19th-century women had all these skills and worked themselves to the bone. But actually witnessing it and seeing how I fall way short depresses me.

The 21st-century "superwoman," who holds down a big, important job and cooks and cleans for a husband and kids, can't carry wifey's jock strap. If she wore one, I mean.

So why did I come to the past?

The impetus for every action man or woman takes: Boredom.

Here I was, daughter of Phil Levy, the top-billing partner at Beerbohlm & Klatsch, respected attorney, community leader, donor to countless charities.

Then there's my mom, devotedly working the trenches for him, doing the actual volunteering and spending her time on his charity projects. Dad had the vision; Mom the talent for execution.

If these two overachievers weren't enough, my two brothers became attorneys, one in New York, the other in Washington, D.C. Benny, the latter, brushes shoulders with senators and congressmen. Jakey, the former, works for Wall Street corporations by day and sleeps in his huge Connecticut home at night.

I'm the family's black sheep, as you probably guessed. I didn't start out that way. I always stayed out of trouble growing up. Meaning, I was smart enough not to get caught when I was causing trouble. Hell, I graduated with a B.A. in English from Northwestern. That counts for something.

But I didn't meet Mr. Right in college like all of my Seven Sisters sisters, who married doctors or lawyers right out of school and could afford to be low-paid editors at New York publishing houses or fashion magazines.

No, I didn't follow that track. I stayed in Chicago and eventually married Dan for love, not money. Or was it lust? Dan told me I had the prettiest pussy on earth, and he appeared to literally worship it, at least for awhile. Then he kind of took it for granted like the rest of me.

My parents were royally pissed because I didn't marry a nice, upwardly mobile, if predictable, Jewish boy, so they gave Dan and me minimal financial help. It kills me thinking about it to this very day, one hundred and seventy-some years in the past.

Dan didn't have the income I was accustomed to and required (and my friends who married doctors and lawyers enjoyed), so I took a job as the office supervisor at the U of C physics department to make ends meet. My job sounds kind of lowly, and it was, but a non-college grad probably couldn't do it.

However, to someone from U of C, even a Northwestern grad is part of an inferior race. I was treated like a slave until I finally told the department chairman to stick his wife's birthday invitation list up his ass, I was busy with real work.

After that, things got better. All of the male professors, visiting fellows and graduate assistants (99.99% of who I saw at work) started taking an interest in their spunky office administrator.

I saw every one as they visited me for filing, photocopying, office keys, batteries, lab scheduling and general information that their lofty brains were too preoccupied with equations to learn on their own.

The only one that stood out from the pimply herd was Bruce. An MIT grad with a doctorate in astrophysics, he was worldlier than the rest, he had a better sense of humor, and he certainly looked better.

Still trim at forty-two, his waist wedged nicely into his tight blue jeans, and he had the most intelligent eyes I'd ever seen. His hair and nails were perfectly clipped, unlike Dan, whose head always looked shaggy, his nails chewed to the quick.

We engaged in innocent flirtation at first. When I got to learn more about him — he just happened to be a world-renowned physicist who approached Einstein in stature — I became more intrigued. I began to imagine sucking his cock.

Bruce's work brought a lot of money into the department, and the chairman made his projects a priority. This meant I worked with his team the most due to their high volume of administrative requests. I came in contact with him about five times every day, and sometimes I had to work overtime for him.

After a few months of hearing our atoms scream out shrilly for each other, we finally did the dirty deed one Saturday on a cot he kept in his office for all-night equation-solving marathons.

Why did I cheat on my husband of six years? What would YOU choose if these were your choices: a well meaning but clueless computer geek with a weakness for drugs, alcohol and strong Jewish women? Or a brilliant, famous, sexy, globetrotting scientist?

I thought so.

How did I get selected for this project? I was the only fit and fertile female in the vicinity. The team wanted to send a female back in time with Bruce. Even though I wasn't a scientist — the only woman on the physics faculty at the time was a fifty-nine year-old lesbian from Holland — I otherwise fit Bruce Bilson's bill.

In short, I attached myself to a shooting star. Literally. The matter making up our bodies met anti-matter inside a miniature black hole artificially induced in a particle accelerator. We traveled backward in time together, the first humans to ever do so.

As the female party, I expect I'll get second billing in the news reports about our trip. I'm Eve to the more interesting Adam. As director of the project, plus being the first time pilot in history, Bruce naturally attracts top billing.

Still, I'm Eve, mom to a race of dwellers in a new time thread.

Yet you can't become a mom with the lack of intimacy, sexual and every other kind, I'm currently experiencing. Bruce is always away from the house. And I'm left here alone, contemplating my coke habit and wishing I had it still.

Sure, we spend a couple of Saturdays a month in town together on what the locals call "Market Day." Everybody from miles around flocks to the grocer, druggist, butcher and baker's shops, which open early and stay open late.

But everybody's so dirty, and the stores are so crowded, and the men are so drunk, that I'm grossed out by the whole scene, and I elbow Bruce that we have to hurry home. Meantime, he's accosting every passing man, talking up the miracles of petroleum.

Not that I can claim anymore that I'm cleaner than everyone else in Fredonia. Guess what I should've thought to bring on this trip, only I didn't, and I'm regretting it five days every month? Tampons.

I hated maxi pads growing up, and here I am using rolled up cotton swabbing, an even cruder method.

Plus I get diarrhea pretty often, at least once a week, ever since the chlorine ran out and I have to drink untreated water. Bruce predicted that my diarrhea would stop in few weeks as my system got used to the water. Only it's been a few months now.

I saw the druggist in Fredonia one Market Day, the same man that counseled me to roll up cotton swabbing for my period, to see if he could give me anything. He handed over a brown powdery concoction, which I immediately downed.

"Eww. This tastes like dirt!" I exclaimed.

"That, indeed, is what it is — clay I dug up from a creek bed this very morning. It's the best antidote for diarrheic conditions. Binds everything together in a solid lump. Which you evacuate after another tincture I am going to give you."

"Tincture?"

"Just some tree bark boiled up. I call it Cannon Shot. I'm thinking about patenting it."

"Take it," urged Bruce. "Remember, lots of doctors use these kinds of alternative medicines where we come from."

Easy for Bruce to say; he didn't have to take the medicine, which tasted exactly how you'd expect boiled tree bark to taste.

Damn if it didn't work, though. After running to a privy (don't even get me started on those) and shitting out what felt like a basketball, I was fine.

I tried to speak with Bruce about our intimacy issues last week. I reminded him that I left Dan on account of the very same lack of intimacy in our marriage.

Bruce responded that he loved me, but he was the strong silent type. "I don't just blurt out everything like you," he said. "You have to coax the details out of me sometimes."

"Sometimes?" I said. "Lately, you don't communicate at all — not by speech, or gesture, or touch."

Come to think of it, Dan said something similar once. "You want me to spill my guts about every little thing. Well, you know what? Your guts are always spilled across the table. You never leave me room to spill mine."

It makes me wonder sometimes if I expect too much from these dim creatures called men.

Bruce promised me that once the oil started pumping, and the dollars started rolling in, he'd have plenty of time to spend with me. He said they were getting close. He and his associates had hired an army of carpenters and blacksmiths that were busy building derricks.

We'll see. As men become richer they generally become more busy, not less. My father and brothers are prime examples of this phenomenon.

I can hear the clopping of horse hooves now, meaning Bruce is back from town. I must wrap things up and hide this journal, but I promise I'll write more later when Bruce is away on some future business trip.

Chapter Three

I didn't get very far in the hours after landing in my new century, perhaps five yards. A huge wave of exhaustion washed over me, perhaps symptomatic of skipping sleep for over a hundred and seventy years, and I lay down and fell asleep almost immediately. I do not know how long I slept — it could have been several hours or several days — but I woke up with an erection that was more insistent than on a typical morning, which suggests it had been more than a catnap. I strongly considered abusing myself until I heard a sneeze behind my head. I tipped my head back to learn the source of this sound: a real-live Indian, studying me!

Fear stuck me in the prostate gland like a spear. However, the Indian did not wield a tomahawk or aim a knife at me. Moreover, it was a female Indian, a squaw with long braided hair and clothed in an indigo dress, who was studying me from a distance of five yards. I perceived one of the fairer and weaker sex less of a threat than a man. In fact, far from hostility, she bore me a concerned expression, as if I needed nursing. I picked myself up off the ground. Simultaneously, the Indian rose to a standing position and spoke a greeting in her language accompanied by a highly stylized hand pantomime. "Bo sho ni tthe na? Ni pi tthe wetth bya yen?"

Finding all her behavior thus far to be non-threatening, my gluteus maximus muscles relaxed somewhat, and I drew down my defenses. With a nervous twitter punctuating my words, I said, waving back, "Hello. I'm Daniel Connor."

"Strong mating spirit found here," responded the Indian, sniffing the ground and air.

"Er, um, yes." In a discreet attempt to quell my tumescence, I swatted at my lap a few times, pretending to dust myself off. "I've told you my name. Now, what is yours?"

"Potawatomi call me Listening Rabbit." Tension appeared to ease within her, too, and she turned flirtatious, coquettishly flicking over her shoulder a braid of raven hair, which she then petted. After a short interval engrossed in this activity, she added, "Log house mates call me Bunny."

I took in the scene, trying to keep my mind open to all of the possibilities. I was a relatively young man, whose wife had recently jilted him, gripped moments earlier by seriously insistent manly urges.

However, sad to tell the story, I just wasn't attracted to Bunny, and not because she was an Indian. How can I say this delicately? — I cannot, seemingly — she was a rather homely creature. Flat-chested, chicken-legged, she resembled nothing so much as a young man of twenty. I decided to limit our intercourse to a strictly business nature.

"It's very nice to make your acquaintance, Listening Rabbit." She continued to pet her hair and look at me expectantly. I did not really know what further remained to be said, plus my imagination began to conjure up the presence nearby of many more of her tribe, who might not act as benignly toward me as she. So I retrieved my two packs containing my survival gear and gold medallions from my capsule. I strapped on my packs and from my pants pocket drew a compass, which would direct me in an easterly direction toward the frontier village of Chicago. "I'm afraid I've got to get going," I said, looking over my compass dial into the distance, calculating the best trail to blaze through the woods that surrounded us.

As I turned to go, the Indian woman said, "You from future time." Pointing at me, she nodded faster and faster and broke into a broad smile missing several teeth, pleased that she had correctly deduced my origins.

This got my attention to say the least, and I halted after one step. I examined her face closely, gauging whether I could get away with denying the truth of my situation. No chance, I concluded: she looked resolute, like it was an article of faith with her, which I supposed it was, given the awe of supernatural phenomena that resides in the Indian breast.

"How do you know that about me?" I asked.

"Dust from long trail on you," she replied, flourishing her hands upward from my midsection toward my face. "Long-long-LONG trail!"

I looked myself over and did not notice an abundance of trail dust. Then it hit me: Listening Rabbit had perceived some essence on my person and called it "trail dust." What she probably observed was some energy field clinging to me after my journey through time. How her gaze penetrated beyond the boundaries of what can be seen by the naked eye I could not venture to guess. Clearly she possessed mystical powers.

"Keep this between you and me. Please." Again, I aimed myself toward where my compass told me Chicago lay. "Good-bye, Listening Rabbit. I must continue on my way. It was nice to meet you."

"Me come with you?"

I had been vaccinated against deadly diseases and instructed in basic survival techniques before departing the twenty-first century. I had been warned about poorer diets and shorter life expectancy in antebellum America. But nobody had prepared me for this scenario — an Indian asking to accompany me on my adventures. I tried to dissuade her from her aim, asking, "What about your life here?"

"Nothing left here." For the first time during our encounter a melancholy air attended her. I refrained from asking her to explain this statement, fearing that her band or tribe had been wiped out at the hands of another tribe or white frontiersmen. Perhaps I should have taken pity on her, the sole survivor of a massacre, like she had taken pity on me, a city boy from another century fairly out of his element in the wilderness.

"You don't even know where I'm going. Wherever I end up, I'm pretty sure there are few, if any, Indians there."

"Me no care." She looked profoundly sad now, from the original incident that had caused her to feel so bereft coupled with the summary rejection she had received from me.

In one of those moves that have characterized my entire life, but have paid off dearly in terms of money or sentiment, I took a suggestion under consideration and concluded, "What the hell?"

"You may come along with me. But on this condition. You have to help me out with things. Cooking, cleaning, whatever. I'll pay your way, plus you'll get a salary." I did not intend to act discriminatorily, but those were the skills I presumed she had, and they were the things I needed the most help with, inhabiting now the nineteenth century without my accustomed twenty-first-century conveniences.

An elated Listening Rabbit rushed over to me and laid her head on my right shoulder while throwing her arm around me and embracing my neck. Meanwhile, her other hand slipped down the front of my trousers, gripped my manhood and began to stimulate it. "Oh, no," I thought. "She thinks I just proposed marriage."

Fighting the impulse to push her off me, I gently removed her hand from my unmentionables and tried patiently to explain, "That's not part of the job I'm offering. It's a professional relationship I'm proposing..."

Listening Rabbit backed away from me looking embarrassed and a little disappointed that she was not entering into the Indian equivalent of a marriage compact. Her sheepish look then lifted, and she nodded her assent to my terms.

Putting her to work immediately, I slipped off the smaller pack from my front and handed it to her. She took her new position quite seriously it appeared, for she demanded that I also pass her the second pack containing about twelve pounds of gold, which she lugged onto her back. My chivalrous impulses took over and I insisted that she could not possibly carry two packs; being the man in our partnership, I would carry the heavier one. She refused to acknowledge my protestations and carried both packs on her strong shoulders for the remainder of our travels, never slowing, never tiring, never complaining.

"And call me Bunny," she admonished me. I had acquired a servant who most definitely was the boss of her household.

The next two days were spent homing in on the village of Chicago. The only mechanisms Bunny and I had to guide us were my compass readings and Indian or animal trails that bypassed the biggest natural barriers like rivers and swamps. The greatest obstacles I personally confronted were the myriad spider webs. When run into by face or chest, they flexed a moment, then snapped, sending filaments flying, including one strand to which a very angry spider clung. Strung at eye-level between every pair of trees, they called to mind badminton nets in their positioning and tensile strength.

One could not blame the spiders for setting their traps in the forest, for it supported a trillion potential victims per square acre. Lunch or supper flew only a few yards away. I was constantly reminded of this unhappy fact by the swarms of mosquitoes landing on me and fruitfully striking blood through my heavy cotton shirt, denim pants, and wool socks. I discovered, too late, that insect repellent was missing from my provisions, leaving me to slap and swat myself as I marched, looking to all the world (or at least to Bunny and the animals of the forest) like a flagellant.

Bunny, the inheritor of generations of Indian wisdom, had no such problem. Slathered on her skin was a liberal amount of bear grease, which successfully kept the mosquitoes at bay. The awful smell, like rancid bacon grease, would keep most other creatures at a distance, too, and when she applied it as we hit a marshy bit of terrain I was introduced to the first of many nineteenth-century offenses to my olfactory sense. When she offered to share the use of this foul concoction, I could not bring myself to scoop any on my fingers, let alone spread it on my person, and I continued to suffer the stings and bites from the insect kingdom.

We crossed the Du Page River near modern-day Warrenville, Illinois, where Bunny knew of a ford. Alone, I believe, I would have found a place to cross the river, but the hunt may have held me up an hour or more, so I was grateful for Bunny's travel tip. A settlement consisting of two or three houses and attendant barns and outbuildings greeted us.

Bunny insisted that we hold back from crossing until dusk. I understood her reasoning: she did not want to spook the white inhabitants by her presence, which could provoke them into attacking us peremptorily, even though we posed them no threat. With a backpack full of gold additionally to worry about, I acceded to her wishes, and we slipped across the river at nightfall, crossing easily through slow-moving water only a few inches deep.

White people safely behind us, we set up camp for the night next to a creek one or two miles east. I had Bunny set the packs down, and then I proceeded to amaze her by reaching inside them and withdrawing ultra-lightweight, high-performance camping equipment. I unrolled my Gortex (synthetic, water-proof fabric) sleeping bag and blew up my inflatable pillow. I unfolded mosquito netting that would, with the aid of an aluminum substructure, form a tent around my head and face, protecting these portions of my body from mosquitoes out for an evening snack. I unscrewed a dropper bottle containing liquid chlorine to purify my drinking water, and placed two drops into creek water Bunny had poured into my canteen. I un-zippered a foil package and from it ate beef jerky and dried fruit.

I should mention that my youth had fully prepared me to travel to frontier America and survive its deprivations. From age eleven to sixteen, I was a member of the Boy Scouts (a club for boys modeled after the U.S. Calvary, complete with neckerchiefs), which taught camping, hiking, swimming, and other outdoor skills. I attained the rank of Life Scout, one level below the top rank of Eagle, before succumbing to the attractions of females and intoxicating beverages, neither of which had a place in the organization. I continued to camp throughout my college years with like-minded friends (we mostly stood around bonfires drinking beer and slept inside pup tents), until I met Rachel, whose tastes ran to luxurious hotels. I wondered how she was faring in frontier conditions possessed of the notion that "camping" was staying overnight at a low-budget roadside inn.

Bunny un-wadded a beautifully embroidered blanket with a large abstract flower design and spread it onto the ground next to my bedding. She sat down and produced from somewhere a handful of nuts and berries that she nibbled. Soon after our respective suppers we fell asleep beneath the stars, exhausted from our active day, not caring one jot that insects buzzed insistently around our ears.

At dawn the next morning I awoke first. I traipsed down to the creek, splashed water on my face and looked around for a discreet place to relieve myself. An ancient oak tree with a trunk the diameter of a flour barrel provided me the proper camouflage. When I returned to the campsite, I was met with a surprising sight: behind and to one side of a tree stood Bunny; on the other side a stream of urine was visible. Obscured by the tree trunk were Bunny's organs of generation, which apparently were of the male variety rather than the female. It then dawned on me: Bunny dressed up in women's garb and had adopted a woman's station in life, but in physical actuality she belonged to the male sex!

While enjoying her long, leisurely piss, she looked around absently until she fixed her attention on me, who watched her no doubt with a stunned look. She burst into a broad, gap-toothed smile, obviously tickled that she had fooled me for so long.

Now, in the modern world among most classes of Americans, when this situation presented itself, it raised extremely few eyebrows, usually only on the foreheads of the excessively devout. Transvestites fascinated journalists and titillated the public; college professors studied the phenomenon of men dressing as women with great seriousness. Still, I was shocked, although several curious things about Bunny now made perfect sense, like her masculine looks, physical strength, and estimable endurance.

"PLEASE explain what I just witnessed," I demanded of Bunny as we began packing our gear before commencing the next leg of our journey.

"Bunny two-spirit Indian," she said. "White man call berdache."

"Bardash?"

"Berdache. Man and woman in same body. Share two spirits."

She proceeded to tell me the story of her life. At a young age she displayed less interest in and aptitude for work traditionally associated with the male sphere and a singular talent for women's work — cooking, cleaning, cultivating, sewing, child rearing, &c. The elders in her tribe recognized her propensities and decided to test them to determine her path in life. They placed a basket and bow and arrow under a bush and set it aflame, and they observed which item she saved from the fire. When she retrieved the basket, her fate was sealed. Squaws took over her education in the domestic arts, and the tribe's medicine men worked to develop the mystical powers often exhibited by two-spirits.

At the age of eighteen, she married a Potawatomi warrior slightly older than she named Broken Eagle. Despite their physical distance from true womanhood, two-spirits were valued mates. They applied male strength to female chores — they fetched more water and firewood, hoed more garden furrows, and butchered more game than their sisterly counterparts. Plus, and this provoked nary a blush from Bunny but much redness from me, she and her husband managed myriad ways of making love, even if their marriage failed to produce any children.

We had walked perhaps eight miles before I was fully informed about Bunny's history due to her limitations with English vocabulary and my imperfect understanding of Indian lifestyles. She brought me up to date on her most recent experiences during an extended crying spell that erupted at lunchtime and lasted much of the afternoon. From hour to hour her weeping varied in intensity, sometimes quiet sniffles, sometimes loud lamentations. The cause? Broken Eagle had recently broken her heart.

"Broken Eagle left me for woman. Real one," she sobbed. Broken Eagle, it seemed, craved children and not so subtly sought another mate who could fulfill his wish. When word went out to the squaws of their band, several presented themselves as candidates, to Bunny's extreme humiliation. Broken Eagle sampled their wares, made his pick and cast Bunny out of his bed. "Dog-sucking whores," she spat, cursing the women who had so disrespected her union with Broken Eagle.

When she had run into me, Bunny had been wandering in the wilderness for several days on a vision quest to determine what she should do next, travel to another village and begin life afresh, or stay in her village and receive the same social opprobrium as the divorced woman experiences in polite white society.

"I'm very sorry," I said. "This explains what you said earlier. That there's nothing left for you here."

"Can't go back to tribe. Broken Eagle shame Bunny." No doubt my appearance influenced her decision; to Bunny, I must have been sent by the Great Spirit himself to rescue her from her dilemma. Intense, focused meditation and prayer during Bunny's vision quest had summoned the power of the supernatural, which answered her call with a stranger who had dropped in from the twenty-first century.

By the time Bunny's tears had finally dissipated it was early evening and time again to make camp. Despite physical exhaustion from our twenty-five mile hike, plus emotional exhaustion from Bunny's sad story, I told her the sorry saga of Rachel, Stompke, and Fermilab as we settled in for the night. Despite language barriers, she understood enough English to comprehend the essential principles, conflicts, and motivations involved, having had just lived through a similar experience herself.

Moreover, being something of a mystic, she had little trouble grasping the concept of time travel. I got the impression that certain of her people, e.g., medicine men, traveled in time, if only on some spiritual plane. Ironically, as I would discover later, the most civilized, educated whites could not fathom the physics behind my journey, whereas a member of the "primitive" Indian race had zero problems visualizing the awesome powers unleashed.

When the hour had grown very late, we fell asleep beside the Des Plaines River with the expectation that we would reach Chicago sometime the next morning. There I hoped to catch word on Rachel and Bilson's situation, and then follow up on the information appropriately and devastatingly.

My mental agitation from traveling into the past had subsided enough by the third day that I began to enjoy the scenery we passed. For the most part this consisted of hardwood forest. Oak, maple, birch, ash, willow, and sycamore trees loomed around us, growing so thick that their branches merged into a leafy canopy that kept the summer sun at bay. Squirrels and chipmunks skittered across our path, and a few deer poked their heads up, pricked their ears, and then darted off. At one point we glimpsed a long-legged canine, a wolf or coyote maybe, and watched it lope away.

We heard silence but for locusts or cicadas buzzing. I could not get over the absence of modern, industrial-age sounds (the future is a very noisy place) — I heard no trains, automobiles, aeroplanes (flying omnibuses), sirens (announcing the arrival of police or firemen), or jackhammers (gas-powered sledges). The most noise I heard was made by myself earlier that morning when I yelled at Bunny across the creek, whence she had gone to gather berries, reminding her to fill our canteens before we broke camp.

Upon reaching what Bunny assured me was the Chicago River, we turned northward and followed it for a few miles until, sure enough, smoke from numerous fires hung above the horizon, indicating that we had nearly arrived at our destination. The village itself came into view only a few minutes later. Clustered around the confluence of the Chicago River's various branches and eastward along the main branch that emptied into Lake Michigan, the town amounted to not many more dwellings than Warrenville, where we had forded the Du Page River.

To the southeast of the river fork stood the Sauganash Hotel, which Stompke had instructed me to search out upon my arrival. My heart started thumping wildly, as I expected to learn here the disposition of Bilson and his mistress — my wife Rachel.

The Sauganash was a two-story L-shaped structure covered in whitewashed siding. As Bunny and I entered the establishment I saw that one part of the L, facing the river, comprised the lobby, a tavern, and common area; I presumed the other part contained guest rooms. Behind a handsome maple desk stood a not-so-handsome man with wiry red hair and sideburns, bulbous nose, and predatory eyes.

"Good morning, sir." He pronounced "morning" as "marning" and "sir" as "sar" in what I labeled "French brogue," a blend of French-Creole and Scotch-Irish. I wondered if I should expect to experience translation problems between nineteenth-century and twenty-first-century American dialects. Already, I was having difficulty understanding the very first white person I talked to in the 1800s.

"We'd like two rooms," I said.

"Ooh, I'm sorry, sir. It's, um, well. You see, sir, there's a 'No Indians' policy."

Bunny snorted, expecting as much.

"Listening Rabbit here is my servant. I'm responsible for housing and feeding her. Clothing her, too, if anyone sells women's clothes around here."

"Ooh, well, yes, sir. It's just that since the Indian troubles began downstate, the guests, sir, they fear Indians staying amongst them. They worry, sir, that their throats will be slit while they sleep, sir."

I knew what to do. I retrieved from my pocket a gold coin, worth I supposed hundreds in 1833 dollars. "How many days will that give us?" I asked.

The hotelier picked up the coin and examined it as close to his eyes as his rotund nose would allow. "That would put us at about a month, sir."

I suspected that the coin was worth enough money to pay for three months, but I did not quibble on this point. I needed to put a roof over Bunny's head. "And that includes Listening Rabbit, too? She gets a room?"

"Yes indeed, sir. That's fine, sir. Just please, sir, keep her under your hat, sir."

As he led us up the stairs to the second floor where our rooms were located, the hotel proprietor introduced himself as "Beaubien, Mark Beaubien" and instructed me (he, like everybody else we would encounter, tended to ignore Bunny) "not to hesitate to ask, sir, if you need anything whatsoever, sir." The rooms at the Sauganash were rustic but reasonably clean and livable. I had requested a room with a bathtub and looked forward to immersing myself in a steaming hot bath to wash off the dirt of several days and two centuries. I intended to make Bunny take a lengthy bath, too, in order to dissolve that damnable bear grease smell.

It did not take long for me to ascertain the whereabouts of Rachel and Bilson. After our baths, Bunny and I took an early supper in the hotel dining room. Beaubien himself served us warmed salted pork and boiled potatoes. A bottle of whiskey was available for us to wash down our dinners. "I'm sorry, sir. They departed about a month ago, sir, on a schooner that set sail for Buffalo."

"Did they mention if they were going beyond Buffalo?" I asked.

"I'm sorry, sir, they did not. According to the gentleman, they planned to examine their prospects in western New York, and then decide whether to move further eastward, either to Boston or perhaps to the city of New York. And it's plenty curious, too, sir, that they were traveling east. Everybody else, sir, moves west. West is where you'll find the future of this great nation, if you wish to know, sir."

I eyed Beaubien a little coldly; I likewise intended to travel east in pursuit of Rachel and Bilson. In Beaubien's mind, Chicago was the ultimate destination, the honest-to-goodness up-from-your-bootstraps frontier, where a man could literally do anything if he threw his mind, back, and mouth into it.

"When is the next boat? I've got to catch them," I said.

"Ooh, I'm sorry, sir. Probably not for a month. The last one left less than a fortnight ago, sir. Of course, it's always possible, sir, a boat will show up sooner, but I shouldn't count on it, sir."

"Then Listening Rabbit and I will stay here at your hotel in the meantime."

"Excellent, sir." Beaubien's smile grew to its largest size yet after an already impressive string of sycophantic and obsequious smiles. The corners of his mouth raised his cheeks so high that the lines around his eyes nearly crinkled into dollar signs.

In honor of our arrival and projected long-term stay (and the steady income Beaubien could count on for at least a month), he insisted on bringing out his fiddle and serenading us. He stomped his foot arhythmically and sawed out an out-of-tune reel that two-legged dancers could not dance to but perhaps one-legged dancers could. Midway through the second number, which did not improve on the first, suggesting to my ears that he was a bad fiddle player and not merely in the process of warming up, Bunny and I speeded up our eating pace and bid a hasty *adieu* for the night.

Safely in my room shut away from the horrible squawking, I thought up excuses on Beaubien's behalf for why he played so poorly. Obviously, he played with relish, but years of practice hadn't improved his technique one iota. Informed that prior to opening the hotel he had operated a ferry across the Chicago River, I theorized that his fingers were too thick and gnarled from gripping ropes to ply the strings with the proper dexterity.

While waiting for my ship to arrive from the east, I spent much time exploring the surrounding countryside. Here and there a small grove of trees grew. Sundry low spots contained standing water from river water that had channeled its way into the depressions in ingenious patterns, affording the birds a sanctuary and the mosquitoes a nursery. The Fort Dearborn stockade loomed on the highest ground, if five feet above lake level can be considered high. After a four-year vacancy, the fort only recently had been reoccupied, when Indian troubles erupted in western Illinois, where I fervently hoped they would remain.

On a few hot and sunny days Bunny joined me in exploring the sandbar jetting into Lake Michigan. Twenty yards offshore, it bottled up the river as effectively as a navy frigate. Many years would pass before the city fathers persuaded the national government to pay for having it dredged to enable the opening a new Great-Lakes port. For now, however, it was our humble destination.

Normally, one could walk across a causeway to reach the main hump of sand; however, at high tide, this narrow strip disappeared below the surface, so wading through chilly knee-deep water was required to ascend what became an island.

One day Bunny and I sat on the sand watching the waves gently lap the shore, as was our habit. Until then, to preserve my health, I had not yet ventured into the water. But it was insufferably hot and humid, and the deerflies were intolerably aggressive in their biting, so a dip in the lake, despite its cold temperature and the high probability it contained raw sewage and wastewater from people living upriver, looked eminently reasonable. I stripped to my underwear, consisting of what are known as "boxer shorts" in the modern world, and stepped into the water. Copying me, Bunny lifted off her tunic, revealing underwear sewn from what looked to be dirty rags, and she accompanied me into the water.

"Lake cold," said Bunny.

"Is Lake Michigan ever warm?" I responded. The water got gradually deeper the further in we went, while the cold crept an excruciatingly slow crawl past my ankles, shins, knees, thighs, and groin.

When we had waded to a depth of three feet, about twenty yards from shore, I dove underwater. After resurfacing I paddled in prodigious circles and figure eights around the murky green lake, grateful to have my hair, neck and face treated to the bracing liquid. Bunny had fun twisting and flailing like a prepubescent girl in shallower water, as she could not swim. Soon enough, however, in spite of our best exertions, the water grew bone-numbingly cold, and we were compelled to get out.

The footing the last few feet was like spilled marbles, causing us to struggle mightily, slipping and sliding on a layer of gravel deposited by a thousand years of breaking waves. After conquering this obstacle, we clambered back onto the sandbar and collapsed onto our backs where we huffed and puffed to catch our breath.

After spending a moment in this relaxed attitude, glad to feel the sunrays pelting my body and drying me, I glanced over at Bunny. My eyes were drawn naturally to her only moving part, her heaving chest. I turned away abruptly, registering the fact that Bunny was going around bare-breasted, and her nakedness was inappropriate. Granted, Bunny was male, but she performed for the entire world the role of female. I had to explain how she was immodestly dressed for the white civilization she was entering, and she must cover up. I had brought a kerchief for mopping the sweat off my brow and retrieved it from the pocket of my pants. We wrapped it around her chest and tied it in back. I informed her that where I had come from we called this a bikini, and all the young fashionable women wore them to swim. Bunny pranced around chanting "bikini-bikini-bikini" and snickering at the word's silly sound.

I determined to purchase a couple of dresses and proper undergarments for her when we reached Buffalo, as I had earlier discovered that every store in town (there were only two) failed to stock women's clothing. I could have bought her overalls or deerskin pants but no women's fashions, not even a simple calico frock.

The radius of my wanderings widened as the weeks wore on. When I had exhausted the land given over to meadow, marsh, and garden, I began to explore the vast forest surrounding the settlement. Leery of exploring alone in those forbidding woods, I asked Bunny to accompany me. I did not believe that Bunny would be of any help in a fight, but I had her tag along with me regardless, calculating that two humans tromping in the woods would scare off more than ninety percent of potential threats, like wolves, bears, or renegade Indians.

"White man, too. He big threat," said Bunny.

We had halted our hike to spy a herd of three white-tailed deer dining on a young tree's leaves. Astonished again at Bunny's insight, I turned around and said, "You're definitely right about the white man." In a brief moment of gravitas I wondered if Bunny could foretell the later near-extermination of Indians at the hands of white men.

"Shoot bullet in butt!" she jested, looking around at her behind, then shaking it a few times for effect. She jokingly referred to her buttocks and performed this lewd and obscene display at least four or five times every day for days thereafter. I attempted to quiet her, but it was too late — the deer had run off and disappeared deeper into the forest.

On the August day these words were spoken, we followed the Chicago River down its south branch. Decades later this section of the river would be jammed with sailing ships loading and unloading. A hundred years later, skyscrapers hugging each bank would turn this flat ground into a river canyon.

When we reached a small clearing approximately two miles from the Sauganash Hotel, we sat and rested on a fallen log and gazed at the lazily flowing river. Normally, given our proximity to the river, one would smell a fishy odor rising from the water. Here, there was a powerful scent of skunk. I held my nose and said to Bunny, "I guess we stirred up a skunk."

"No skunk. Skunk plant. Che-ka-gou."

"Wild onion, yes. What Chicago is named after."

"No onion. Rope plant." She uprooted a nearby stalk. "Make rope this way." She peeled the stalk apart into several strands and proceeded to weave them together. Within two minutes, she had woven a three-foot length of what looked to be extremely sturdy rope.

As she did her trick, it dawned on me that all around us stood hemp plants, a few in excess of six feet tall, each one heavy with flower buds that caused its branches to sag. If Bunny could be believed, then Chicago was named after skunkweed!

I asked to borrow her carrying bag, a lovely creation made of deerskin and decorated with dyed porcupine quills sewn into flower designs. While she looked on with a curious expression, I began to harvest the buds off a nearby hemp plant and stuff them into her bag.

I couldn't really share with Bunny, nor anyone I met from 1833, this hugely funny news: that Chicago, known the world over for its work ethic, was named for a plant worshiped by young twenty-first-century wastrels not unlike myself. "Where I'm from, we smoke this. Like tobacco in a pipe. It makes you silly, like whiskey."

"Smoke chekagou? No, can't!" she said and laughed nervously, as if I were teasing her, getting her to do it as a practical joke.

"Really. We'll try to borrow a pipe from somebody back at the hotel."

"Me like whiskey..."

It was decided. I clasped her bag shut and we hiked back to the hotel. A good omen of this specimen's quality: my fingers were sticky.

It turned out that Beaubien sold several pipe models along with a variety of cigars from behind the front desk. I selected an inexpensive corncob pipe, despite intense pressure from the hotelier to buy a hand-carved mahogany pipe "more befitting your social position and pocketbook, sir."

"And will you be taking a pouch of our finest Tennessee tobacco, too, sir?" he added, reaching under the counter for a small leather bag.

Not to seem suspicious, I agreed, even though I had never smoked tobacco. Then I remembered that the social opprobrium and legal penalties for smoking marijuana did not apply here on the frontier, and I did not need to disguise my activities. I reached this conclusion too late, as Beaubien already had my money and we were outside the hotel rushing to a nearby grove of trees to smoke the hemp I had earlier picked.

I quickly crushed a bud into a ball and stuffed it in the pipe bowl. I lit the pipe with a Locofoco-brand match, recently invented in the East and stocked in Chicago's general store. Locofocos were sold in red pocket-sized boxes emblazoned with the silhouetted head of Chief Locofoco, allegedly a real Indian. I sucked in the smoke and held it deep in my lungs for ten seconds' duration. Then I exhaled a huge brown cloud while passing the pipe to Bunny.

Bunny inhaled too much and began to cough violently. I patted her on the back and remembered that every woman with whom I had tried smoking marijuana had started out this way, extending from Rachel backward into my early adolescence. I took a turn and again passed the pipe to Bunny. She did much better the second time, exhaling with nary a peep.

After six or seven puffs, I began to feel light-headed. Bunny's crescendo of giggling alerted me that she also had begun to feel the smoke's intoxicating effects.

"I'm going to pack a trunk of this and take it east with us!" I announced.

"No can carry. Too many packs already," Bunny responded. Then she tilted her shoulders back, faced the sky, and let out a war whoop that pierced the trees and meadows like a flurry of arrows.

Her scream startled me, and I felt anxious that she might go mad and attack me for my perceived importunity. She was, after all, an Indian unaccustomed to civilized habits, let alone bad twenty-first-century habits. I feared she might be driven into lunacy by smoking marijuana through some biological or cultural incompatibility. When her howl subsided into paroxysms of laughter I felt great relief and chided myself for thinking such groundless thoughts.

"I'll carry it then!" I promised, my mood again merry. And I did carry it — with us on our boat I took a small chest containing about five pounds of choice hemp, which lasted Bunny and me several months before it went stale, forcing us to seek out new sources in our next locale.

For two hours and more, an air of jocularity reigned, as we laughed so fantastically hard and long about things that we gave ourselves headaches by the end. I believe I laughed hardest when Bunny referred to the bad fiddler Beaubien as "Coyote with Broken Bark," the nickname for our host that would ever afterward stick in our memories.

Next morning, our hilarity dimmed considerably when at breakfast we met the commandant of Fort Dearborn, Captain Abraham Whistler. Beaubien brought to our table, shared communally, steak and hotcakes along with a bottle of "breakfast whiskey, sirs." In command of men who did more before nine o'clock than most people did all day, the Captain had taken a break from supervising his soldiers who were busy building ever-more elaborate defenses around the fort. One week it was a system of pointed stakes planted in the ground at an angle facing the prospective enemy. The next week he ordered his men to dig a series of trenches of increasing circumference outside the walls of the fort. I asked him why he appeared to be taking such pains to reinforce the battlements.

"Purely precautionary measures," he explained. "Indians led by Chief Blackhawk in the Iowa Territory are remonstrating with our friendlier Indians in Illinois to join an alliance whose aim is to fend off whites settling along the Rock River."

"That's a ways away, is it not?" I asked.

"Closer than you might at first imagine. These bands of Indians strike lightning-quick. One minute you're digging turnips. The next minute you're lying dead watering the turnips with your blood. This unhappy situation has already befallen a few settlers only one or two counties west of here."

"But will they attack a fort?"

"In 1812 they attacked the first Fort Dearborn and butchered over ninety. Then they burned the fort to the ground. I shall not allow history to repeat itself while I am commanding officer here. I have my sworn duty, plus there is a strong duty owed to my grandfather, who built the first fort on this site. I will not see his legacy destroyed a second time."

"Just how concerned should I be about an Indian attack?"

"Not very concerned I should say, as we are making preparations for the fort's defense. Any day I'm expecting reinforcements led by General Winfield Scott to arrive from the east. General Edmund Gaines, stationed down in St. Louis, is marching north and will meet Scott's forces around Rock Island, on the Mississippi, whereupon this pincer tactic will squeeze any hostile bands they encounter like bloody ticks."

"What about Listening Rabbit? I don't want any harm to come to her from your soldiers acting overzealously in patrolling the town. Look at her. She's clearly harmless."

Until this point Whistler had failed to lay eyes upon Bunny, who all this time quietly ate. Once the Captain finally acknowledged her presence, his face registered alternating amounts of distaste and disgust, not only for Indians generally, but for this homosexual Indian specifically. I personally enjoyed the Captain's discomfort and was fabulously entertained as his eyebrows, nose and mouth went through myriad contortions while he feigned nonchalance but betrayed prejudice. That I possessed a stock of gold worth thousands of dollars accounted for ninety percent of why we were having this conversation. If I were a settler of modest means, I believe Captain Whistler would have ignored my pleas and ejected Bunny from the neighborhood long ago.

Push never came to shove, however, because our boat arrived on August 12, three days early. Schooners from Buffalo and further east fed the nascent city of Chicago three times a year: in late March/early April, the middle of August, and late October/early November. From November to March ice threatened the boat's wooden hulls. Gangs of Creole blacks unloaded the boat's cargo in the most laborious manner possible, via multiple trips on *bateaux* between the beach and the ship anchored some fifty yards offshore. This process took two days.

In the meantime the ship's crew reveled, drinking whiskey, shooting off guns, fighting, and falling down drunk in the mud flats pock-marking the town. The officers, Captain Bloodwood, and his First Mate Andrew Minty, stayed in relative civility with us at the Sauganash Hotel. Beaubien introduced us soon after their arrival when our paths crossed in the lobby. Verily bored out of my skull stranded in a frontier town with few entertainment prospects, I was disappointed to learn that the ship would stay at last a week before leaving.

"When it does leave, how do I book my passage?" I asked.

"Passage?" asked the Captain, squinting quizzically.

"Yes, for Listening Rabbit and me."

"It's right strange. I never transport people back the other way to Buffalo. But you're the second party in two trips that wanted to sail back with me. The last ones were in April, a man and woman." He squinted harder, examined my person, and no doubt saw resemblances between their twenty-first-century wardrobe and mine.

"A woman with dark, frizzy hair? She's my wife."

"I'm very sorry, Mr. Connor." Everything made sense to the Captain now, and he turned from suspicious to sympathetic. "I feel simply awful, as if I bear some responsibility for abetting her getaway. Our shipping line has a strict policy on making sure our cargoes are legally and morally above-board." He stopped when he noticed I was reacting to him calling my wife immoral. He need not have been concerned about insulting me; by leaving me for another man I thought that Rachel was immoral, too.

"Yes, well, I mean to pursue them and win her back." A little surprising was my sudden concupiscence when imagining Rachel and Bilson's congress — not as some weak, pathetic cuckold but as a battle-hardened gladiator poised to vanquish a sexual foe. I looked forward to the immense pleasure I would receive one day from Rachel while I busily outperformed Bilson in her bedchamber.

"Capital idea!" the Captain exclaimed. "I shall atone for my earlier misdeed by taking you to her, at least as far as Buffalo. Perhaps my company's agents can assist you in tracking her whereabouts once you arrive."

"Any help would be appreciated."

"Pending favorable winds, we leave at first light Saturday morning. Come down to the beach with your luggage Friday afternoon, and my men will bring you and it aboard."

"Listening Rabbit, too. She's traveling with me."

"An Indian? The company has a 'No Indians' policy, I'm afraid. She will have to be left behind." He moved his lips closer to my left ear and whispered this sage advice: "Don't think you can solve one moral dilemma by starting another."

"It's nothing like that, I can assure you. Listening Rabbit is my employee, not my whore."

"Still, Indians are unpredictable. They don't have any learning. They smell."

"She speaks decent enough English. And she took readily to soap and water, when I introduced them to her upon our arrival in town."

"The company's policy is very explicit..."

"I can pay good money."

"Really, I cannot. I do not wish to be out of a job."

Once again, a Krugerrand came to our rescue. "I can pay our way with solid gold," I said, retrieving a coin from my pocket and handing it to the Captain. His eyes glinted brighter than the coin he beheld.

"I suppose it would be all right. With just you two aboard there wouldn't be any other passengers to complain. Perhaps you have another gold coin? To split among my crew to ensure their silence?"

Like at a play or other entertainment, I felt as though I was eating all my popcorn before the main event. I envisioned spending all of my gold in Chicago before my trip truly got off the ground. "All right. But remember: She's a regular passenger and gets treated as such."

"I'll make certain you and the Indian lass have the most commodious beds that can be arranged. As you will most certainly be the only passengers, you will get the men's and ladies' sleeping quarters all to yourselves."

"Your passengers last spring, the man and woman — did they share quarters?"

"Aye, sir, they did. We understood they were a properly married couple and didn't foresee the harm it would cause." No questions asked, he probably struck the same deal with them, two gold coins for passage and the crew's silence, handily profiting from both sides of the conflict.

"No worries," I assured the Captain. "That is my — and shall become — their business.

Chapter Four

October 6, 1833

I'm worried about Bruce. It's the first time he's been away for an extended period of time since we left Fredonia. I trust the secrets regarding our origin and his abortive career in oil will be safe as he travels around to the Canadian side of Niagara Falls.

Honeymoons. That's what I'm reminded of when I think about Niagara Falls. It's supposed to feel like I'm on a honeymoon with Bruce. But the honeymoon ended almost as soon as it began. This fact depresses me.

I actually found myself the other day yelling "SHUT THE FUCK UP!" at the Falls. I was sick of the nonstop reminder that romance has exited from my life. I hope it's staying away only temporarily.

After a rocky first few months in Fredonia, things were looking up. Bruce's oil well started producing. Oil was so plentiful around town that they struck it only fifty-five feet below ground.

When the hundredth barrel was sold, all of the doubters and naysayers changed their minds about oil's potential, and they practically threw bags of money at Bruce, engaging his expertise in drilling wells on their property.

Within a few weeks, eight wells were pumping away, and Bruce along with a few town fathers were planning how they might take advantage of the nearby Erie Canal in marketing their oil to New York City. "Burns cleaner than wood or gas" became their slogan.

Bruce surprised me by making good on his promise to spend more time with me when the well began producing. He stopped working nights and weekends and kept more of a nine-to-five work schedule.

We even discussed sailing to Europe, where we would go on the Grand Tour, traveling first class all the way. I could finally learn for myself why Henry James made such a big deal out of the experience in so many thick novels I was forced to read in college.

As Bruce's popularity grew, so did mine. I began to live the part my parents had planned for me. Bruce wasn't Jewish, but he had the doctor title and made lots of money. Affording me, his "wife," a heightened status in the community.

Unlike the early weeks when Bruce struck out alone and entered the haunts of the local male culture (arriving home stinking of cigars) to seek investors, I was now able to accompany him.

"Accompany" is perhaps too strong a word. For as soon as we passed through the door of someone's home, we had to separate and join our respective male and female realms.

Naturally, the desirable spot was with the men. They discussed business and the issues of the day, particularly slavery and the tariff (whatever that is), or they told dirty jokes involving politicians they hated having sex with farm animals.

Women, by contrast, were stuck preparing food for the gathered horde. Their discussion topics centered on their children, childbirth, children's diseases, children's behavior, children's education and pregnancy. Guess how a childless woman like myself handled that?

I have considerable difficulty communicating with people, even on topics I'm more familiar with than children. This is due, I think, to the absence of modern metaphors that I grew up expressing myself with.

For example: "It doesn't take a rocket scientist to..." or "Nuke it in the microwave" or "Shift into high gear." I can't use statements like these or hundreds of others to express myself anymore.

Women have to talk, they have to constantly discuss their experiences and feelings. I like to think it's because we're honest and open, although I realize men like Dan and, increasingly, Bruce, think it's because we're nags and shrews.

Whoa, I went off on a tangent there, didn't I?

So the men yukked it up in the parlor or on the front porch, while the women shucked corn, snapped beans, peeled potatoes and baked bread in advance of the main event, stewing beef, roasting pig or grilling lamb (sometimes goat).

I remember the first such occasion vividly. I handled the shucking, snapping and peeling fine. Then they started barking orders at me from every direction. "Whip up some biscuits! Mix up some gravy! Mash up some taters!"

Lacking powdered mixes and the printed instructions on their boxes, I froze. Observing my indecision, the eldest among us, a crone called Prudence Crandall, shouted, "For goodness' sake, Rachel. Do something, don't just stand there waiting for the devil to find you something to do."

That was it. I burst into tears and ran outside. I found a tree near the house, which I hugged as I bawled miserably.

A few moments later Prudence led the other women outside to see what was the matter with me. When I confessed I didn't know how to do any of the stuff they were asking, Prudence became surprisingly understanding and took me in her arms.

"There, there, child," she said to comfort me. Then to the others, "Mrs. Bilson is a rare bird for these parts, a TRUE LADY whose station in life has precluded her from working in a kitchen. I assume you had servants to cook and clean for you where you're from?"

"Um, yes," I said. Far from thinking I was lazy or incompetent, they thought I was rich and therefore above doing everyday household chores! "Millicent used to do our cooking."

Never mind that Millicent was a goofy name that Dan and I used to call our microwave oven — Millicent the Microwave. "What did Millicent make today?" he'd ask when getting home from work. "Leftover Hunan beef" or "pizza bagels," I'd answer.

From that point forward, the ladies of Fredonia took me under their wings. They taught me how to make stew, biscuits, gravy, succotash, bread and a variety of meats. My mother would die if she saw me roasting a pork loin.

Still, women's work and women's company remained supremely boring. How I wished I could join the men, drink whiskey with them, and take part in their conversations! Yet, because of my gender, I was consigned to the company of well-meaning, if completely out-of-it, wives.

This really was my only complaint during those days: the unrelenting boredom of staying home alone or hanging out with cooking, sewing, quilting and childrearing women while Bruce wooed their husbands into funding his grandiose schemes.

Trouble came out of nowhere, as trouble always does. One of Bruce's wells caught fire early on the morning of September 19th. We're still not sure how.

The "what" of what happened isn't in doubt, however. There was a strong wind that day that blew the flames in the direction of town, which was engulfed and totally destroyed in less than two hours. Every single house, store, barn, tavern and outhouse burned to the ground.

Our house, being outside of town, was spared. In fact, neither Bruce nor I knew what had happened until later that day when a mob showed up on our property, demanding that Bruce come outside. We had seen the smoke off in the distance, but we figured it was a simple house fire that the inept volunteer fire department had trouble putting out.

I had always heard of people shaking so hard that their knees knocked together when they were scared, but I always dismissed it as exaggeration. Until I saw it happen to Bruce.

Thinking it better for both of us if he went out to meet the mob rather than have them break down the door and come inside looking for us, he told me to stay put while he headed outside. From the window, I saw lots of angry gestures aimed at Bruce and heard many accusations against him that I knew were completely untrue.

The truth doesn't mean very much to a determined mob, though. They grabbed hold of him and threw him into the back of a horse wagon and carted him away. I had to summon all my strength not to scream "NO! STOP!" for I didn't want to call attention to myself and be dragged away, too.

Many hours passed before I heard any news about Bruce's fate. Around dusk a committee of several men knocked on the door. "It's done, ma'am," their leader, a mustachioed man I knew to be mayor of Fredonia, informed me.

"You ... you mean he's dead?" I asked, fearing the worst.

"No, of course not. Today the town may have had vengeance on its mind, but we're not a bunch of ruthless murderers. Your husband was tarred and feathered and ridden out of town on a rail."

"Where is he now?" I asked, relieved but still very much concerned that my "husband" was missing in action.

"I'm not precisely certain, ma'am."

"The last I saw of him," said another man in a bloody butcher's apron, "he was splashing about in the river trying to shed his clothes and wash off the tar."

"Lots of luck with that!" said a third man whose face and clothes were soot-blackened. The entire party broke out laughing.

"Where will I find him?" I asked.

"Ask yourself this, ma'am: are you sure you want to find him?" asked the mayor. "After all, he's a marked man, guilty of burning down our town."

"Yes," I admitted, despite Bruce's extreme unpopularity.

"If I were you I would leave the rascal behind to fend for himself in the forest. We shall see how far his highfalutin philosophy and scientific theories take him there," advised the butcher.

"Um, yes," agreed the mayor. "Which brings me to the unpleasant task I am here to undertake. I am afraid that you will have to depart our town as well."

"Depart your town? Why?"

"If you remain, I am certain that Mr. Bilson will try to rejoin you eventually. And we cannot allow the destroyer of our town to live among us as we rebuild. It will make our citizens uncomfortable and will pose a danger to both you and your husband."

"It may not have looked organized," said old sooty-face, "but the mob today was of a single mind to punish Mr. Bilson for his misdeeds. Yet, everyone agreed that it would be wrong for him to pay with his life."

"Nevertheless," continued the butcher, "there might be a resident or two who lost everything in the fire that might desire a more fatal punishment to befall your husband."

"Just where the fuck am I supposed to go?" I asked, throwing out the window any notion that I'd had to utilize language suitable for nineteenth-century ladies.

"You shall have the night to pack your things," said the mayor. "On the morrow you shall catch the stagecoach to Albany. Your fate will then be in your own hands."

"This fucking sucks," I grumbled, and I went back inside our house, which would soon be taken over by the town and sold to help defray damages caused by the fire. I packed as many of our things as a stagecoach could realistically be expected to carry, including my Krugerrands.

Thank God I kept my gold hidden in the house under a loose floorboard. If it had been deposited in the Bank of Fredonia, it would've either been lost in the fire or confiscated by the town fathers who'd come to boot me out of their town.

Next morning, a buggy arrived to pick up me and my luggage. We rode straight to what was left of the stagecoach depot, and the Albany stagecoach arrived a little bit later. I climbed into the passenger compartment, the driver cracked his whip and we lurched off.

When we were a couple of miles outside town, I faked being sick and got the driver to stop. I offered him a gold coin if he took a short detour to help me look for Bruce. The other passengers put up a fuss, but when I offered them gold coins, too, they agreed to go along for the ride.

We turned onto a road that took us alongside the river, where we checked out a few bends and fords the driver knew about. Sure enough, within about a half-hour we found Bruce sitting on a riverbank naked as a jaybird, trying to weave himself a grass skirt.

He was pretty scuffed up, and I noticed a few burn blisters on his neck and shoulders, but otherwise he seemed in okay condition. I dug out an outfit for him to wear, and he dressed behind a tree.

All the while, the other lady in the coach, whom I'll call Little Miss Prissy-Priss, felt faint at the sight of a naked man and fanned herself with a copy of *The Lady's Home Companion*.

Once clothed, Bruce hopped aboard, and we got underway again. We instructed the driver to let us off at the next stop where we could catch a stagecoach to Buffalo. Already, Bruce was calculating his next move, which has brought us to Niagara Falls.

Bruce is certainly a lot poorer than when we started this process. Until he gets back on his feet, it's up to me to support us. We're currently staying at a roadside inn not far from the Falls. People from all over — New York City, Boston, England, France — stay here on their tour of the Falls.

It's the first time since we left the twenty-first century that I feel like I'm hanging out with a reasonably cosmopolitan crowd.

Mindful that we could run into visitors from Fredonia, Bruce has grown a beard (ugh! I *hate* beards) to disguise himself. He's also going by a new name, William Bruce.

His goal at present is to attract investors for a brand-new scheme: he plans to generate electric power from the Falls.

It's an uphill battle, he says, because the practical uses of electricity aren't immediately apparent to people. Obviously, things like toasters and computers haven't been invented yet.

So he has to build a generator and rig up some light bulbs, which he also has to fabricate, to demonstrate the miracle of electricity. Given his knowledge of physics and engineering, these will be a cinch to throw together, or so he claims. All he needs is some cash.

Guess who's fronting the cash? Yours truly, diary, Rachel. I told him it was okay, as long as he's ultra-careful and nothing happens here like what happened in Fredonia.

I'm still not sure why we don't move to New York City and just live off our gold. Barry Stompke had told us we wouldn't have to work a day in our lives. In New York City I could just relax and enjoy life, rather than worrying about Bruce's projects blowing up in our faces.

Chapter Five

Late August 1833 found me sailing on the schooner Cuyahoga Maid north along the western shore of Lake Michigan. The Cuyahoga Maid was an eighty-foot fore-and-aft jib sailboat that was typical, I learned, of travel on the Great Lakes. A newfangled steamboat plied the waves of Lake Erie from Buffalo to Detroit, but no steam vessel had yet ventured into Lake Michigan. For five days we zigzagged past the harbors of Kenosha, Milwaukee, and Sheboygan to our first destination, Green Bay, where we anchored for one day while the crew and soldiers from the fort onshore lazily loaded and unloaded provisions.

I found my sea legs pretty well. With nothing but idle time on my hands — I could have killed myself for not bringing a book along — I lounged on the top deck and enjoyed the scenery we passed, consisting predominantly of forest punctuated by shoals and beaches, river mouths, and sandy bluffs. In recent years I had a fair amount of experience sailing — my father had taken me out on his boat a couple of times when I visited him in San Diego. And, though they didn't own a boat themselves, my in-laws had socialized with many families who did, and I was allowed to tag along with them to this or that function. In the months leading up to my wedding, my father and my in-laws' friends threw Rachel and me no less than four parties and showers on their boats harbored at Chicago or San Diego.

Bunny certainly enjoyed the shipboard perspective of the forest at our left — "All this land belong to my people," she boasted — but she got pretty seasick from the waves and swells into which our bow bashed as we tacked, and she often stayed below-deck, electing to suffer in private.

Accommodations were not as decent as at the Sauganash Hotel, but I found them comfortable enough. I had the male passenger cabin all to myself. It was a modest affair, really more an aisle between two rows of short bunk beds stacked four-high. I'm glad Bunny and I were the only passengers, because it would have been cramped and uncomfortable with seven other men in this room. We took our meals in the galley with the crew save either the Captain or First Mate, who variously excused themselves when it was their shift at the wheel. The food was not horrible, but it was not terribly good either; despite the thousands of highly edible lake fish swimming all around us, we and our mates subsisted mainly on beef and pork fished out of barrels accompanied by hard-as-rock bread and a tumbler or two of whiskey.

Thinking back, it's amazing that we never ran aground or wrecked upon the shore, considering how much whiskey was on board the Cuyahoga Maid. The Captain explained that potable water was in short supply aboard his ship (while we sailed on one of the largest bodies of fresh water in the world). After the first day, when everybody's canteen was emptied, the only liquid the crew consumed when away from port was whiskey, a barrel of which sat, along with a ladle, near the wheelhouse, where any man could at any time grab a quick sip when he found the need. As I traveled on the Cuyahoga Maid, I visited this amenity often and played to the absolute hilt the role of drunken tourist on a pleasure sail.

Hauling a cargo of badger, beaver, and raccoon pelts detracted somewhat from the pleasure cruise aspect of our journey, however. These were piled everywhere in the hold and smelled immensely rank. Freshly taken in the woods surrounding Chicago, they were heading to New York City, where tanning factories would treat them before turning them over to John Jacob Astor's American Fur Company. One day, just as I was getting acclimated to the stink, Captain Bloodwood passed me in the hold and remarked after a few opening pleasantries, "I trust you know what you're doing with your Indian. But I warn you: Be vigilant around her every minute. You wouldn't want your scalp to end up in a pile such as these."

Involuntarily, I patted the top of my head to ensure my hair was still in its proper place. Catching the import of my action, the Captain roared with laughter, slapped my rump jocularly, and cackled the rest of the way to his cabin. I decided that, though I trusted him to steer a proper course to Buffalo without sinking, I would not be trusting Captain Bloodwood as a source of important information or advice as I formulated my plans.

The rest of the crew consisted of First Mate Minty and three other gentlemen, one being cross-eyed, another lame in one leg, and a third missing three fingers on his left hand. All took a keen interest in Bunny, probably the only "woman" they had seen in weeks or months. Such was the male-female ratio on the frontier, where even in a growing town like Chicago sailors could stay ashore for a week and never glimpse a member of the opposite sex. Indeed, they argued over who got to sit next to her at meals and who got to dance with her when Minty brought out his banjo and strummed a few chanteys. Captain Bloodwood seemed to know Bunny's secret, and, after my jarring experience with him down in the hold among all those bloody furs, I perceived that he rather enjoyed watching his otherwise rough and ready men act like silly romantics, fooled by her disguise.

After five days we passed through the Strait of Mackinaw and entered Lake Huron. Our next destination was Detroit. We traveled down the eastern shore, easily the remotest and farthest-fetched of the locales that we passed. There along the shore we saw little but dense forests of Douglas firs and nary another person including Indians. That was all right with Bunny; the richer, snootier Hurons were not her favorite people. This land was likewise remote in the twenty-first century, the iron and copper mines and fisheries that evolved later all but exhausted, leaving behind ghost towns and defunct harbor villages.

Four and a half days later, we passed through Lake St. Clair and in the early evening of August twenty-something docked at Detroit. The Motor City (thus nicknamed in honor of the horseless carriages later produced there) hadn't yet discovered motoring, of course, but nevertheless here in its early days carried on a brisk commerce in furs, ores, and timber. Our boat took on additional bundles of furs and, regrettably, passengers. Rather than share close quarters with three crudely dressed and foul-smelling woodsmen, I elected to transfer Bunny and myself to private berths on the steamboat Lady of the Lake, a palatial paddle-wheeler that specialized in hauling passengers, which had the extra bonus of reaching Buffalo three days sooner than the Cuyahoga Maid. An express boat that confidently steamed right across Lake Erie rather than hug the shoreline like the Cuyahoga Maid, it connected all three points of the Detroit-Cleveland-Buffalo triangle.

My quarters on the Lady of the Lake were luxurious compared to those in the Cuyahoga Maid. Though tiny, my room contained a real bed with straw mattress and a decorative hook on which I could hang my clothes. I spent much of the eight days we sailed on the steamboat standing or sitting on the roof of the wheelhouse. To my left the paddlewheel churned. Also, the Lady's crew was much more professional, that is to say more invisible, than the Maid's, and steadily kept to their business of running the ship.

We ate separately from the crew with the other passengers. Each night our fare consisted of warmed over lake perch from a barrel, boiled potatoes, and whiskey. The passengers were a gregarious bunch, but nearly everyone avoided Bunny and me, I think due to her race and the prejudices attendant on it. I had expected as much, as did Bunny, too. It was just as well, we found, that the other passengers kept their distance from us, for never in my life had I seen such a demonstration of crude eating habits — slurping, gulping, and sucking; spitting, drooling, and salivating; talking with mouths full; drying wet mouths on sleeves; wiping greasy hands on pants; throwing bones, seeds, and pits onto the floor; eating with fingers rather than spoons.

At long last, Bunny and I landed in Buffalo, our final destination. Bunny and I jumped over the Lady of the Lake's safety rail and onto a combination timber and cement dock that had all of the sloppy construction and haphazard angles of a beaver dam, except this structure had been built, I presumed, by adult men. I kept a tight grip on my gold bag, while Bunny clenched my provisions. We made our way inland through a sea of dirty-faced urchins who offered to carry our bags, while not so subtly trying to pry them loose from our hands.

The pack of would-be luggage handlers orbiting us broke off as we proceeded up the hill toward the center of town in search of the Eagle Tavern, which a passenger on the Lady of the Lake, Peter Witherspoon, a self-described "investment subscriber," had highly recommended. Witherspoon braved Bunny's savage looks and sat to dine with us on the last night of our cruise. "The Sauganash in Chicago is a decent place to stay by frontier standards. But the Eagle Tavern — now there's an honest-to-God hotel. They only have the resources to build and administer such an edifice in the East. The West is where you'll find your fortune, but the East is where you'll best spend it." I was cheered by this interpretation, considering that my fortune, already vast by nineteenth-century standards, lay underneath my chair where I sat eating. I had the potential to be housed and fed very comfortably when I reached civilization in the East.

At three stories, making it Buffalo's tallest structure, the Eagle Tavern was easily located. It was a handsome brick affair that gave me hope that accommodations in the nineteenth century were not uniformly shitty. Its insides could have been mistaken for a modern-day hotel in any large city. There was a well-lit, airy lobby, a spacious restaurant and bar, and an extremely attentive staff, from the porters at the front door who took Bunny's bag, to the desk clerk, who cheerily locked my gold in the hotel safe. There were even two meeting rooms, named Erie and Ontario, where itinerant lecturers spoke and new religious sects worshipped.

I reserved two adjoining rooms on the third floor; I instructed Bunny to go to her room and rest, while I retired to my own room and collapsed on the very wide and puffy featherbed. Tomorrow morning I would order us up breakfasts and hot baths, and then set about the business of locating my wife and her curséd paramour. Later that night, perhaps at ten or eleven o'clock, I awoke, lit a candle, smoked a pipe load of chekagou, and curled back into bed where I studied the snapshot of Rachel I had brought with me to the past. Despite her betrayal of our marriage vows and of me personally, as I looked at her likeness I thought of a hundred and one reasons why I should try to win her back. Following here are ten: her chin, earlobes, cheekbones, shoulders, navel, and, of course, her sublimely sculpted labia.

After our morning meal and ablutions, I questioned the desk clerk as to whether he had glimpsed Rachel or Bilson in the lobby or halls of his hotel.

"I am most sorry, sir, I have not. It might prove profitable to ask others on the staff if their memories serve." I had to think for a second what Cliff, as his name-plate identified him, had answered. Upon digesting his fancily delivered words, I made plans to speak with other hotel staff members. Meantime, until the next clerk came on, at two o'clock, there was time to kill, so I took Bunny on a search for a dressmaker's shop to purchase her an appropriate wardrobe.

We found a European-style boutique only two doors from the Eagle Tavern, Abigail's Ladies' Apparel. We entered a perfumed emporium of women's clothing, ranging from plain day frocks to elegant eveningwear. I was familiar with the territory; Rachel dragged me into such shops all of the time in our early years together until one afternoon I cried "Enough!" and never again had to stand idly by while she rifled through rack after rack of marked-down designer wear. I was unfamiliar with many items — devices made of leather, iron and bone, which, judging from their shapes and angles, attached to ladies' stomachs, hips, and posteriors.

Bunny was immediately drawn to the crinoline dresses, scarlet skirts, and silk accents. "Pretty cloth," she said, running the fronts and backs of her hands along the material. "Why so much like a bag?" she asked, holding up a skirt that looked as though it fit a two-hundred-fifty-pound woman.

The clerk, an amiable middle-aged sort with graying blonde hair and an over-abundance of perfume on her person, hoisted up for our eyes a thing called a bustle intended to fill the excess fabric of the skirt. Refreshingly nonplussed by Bunny's race, she gathered up an additional twenty items, most of which consisted of underwear items, and proceeded to the rear of the store. She directed Bunny into a dressing room and followed her inside.

This ought to be good, I thought.

Moments later a shrill scream pierced the air. The clerk flung open the door and galloped into my arms.

"She's a ... he's a ... MAN!" She gave me a mortified look and buried her face in my shoulder. (I forget even today about the nineteenth-century aversion to nudity, even in natural, non-prurient circumstances. Only last week, I outraged other swimmers on a sandy beach on Long Island, where I was holidaying, by going topless wearing only swimming trunks.)

"Yes, she is actually a he. But in how he acts and dresses, he might as well be a she."

Bunny poked her head out of the changing room and urgently protested her innocence. "No want to pound possum with her! No want to pound possum with her!" I gathered that "pounding possum" meant the physical act of love.

The clerk looked at Bunny and back at me, utterly confused. Then her face melted into a look of sheer horror as she envisioned Bunny and I living together as a married couple. An Indian squaw and a white man made a strange enough pair of birds, though nothing beyond the large number of strange sorts drawn to this place by Erie Canal traffic. But an Indian drag queen in bed together with a white man — that was unthinkable. She backed away from Bunny and me, appearing as if she were about to bolt out the door, find a constable, and accuse us of sodomy.

"Really, it's all right. He's harmless. As you probably noticed, he's not very far removed from the woods, where he's lived like a squaw all his life. Out east with me, he needs to look presentable. Please," I said, attempting to place my hand on hers, "get something for him to cover up his nakedness, then go in there and help him dress like a civilized lady."

She shrank from my reach. "It's just that it's so ... so ... *improper*," she whispered, shuddering.

"Please. We're counting on your obvious sense of professionalism and decorum."

My calm demeanor and flattering words had the intended effect — the clerk inhaled deeply for courage and returned to the dressing room to continue dressing Bunny.

Twenty minutes later, Bunny emerged to model her new duds. She flounced and danced around the store, spinning this way and that, to afford me a three-hundred-sixty-degree view of her and her expanded rear end. The frilly, ruffled clothing and the elaborate understructure girding it feminized Bunny: she was bustier and rounder in the rump, more womanly in other words, than before entering the dressing room. I asked her to re-enter the magic booth and perform another transformation, this time wearing a royal-blue velvet dress I picked off the rack. She modeled that, too, smiling radiantly at what appeared to be a high moment in her life, when she could completely indulge her girlish fantasies. Two months before, when we met outside Chicago, Bunny would never have dreamed of being able to doll up like this in fancy white women's clothes.

Realizing that Bunny needed more practical everyday wear, I had her try on a couple of plain checked frocks. To complete her wardrobe we had only to visit a shoemaker to have a pair of shoes made for her. I handed the clerk a gold coin as payment; she disappeared in the back of the store for a moment and returned with my change, comprised of English pounds and shillings, Spanish reales, and one or two copper coins minted locally. This more than paid for Bunny's shoes plus a complete wardrobe for me, purchased the next afternoon during a visit to a men's clothier. The underwear, shirts and trousers proved to be the stiffest, scratchiest clothes I had ever worn, but at least I looked the part of a nineteenth-century gentleman, dressed in a black waistcoat and gray pantaloons, white shirt, black vest, and silk cravat.

Promptly at two, Bunny and I returned from the dress shop to the hotel, where we met Ward, the afternoon and evening desk clerk. Although it wasn't gold, we hit pay dirt, silver rather, with Ward, who told us that he remembered

Rachel and Bilson quite well. They had stayed for about a fortnight, whereupon they had departed to parts unknown.

"Their clothes were a queer brew. They looked casual and Western, like you would plow or smith in them. Yet they looked professionally made, definitely not homespun." Ward eyeballed Bunny and me warily as he began to imagine all kinds of twisted plots our foursome — Rachel, Bilson, Bunny, and I — was wrapped up in.

"Regarding the subjects of your query, you should speak about them with Mr. Rathbun."

"Rathbun?"

"The owner of the Eagle Tavern in addition to, I would conservatively estimate, half of Buffalo. When these particular guests in question stayed at our hotel, Mr. Rathbun took an interest in them."

"An interest?"

"Yes, he dined with them many nights in his private suite upstairs."

"What did they discuss?"

"I could not say for certain. Purchasing shares in Mr. Rathbun's new joint-stock company perhaps? He's presently selling stock to his latest real-estate venture with more religious fervor than a tent revivalist."

"How can I make an appointment with Mr. Rathbun?"

"I shall tell him of your interest in an audience. You're in Rooms 12 and 14?"

"Yes."

"I shall contact you presently, when I receive instructions from Mr. Rathbun."

"Thank you." Bunny and I turned to leave.

"And sir? I don't know if you remember, but I checked you into the hotel last night. May I say, sir, that the lady looks lovely today? That's a very becoming dress. Is it new?" he asked Bunny, who, dying to talk to the young man who had complimented her, but feeling shyness and embarrassment wash over her, ducked behind me where she hid and giggled. The big, cosmopolitan city of Buffalo, it appeared, held no prejudices against Indians, perhaps due to its removal from the frontier, where Indians posed more of a threat to the white population.

An hour or two later a knock at my door summoned me from my bed where I lay reading the *Commercial Advertiser*, a newspaper that had arrived free outside my room's door sometime during the previous night. I scanned the four-page rag for any news of Rachel and/or Bilson. Mostly therein I found overly long articles pertaining to boat cargoes, bankruptcies, lost farm animals, and stabbings at the waterfront. Evidently, nineteenth-century newspapers had different ideas of newsworthiness compared to twenty-first-century journalistic enterprises. Brevity, too, for exceedingly long articles were laid out top to bottom in five narrow columns with neither scrolls nor illustrations to break up the high volume of words. Though only a single eleven-by-seventeen-inch sheet folded in half, it took most of the afternoon to read its contents.

After similarly ousting Bunny from her room, a tall, gangly deaf and mute bellhop motioned for us to follow him down the hall. With great mimed fanfare, he ushered us into the private suite of the man who owned half of Buffalo.

"I'm Benjamin Rathbun," said a man seated at a desk on which sat a quill, an ink bottle, a blotter, and nothing else.

"The 'Builder of Buffalo,'" said a man standing to the left of the first man next to the broad third-floor window and its panoramic view of Lake Erie.

"This is my younger brother, Lyman Rathbun," said Benjamin Rathbun.

"I handle all of my older brother's accounts," said Lyman Rathbun.

"Pleased to make your acquaintance," I said to Lyman.

"An honor to make yours," said Benjamin. Benjamin was a compact man with a large head and gray locks whose lips pursed severely when he wasn't speaking. Lyman was less compact than his brother, with a larger head, graying locks, less severe features, and small-pox scars, which I later found to be ubiquitous on nineteenth-century faces.

"And who is this ... um ..." asked Lyman.

"... lovely lass?" asked Benjamin.

"Yes, your lovely Indian lass here — what is her name?" asked Lyman.

"Listening Rabbit," I answered. "She's my maidservant. She's Potawatomi, from Chicago." Already in this conversation, in the midst of introductions, I felt dizzy as the two Rathbun brothers finished each other's sentences in rapid-fire manner.

Bunny curtsied and greeted the brothers in her native language. As her knees bent and straightened, all twelve of her skirts and underskirts rustled, sounding like a small wind-blown forest.

"How can my brother and I be of assistance?" asked Benjamin.

"Yes, how may we help you?" asked Lyman.

"Your evening desk clerk, Ward, informed me that you were recently acquainted with a couple that stayed at your hotel a few months ago. Bruce Bilson and Rachel Levy?"

"Indeed, we dined on several occasions back in the summer," said Lyman.

"Quite wealthy," said Benjamin.

"Gold-rich, as they say," said Lyman.

"Mysterious, though," said Benjamin. "Very circumspect in their dealings."

"Most mysterious," said Lyman.

"And here you show up," said Benjamin.

"Asking after them," said Lyman.

"With — may we be frank here, Mr. Connor?" asked Benjamin.

"— a hoard of gold worth many thousands," said Lyman.

"From frontier territory where most families don't use cash but rather the barter system," said Benjamin.

"Specie with strange Dutch-like inscriptions referring to Africa," said Lyman.

"Just like Bilson and his mistress," said Benjamin.

"You want an explanation for my presence," I said.

"Not an explanation ...," said Benjamin.

"We're much too discreet to demand an explanation," said Lyman.

"... just to remark in passing that my brother and I, as does everybody else who has come in contact with you and the party you are pursuing, find it ...," said Benjamin.

"Unusual," said Lyman.

"Odd," said Benjamin.

"Yes, well. That *is* all my business, isn't it?"

"Absolutely," said Benjamin.

"Positively," agreed Lyman.

"So. What news do you have of them, if any?"

"Mr. Bilson planned to settle a few miles south of here," said Benjamin.

"In Fredonia," said Lyman.

"He had in mind a mad scheme to drill for oil," said Benjamin.

"Said it would burn like gas or peat," said Lyman.

"According to Mr. Bilson, the likeliest place to find oil was in the vicinity of underground salt mines," said Benjamin.

"We told him to try either Syracuse or Fredonia," said Lyman.

"I have to get there immediately," I announced. Ever alert to signs of swift change during her employment with me, Bunny stopped primping and posing in front of an elaborate mirror, which had occupied her during my conversation with the Rathbuns, and she stood beside me ready to leave for our next destination.

"A stage to Fredonia departs sometime tomorrow, but I do not know the precise time," said Benjamin.

"You'll have to check the schedule at the depot. Or maybe one of the hotel's concierges could direct you," said Lyman.

"Could I hire somebody to take me tonight?" I asked.

"You could," said Benjamin.

"But I wouldn't recommend it," said Lyman.

"Riding through not completely settled territory, with people whom you do not know," said Benjamin.

"Hauling gold," said Lyman.

"At least with a stage coach you are working with a bonded company," said Benjamin.

"With trusted drivers," said Lyman.

"We could even supply you with a guard," said Benjamin.

"I see your point," I said. Bunny stood down.

"Stay in my hotel for one more night," said Benjamin.

"It is the finest in Buffalo," chimed in Lyman.

"Get a good night's sleep and travel to Fredonia tomorrow," advised Benjamin.

"I will. Thank you for your advice," I said. And I was truly thankful for their graciousness towards Bunny and me. Sober, eminently reasonable men — Benjamin Rathbun bore the aspect of a minister — I found myself trusting their counsel, much as I had placed my faith in the guidance of similar avuncular managers and mentors in my former life.

"Maybe you could help us," said Benjamin.

"Now that we have helped you," said Lyman.

The brothers commenced their sales pitch. "It is generally known in Buffalo that my business transactions have been of an immense amount and various in their character," said Benjamin.

"My brother is extensively engaged in the building business in all of its various branches," said Lyman.

"The improving of real estate, dealing in lands," said Benjamin.

"Merchandising on a corresponding scale," said Lyman.

"Manufacturing post coaches and pleasure carriages in all of their variety, running various lines of stages and omnibuses," said Benjamin.

"You will ride on one of my brother's stages to Fredonia, as a matter of fact," pointed out Lyman.

"And I'm involved in many other minor branches of business," said Benjamin.

"My brother's companies employ over twenty-five-hundred workers," said Lyman.

"We have especially ambitious plans for the coming year," said Benjamin.

"Yes, we aim to build one-hundred structures in 1833," said Lyman.

"Let me show you a few of the buildings we have put up already," said Benjamin, steering me over to the window.

"That is the Unitarian Church. There is the Washington Block," said Benjamin, pointing in various directions.

"That is the Webster Block. There is the new jail," said Lyman, also pointing.

"Over here is the American Hotel. Over there is the United States Hotel," said Benjamin.

"Neither, of course, is as fine as the one you are staying in right now," said Lyman.

"Talk to anyone in Western New York. I have a proven track record in financing and building stately public buildings," said Benjamin.

"As well as superb private dwellings," said Lyman.

"The question at hand is this," said Benjamin.

"Would you care to invest in my brother's new real-estate-development firm?" asked Lyman.

"You will quadruple your investment within five years," promised Benjamin.

"Hmm. I don't know. Isn't real estate risky?" I asked.

"The goal is to buy up land," said Benjamin.

"And not to be the last one holding the deed," said Lyman.

"The last-one-out theory," said Benjamin.

"Sell at the last possible moment before prices fall," said Lyman.

"As they inevitably do," said Benjamin.

Lyman reached inside his purple waistcoat and pulled from his pocket a folded paper document. "This is a note for one thousand dollars co-signed by Hiram Pratt," said Lyman.

"Along with Lyman and myself, Mr. Pratt is one of Buffalo's leading citizens," said Benjamin. "I do not doubt that he shall be elected mayor or even governor one day," said Benjamin.

"In return for a loan from you of one-thousand dollars, in gold, we could give you this note as collateral," said Lyman.

"And invest the proceeds in our real-estate venture," said Benjamin.

"Remember, that is one-hundred buildings in three-hundred-sixty-five days," said Lyman.

"I need to think about it," I answered. Once again paying attention, Bunny looked at me and shook her head, putting in her two cents, gathered from her intuitive sense alone, for I have no doubt she could not much understand my dealings with the Rathbuns other than they were offering me some trade. Having witnessed her supernatural power in action before and finding it dead-on correct, I deferred for now to her "sixth sense" and told them that I would give them an answer on the morrow.

Beside the fact, I could not abide eating dinner with this conversational tag team, these experts at the game of verbal shuttlecock, who expected a tip for passing information, just like their desk clerks earlier, only in the Rathbun's league they expected the tips to be correspondingly larger. "I'd like to get some air, and Listening Rabbit wishes to go outdoors," I announced, preparing to leave. "Where can we go to buy dinner and see a bit of the local scenery before we have to leave tomorrow?"

At Lyman Rathbun's suggestion, we directed ourselves toward some "colorful scenery, all right" in the area near the terminus of the Erie Canal, the city's "Infected District." Normally, he explained, he would never send his guests to this neighborhood; the Eagle Tavern's high-class clientele abhorred the place.

"But," chimed in Benjamin, "in light of your Indian, ahem, guest, who will not be allowed in the politer precincts of the city, it is there that you will find the best welcome."

"But mind whom you touch," warned Lyman, "however casually, for he or she can visit upon you every misfortune from syphilis to head lice to money missing from your wallet."

In our city finest, Bunny and I strolled through the newly incorporated city of Buffalo, New York. We headed downhill toward the waterfront, turned left and walked a half-mile to the Erie Canal. The Infected District consisted of a few streets crisscrossing where man-made river met nature-made lake. The area bustled — men rolling barrels every which way; unescorted ladies roving in packs; horses pulling carts loaded with crates; horse shit *everywhere*; cries of anger, pain, strain, and angst. Blocky boats jammed the canal floating end-to-end for more than a mile. Present, too, were all of the extras a town attracts when aswarm with money, namely, prostitutes, petty thieves, alcoholics, gamblers, and confidence men.

"Sailor! Want your willy sucked?" boldly asked a woman in a threadbare second-hand designer dress whom we passed on the wooden plank sidewalk.

"Excuse me?"

"C'mon! That skinny, flat-chested squaw can't pop your cork like I can." The hooker's face could only be described as asymmetrical — she had a black eye, and her left cheek was red and swollen. A poorly healed knife wound crossed her forehead, intersecting the heavy lines found thereon. She was missing a gaggle of teeth.

"Um, very sorry. Not interested," I said as I walked on.

In my wake followed Bunny, who hauled off and, as we indelicately put it in 2015, bitch-slapped the woman on the unmarked cheek and knocked her to her knees. Over the woman's prone body she declared, "Connor heap-big gentleman," I suspect as much for the injury done by the woman to her feelings, calling her a flat, skinny squaw, as to me.

"Bunny! You can't just hit people!" I scolded, while helping the woman to her feet. "A thousand pardons," I said. "Bunny gets a little over-protective. Are you all right?"

"Yes, thank you. Sorry to have bothered you, sir," said the hooker. Her face now appeared more symmetrical, with a new shiner surrounding her right eye and a rapidly purpling welt on her right cheek to match the injuries inflicted on the left side of her face.

Bunny stood apart from us and pouted after my admonishment. "Bunny sorry," she muttered, face turned away from the woman and me so she could protect her pride but still remain audible to us. I gave the woman a shilling piece for her pain and quickly whisked Bunny and myself away.

But no sooner had we extricated ourselves from that predicament than a new situation, thankfully not involving us directly, erupted a few feet away. A seventeen- or eighteen-year-old youth conked an old gentleman on the head and threatened to beat him further unless he gave up his wallet immediately. Leery of getting involved, I held Bunny back from rushing in and breaking up the assault. For one thing, I didn't know how the hoodlum might be armed, with a knife, perhaps, or a pistol.

The old man shook off the shock of getting cold-cocked and removed from under his overcoat a coiled bullwhip. The youth slipped a knife from its sheath, but before he managed to point it the old man cracked his whip and tore the knife out of his hand, leaving two fingers dangling from tendons and bleeding profusely. The old man followed rapidly with a strike to the face that lopped off the tip of the robber's nose. The youth collapsed onto the gravel sidewalk to howl and lick his wounds, but the old man was not finished. He gave him twenty lashes, leaving the youth's back a pulpy mess of carved skin and torn wool. The youth passed out from pain and shock (I saw him breathing so knew he wasn't killed); the old man calmly re-coiled his whip, attached it to his belt, and went on his merry way.

Stunned, Bunny and I shuffled away from the scene, letting a watchman or constable or Good Samaritan tend to the severely chastened would-be robber. Deciding we had had enough of Buffalo's street life, Bunny and I ducked into a restaurant whose sign out front promised fresh lake perch and cold English ale. While we feasted on fried fish and drank many pints of ale, I informed Bunny that I wanted to learn how to handle a whip like that old gentleman who had done in that delinquent youth. "Who can teach me?" I asked.

"Bunny not know. Can't fight with bow and arrow or tomahawk. But she can cook big pot of acorn stew!"

"I know! We'll go to a stable. They're bound to have whips there." We asked our waiter where we could find the nearest stable. He answered us, we settled our bill, and we took off across the street and down the block to Merle's Stable. On the wall inside the shack where Merle conducted business hung several coiled whips of various lengths and diameters.

Merle, a grizzled but affable character who often smiled and flashed brown tobacco-stained teeth, had to redirect us to a "Feed and Seed" store where such items were bought. The whips hanging on his wall were not for sale but were used in his business to handle recalcitrant horses. The Feed and Seed was closed for the night, Merle informed us, so we deferred my purchasing errand until the next day before leaving town. Having had my fill of fish, ale, and Buffalo's Infected District, I suggested to Bunny that we turn in early, visit the Feed and Seed first thing in the morning, and then catch our stage to Fredonia. We returned to the Eagle Tavern without further incident and put my plan into action.

The next morning I bought a ten-foot beginner's model bullwhip at the Feed and Seed Emporium, an amazing establishment that sold everything from farm implements and blacksmith accessories, to seed corn and cattle feed, cooking pots, oil lanterns, and washtubs. The store sold whips as long as twenty-two feet for professional drivers driving large teams of horses. A beginner like me, the clerk coached, had best start out with an eight- or ten-foot whip. He demonstrated cracking the whip vertically so it struck the floor (and stirred up a major dust tornado) and horizontally using a sidearm motion. He advised me to practice these two moves and take things from there.

Confident that I would later meet someone who could coach me further in my quest to become competent in defending myself with a bullwhip, I hustled Bunny over to the depot where we bought tickets to ride on the eleven o'clock stage to Fredonia. In the remaining interval we had simply to retrieve our luggage, settle our hotel bill, and go.

I had forgotten about my promise to consider the Rathbun brothers' business proposal. By the fireplace in the lobby of the Eagle Tavern, Benjamin and Lyman sat in chairs awaiting me. I was prepared to offer them the money they had requested just to escape their presence before the aggressive sales job got rolling again.

After a porter brought down my things and I had recovered my gold from the hotel safe, I counted out four Krugerrands worth about one thousand dollars and dropped them into Lyman's left hand. Simultaneously with the right hand Lyman handed me the note seen last night on which Benjamin Rathbun's signature now joined Hiram Pratt's.

"This note represents a share of the company and its profits," said Benjamin.

"But heed: do not wait too long before selling it," said Lyman.

"The key is to get into the market and get out again before prices fall," said Benjamin.

"Thanks for the advice," I said. But I didn't follow Benjamin Rathbun's advice. I hung onto the note long enough for it to emerge later, in 1837, that the Rathbun brothers were engaged in a scheme by which they sold fraudulent shares in Benjamin's enterprises backed by forged notes. The signature of Hiram Pratt appearing on my note was forged by Benjamin's nephew, Lyman Rathbun Howlett, who was all of fourteen years old at the time. Projecting to all the world a cherubic face and innocent disposition, in reality Lyman the Younger was a scamp and a rascal who privately apprenticed in the art of white collar crime with his uncle Benjamin.

Although Benjamin blamed his by-then-dead brother for masterminding the fraud, a jury found him guilty of being an accessory to fraud, and he served three years in the Buffalo jailhouse that his construction company had built. The note in my possession was worthless, of course, but not so the lesson I learned from my experience, to wit: do not invest in real estate or farm commodities, only put your money into steel, railroads, and power utilities.

It turned out that Bunny and I were the Fredonia stage's only passengers. The coach itself was a handsome affair sporting a polished maple body, rugged spoked wheels, a team of four horses, and a nearly toothless driver wearing a top hat. The passenger compartment was upholstered with leather and featured a cupboard inside of which could be found a water canteen, corn whiskey, and strips of deer jerky to snack on during the trip. Having only once ridden on such a vehicle at a theme park (the modern-day version of a county fair or carnival) when I was a child, I looked forward to the ride.

That is, until we got underway and my rear end confronted the seat and floor and side of the coach as we banged and bumped along rocky dirt "roads" hardly deserving of the name. Bunny, too, was thrown all around the coach — once or twice we slammed into each other — and I regretted that there were not more passengers to wedge everybody into place. Four-and-a-half hours later (a forty-five-minute trip on modern highways), we arrived in Fredonia, New York, and were confronted with a scene of near-apocalyptic devastation. Practically the whole town had burned down and lay in a smoking ruin. I fervently prayed — very unlike me — that Rachel was not lying dead underneath a pile of burnt rubble. Bunny and I desperately sought out anyone who could answer our questions about what had so recently transpired there.

Chapter Five

Late August 1833 found me sailing on the schooner Cuyahoga Maid north along the western shore of Lake Michigan. The Cuyahoga Maid was an eighty-foot fore-and-aft jib sailboat that was typical, I learned, of travel on the Great Lakes. A newfangled steamboat plied the waves of Lake Erie from Buffalo to Detroit, but no steam vessel had yet ventured into Lake Michigan. For five days we zigzagged past the harbors of Kenosha, Milwaukee, and Sheboygan to our first destination, Green Bay, where we anchored for one day while the crew and soldiers from the fort onshore lazily loaded and unloaded provisions.

I found my sea legs pretty well. With nothing but idle time on my hands — I could have killed myself for not bringing a book along — I lounged on the top deck and enjoyed the scenery we passed, consisting predominantly of forest punctuated by shoals and beaches, river mouths, and sandy bluffs. In recent years I had a fair amount of experience sailing — my father had taken me out on his boat a couple of times when I visited him in San Diego. And, though they didn't own a boat themselves, my in-laws had socialized with many families who did, and I was allowed to tag along with them to this or that function. In the months leading up to my wedding, my father and my in-laws' friends threw Rachel and me no less than four parties and showers on their boats harbored at Chicago or San Diego.

Bunny certainly enjoyed the shipboard perspective of the forest at our left — "All this land belong to my people," she boasted — but she got pretty seasick from the waves and swells into which our bow bashed as we tacked, and she often stayed below-deck, electing to suffer in private.

Accommodations were not as decent as at the Sauganash Hotel, but I found them comfortable enough. I had the male passenger cabin all to myself. It was a modest affair, really more an aisle between two rows of short bunk beds stacked four-high. I'm glad Bunny and I were the only passengers, because it would have been cramped and uncomfortable with seven other men in this room. We took our meals in the galley with the crew save either the Captain or First Mate, who variously excused themselves when it was their shift at the wheel. The food was not horrible, but it was not terribly good either; despite the thousands of highly edible lake fish swimming all around us, we and our mates subsisted mainly on beef and pork fished out of barrels accompanied by hard-as-rock bread and a tumbler or two of whiskey.

Thinking back, it's amazing that we never ran aground or wrecked upon the shore, considering how much whiskey was on board the Cuyahoga Maid. The Captain explained that potable water was in short supply aboard his ship (while we sailed on one of the largest bodies of fresh water in the world). After the first day, when everybody's canteen was emptied, the only liquid the crew consumed when away from port was whiskey, a barrel of which sat, along with a ladle, near the wheelhouse, where any man could at any time grab a quick sip when he found the need. As I traveled on the Cuyahoga Maid, I visited this amenity often and played to the absolute hilt the role of drunken tourist on a pleasure sail.

Hauling a cargo of badger, beaver, and raccoon pelts detracted somewhat from the pleasure cruise aspect of our journey, however. These were piled everywhere in the hold and smelled immensely rank. Freshly taken in the woods surrounding Chicago, they were heading to New York City, where tanning factories would treat them before turning them over to John Jacob Astor's American Fur Company. One day, just as I was getting acclimated to the stink, Captain Bloodwood passed me in the hold and remarked after a few opening pleasantries, "I trust you know what you're doing with your Indian. But I warn you: Be vigilant around her every minute. You wouldn't want your scalp to end up in a pile such as these."

Involuntarily, I patted the top of my head to ensure my hair was still in its proper place. Catching the import of my action, the Captain roared with laughter, slapped my rump jocularly, and cackled the rest of the way to his cabin. I decided that, though I trusted him to steer a proper course to Buffalo without sinking, I would not be trusting Captain Bloodwood as a source of important information or advice as I formulated my plans.

The rest of the crew consisted of First Mate Minty and three other gentlemen, one being cross-eyed, another lame in one leg, and a third missing three fingers on his left hand. All took a keen interest in Bunny, probably the only "woman" they had seen in weeks or months. Such was the male-female ratio on the frontier, where even in a growing town like Chicago sailors could stay ashore for a week and never glimpse a member of the opposite sex. Indeed, they argued over who got to sit next to her at meals and who got to dance with her when Minty brought out his banjo and strummed a few chanteys. Captain Bloodwood seemed to know Bunny's secret, and, after my jarring experience with him down in the hold among all those bloody furs, I perceived that he rather enjoyed watching his otherwise rough and ready men act like silly romantics, fooled by her disguise.

After five days we passed through the Strait of Mackinaw and entered Lake Huron. Our next destination was Detroit. We traveled down the eastern shore, easily the remotest and farthest-fetched of the locales that we passed. There along the shore we saw little but dense forests of Douglas firs and nary another person including Indians. That was all right with Bunny; the richer, snootier Hurons were not her favorite people. This land was likewise remote in the twenty-first century, the iron and copper mines and fisheries that evolved later all but exhausted, leaving behind ghost towns and defunct harbor villages.

Four and a half days later, we passed through Lake St. Clair and in the early evening of August twenty-something docked at Detroit. The Motor City (thus nicknamed in honor of the horseless carriages later produced there) hadn't yet discovered motoring, of course, but nevertheless here in its early days carried on a brisk commerce in furs, ores, and timber. Our boat took on additional bundles of furs and, regrettably, passengers. Rather than share close quarters with three crudely dressed and foul-smelling woodsmen, I elected to transfer Bunny and myself to private berths on the steamboat Lady of the Lake, a palatial paddle-wheeler that specialized in hauling passengers, which had the extra bonus of reaching Buffalo three days sooner than the Cuyahoga Maid. An express boat that confidently steamed right across Lake Erie rather than hug the shoreline like the Cuyahoga Maid, it connected all three points of the Detroit-Cleveland-Buffalo triangle.

My quarters on the Lady of the Lake were luxurious compared to those in the Cuyahoga Maid. Though tiny, my room contained a real bed with straw mattress and a decorative hook on which I could hang my clothes. I spent much of the eight days we sailed on the steamboat standing or sitting on the roof of the wheelhouse. To my left the paddlewheel churned. Also, the Lady's crew was much more professional, that is to say more invisible, than the Maid's, and steadily kept to their business of running the ship.

We ate separately from the crew with the other passengers. Each night our fare consisted of warmed over lake perch from a barrel, boiled potatoes, and whiskey. The passengers were a gregarious bunch, but nearly everyone avoided Bunny and me, I think due to her race and the prejudices attendant on it. I had expected as much, as did Bunny, too. It was just as well, we found, that the other passengers kept their distance from us, for never in my life had I seen such a demonstration of crude eating habits — slurping, gulping, and sucking; spitting, drooling, and salivating; talking with mouths full; drying wet mouths on sleeves; wiping greasy hands on pants; throwing bones, seeds, and pits onto the floor; eating with fingers rather than spoons.

At long last, Bunny and I landed in Buffalo, our final destination. Bunny and I jumped over the Lady of the Lake's safety rail and onto a combination timber and cement dock that had all of the sloppy construction and haphazard angles of a beaver dam, except this structure had been built, I presumed, by adult men. I kept a tight grip on my gold bag, while Bunny clenched my provisions. We made our way inland through a sea of dirty-faced urchins who offered to carry our bags, while not so subtly trying to pry them loose from our hands.

The pack of would-be luggage handlers orbiting us broke off as we proceeded up the hill toward the center of town in search of the Eagle Tavern, which a passenger on the Lady of the Lake, Peter Witherspoon, a self-described "investment subscriber," had highly recommended. Witherspoon braved Bunny's savage looks and sat to dine with us on the last night of our cruise. "The Sauganash in Chicago is a decent place to stay by frontier standards. But the Eagle Tavern — now there's an honest-to-God hotel. They only have the resources to build and administer such an edifice in the East. The West is where you'll find your fortune, but the East is where you'll best spend it." I was cheered by this interpretation, considering that my fortune, already vast by nineteenth-century standards, lay underneath my chair where I sat eating. I had the potential to be housed and fed very comfortably when I reached civilization in the East.

At three stories, making it Buffalo's tallest structure, the Eagle Tavern was easily located. It was a handsome brick affair that gave me hope that accommodations in the nineteenth century were not uniformly shitty. Its insides could have been mistaken for a modern-day hotel in any large city. There was a well-lit, airy lobby, a spacious restaurant and bar, and an extremely attentive staff, from the porters at the front door who took Bunny's bag, to the desk clerk, who cheerily locked my gold in the hotel safe. There were even two meeting rooms, named Erie and Ontario, where itinerant lecturers spoke and new religious sects worshipped.

I reserved two adjoining rooms on the third floor; I instructed Bunny to go to her room and rest, while I retired to my own room and collapsed on the very wide and puffy featherbed. Tomorrow morning I would order us up breakfasts and hot baths, and then set about the business of locating my wife and her curséd paramour. Later that night, perhaps at ten or eleven o'clock, I awoke, lit a candle, smoked a pipe load of chekagou, and curled back into bed where I studied the snapshot of Rachel I had brought with me to the past. Despite her betrayal of our marriage vows and of me personally, as I looked at her likeness I thought of a hundred and one reasons why I should try to win her back. Following here are ten: her chin, earlobes, cheekbones, shoulders, navel, and, of course, her sublimely sculpted labia.

After our morning meal and ablutions, I questioned the desk clerk as to whether he had glimpsed Rachel or Bilson in the lobby or halls of his hotel.

"I am most sorry, sir, I have not. It might prove profitable to ask others on the staff if their memories serve." I had to think for a second what Cliff, as his nameplate identified him, had answered. Upon digesting his fancily delivered words, I made plans to speak with other hotel staff members. Meantime, until the next clerk came on, at two o'clock, there was time to kill, so I took Bunny on a search for a dressmaker's shop to purchase her an appropriate wardrobe.

We found a European-style boutique only two doors from the Eagle Tavern, Abigail's Ladies' Apparel. We entered a perfumed emporium of women's clothing, ranging from plain day frocks to elegant eveningwear. I was familiar with the territory; Rachel dragged me into such shops all of the time in our early years together until one afternoon I cried "Enough!" and never again had to stand idly by while she rifled through rack after rack of marked-down designer wear. I was unfamiliar with many items — devices made of leather, iron and bone, which, judging from their shapes and angles, attached to ladies' stomachs, hips, and posteriors.

Bunny was immediately drawn to the crinoline dresses, scarlet skirts, and silk accents. "Pretty cloth," she said, running the fronts and backs of her hands along the material. "Why so much like a bag?" she asked, holding up a skirt that looked as though it fit a two-hundred-fifty-pound woman.

The clerk, an amiable middle-aged sort with graying blonde hair and an over-abundance of perfume on her person, hoisted up for our eyes a thing called a bustle intended to fill the excess fabric of the skirt. Refreshingly nonplussed by Bunny's race, she gathered up an additional twenty items, most of which consisted of underwear items, and proceeded to the rear of the store. She directed Bunny into a dressing room and followed her inside.

This ought to be good, I thought.

Moments later a shrill scream pierced the air. The clerk flung open the door and galloped into my arms.

"She's a ... he's a ... MAN!" She gave me a mortified look and buried her face in my shoulder. (I forget even today about the nineteenth-century aversion to nudity, even in natural, non-prurient circumstances. Only last week, I outraged other swimmers on a sandy beach on Long Island, where I was holidaying, by going topless wearing only swimming trunks.)

"Yes, she is actually a he. But in how he acts and dresses, he might as well be a she."

Bunny poked her head out of the changing room and urgently protested her innocence. "No want to pound possum with her! No want to pound possum with her!" I gathered that "pounding possum" meant the physical act of love.

The clerk looked at Bunny and back at me, utterly confused. Then her face melted into a look of sheer horror as she envisioned Bunny and I living together as a married couple. An Indian squaw and a white man made a strange enough pair of birds, though nothing beyond the large number of strange sorts drawn to this place by Erie Canal traffic. But an Indian drag queen in bed together with a white man — that was unthinkable. She backed away from Bunny and me, appearing as if she were about to bolt out the door, find a constable, and accuse us of sodomy.

"Really, it's all right. He's harmless. As you probably noticed, he's not very far removed from the woods, where he's lived like a squaw all his life. Out east with me, he needs to look presentable. Please," I said, attempting to place my hand on hers, "get something for him to cover up his nakedness, then go in there and help him dress like a civilized lady."

She shrank from my reach. "It's just that it's so ... so ... *improper*," she whispered, shuddering.

"Please. We're counting on your obvious sense of professionalism and decorum."

My calm demeanor and flattering words had the intended effect — the clerk inhaled deeply for courage and returned to the dressing room to continue dressing Bunny.

Twenty minutes later, Bunny emerged to model her new duds. She flounced and danced around the store, spinning this way and that, to afford me a three-hundred-sixty-degree view of her and her expanded rear end. The frilly, ruffled clothing and the elaborate understructure girding it feminized Bunny: she was bustier and rounder in the rump, more womanly in other words, than before entering the dressing room. I asked her to re-enter the magic booth and perform another transformation, this time wearing a royal-blue velvet dress I picked off the rack. She modeled that, too, smiling radiantly at what appeared to be a high moment in her life, when she could completely indulge her girlish fantasies. Two months before, when we met outside Chicago, Bunny would never have dreamed of being able to doll up like this in fancy white women's clothes.

Realizing that Bunny needed more practical everyday wear, I had her try on a couple of plain checked frocks. To complete her wardrobe we had only to visit a shoemaker to have a pair of shoes made for her. I handed the clerk a gold coin as payment; she disappeared in the back of the store for a moment and returned with my change, comprised of English pounds and shillings, Spanish reales, and one or two copper coins minted locally. This more than paid for Bunny's shoes plus a complete wardrobe for me, purchased the next afternoon during a visit to a men's clothier. The underwear, shirts and trousers proved to be the stiffest, scratchiest clothes I had ever worn, but at least I looked the part of a nineteenth-century gentleman, dressed in a black waistcoat and gray pantaloons, white shirt, black vest, and silk cravat.

Promptly at two, Bunny and I returned from the dress shop to the hotel, where we met Ward, the afternoon and evening desk clerk. Although it wasn't gold, we hit pay dirt, silver rather, with Ward, who told us that he remembered

Rachel and Bilson quite well. They had stayed for about a fortnight, whereupon they had departed to parts unknown.

"Their clothes were a queer brew. They looked casual and Western, like you would plow or smith in them. Yet they looked professionally made, definitely not homespun." Ward eyeballed Bunny and me warily as he began to imagine all kinds of twisted plots our foursome — Rachel, Bilson, Bunny, and I — was wrapped up in.

"Regarding the subjects of your query, you should speak about them with Mr. Rathbun."

"Rathbun?"

"The owner of the Eagle Tavern in addition to, I would conservatively estimate, half of Buffalo. When these particular guests in question stayed at our hotel, Mr. Rathbun took an interest in them."

"An interest?"

"Yes, he dined with them many nights in his private suite upstairs."

"What did they discuss?"

"I could not say for certain. Purchasing shares in Mr. Rathbun's new joint-stock company perhaps? He's presently selling stock to his latest real-estate venture with more religious fervor than a tent revivalist."

"How can I make an appointment with Mr. Rathbun?"

"I shall tell him of your interest in an audience. You're in Rooms 12 and 14?"

"Yes."

"I shall contact you presently, when I receive instructions from Mr. Rathbun."

"Thank you." Bunny and I turned to leave.

"And sir? I don't know if you remember, but I checked you into the hotel last night. May I say, sir, that the lady looks lovely today? That's a very becoming dress. Is it new?" he asked Bunny, who, dying to talk to the young man who had complimented her, but feeling shyness and embarrassment wash over her, ducked behind me where she hid and giggled. The big, cosmopolitan city of Buffalo, it appeared, held no prejudices against Indians, perhaps due to its removal from the frontier, where Indians posed more of a threat to the white population.

An hour or two later a knock at my door summoned me from my bed where I lay reading the *Commercial Advertiser*, a newspaper that had arrived free outside my room's door sometime during the previous night. I scanned the four-page rag for any news of Rachel and/or Bilson. Mostly therein I found overly long articles pertaining to boat cargoes, bankruptcies, lost farm animals, and stabbings at the waterfront. Evidently, nineteenth-century newspapers had different ideas of newsworthiness compared to twenty-first-century journalistic enterprises. Brevity, too, for exceedingly long articles were laid out top to bottom in five narrow columns with neither scrolls nor illustrations to break up the high volume of words. Though only a single eleven-by-seventeen-inch sheet folded in half, it took most of the afternoon to read its contents.

After similarly ousting Bunny from her room, a tall, gangly deaf and mute bellhop motioned for us to follow him down the hall. With great mimed fanfare, he ushered us into the private suite of the man who owned half of Buffalo.

"I'm Benjamin Rathbun," said a man seated at a desk on which sat a quill, an ink bottle, a blotter, and nothing else.

"The 'Builder of Buffalo,'" said a man standing to the left of the first man next to the broad third-floor window and its panoramic view of Lake Erie.

"This is my younger brother, Lyman Rathbun," said Benjamin Rathbun.

"I handle all of my older brother's accounts," said Lyman Rathbun.

"Pleased to make your acquaintance," I said to Lyman.

"An honor to make yours," said Benjamin. Benjamin was a compact man with a large head and gray locks whose lips pursed severely when he wasn't speaking. Lyman was less compact than his brother, with a larger head, graying locks, less severe features, and small-pox scars, which I later found to be ubiquitous on nineteenth-century faces.

"And who is this ... um ..." asked Lyman.

"... lovely lass?" asked Benjamin.

"Yes, your lovely Indian lass here — what is her name?" asked Lyman.

"Listening Rabbit," I answered. "She's my maidservant. She's Potawatomi, from Chicago." Already in this conversation, in the midst of introductions, I felt dizzy as the two Rathbun brothers finished each other's sentences in rapid-fire manner.

Bunny curtsied and greeted the brothers in her native language. As her knees bent and straightened, all twelve of her skirts and underskirts rustled, sounding like a small wind-blown forest.

"How can my brother and I be of assistance?" asked Benjamin.

"Yes, how may we help you?" asked Lyman.

"Your evening desk clerk, Ward, informed me that you were recently acquainted with a couple that stayed at your hotel a few months ago. Bruce Bilson and Rachel Levy?"

"Indeed, we dined on several occasions back in the summer," said Lyman.

"Quite wealthy," said Benjamin.

"Gold-rich, as they say," said Lyman.

"Mysterious, though," said Benjamin. "Very circumspect in their dealings."

"Most mysterious," said Lyman.

"And here you show up," said Benjamin.

"Asking after them," said Lyman.

"With — may we be frank here, Mr. Connor?" asked Benjamin.

"— a hoard of gold worth many thousands," said Lyman.

"From frontier territory where most families don't use cash but rather the barter system," said Benjamin.

"Specie with strange Dutch-like inscriptions referring to Africa," said Lyman.

"Just like Bilson and his mistress," said Benjamin.

"You want an explanation for my presence," I said.

"Not an explanation ...," said Benjamin.

"We're much too discreet to demand an explanation," said Lyman.

"... just to remark in passing that my brother and I, as does everybody else who has come in contact with you and the party you are pursuing, find it ...," said Benjamin.

"Unusual," said Lyman.

"Odd," said Benjamin.

"Yes, well. That *is* all my business, isn't it?"

"Absolutely," said Benjamin.

"Positively," agreed Lyman.

"So. What news do you have of them, if any?"

"Mr. Bilson planned to settle a few miles south of here," said Benjamin.

"In Fredonia," said Lyman.

"He had in mind a mad scheme to drill for oil," said Benjamin.

"Said it would burn like gas or peat," said Lyman.

"According to Mr. Bilson, the likeliest place to find oil was in the vicinity of underground salt mines," said Benjamin.

"We told him to try either Syracuse or Fredonia," said Lyman.

"I have to get there immediately," I announced. Ever alert to signs of swift change during her employment with me, Bunny stopped primping and posing in front of an elaborate mirror, which had occupied her during my conversation with the Rathbuns, and she stood beside me ready to leave for our next destination.

"A stage to Fredonia departs sometime tomorrow, but I do not know the precise time," said Benjamin.

"You'll have to check the schedule at the depot. Or maybe one of the hotel's concierges could direct you," said Lyman.

"Could I hire somebody to take me tonight?" I asked.

"You could," said Benjamin.

"But I wouldn't recommend it," said Lyman.

"Riding through not completely settled territory, with people whom you do not know," said Benjamin.

"Hauling gold," said Lyman.

"At least with a stage coach you are working with a bonded company," said Benjamin.

"With trusted drivers," said Lyman.

"We could even supply you with a guard," said Benjamin.

"I see your point," I said. Bunny stood down.

"Stay in my hotel for one more night," said Benjamin.

"It is the finest in Buffalo," chimed in Lyman.

"Get a good night's sleep and travel to Fredonia tomorrow," advised Benjamin.

"I will. Thank you for your advice," I said. And I was truly thankful for their graciousness towards Bunny and me. Sober, eminently reasonable men — Benjamin Rathbun bore the aspect of a minister — I found myself trusting their counsel, much as I had placed my faith in the guidance of similar avuncular managers and mentors in my former life.

"Maybe you could help us," said Benjamin.

"Now that we have helped you," said Lyman.

The brothers commenced their sales pitch. "It is generally known in Buffalo that my business transactions have been of an immense amount and various in their character," said Benjamin.

"My brother is extensively engaged in the building business in all of its various branches," said Lyman.

"The improving of real estate, dealing in lands," said Benjamin.

"Merchandising on a corresponding scale," said Lyman.

"Manufacturing post coaches and pleasure carriages in all of their variety, running various lines of stages and omnibuses," said Benjamin.

"You will ride on one of my brother's stages to Fredonia, as a matter of fact," pointed out Lyman.

"And I'm involved in many other minor branches of business," said Benjamin.

"My brother's companies employ over twenty-five-hundred workers," said Lyman.

"We have especially ambitious plans for the coming year," said Benjamin.

"Yes, we aim to build one-hundred structures in 1833," said Lyman.

"Let me show you a few of the buildings we have put up already," said Benjamin, steering me over to the window.

"That is the Unitarian Church. There is the Washington Block," said Benjamin, pointing in various directions.

"That is the Webster Block. There is the new jail," said Lyman, also pointing.

"Over here is the American Hotel. Over there is the United States Hotel," said Benjamin.

"Neither, of course, is as fine as the one you are staying in right now," said Lyman.

"Talk to anyone in Western New York. I have a proven track record in financing and building stately public buildings," said Benjamin.

"As well as superb private dwellings," said Lyman.

"The question at hand is this," said Benjamin.

"Would you care to invest in my brother's new real-estate-development firm?" asked Lyman.

"You will quadruple your investment within five years," promised Benjamin.

"Hmm. I don't know. Isn't real estate risky?" I asked.

"The goal is to buy up land," said Benjamin.

"And not to be the last one holding the deed," said Lyman.

"The last-one-out theory," said Benjamin.

"Sell at the last possible moment before prices fall," said Lyman.

"As they inevitably do," said Benjamin.

Lyman reached inside his purple waistcoat and pulled from his pocket a folded paper document. "This is a note for one thousand dollars co-signed by Hiram Pratt," said Lyman.

"Along with Lyman and myself, Mr. Pratt is one of Buffalo's leading citizens," said Benjamin. "I do not doubt that he shall be elected mayor or even governor one day," said Benjamin.

"In return for a loan from you of one-thousand dollars, in gold, we could give you this note as collateral," said Lyman.

"And invest the proceeds in our real-estate venture," said Benjamin.

"Remember, that is one-hundred buildings in three-hundred-sixty-five days," said Lyman.

"I need to think about it," I answered. Once again paying attention, Bunny looked at me and shook her head, putting in her two cents, gathered from her intuitive sense alone, for I have no doubt she could not much understand my dealings with the Rathbuns other than they were offering me some trade. Having witnessed her supernatural power in action before and finding it dead-on correct, I deferred for now to her "sixth sense" and told them that I would give them an answer on the morrow.

Beside the fact, I could not abide eating dinner with this conversational tag team, these experts at the game of verbal shuttlecock, who expected a tip for passing information, just like their desk clerks earlier, only in the Rathbun's league they expected the tips to be correspondingly larger. "I'd like to get some air, and Listening Rabbit wishes to go outdoors," I announced, preparing to leave. "Where can we go to buy dinner and see a bit of the local scenery before we have to leave tomorrow?"

At Lyman Rathbun's suggestion, we directed ourselves toward some "colorful scenery, all right" in the area near the terminus of the Erie Canal, the city's "Infected District." Normally, he explained, he would never send his guests to this neighborhood; the Eagle Tavern's high-class clientele abhorred the place.

"But," chimed in Benjamin, "in light of your Indian, ahem, guest, who will not be allowed in the politer precincts of the city, it is there that you will find the best welcome."

"But mind whom you touch," warned Lyman, "however casually, for he or she can visit upon you every misfortune from syphilis to head lice to money missing from your wallet."

In our city finest, Bunny and I strolled through the newly incorporated city of Buffalo, New York. We headed downhill toward the waterfront, turned left and walked a half-mile to the Erie Canal. The Infected District consisted of a few streets crisscrossing where man-made river met nature-made lake. The area bustled — men rolling barrels every which way; unescorted ladies roving in packs; horses pulling carts loaded with crates; horse shit *everywhere*; cries of anger, pain, strain, and angst. Blocky boats jammed the canal floating end-to-end for more than a mile. Present, too, were all of the extras a town attracts when aswarm with money, namely, prostitutes, petty thieves, alcoholics, gamblers, and confidence men.

"Sailor! Want your willy sucked?" boldly asked a woman in a threadbare second-hand designer dress whom we passed on the wooden plank sidewalk.

"Excuse me?"

"C'mon! That skinny, flat-chested squaw can't pop your cork like I can." The hooker's face could only be described as asymmetrical — she had a black eye, and her left cheek was red and swollen. A poorly healed knife wound crossed her forehead, intersecting the heavy lines found thereon. She was missing a gaggle of teeth.

"Um, very sorry. Not interested," I said as I walked on.

In my wake followed Bunny, who hauled off and, as we indelicately put it in 2015, bitch-slapped the woman on the unmarked cheek and knocked her to her knees. Over the woman's prone body she declared, "Connor heap-big gentleman," I suspect as much for the injury done by the woman to her feelings, calling her a flat, skinny squaw, as to me.

"Bunny! You can't just hit people!" I scolded, while helping the woman to her feet. "A thousand pardons," I said. "Bunny gets a little over-protective. Are you all right?"

"Yes, thank you. Sorry to have bothered you, sir," said the hooker. Her face now appeared more symmetrical, with a new shiner surrounding her right eye and a rapidly purpling welt on her right cheek to match the injuries inflicted on the left side of her face.

Bunny stood apart from us and pouted after my admonishment. "Bunny sorry," she muttered, face turned away from the woman and me so she could protect her pride but still remain audible to us. I gave the woman a shilling piece for her pain and quickly whisked Bunny and myself away.

But no sooner had we extricated ourselves from that predicament than a new situation, thankfully not involving us directly, erupted a few feet away. A seventeen- or eighteen-year-old youth conked an old gentleman on the head and threatened to beat him further unless he gave up his wallet immediately. Leery of getting involved, I held Bunny back from rushing in and breaking up the assault. For one thing, I didn't know how the hoodlum might be armed, with a knife, perhaps, or a pistol.

The old man shook off the shock of getting cold-cocked and removed from under his overcoat a coiled bullwhip. The youth slipped a knife from its sheath, but before he managed to point it the old man cracked his whip and tore the knife out of his hand, leaving two fingers dangling from tendons and bleeding profusely. The old man followed rapidly with a strike to the face that lopped off the tip of the robber's nose. The youth collapsed onto the gravel sidewalk to howl and lick his wounds, but the old man was not finished. He gave him twenty lashes, leaving the youth's back a pulpy mess of carved skin and torn wool. The youth passed out from pain and shock (I saw him breathing so knew he wasn't killed); the old man calmly re-coiled his whip, attached it to his belt, and went on his merry way.

Stunned, Bunny and I shuffled away from the scene, letting a watchman or constable or Good Samaritan tend to the severely chastened would-be robber. Deciding we had had enough of Buffalo's street life, Bunny and I ducked into a restaurant whose sign out front promised fresh lake perch and cold English ale. While we feasted on fried fish and drank many pints of ale, I informed Bunny that I wanted to learn how to handle a whip like that old gentleman who had done in that delinquent youth. "Who can teach me?" I asked.

"Bunny not know. Can't fight with bow and arrow or tomahawk. But she can cook big pot of acorn stew!"

"I know! We'll go to a stable. They're bound to have whips there." We asked our waiter where we could find the nearest stable. He answered us, we settled our bill, and we took off across the street and down the block to Merle's Stable. On the wall inside the shack where Merle conducted business hung several coiled whips of various lengths and diameters.

Merle, a grizzled but affable character who often smiled and flashed brown tobacco-stained teeth, had to redirect us to a "Feed and Seed" store where such items were bought. The whips hanging on his wall were not for sale but were used in his business to handle recalcitrant horses. The Feed and Seed was closed for the night, Merle informed us, so we deferred my purchasing errand until the next day before leaving town. Having had my fill of fish, ale, and Buffalo's Infected District, I suggested to Bunny that we turn in early, visit the Feed and Seed first thing in the morning, and then catch our stage to Fredonia. We returned to the Eagle Tavern without further incident and put my plan into action.

The next morning I bought a ten-foot beginner's model bullwhip at the Feed and Seed Emporium, an amazing establishment that sold everything from farm implements and blacksmith accessories, to seed corn and cattle feed, cooking pots, oil lanterns, and washtubs. The store sold whips as long as twenty-two feet for professional drivers driving large teams of horses. A beginner like me, the clerk coached, had best start out with an eight- or ten-foot whip. He demonstrated cracking the whip vertically so it struck the floor (and stirred up a major dust tornado) and horizontally using a sidearm motion. He advised me to practice these two moves and take things from there.

Confident that I would later meet someone who could coach me further in my quest to become competent in defending myself with a bullwhip, I hustled Bunny over to the depot where we bought tickets to ride on the eleven o'clock stage to Fredonia. In the remaining interval we had simply to retrieve our luggage, settle our hotel bill, and go.

I had forgotten about my promise to consider the Rathbun brothers' business proposal. By the fireplace in the lobby of the Eagle Tavern, Benjamin and Lyman sat in chairs awaiting me. I was prepared to offer them the money they had requested just to escape their presence before the aggressive sales job got rolling again.

After a porter brought down my things and I had recovered my gold from the hotel safe, I counted out four Krugerrands worth about one thousand dollars and dropped them into Lyman's left hand. Simultaneously with the right hand Lyman handed me the note seen last night on which Benjamin Rathbun's signature now joined Hiram Pratt's.

"This note represents a share of the company and its profits," said Benjamin.

"But heed: do not wait too long before selling it," said Lyman.

"The key is to get into the market and get out again before prices fall," said Benjamin.

"Thanks for the advice," I said. But I didn't follow Benjamin Rathbun's advice. I hung onto the note long enough for it to emerge later, in 1837, that the Rathbun brothers were engaged in a scheme by which they sold fraudulent shares in Benjamin's enterprises backed by forged notes. The signature of Hiram Pratt appearing on my note was forged by Benjamin's nephew, Lyman Rathbun Howlett, who was all of fourteen years old at the time. Projecting to all the world a cherubic face and innocent disposition, in reality Lyman the Younger was a scamp and a rascal who privately apprenticed in the art of white-collar crime with his uncle Benjamin.

Although Benjamin blamed his by-then-dead brother for masterminding the fraud, a jury found him guilty of being an accessory to fraud, and he served three years in the Buffalo jailhouse that his construction company had built. The note in my possession was worthless, of course, but not so the lesson I learned from my experience, to wit: do not invest in real estate or farm commodities, only put your money into steel, railroads, and power utilities.

It turned out that Bunny and I were the Fredonia stage's only passengers. The coach itself was a handsome affair sporting a polished maple body, rugged spoked wheels, a team of four horses, and a nearly toothless driver wearing a top hat. The passenger compartment was upholstered with leather and featured a cupboard inside of which could be found a water canteen, corn whiskey, and strips of deer jerky to snack on during the trip. Having only once ridden on such a vehicle at a theme park (the modern-day version of a county fair or carnival) when I was a child, I looked forward to the ride.

That is, until we got underway and my rear end confronted the seat and floor and side of the coach as we banged and bumped along rocky dirt "roads" hardly deserving of the name. Bunny, too, was thrown all around the coach — once or twice we slammed into each other — and I regretted that there were not more passengers to wedge everybody into place. Four-and-a-half hours later (a forty-five-minute trip on modern highways), we arrived in Fredonia, New York, and were confronted with a scene of near-apocalyptic devastation. Practically the whole town had burned down and lay in a smoking ruin. I fervently prayed — very unlike me — that Rachel was not lying dead underneath a pile of burnt rubble. Bunny and I desperately sought out anyone who could answer our questions about what had so recently transpired there.

Chapter Six

Bunny and I squinted our eyes, plugged our noses, and locked our lips to prevent the dense smoke hanging in the air from entering our bodies. Fredonia was a wreck — a black splotch of smoldering debris set on stately lakeside property. I thought, "Great! My new suit is probably ruined, unless I can find a dry cleaner (fat chance of that)." Bunny previously had looked as though she had tossed aside all of her doubts about accompanying me east, but now they had all come rushing back. Never mind, we only had to wait a day until the next stage came, and we could catch it back to Buffalo. Meantime, we had twenty-four hours to learn the fate of Rachel and Bilson. I hoped I wouldn't have to bury her. Him? I'd just as soon let the buzzards eat his stinking body and spit out his vile bones.

We wandered aimlessly amid collapsed buildings whose contents of dry goods or foodstuffs lay scattered about, charred. A few smoking stakes and pickets sticking upright out of the ground were all that remained of houses and barns. Here and there dead livestock stood or lay in the torched straw of former barns and pastures, roasted in their skins. "Graveyard," suggested Bunny. "People bury dead."

I followed her in the direction that her sixth sense told her stood the town's cemetery until we found it — a pathetic handful of stone markers dotting a meadow. Strangely, no grave appeared freshly dug. Moreover, nobody congregated at the site, so we had to move elsewhere for an explanation of the destruction surrounding us. "River," said Bunny, leading me in the direction of a stream she smelled either in her nose or perceived in her mind. There, finally, we met with a resident, Eustis Blake, a grizzled old-timer with a smudged black face, who told us the story.

Eustis hailed from the new site of Fredonia, "a half-mile to the other side of the creek," he explained. My heart brightened; Rachel could be mere footsteps away. As we spoke, our interlocutor busied himself with filling a large leather bucket with river water.

"What in God's name happened here?" I asked. Bunny was all ears.

"Durned fool tried drilling for oil up on Clavey Road by the salt mines," said Eustis.

"And ...?"

"The cusséd stuff blowed up on him. Flaming oil spurting up out of the ground got caught in a wind and sprayed the whole dang town with liquid fire. Being fifteen-sixteenths wood, the whole kit and caboodle burned down quicker than you can say 'Andrew Jackson.'"

"What about the town's residents? Surely, many must have been killed?"

"Well, I know a few people that lost some cattle, pigs, and horses, but I don't think anybody lost any kin. Practically the whole town, excepting them that had relations who could take them in elsewhere, is camped across the river. Soon we plan to raise some buildings and rebuild Fredonia in a new location and let the earth reclaim the wasteland you see here."

"Can we return with you to the campsite?" I asked. "I may know people there. Maybe I could help."

"That's right neighborly of you, mister. Follow me. We're just over that hill."

Bunny and I followed Eustis over the hill; a campground of shacks, canvas tents, and lean-tos came into focus. Smoke rose from this settlement, too, only it came from controlled and contained fires. I did not glimpse Rachel or Bilson milling about the shantytown, where everybody looked occupied in planning and preparing to rebuild.

We arrived at Eustis's tent, a small canvas job with a dirt floor, containing nothing but a bedroll and a wooden trunk holding Eustis's mementos. "Sit here," he told Bunny and me, indicating a log he had set up outside his tent flap — its porch, if you will. "I'll go pour some water."

Eustis returned with a trio of tin cups brimming with smoky-flavored water and sat beside us on the log. He took great interest in my adding a drop of chlorine to the cup of water he had handed me. "Purely medicinal," I said.

"Sorry to pry," Eustis apologized.

"Nothing to be sorry for. Listen, I'm very interested to learn the fate of one person in particular who I was told lived in Fredonia. Rachel Levy? She would have been traveling with a man named Bruce Bilson."

"BILSON? Why that's the villain who burned down our town!"

"You're joking."

"I curse the day he appeared among us!"

"And Rachel?"

"His woman. A Jewess, I heard."

"Are they here still or did they leave after the fire?"

"They left all right. Bilson was tarred and feathered and run out of town on a rail." Bunny and I gaped at each other while Eustis told us the sordid tale.

"Bilson came here on the stage one day, same as you. Right away he got to throwing money around. Pure gold. I ain't never seen real gold before. Silver's the closest precious metal I'd ever seen, and I ain't seen much of that in fifty-one years."

Bilson had deposited his money in the local bank. Banker Freeman McNeil, born in 1776, hence his name, accepted his gold gladly. Together, they drummed up a scheme to drill for petroleum in the surrounding countryside.

Next, they had to line up investors. They invited the ten or fifteen richest men in town to one of the local meetinghouses, where Bilson had set up a practical demonstration of the benefits of oil. Using the output from his well, he lit the interior with oil-fed lanterns. And he had refitted a Franklin stove to burn oil, which on one of the first really cold days of autumn had made the meetinghouse a toasty, inviting environment. All of the important men marveled at the oil heater, impressed at the steady heat it gave off as opposed to a wood-burning stove, whose temperature varied depending on the fire's fury, and they immediately recognized the practical value of oil. Each enrolled in the initial stock offering by pledging to invest anywhere from five hundred to three thousand dollars in an oil-drilling venture.

In short, Bilson had arrived from the future and engaged in a get-rich-quick scheme employing his advanced physics and engineering knowledge.

Things had gone swimmingly for a while as the black gold was pumped from the ground and sold to people in the area to warm their homes with an admittedly dirty but even heat from a power source free to anyone who could coax it out of the ground. Bilson's go-getter banker and his booster cronies loved the return on their investment. Bilson, with the biggest stake in the scheme, had made out the handsomest.

Then a well had caught fire; nobody quite for sure knew how. It could have been an accident — ignited by a worker lighting his pipe. Or it could have been set deliberately by a salt-mine operator angry that oil was seeping into and contaminating his salt mine. In these days, before scientific fire investigations, no one knew if the cap on the well had popped off from an underground eruption or had been axed off by a saboteur.

For the purposes of the mob that assembled to punish Bilson, the proximate cause of the fire did not much matter. As people gathered across the river in the aftermath of the disaster, filthy, tired, and ruined, their anger swelled until someone accused Bilson of causing the fire. It was he, after all, who had drilled the original well and talked the people into heating their homes and barns with oil. A chorus of accusations and threats followed, along with some pushing and shoving, until a member of the nascent mob suggested that Bilson be jailed. That proved problematic, because the jail had burned down along with the rest of the town. Someone else raised the stakes considerably when he proposed that Bilson be hanged. Agreeing that that punishment was too drastic, the mob sought another remedy.

Things proceeded along these lines until someone shouted out a solution that garnered the mob's unanimous assent: "Let's tar and feather the rascal!"

An enthused, sadistic cheer went up, and the mob immediately set about its task. A group of men seized Bilson and tied his hands behind him. A second group filtered through the former town to locate the appropriate tools that may have survived the fire — tar, chickens, and paintbrushes.

The tar could still be found inside a fireproof bucket. It didn't have to be heated; it already was plenty hot and viscous due to the inferno that had engulfed the barn it sat next to. An army of women, the mob's ladies auxiliary if you will, set to plucking a number of chickens found asphyxiated in coops inside a heavily damaged barn. Their feathers were scorched but otherwise serviceable and were bagged in burlap sacks. A few of the town's Irish servants dug through the ruins of their rooms and returned to the town-wide scavenger hunt carrying burnt brushes and whisk brooms.

The two or three most vocal and alarmist of the mob proceeded to dip the brushes into the hot tar and slop it onto a screaming Bilson. One painted his front, another his back, and a third dumped the remaining tar in the bucket over his head. Others, including children, grabbed handfuls of chicken feathers and tossed them at Bilson. These struck him with the force of, and leaving a splatter pattern similar to, loosely packed snowballs. Covered head-to-toe with feathers, Bilson was seated on a rail and hoisted aloft by two of the town's most strapping fellows and thereupon thrown into the river, where he sat on the shallow bottom and wailed.

"He's lucky he didn't get the Tory Treatment," said Eustis. "That's where they strip you first and you get second- and third-degree burns. Plus you have a devil of a time scrubbing off all that tar." As it was, with Bilson fully clothed and chapeauxed, Eustis reported blisters bubbling up around Bilson's hairline and on the back of his neck.

"But what of Rachel?" I asked.

"None of our townsfolk held her responsible for the disaster. We're a Christian town after all. I hope that she remembers the Christian mercy extended to her. Who knows? Maybe she'll see that Jesus shines with the one-true light and she'll be converted from her heathen, Jew ways."

"So where is she?" I demanded. I had to get to the crux here; I had neither the time nor the energy to take Eustis to task for his anti-Semitism, which Rachel had conditioned me to denounce loudly whenever I heard it. I had a long history of taking on family, friends, and even my boss once over the issue, but now I had more pressing matters.

"We let her gather her possessions and withdraw her gold from the bank" — minus a hefty 'donation' to help fund the new town — "and the next morning we put her on a stage to Albany. From there it's anybody's guess where she went. I suspect she bribed the driver to drive out into the woods and search for Bilson. He hasn't shown up on anybody's doorstep yet. Not that anybody would let him in, being banished and suchlike."

"You're sure she wasn't hurt?" I asked.

"No need to concern yourself with that. She was treated with the respect owing to a proper lady."

I breathed a sigh of relief and huddled with my thoughts out walking in the surrounding woods for a while. I left Bunny behind with Eustis, who had begun flirting with her. First, I was crushed that Rachel had escaped my grasp by mere days for a second time. I would get within a few miles or feet of her, only to find she had vamoosed days or mere hours before.

Second, I had to figure out what to do next, for Bunny and I certainly could not stay in a Fredonia, which presently consisted of one part hope and two parts charcoal. Faced with the choice of three-and-a-half days on a stagecoach to Albany, whose route no doubt took it over every single bump and large rock between the two points, and four days on a packet boat from Buffalo on a smooth-flowing Erie Canal, I opted for the latter.

I did not know whether I would locate Rachel — and possibly Bilson also — in Albany. More in line with her tastes, she had probably sailed down the Hudson River to New York City, where she could join the teeming crowds of shippers and shopkeepers, bankers and builders, hoteliers, and lawyers residing there, and she could feel the adrenaline rush of living in the nation's largest and most important urb. Albany may have been the state's capital city, but it could not hold a candle to the bright lights of old Broadway.

Meanwhile, before the stage to Buffalo returned at three o'clock the next afternoon (for the hour was getting late), Bunny and I attempted to settle in for the night. Eustis's neighbor, Gabriel Littlefield, a freckled, bucktoothed shop clerk raised in the farming hinterlands and presently living on his own in the county seat, offered to share the canopied space under his lean-to. I accepted his offer and unrolled my space-age sleeping bag beside his bedroll under the primitive shelter he had constructed.

Bunny accepted Eustis's offer to bunk with him. I knew that hanky-panky would result, but I accepted the situation. How could I not? Bunny was a free woman; she could sleep with whomever she chose. True, I feared the consequences when or if Eustis discovered Bunny's true gender. But I imagined that she had rehearsed ways of hiding her sex, and her secret might not come uncorked. Then again, Bunny may have tipped off Eustis when I was not standing within eyeshot or earshot, and it turned out that he liked that sort of thing. Besides, both appeared fully cognizant that they would enjoy only a single night of love together before Bunny and I had to depart on the morrow.

Next morning, I woke early and enjoyed breakfast with Gabriel, who had rustled up quail eggs somewhere. Fried for a few moments over a campfire, they tasted good, though they were rather less than satisfying due to their miniscule size. Still, it was some nutrition to tide me over on my upcoming ride.

Bunny and Eustis emerged from his tent sometime later. He had a smile as big as Lake Erie on his face, and she had a highly contented look on hers. Their liaison appeared a rousing success. Eustis said as much when he cornered me and boasted of his conquest. He had sidled up to me as I stared into a shard of mirror glass strung up on a nearby tree and shaved with a straight-razor I bought in Buffalo, cold river water, and lye soap, freshly made from Fredonia's ashes by one of the women who looked after Eustis. A horse-faced spinster named Nelly Nickerson, she popped in on him periodically to make certain he ate at least one square meal per day, laundered his drawers at least weekly, and didn't go too long without a bath. As part of her charity to the crude but honest bachelor, she dropped off a supply of the harsh soap, and I borrowed a cake with Eustis's blessing. He used it to clean everything from his face and hands to his coffeepot and saddle.

Eustis spoke enthusiastically but softly so Bunny would not likely overhear. "Did you know that Indian squaws like it from behind?" He glanced around to see if Bunny or anyone else was within earshot. "Your little Indian friend is tighter than a hen!"

I could not believe Eustis was telling me this. "Is that so?" I asked, rapidly shaving and acting disinterested to discourage any further disclosure about last night's amorous adventure.

"Honest Injun!" he swore, raising his hand. Then he guffawed, realizing he had made something of a pun. Divulging no further information (thank God), he left me alone and spent the rest of the morning marching about the settlement like a rooster that had gotten very lucky all night. I wondered how impressed with himself he would feel if he knew that Bunny was not a hen, but a rooster like he.

The stage finally came at around four o'clock, about an hour late, and Bunny and I departed. But not before she and Eustis hugged and kissed so much that I feared the sparks they threw off would re-ignite the town. An "all aboard" notice from the stage driver finally impelled them to unlock lips, and she joined me inside the coach. The ride was unremarkable, except for the promise I made to myself, as the victim of wooden wheels grinding against granite rocks, to invest some of my fortune in rubber tires if the opportunity ever arose.

Back in Buffalo, we slogged a short distance across a muddy field from the stagecoach depot to the Erie Canal terminal. Passengers awaiting the next packet boat east stood around reminding me that Bunny and I had entered civilization for good, and empty boats were a thing of the past. We bought our tickets, handed over our baggage (minus my gold, which I hung onto), and waited for a team of horses to be hitched up to our boat. Finally, we got underway, accelerating to a whopping four-miles-per-hour before it was time to change horses a couple of hours later.

The packet boat we rode spanned eighty feet, but it was only fourteen feet wide to fit within the banks of the canal. By standards I had witnessed thus far in my sojourn, accommodations were luxurious — the dining room featured tablecloths and fine pewter utensils, and it served fresher, tastier fare than the boats I had earlier sailed on. The sleeping compartments were divided between males, who slept fore in the parlor and bar, and females, who slept aft in the dining room. Hidden behind heavy green velvet drapes along the walls of both rooms were pull-down beds with feather mattresses that offered a comfortable night's sleep, if you could ignore the pungent odors of feet and ass hanging in the air with everybody's boots and trousers cast off at bedtime.

Most impressive, the ticket agent had staged no fuss on account of Bunny's nonwhite origins when I paid our fares. Out east, people appeared less rattled by the sight of an Indian; as this was no longer frontier territory, Indians posed little threat to them like back in Chicago, which stood at the tense border between white and Indian country. In the more enlightened east, if you had the coins to pay for your passage, then you were let on the boat without argument. Commerce in Western New York seemingly had taken a permanent vacation from prejudice.

Still, I was mindful of Bunny's potential to unnerve the female passengers by her presence. The company may have had no qualms about allowing her onboard, but the general passenger might fear her, particularly the ladies, if it were found out she was male. To avoid a general panic in the ladies' quarters, I instructed her not to undress or bathe within eyesight of her roommates. I felt that placing her in the ladies' midst perhaps undermined their privacy, but I believed it was the best solution, for her presence in the men's quarters would have raised many uncomfortable questions and subjected her to verbal, if not physical, abuse.

I repeated my habit of spending much time atop the boat. Stationed around the deck were lounge chairs and tables at which passengers played checkers or dominoes in the heavily slanted autumn sun. Waiters carried on a brisk business, carting trays of glasses holding whiskey up and down the barroom stairway. I drank my share, although I was getting tired of whiskey, the only spirit available west of the Appalachians. A waiter informed me that rum and beer in addition to wine and gin could be bought on Hudson River boats.

Reclining in a lounge chair, enjoying an alcoholic beverage on a boat amidst unspoiled scenery exploding with the orange, yellow, red, and purple hues of fall: you would think it was an exercise in perfect relaxation. Indeed it was; that is until a deckhand shouted "BRIDGE!" and everybody had to crouch or lie flat against the deck as we flowed under the arch of a solid stone bridge in well-to-do villages or between the spans of a rickety wood planking bridge in not-so-well-to-do villages. Ducking under bridges presented a rather comic scene as ladies and gentlemen in their traveling finery prostrated themselves for a moment, then rose up again and continued their conversations and card games as if nothing had interrupted them.

Without waves to trouble her sense of balance, Bunny joined me on the top deck and thoroughly enjoyed gazing at the passing scenery. After about two hours, however, she confessed to me, "Bunny bored."

"Me, too. Let's play a game of cards."

"Don't know how."

"I'll teach you." So I bought a pack of playing cards from the bartender downstairs, and I attempted to teach Bunny the simplest card game I knew, Go Fish.

It took a few hands for her to understand the game. But she proved a quick study at counting the spots on the cards and decoding their four possible shapes. I won the first three hands until her luck and skill converged so that she finally won a hand.

"Yip yip yippee!" she crowed, then engaged in a celebratory dance — she raised her arms and waved her hands, jiggled her posterior, and brayed at the sky in triumph. As she busied herself dancing and gloating, she completely missed hearing the word "Bridge!" bellowed by the nearby helmsman. While I dropped to the deck, an immobile cut-limestone bridge slammed into Bunny and swept her into the canal.

"MAN OVERBOARD!" I yelled, uncertain what else to do. I hastily added, "WOMAN OVERBOARD!" hoping that people had interpreted my first exclamation as general and not literal.

I scrambled to my feet and saw a quickly receding Bunny struggle. I threw off my jacket and shoes — queer, dainty things that reminded me of modern-day women's pumps — and dove in after her.

That the water was only five feet deep encouraged my heroics. Bunny flailed toward me as I paddled toward her. "It's not deep!" I called. "You can stand here!"

Bunny was panicking, though, and her head dipped below the surface a few times and she bobbed back up coughing and choking. Meantime, sailors on the stopped boat threw a rope to me, which I clenched in my teeth, and swam the last few strokes to Bunny. "Here! Hold the rope! They'll tow us in!"

I spun Bunny around onto her back and put the rope in her hand. The sailors began tugging us toward the boat. Once thither we climbed up a side ladder and landed in a sopping heap on the deck, whereupon Bunny vomited on the boots of the captain, who had come to the stern to oversee the rescue.

"Is the Indian lass all right?" asked the captain.

"Bunny's ribs hurt," she complained.

"I'll check the manifest and see if there's a doctor on board," said the captain. "My apologies for your accident."

"No, I'm sorry," I said. "We weren't paying attention."

"Pay no mind. This doesn't happen on every trip, but it happens oftener than you would think."

The crew found a Dr. Bonham drinking in the dayroom. Drunkenly announcing a medical emergency and demanding everybody leave the room — to loud groans and complaints — he asked Bunny to remove her clothes and lie on the bar. Bunny reluctantly slipped out of her dress after the card sharks, traveling salesmen, and real estate speculators had quit their games, scooped up their drinks, and filed out of the parlor.

This was it, I feared — the doctor would find us out and the captain, already peeved at his ruined boots, would throw us off the boat in some dinky burg, and we'd be stuck riding a vertebrae-crushing stagecoach the rest of the way to Albany. But the doctor, drunk and preoccupied with lighting his cigar with damp Locofocos, neither noticed Bunny's lack of feminine curves nor had occasion to peek below her underwear once he focused through blurry eyes at the bruises swelling up and down her left side. He diagnosed her as "badly bruised," examined her no further, and returned to his place at the end of the bar over which he reached for a bottle and poured its contents into his glass. I wondered where he'd been trained and how he came to be called a "doctor" — unaccredited college and forged diploma were my guesses. Happily, after much rest below-deck, Bunny's bruises and her embarrassment had faded by the time we reached Albany.

Meantime, I commenced my whip-training, and my embarrassment was about to begin. Most passengers sat aft, so I took over the space behind the bow. I borrowed an empty barrel from a crew member and set it upside down. Upon it I placed my top hat, which would serve as my target. Like the Feed and Seed clerk had shown me, I twirled the whip a couple of times overhead and let fly at my hat. Naturally, I missed widely, as I did on many subsequent attempts. I failed even to achieve the characteristic "crack" sound associated with whips in the early going. On one try, I managed to strike my left shoe, peeling off the polish down to bare leather and making my toes smart greatly. Needless to say, this encouraged my whiskey consumption further as I attempted to anaesthetize myself from such self-inflicted injuries.

Repeated attempts started to reap rewards, however, and by the second afternoon of my practice regimen, I was able to strike the barrel regularly and even hit my top hat a couple of times, knocking it off the barrel and nearly into the canal. Curious spectators occasionally came forward to watch me, but they tended to drift away upon discovering how inexpert I was with my weapon. Nevertheless, by our last day aboard the boat, I was hitting my hat fairly frequently and even felt confident enough in my growing skill to turn my attention to passing saplings, which I was able to slice in half about one out of three times. Still, there was much practicing to be done, and whenever I had time to kill in places that Bunny and I would visit in the future, I brought out my top hat, transformed after awhile into a chewed-up felt rag, and worked at refining my technique.

After the agonizingly slow ride on the Erie Canal, we gladly transferred to a swift steam-powered boat that carried us down the Hudson River to New York City in a day and a half, no-time-flat by nineteenth-century standards. As our boat plowed the majestic river, past narrow channels with cliffs slicing up so high that clouds collected around their peaks, its paddle wheel chugging, I couldn't help but think of the words by the twentieth-century bard John Fogerty, who sang, "Big wheel keep on turnin', Proud Mary keep on burnin'. Rollin' ... rollin' ... rollin' down the river."

At long last we set our eyes on the Big Apple, New York City's twenty-first century nickname, where I expected, sooner or later, to run into Rachel and Bilson, and where the travel portion of this narrative halts.

I could not help but be struck by the contrast between the giant megalopolis of 18 million when I was born and its current size — at 170,000 it had had the same population as 2015 Peoria, Illinois. Like every other town on the water I had seen, its shoreline was assaulted by wave upon wave of cargo ships, dumping off loads of lumber, food, ore, fur, and rum while taking on manufactures to be returned to the western provinces in trade. Much of the sound you heard in New York, distinctly if you stood close by or a general background din further inland, was boatmen arguing and fighting over collisions in the harbor or tangled sailboat rigging.

Bunny and I were hustled off the boat by a rude and pushy Irish porter, and our bags were tossed overboard and landed on the pier with a plop. A pack of street urchins converged like curs on entrails ready to swipe any portion of our luggage. If not for Bunny letting out a bloodcurdling war whoop and waving at them threateningly, our possessions would have likely blown the ways of the four winds. The youths took one look at her savage visage and hastily retreated after observing from their street-life vantage that Bunny was the real deal — a genuine "red Indian" that would scalp you as soon as look at you.

"Well done!" I praised. "Remember that for other scrapes we get into."

"Dog-sucking whores!" spat Bunny, lifting our bags onto her shoulders and following me toward the Customs House.

I feared this place a little, for my bags contained numerous items to raise suspicion. Gold, for instance. High-tech, twenty-first-century camping gear. Chekagou. The latter two items provoked no comment as the clerk poked through my things with a stick. But the former evoked a shocked gasp and drew over the supervisor, who promptly and enthusiastically inserted his nose into my business.

"The New York State civil code requires you to declare all precious metals and legal tender before entering the port," the Senior Clerk informed me.

"Okay," I said.

"Have you an estimate of how much this gold is worth, sir?"

"Not exactly. I expect to deposit it all in the bank once we're done here and let them tell me how much it's worth."

"We shall have to weigh it then. DRUMMOND!" he shouted at the clerk who had first inspected my luggage. "We need an assayer here immediately!"

"Yes, Drummond," I commanded, "Assayer A.S.A.P."

"I beg your pardon?" asked the Senior Clerk, suspecting that I had mocked him, which in fact I had. But he became too fascinated with my utterance to protest.

"A.S.A.P.," I explained. "'As soon as possible.' It's a saying where I'm from."

"I like it — big round vowels, percussive consonants. DRUMMOND! Assayer, A.S.A.P.!" he bellowed. Then to me, quietly: "I'm sorry, Mister...?"

"Daniel Connor."

"... Mr. Connor. I'm sorry, but we cannot let you pass until we settle this matter. For the amount of money involved here we're required to call in the big guns — someone from a reputable bank with a secure vault who knows about current exchange rates. We're not equipped to provide these services here. I hope you understand."

I said that I sort of understood. I accepted the senior clerk's invitation to sit in his office while we waited for Drummond to return with a representative from the National Bank of the City of New York, a rock-solid institution, he said, with a long list of depositors, including wealthy merchants, furriers, and manufacturers.

While I relaxed with a snifter of whiskey confiscated that morning from a Canadian smuggler, the senior clerk made Bunny wait outside his office — this in spite of her expensive wardrobe, consisting of a kelly-green velvet dress trimmed with white lace and a silver necklace that came from her seemingly bottomless leather bag, now forsaken for a dainty yellow cinch purse. Hanging from her neck by a silver chain, the elaborately etched medallion shone brilliantly and lent needed relief to Bunny's otherwise two-dimensional chest. Her necklace would have fetched a hefty sum at one of the modern world's Native American (the twenty-first-century term for "Indian") art galleries. Yet the senior clerk chose to ignore all of this evidence that Bunny was due the respect of a lady and surrendered to his prejudice, causing me to reconsider my recently acquired belief that prejudice and intolerance were based on class and not race.

After an interminable interval, an out-of-breath Drummond returned with another puffing and wheezing individual, Roger Chillicothe, Senior Teller at the National Bank of New York.

Chillicothe, a gaunt character in an exaggeratedly tall top hat and woolen scarf hiding all of his face except his eyes, closely examined about twenty of the identical coins. "Strange Dutch inscriptions," he commented, his voice the timbre of a creaking door. He weighed a few on a balance-beam scale he produced from a satchel. "Each weighs an ounce," he determined, and then he proceeded to count every single coin, placing stacks of ten in neat rows across the Customs House counter. "Almost one hundred," he tallied.

Upon completing a few calculations in his notebook, he made his pronouncement: "You have here in gold specie of uncertain origin sixty-seven thousand two-hundred-twelve dollars and eighteen cents. Mr. Connor, may I please present my credentials on behalf of the National Bank of the City of New York?" he asked, handing me a finely engraved business card. "Sir, our bank would sincerely appreciate the opportunity to become the depository of your fortune. In the hands of Mr. Gallatin, president of our bank, your money will compound to no end. Look around us here," he said, directing our eyes to the surrounding construction, shipping, and manufacturing noisily occurring outside the senior clerk's office window. "Boundless opportunities for a man in possession of a boatload of cash like yourself."

I definitely liked the idea of this, becoming a member of the idle rich class with Bunny as my butler. Buy a house on Fifth Avenue, country in the Hamptons, maybe run for political office someday. "It's a safe bank?" I asked. "Big, thick walls around your vault?"

"The thickest, sir," Chillicothe drolly replied.

"You've got a deal," I stuck out my hand to shake, but Chillicothe stared at it uncomprehendingly. Obviously, he was a social handicap, but he ciphered big numbers flawlessly, not unlike Barry Stompke whom I had left in my cosmic dust at the University of Chicago.

"Sir, I must insist: there is too much money here for you to carry on Manhatta Isle. There are ruffians lurking around every corner poised to bop you on the head and steal everything but your undergarments, and a few will steal even those. I shall summon a lead-lined coach with a full complement of armed guards to transport us to the bank. Only a large militia could stop us."

"Sounds good," I said, thinking it sounded excessive. But then he was bound to know more than I about local dangers. Still, with Bunny at my side, I felt invincible.

"Please grant me an hour or thereabouts to plan and execute the operation. With Coast Guard and Army officials stationed here at the Customs House, your gold and you ought to be safe until my return."

The plan unfolded flawlessly. Chillicothe showed up in about fifty-five minutes. In a three-minute span, he stationed guards up and down the hall from the Senior Clerk's office all of the way to a side door, which opened onto a dock peopled with burly guards wearing side arms. In an operation worthy of the President's Secret Service, Bunny, gold, and I were ushered out of the Customs House and into an armored coach pulled by a team of twelve horses. From narrow slits I saw the guards from the dock all clamber onto the sides and top of the coach, and we sped off at the crack of the driver's whip. We traveled at a fast gallop through the crowded streets of New York, nearly running over numerous pedestrians, pigs, and dogs in our path.

A few minutes later, we came to a jarring halt behind the stately granite National Bank of New York. The guards leaped off the coach and drew their weapons on phantom assailants hidden behind hay wagons, water troughs, and ashbins, meaning to rob me of my gold. The security guard accompanying us inside the coach threw open the door and shoved my gold, Bunny, and me down a ramp, through an exterior basement door, and into the bowels of the bank building. Once we were safely inside, an armor-plated door clanged shut, locking out all pursuers and blocking out all natural light. Congratulating one another, the guards immediately threw down their guns, tossed off their overcoats, and winged aside their hats. Another cash deposit made successfully.

Witnessing these precautions with our lives in relation to my hoard of gold, a shudder befell me as I recognized that Bunny and I had been traveling in a seriously understaffed manner. We could have been robbed, shot, or scalped in the West as easily as we had landed safely in the East.

A sallow, spectral Chillicothe emerged from down a long black passageway, looking very much like Lucifer with lantern raised in one hand and ledger book and ink feather clutched in the other. On the back of a guard whom Chillicothe impressed for the occasion, I signed a receipt for sixty-seven thousand two-hundred-twelve dollars and eighteen cents deposited into the National Bank of New York. Given the dungeon-like setting, Chillicothe's avuncular undertaker character, and my own imagination tutored by devil-possession tales and horror cinema (motion pictures depicting scary subject matter), the bank could not have more perfectly dramatized the experience of selling one's soul for earthly riches. I wondered if Daniel Webster could defend me should I ever require someone of his worldly experience and supernatural negotiating abilities in extricating me from a tumble into the proverbial pickle barrel.

"Where shall I list you as dwelling?" asked Chillicothe, squinting at my receipt and amending it here and there with his quill.

"Um, I don't know yet. We hadn't gotten that far in our plans when we were detained at the Customs House."

"Might I suggest the City Hotel? It's the finest lodging place in North America."

"Fine." Bunny and I began to walk with him down the dark corridor and up some stairs toward a better-lighted space, judging by a white rectangle ahead indicating the presence of a door leading to a brighter place.

We climbed about four steps and passed through the aforesaid door and into the blinding sky-lit lobby of the National Bank of New York, whereupon we climbed another staircase, this one carved from elegant marble, to the second floor. After a short trip through a hallway decorated with a lush maroon carpet and portraits of characters in powdered wigs lining the walls, we arrived at the outer office of Albert Gallatin, President of the National Bank of New York.

"You may call him Mr. Gallatin or Mr. Secretary. He goes by either appellation," creaked Chillicothe.

"Mr. Secretary?" I asked. I thought I was supposed to speak with the president of the bank, not some lowly secretary.

"Secretary of the Treasury. Under Mr. Jefferson."

"*Thomas* Jefferson?"

"The one and only. Of course, this was when Mr. Gallatin was a young man with a more energetic constitution."

"Wow. I'm about to meet with a man who actually knew Thomas Jefferson."

"All of Mr. Gallatin's guests say the same thing. Meeting him is a momentous occasion for everyone." Least of all someone educated in the twenty-first century, when Jefferson was thought of more highly than every other founding father, Washington included.

Gallatin's door swung outward and the man himself emerged from the cramped office. At first he appeared of the same powdered wig ilk as the men in the paintings. But on closer inspection his long white hair and ponytail were authentic outgrowths of his head and not placed atop it as mere ceremonial decoration. His eyes had the mischievous gleam and his mouth the impish curl of a public man who had seen everything there was to see, and all that kept him interested at present were amused thoughts about other men's folly. In truth, he resembled more than a little Charlie Watts, drummer of the Rolling Stones, a modern musical quintet of note.

"Felicitations!" he said, greeting me. He turned to Bunny and to our mutual amazement uttered, "Kweh, ya winoh!"

"Bo sho," Bunny tartly responded. Then she upbraided Gallatin in her native tongue and spat on his fine Turkish rug. Oh, God, I thought, here I had just recently met the man, and Bunny had spoiled the occasion with some Indian deprecation.

Gallatin apologized for his impertinence in the Potawatomi language, which greatly pacified Bunny, who immediately became his friend for life. He said something more in Potawatomi after which Bunny flounced around the tight confines of the office, her behavior evidently the product of a compliment about her dress.

"Sorry about the misunderstanding with your Indian maid," Mr. Gallatin said to me. "Sometimes I do overstretch my reach."

"You accidentally insulted her?"

"I'm afraid so. I greeted her in Huron and she's Potawatomi. She did not take too kindly to that."

"Sorry about your rug. What did she say before she spat?"

"She called the Huron a 'pack of dog-sucking whores.'"

"How do you know her language?"

"A hobby of mine, collecting languages. I can speak over a dozen. Greek and Latin naturally, plus English, French, Russian, and German. Most recently, I've investigated the native languages of the North American continent, including the Iroquois and Algonquin language families. I've attained a reasonably solid knowledge of Cherokee — shame on what dear Mr. Jackson perpetrated there with his Trail of Tears! — and, of course, our local Delaware."

"And you have time to run a bank?"

"Mr. Chillicothe runs the day-to-day operations of the bank. I'm purely a figurehead here. Put out to pasture upstairs away from the action downstairs, to serve out my dotage. Hence, my time for such gentlemen's pursuits as writing my memoirs and researching languages."

A stunned "Interesting!" was all I could muster in the presence of such a monumental over-achiever as Albert Gallatin, who, now and later, would prove a good and useful friend.

"Every so often they trot me out to meet depositors such as yourself. 'Meet Mr. Gallatin,' they say. 'He knew Jefferson personally.' Inevitably, I'm forced to recite some anecdote pertaining to the President and answer questions about his private life. 'Mr. Gallatin, is it true that Jefferson fathered a child by a slave?' everybody asks. I answer that I'm quite certain I don't know, that in fact I'm the wrong person to ask, and, moreover, that Mr. Jefferson's private business was none of their bloody concern. Accursed Federalists!"

"I won't ask anything about Thomas Jefferson," I said, although I was dying to. I wanted to hear about the great man's inventions, his passion for science, his appreciation of wine, those sorts of things, not his love life.

"Much obliged. Now, how can we put your money to work at the National Bank of the City of New York? There are a number of investments and trusts we could create, real estate primary on the list. Whole territories yet to be seen by white men ready to be opened for sale. Then there are shipping companies, bridge- and canal-building companies, road-laying companies, woolen mills..."

"Railroads and steel."

"Those are infant industries with opposite trajectories. These steam locomotives they use often blow up and have killed a number of people and livestock. Until their machine shops can turn out a reliable boiler, an investment there will yield flat returns. Steel, on the other hand, with this new Bessemer Process, will undoubtedly grow very big. Chillicothe can devise a portfolio of real estate trusts, bonds, gold, and steel."

"And railroads, too," I insisted.

"I suppose we could buy up some railroad notes at ten cents on the dollar. Later you might be able to sell them for twenty or twenty-two cents in an upward-trending stock market."

"I'll leave the details to you and Chillicothe. But please run everything past me before moving forward with buying or selling or trading anything on my behalf."

"By all means. And hark: once you become acquainted with the city and its society, my bank can find you a property ideally suited for a single gentleman's interests and diversions. New luxury developments are going up everywhere — Gramercy Park, for example. Or you might find that a restored Colonial-era property closer downtown strikes your fancy. If poor and dangerous by many people's standards, the neighborhood's housing stock is rising in value as gangs of ruffians residing therein surrender their territory to more respectable artisans, coffee houses, bordellos, and restaurants serving haute cuisine."

"I think maybe a new townhouse. What did you mean before when you used the word 'diversions?'"

"Perhaps you might want a big parcel of land outside the city to go turkey shooting."

"Turkey shooting?"

"A very fashionable activity among our gentlemen currently. You may have a taste of it, as it were, at the city's annual pig shoot scheduled in a few weeks."

"Pig shoot?"

"The city's swine have learned to escape northward into the territory north of Twenty-second Street. The country is full of once-domesticated pigs thriving in the wild. Every autumn season, parties of the city's gentlemen armed with old flintlocks and blunderbusses blast up the place and rid the woods and fields of them."

"Interesting. Do they have a big pig roast afterwards, then?"

"Yes, indeed, the nation's largest. All of the city's population is invited. The butchers' union assists with preparation, wives and mothers pack picnic baskets, social clubs donate casks of rum and ale. And let me assure you, nothing is left to waste. Even the intestines and feet are not spared from the civic orgy. These are given to the city's Negroes."

"I'd love to take part," I said, surprising myself with the reply. Never having gone shooting before, and strongly disapproving of firearms all my life, I suddenly had the itch to load a gun, aim it, and fire, in the process sending a pig to its rightful place in the universe, a barbecue pit. Why not enjoy the joys and thrills of life in an earlier, more barbaric era, as long as nobody but pigs got hurt?

"Yes yes yes! I cook up fancy," interjected Bunny, jostling my elbow and nodding enthusiastically. The prospect of my shooting a feral pig had brought out her inner squaw, which hadn't been exercised much lately as we had traveled the past three months from inn to tavern to hotel all across hell's half-acre.

It was settled. Mr. Gallatin promised to contact the event's coordinators and urge them to invite me. I felt elated and panicked simultaneously. This would be my introduction to New York City's high society, where I predicted that my money would buy others' respect. However, if I did not obtain a rifle soon and start practicing, money would be the one and only reason to respect me. To bond properly with my peers, I had to put my manly talents on display for all to see, beginning with shooting, and make a respectable showing, even if I might not bag a pig. Afterward, we would all head to the tavern, a field of battle where I excelled. Drinking all but the burliest men under the table, I would cement my standing in the community as a man's man.

Meantime, Chillicothe returned with an armload of investment prospectuses for me to examine. He ushered us out of the building and into a waiting cabriolet. We merged into the slow-moving horse-and-buggy traffic and aimed for the City Hotel. A four-story edifice that imposingly spanned an entire city block greeted us at the conclusion of our trip.

A snappy, hup-two bunch of bellhops helped us with our bags. I checked Bunny and myself into connecting suites where we quickly plopped into our respective beds, exhausted. I did not know Bunny's situation, but, feeling exhilarated yet anxious about the future, I could not sleep. I stared at a blank wall late into the morning hours, when the outside commotion from "the city that never sleeps" — prostitutes' laughs, alcoholics' cries, and stabbing victims' screams — finally died down. Then, around five, it started all over again with fishmongers' songs, produce sellers' pitches, and teamsters' commands. A new day was dawning, literally and figuratively.

The logistics of relocating from pioneer Chicago to the great metropolis of New York were nearly complete. I was relatively young and rich in New York City, encamped at the city's, maybe the nation's, finest hotel, while I leisurely shopped for a permanent residence. Only one matter remained that required my prompt attention. As the first light of dawn pierced the lace window curtains, I resolved to request a second interview with Mr. Gallatin, a man who clearly had one ear trained to the ground. For I sorely craved any news or gossip he might have read or heard about my wife and her loser boyfriend, the man responsible for burning down Fredonia, New York.

Chapter Seven

August 6, 1834

I was so angry with Bruce that night, I came this close to letting him leave town without me. You can't see me, diary, but I'm holding my thumb and forefinger about a millimeter apart.

"Why can't you leave the universe alone?" I demanded to know, while we hurriedly gathered our clothes and the few other things we could fit in the back of our buggy.

"Because it's there?" he lamely answered, his voice totally lacking his usual arrogance.

I absolutely hated how cliché that sounded. How long have we been hearing that now? Sixty years, ever since that Hilary guy climbed Mt. Everest?

"You've got nothing left to conquer. Back at Fermilab you solved the riddle of time. Where we came from, you're probably more famous than Newton, Einstein and Darwin put together."

"No doubt," he said, arrogance briefly returning. Considering what had just happened, he seriously needed a dose of humility. Arrogance wasn't the proper response when ten of your assistants lay dead in your lab.

"You may be the toast of the 21st century," I shouted, "but you're turning our prospects in the 19th into burnt toast!"

"Look, can I help it if they were a bunch of boneheads that didn't know you can't touch wires carrying twelve hundred volts of electricity?"

"It's 1834! They didn't grow up around electricity like you and I did! They didn't have parents drilling into their heads from birth that you don't stick a fork into an electrical socket!"

"We warned them..."

"You may have warned them. But you didn't PROTECT them. Nothing was insulated. Nobody wore rubber-soled shoes or gloves."

"Like you said, it's 1834. Plastic insulation and rubber-soled shoes haven't been invented yet."

"My point exactly. Did you ever stop to think that people aren't ready for electricity? You can't just say, 'Here's your electricity. Go nuts.' To do it right you have to have a lot of other stuff in place, too. Like plastic and rubber and who knows what all else."

"We did the best we could, given the limited knowledge and resources of today."

"Well, it wasn't good enough. It was irresponsible. Actually, it was probably criminal."

"I'm afraid other people will think so, too. That's why we have to leave town right away. I'm not going through another tar and feather episode."

"To do what? You're broke again, and I'm not willing to fund another disaster."

"I'll think of something. Something on a smaller scale that won't put people's lives in jeopardy."

"Okay. Fine."

To tell the truth, I wasn't okay. Or fine. I felt like I was aiding and abetting a fugitive.

Lord knows, I've tried to live a guilt-free life. I saw how guilt tore up my mother's insides, and she didn't have anything to feel guilty about. She just had the gene that produces Jewish guilt.

I was born with the same gene. As I stuffed my clothes, shoes and Krugerrands into a trunk, it struck me that I was in denial about my guilt for a bunch of things.

Disappointing my parents by underachieving in school. Buying and selling coke. Sneaking lines when Dan was out. Having an affair with Bruce. Running away to the past and leaving my husband.

Now I could add to the list covering up a crime that would probably get you tossed in jail for manslaughter. Or worse. Murder.

Say what you will about Dan Connor, but he'd never flee in the middle of the night to escape justice. He'd definitely stay and face the music. That's what healthy guilt should do — make you take responsibility for your actions.

Bruce is just the opposite. He's a scientist who's unconcerned with morality and feels no guilt. It's all about immutable laws based on chemistry and physics rather than, in the case of Judaism, fifty-seven hundred years of moral tradition that's still evolving.

So why did I run away from Niagara Falls instead of stay? After all, it was Bruce and his partners who were negligent and led to the deaths of ten young men, not me.

Basically, it was my escape hatch. Not from the law or my responsibility for the massacre of Bruce's assistants — although I confess I feared the guilt-by-association thing. No, here was my chance to escape western New York and the unrelenting boredom of living there.

Don't get me wrong. Niagara Falls is a beautiful place, especially in the 1830s, when it's unspoiled by modern tourist traps closing in from every side. But you can stare at it and listen to it for only so long before you eventually get bored by it. The steady roar literally lulls you to sleep.

Plus, the same boring farmers and housewives that surrounded us in Fredonia also live in Niagara Falls. Different faces, but the same tedious quilting bees, canning parties and barn dances.

Actually, everyone was nice as pie — sickeningly sweet and blueberry pie oozing thick syrupy juice. I suppose you can't fault them for it: they're simple people from a simpler time whose tastes are much much MUCH simpler than mine.

It all started out so promisingly when we first got to Niagara Falls. We rented an apartment above Frick's General Store — I insisted we get a place in town this time. I wasn't going to be stuck again in a remote farmhouse where my only company consisted of squirrels, skunks, cows and the occasional bear.

Bruce performed his usual shtick, buddying up to the leading men in town and presenting them with a revolutionary idea: hydroelectric power generated by the Falls. He showed them plans he drew, and he even rigged up a simple battery and small motor to demonstrate the miracle of electricity.

Initially, they were unimpressed. They already were familiar with waterpower — a couple owned sawmills and flourmills and used it themselves. But when they saw how a battery in Frick's General Store could power a motor in a horse stable at the other end of town via a long metal rod, they were sold.

They began throwing money at Bruce, who became de facto mayor of the town, putting every resource available to work on the project.

People were too polite to complain to my face, but I overheard grumbling from people of more modest means without a stake in his scheme that it was impossible to get your horse shoed, because both blacksmith shops in town were tied up making equipment for Bruce.

One of the blacksmiths, Elwood Hopsbawn, donated his whole barn to the cause. Bruce assembled his first dynamo inside, cobbling together a bunch of crude iron parts.

It wasn't pretty, but when he mounted it on a wooden platform in a cavern behind the American Falls (I think I visited the spot wearing a yellow rain slicker when I was a kid on a family vacation), it spun around so fast that its blades were just a blur.

Phase One was a success. Now he had to build a generator to attach to the turbine and harness the energy. With a huge magnetic iron bar hauled from a forge in Erie, Pennsylvania, he built a generator that jumped the power up to twelve-hundred volts.

At the time I remember asking, "What's the point? It's not like there are microwaves and coffee makers to run."

"If you build it, they will come," he said.

"Small appliances or baseball players?" I asked. Again with the clichés — this time from a movie from when I was a kid about a guy who had a silly dream of building a baseball stadium in the middle of nowhere.

Bruce was right. Tinkerers from all across western New York, who'd heard about Bruce's marvelous contraption, flocked to town and began to build smaller-scale versions of Bruce's electric motor.

They offered everything from coins and cash, to cows and pigs, to rum and rye, to be wired to the generator. Each had a small-scale scheme to put the electricity to work. One planned to pump water. Another hoped to build a big fan to dry corn. A third designed an electric butter churn. And so on down the line.

The most enthusiastic of all was Elwood Hopsbawn, who became a close colleague of Bruce's. A talented mechanic as well as a blacksmith, he planned to create an electric light, using the same design Thomas Edison would use fifty years later, which of course Bruce had described for him.

Elwood made great progress with the project. He hired a glass blower from Vermont to make bulbs. He scored some tungsten from Canada that he hammered into thin strips for the filaments. He bought a bell jar and bellows from a scientific supply house in England to suck the air out of the bulbs and create a vacuum to prevent the filament from flaming out after being turned on.

The trickiest part was the base where the positive and negative electricity came up into the bulb and caused the filament to glow. He ended up just mounting the bulb on a square board and hooked the copper wires to the inner works.

It didn't look precisely like a modern-day light bulb, but someone from my world would have recognized it as one. Thanks to Bruce's guidance, the earliest bulbs to roll out of his shop glowed for upwards of six hours before burning out.

"It's only a matter of time before he gets a bulb to last one or two hundred hours," Bruce said. "He has to work the kinks out of the manufacturing process and make the bulb absolutely airtight. Air's creeping in, causing the tungsten to oxidize too rapidly."

That's where things stood, until two nights ago when Bruce paid a visit to Elwood and found ten dead bodies piled up inside Elwood's blacksmith shop, a human chain of scorched and smoking men and boys.

Near as Bruce could figure out, it started with Jefferson Layhorn, Elwood's most senior apprentice. He gripped the positive and negative wires in each hand, looking like he meant to force them apart and prevent a short. Except he had a momentary lapse, forgetting about the electrical properties of the equipment he dealt with.

Eight more apprentices, each apparently as forgetful as the last (or maybe driven by a strong humanitarian sense that outstripped common sense) attempted to pry their dying friends loose from the deadly electric charge, only to find themselves ensnared by it, too.

The last man in the chain was Elwood Hopsbawn, who, to his credit, used a tool instead of his hands to separate his dying apprentices. But he also was electrocuted, because he grabbed a pair of blacksmith forceps made of iron, a conductor of electricity, rather than, say, a non-conducting wooden ax handle.

Suffice it to say it was a grisly mess greeting Bruce, which I'm very glad I didn't see. Before entering the barn I had excused myself to tinkle in the privy at the back of poor Elwood's property.

I was about ready to walk into the barn and see what was up, when Bruce rushed out and blocked my way. "We have to split town," he said, face all ashen. "Now."

After we hastily packed our stuff, Bruce hitched our two horses, Lennon and McCartney, to our buggy, and we rode off stealthily into the night, leaving the citizens of Niagara Falls to discover the dead bodies and wonder about our disappearance.

For all I know, we're wanted by the law. Luckily, the telegraph hasn't been invented yet (maybe Bruce will try his hand at inventing it and fuck that up, too), so it's pretty unlikely the authorities can set up a dragnet and catch us before we reach our final destination.

What is our final destination? The steamboat we're presently riding on is heading down the Hudson River toward New York City. I'm on the deck right now writing this under a gray sky threatening rain.

Adding to the stress of my recent life, I'm afraid the ship's boiler, which is clunking terribly, will blow up any minute and kill everybody aboard. I hear that this happens somewhere in America at least once or twice a week.

If I wasn't so totally self-absorbed, I could maybe enjoy the trip. The scenery is certainly nice — tree-covered hills, geese swimming with their goslings, charming little towns dotting the shore. I like the pretty rock palisades most of all, sheer rock cliffs that the Indians believe were carved by the claws of giant beavers.

But I can't focus on the environment. I'm too busy worrying about the future. I should have plenty of money left to live comfortably in New York City. But what the hell am I going to do with myself? It's clear I can't rely on Bruce's efforts to give our lives direction. A winner in the 21st century, he's a total loser in the 19th.

What would Lydia Maria Child say about my predicament? That's going to be my new mantra, similar to the one born-again Christians spout in the modern world: "What would Jesus do?" Instead of WWJD I will think WWLMCS.

I saw Maria speak back in Niagara Falls a couple of weeks before we left town. I wasn't familiar with her, but I knew I had to see her when I learned how threatening she was to everybody who uttered her name. I heard nonsense like:

"She would have women do men's work!"

"Her words will create an epidemic of divorce!"

"She will persuade women not to bear children!"

"She wishes to free the slaves and unleash a Negro horde to plague our society!"

With my more enlightened 21st-century upbringing, I didn't feel threatened by any of these concerns, though I have to confess I didn't argue the points with anybody. For I had lived long enough in my new century to realize that women were expected to be seen and not heard.

Which is why Maria's visit was so refreshing. Because she wasn't going to let having female reproductive organs intimidate her into silence. I hoped that she would inspire me to regain my old confidence and outspokenness.

The lecture that night was the biggest thing to hit town in a long time, judging by the crowd that surrounded the Niagara Falls meeting hall. Ominously, a few scuffles broke out between townspeople who disagreed about the speakers' right to appear in their town.

Maria was the second speaker in a double bill. First up was a preacher named Theodore Dwight Weld. He was supposed to discuss the immorality of slavery. I would've loved to see him, not only because the topic was important, but also because he was extremely handsome. He resembled a young Warren Beatty.

Unfortunately, I wasn't allowed in the hall, and neither were any other women, due to a prudish custom that didn't allow mixing of the sexes in public places. "Promiscuous assemblies," they called audiences containing both men and women, giving you an idea of their bass-ackward thinking.

So, while the men listened to Reverend Weld, a bunch of us women hung out in front of the meeting hall, gossiping, bitching about housework, breast-feeding babies and evil-eyeing each others' outfits.

Needless to say, Bruce stayed away in keeping with his habit to avoid all controversy and curry favor with his investors. In fact, he begged me not to go, but I told him to eat me, my brain needed more stimulation than sewing circles offered.

Meantime, a mob with a collective IQ of about forty-two beat the sides of the building with their fists and yelled in the windows, trying to disrupt Reverend Weld's lecture, until the sheriff and his deputies shooed them across the street. The scene reminded me of one of those anti-abortion rallies in the 21st century.

After about an hour and a half, Reverend Weld wound up his lecture, and the men left the building. The mothers among us handed the children over to their husbands, and we women filed inside the hot and sticky room and sat on rows of wooden benches. Extremely hard wooden benches.

When everybody was settled, a fortyish woman in a white lace bonnet and long black dress appeared behind the lectern and began to speak. Despite her plain looks and antique clothes, which were outdated even by 1834 standards, she had a loud voice and commanding stage presence, and her charisma shone through the homespun get-up.

A number of women sniffed beforehand that the only reason they'd come was to put her and her modern, anti-Christian, pro-female notions on the spot by asking embarrassing questions. To deflect any criticism that she didn't belong up on stage, she began with a little self-deprecating humor.

"I was gravely warned by some of my female acquaintances that no woman should expect to be regarded as a lady after she had written a book," she said.

She was greeted with knowing laughter from dozens of women who had read her best-selling books. That shut up any potential critics. If she wasn't considered a "lady" by many, at least she was rich enough not to care.

The first half of her talk quite frankly bummed me out, although most of the women sitting around me ate it up. She spouted a bunch of statements that sound like they came straight out of a 4th grade self-improvement manual:

"An effort made for the happiness of others lifts us above ourselves."

"You find yourself refreshed by the presence of cheerful people. Why not make an honest effort to confer that pleasure on others? Half the battle is gained if you never allow yourself to say anything gloomy."

"The cure for all the ills and wrongs, the cares, the sorrows, and the crimes of humanity, all lie in the one word 'love.' It is the divine vitality that everywhere produces and restores life."

After rattling off these and other tips and pointers for conducting yourself, which made me begin to regret that I'd come, she read an excerpt from her extremely controversial, book, *An Appeal in Favor of That Class of Americans Called Africans*.

The excerpt was also very — what do you call it? — *didactic*. But I have to admit I felt inspired nonetheless, because she was so damned *earnest* in her delivery.

(I keep forgetting that it's before the Civil War, and I underestimate the powerful feelings people have about subjects I learned about in high school history class but felt so removed from in time that I could give a shit.)

She told the story of a poor family she met in rural Ohio (or was it Idaho? — I get the two mixed up). They lived in a one-room shack on a crappy little farm swarming with kids, pigs, chickens and, I'm guessing, lots of flies.

Yet something didn't jibe: the wife was too pretty, intelligent and refined to have spent all her life on a farm. And the husband was too good a conversationalist to have been only a simple farmer.

Turns out they were former slaveholders who had moved north from Virginia. After many years of living atop the Southern food chain, their consciences began to bother them, so they freed their slaves, moved to Ohio (or Idaho — whatever), and made a living with their own two hands.

Confessing that the months immediately after their move had been incredibly hard (does this sound familiar, diary?), the woman boasted that she now found the work of a farm wife easy (okay, that doesn't sound so familiar).

"It is a privilege to dispense with the lazy, sluttish, and reluctant service of slaves," Maria quoted the woman as saying. "Never did we feel what it was to be truly free *ourselves*, till we had set *them* free."

The audience applauded passionately; a few of the less lady-like — stocky, ill-dressed women from the hinterlands who probably pulled plows because their husbands couldn't afford horses — whistled through their fingers. I clapped hard, too, for Maria's message rang home loud and clear.

During those early months of our 19th-century sojourn I had learned to squelch every temptation to speak my mind. Sometimes for good reason. I didn't want to get in a heated argument with some idiot about slavery or women's rights and spill the beans about who I was or where I came from.

A lot of the time, though, my silence was due to sheer laziness. It simply took too much energy to correct all the stupid notions spewing out of all the stupid hicks I met everywhere I went.

This is where I'll leave off, diary. New York City is coming into view downriver. I feel like something big awaits me there.

Chapter Eight

Securely ensconced at the City Hotel, I vigilantly pursued my strategy of introducing myself to the city's elite and insinuating myself into their world. This path I hoped would lead me to Rachel, whom I believed to be residing somewhere within the city's limits. A woman of refined tastes with a thirst for excitement, she surely could not remain long in the largely unsettled western half of the state with the biggest, most sophisticated city in the nation beckoning next door.

At the corner of Cortlandt Street and Broadway, the City Hotel was located in the heart of New York's financial district. Rising five stories, it claimed the title of tallest building in the city, excepting a few church steeples that stabbed the sky at a higher altitude. Bunny and I lived thereat while my new residence at Gramercy Park was being built. Given that winter weather rapidly approached and promised to interrupt construction for two or three months at a minimum, I did not expect to settle into my new abode until late the following spring.

Mr. Gallatin recommended that I investigate buying into the Gramercy Park development. The city's population was rapidly outgrowing its boundaries, which extended in those days from the Battery at the southern tip of Manhattan Island to Fourteenth Street. Between these two points lay a maze of streets overrun by immigrants from Ireland, Germany, and the poorer precincts of our own country. Close quarters had bred disease, and rampant poverty had led to violent crime that plagued the entire city. Even denizens of the City Hotel were not immune: every week, stories about a fellow guest getting conked on the head and robbed of his money reached Bunny and me in our rooms on the fifth floor. Built wholly outside of the city (only to be swallowed up a few years later), Gramercy Park offered an antidote to urban decay. My planned residence was part of a development of town homes that encircled a private park and gardens like a medieval fortress.

My biggest challenge in those early days of living in New York entailed keeping Bunny out of trouble. I could tell at least as far back in our journey as Chicago that she hated idle time. At every address we had shared so far, I had found it necessary to explain to her that in the hotel environment a well-paid staff is employed to fetch our water, build our fires, prepare our meals, switch our chamber pots, and sweep our rooms. As guests of the hotel, we need only concern ourselves with matters of business and self-cultivation. Yet, despite my efforts, at the Sauganash Hotel she had argued with Beaubien over building fires in the fireplace. At the Eagle Tavern she had constantly interfered with the culinary staff and was thrown out of the kitchen at least once per day. And now at the City Hotel, she fought with the maids over laundering my clothes and bed linens.

As on several occasions already, Mr. Gallatin presented a solution. He offered to spare one whole hour each day for Bunny to visit his office and converse with him in Potawatomi.

"That's really generous of you," I said, amazed by such a kind gesture from a man as busy as he.

"I would like to believe it is because of my magnanimity that I have made you this proposal," said Mr. Gallatin. "But I confess that I extend this offer purely for selfish reasons."

"How so? You're taking Bunny off my hands and giving me a very valuable hour's worth of peace every day."

"It is true that I am much occupied at present with repealing the Restraining Act, yet another of Mr. Jackson's bright ideas that will kill the banking industry in this country if we do not fight him. Where does it say in the Constitution that each state should have only one chartered bank?"

"I don't know. I'm not very familiar with that issue, I'm afraid."

"My apologies, Mr. Connor. My outburst is a symptom of why I desperately need your Miss Bunny to call on me. The only way I am able to prevent myself from going mad amid all of the political bickering adhering to my position as President of this bank is to pursue, if only for short periods, my hobby of collecting Indian languages. Little else distracts me from my cares."

Whatever benefits Mr. Gallatin accrued from their relationship, I believed that Bunny stood to benefit even more. If nothing else, she would have a regular opportunity to converse in her own language and maintain her roots to her former life. This, I hoped, would pacify her and keep her out of Housekeeping's hair.

So during the winter of 1833-34, Bunny paid a visit each afternoon to Mr. Gallatin at his posh offices above the National Bank of New York. Bunny said he wrote copious notes of their conversations, taking great pains to spell out in written English the phonetics of her language. You can learn the results of their sessions together by reading a book he later published, titled, in the verbose habit of the era, *Synopsis of the Indian Tribes Within the United States East of the Rocky Mountains and in the British and Russian Possessions of North America*. Upon publication in 1836, he mailed an inscribed copy to Bunny, and she treasures it to this day, along with the silver broach fashioned for her grandmother by the Chicago frontiersman John Kinzie.

After a week or so, when I sensed that Mr. Gallatin and I were on comfortable terms, I confided in him about my marital woes (leaving out, of course, precise details of how I had come to be in this part of the world). I told him that I sought his aid in searching for my wife.

"What again was your wife's companion's name?" he asked.

"Bilson. Bruce Bilson."

He closed his eyes, filing through the names and faces of the thousands of people he had met during his sixty years of service to his country. Upon reopening his eyes: "That name is unfamiliar to me."

"And you are sure that nobody else besides me lately has deposited into your bank thousands of dollars in gold coins?"

"I do not mean to boast, really the exact opposite, for it is an awesome responsibility that humbles even an elder statesman like myself, when I say that no money is loaned, deposited, or disbursed in this city without my knowledge. If this humbug Bilson circulates a stock offering or pools funds to underwrite one of his schemes, I shall most certainly hear of it. You have my pledge that if I obtain one whiff of information about your wife or your antagonist, I shall contact you post-haste."

"That is very helpful, Mr. Gallatin, thank you." I hesitated to impose on him more, and then I went ahead and asked, "Can you suggest any additional steps, external to your bank, which I might take to find my wife?"

He scribbled a quick note on his stationery and stuffed it in an envelope. "Here, put this in your pocket. It's an introduction to Mr. Joseph Pemberton, of the Pemberton Detective Agency. If there is any man alive who can track down your wife, it is he. I have used him before when the circumstances required a firm but discreet hand."

"Thank you again, Mr. Gallatin. I don't know how to repay you for all of the time you have spent on my admittedly unique set of problems."

"No need to repay me in any other currency than to keep sending Miss Bunny to my office every afternoon. She is a daily delight."

I came to agree with Mr. Gallatin's assessment of Bunny. She learned a lot about the comportment of civilized ladies from the time they spent together. She ceased for the most part hitting or kicking other people, and she kept to a minimum the blood-curdling screams that so unnerved our acquaintances. She even started speaking English better, which was hard for me to explain, considering that they spoke exclusively in Potawatomi. Then I figured out the answer: as Gallatin dissected Potawatomi grammar with Bunny, she applied the lessons learned about her native language, which I am certain she never formally had studied, to English. Hence, she began talking in complete sentences, using subject, verb, object, and, when inspired, an indirect object in her utterances.

After leaving Bunny to her hour with Mr. Gallatin, I obtained from Roger Chillicothe directions to the Pemberton Detective Agency and proceeded there forthwith. For the very first time I ventured outside the financial district, where I rarely strayed from the short route between the City Hotel and the National Bank of New York. Located in a commercial block at 14 Bowery Street, Pemberton's office was wedged in a second-floor corner of an irregularly shaped brick building emblazoned top-to-bottom with signs advertising various tenants' products and services. Included among the groups of three-foot letters wrapping around the building and spelling out "SAILMAKER" and "CLOTHS & CASSIMERES" and "H. BROOME & SONS," I glimpsed a more modestly sized "PEMB. DET. AGENCY" sign.

I caught Mr. Pemberton in his office a few minutes before he had to leave for an appointment. He sat at a roll-top desk, examining what looked like a plate of dirt through a magnifying glass. I noticed that his knuckles were swollen and his fingers badly gnarled, I guessed from a long career of fist-fighting. I received more evidence of this belief when he turned around in his chair and stood, and I observed the vast network of scars on his face, plus his hopelessly crooked nose, the product of multiple breaks. Barrel-chested, with powerful arms that could probably toss a man clear across a barroom, he was someone with whom I vowed never to tangle.

During introductions, he gathered up a few items, including a knife and pistol, and placed them in pockets under his cloak. "I am most sorry, Mr. Connor, but I must soon excuse myself, for I have another appointment. What is it that I can do for you?"

"I'm searching for my wife, who ran away with another man a few months ago. I followed them as far as Buffalo, but then I lost track of them."

"Why are you in New York City if you believe they are three-hundred miles away in Buffalo? I seldom take assignments upstate. There is plenty enough of trouble in this city to keep two or even three of me fully employed."

"Because I suspect they have come here and gone into hiding."

"And why do you hold this belief?"

"Just knowing my wife's predilections. She could never cope for very long on the frontier."

"Regarding your belief that they have hidden themselves, is there some legal entanglement that they are fleeing?"

"Quite possibly. Arson maybe."

"Sit down here," he said, directing me to one of several chairs around a long wooden table piled high with assorted documents. He handed me some blank sheets of paper and pointed to a quill pen and inkwell. "Write for me as comprehensive a description of your wife and her lover as you can. On separate sheets, put their names at the top of the paper and include below their physical descriptions, distinguishing marks, wardrobe, everyday habits, occupations, and whatever else you can think of that may help in the search. Who knows? We may get lucky and find their names and addresses listed in a city directory, and your case will be closed as soon as it is opened.

"Now, if you will pardon me, I must go. You may leave the information on this table, and I will review it upon my return."

"You look ready for some serious action, with the gun and knife and all."

"A fellow owes one of my clients money, which I have been hired to recover. I understand he is holed up in Five Points, the roughest, most dangerous part of town. It would not surprise me if I had to knock together a few Irish heads during my sojourn there. I shall contact you at your hotel after I have read your materials to inform you whether I have accepted your case."

Pemberton disappeared down the stairway, and I set myself to providing him with the information he requested. Having little experience beyond signing my name or initials with a quill pen, I left behind an ink-smeared mess scrawled in the clumsy hand of a child, which I hoped was sufficiently legible for Pemberton to find useful. Apparently, the documents served, for a couple of days later I received a note from Pemberton accepting my case, along with an invoice for two dollars, the first of many I would receive in subsequent months, as he scoured the island looking for Rachel and Bilson.

After accomplishing my immediate work of distracting Bunny and hiring a detective, it was time for play. Thanks, yet again, to the good graces of Mr. Gallatin, I received my invitation from the Manhattan Civic Improvement Club to participate in their annual pig shoot. "Customarily," he explained, "invitations are sent to the three hundred richest men on the island, popularly known, appropriately enough, as 'The Three Hundred.' Recognizing that you possess more money than at least two of the three hundred, I placed your name on their membership roll."

All of this was well and good, except I did not know how to shoot. To teach myself this manly art, I purchased a hunting rifle and bullets from a hardware dealer on Dock Street, near the waterfront, and I led Bunny on a trip each morning via the Broadway omnibus to the city's northern fringe, where in a meadow we improvised a firing range so I might practice.

On a rocky outcrop, we set up discarded bottles that Bunny had scrounged early each morning from the refuse pile behind the hotel. I stood back perhaps thirty yards, loaded my weapon like the store clerk demonstrated, aimed, held my breath, pulled the trigger, and ... missed horribly. Six days and three boxes of ammunition later, I managed to hit a bottle two times out of every five shots, a forty percent success rate. Despite a second-straight-week of target practice, during which I played whatever mind tricks I could on myself to lie still, breathe slowly, and relax my muscles, I could do nothing to improve my technique and make this percentage rise.

Looking at me after another volley of shots widely missed their mark, Bunny said, concluding that my efforts were hopeless, "Bunny no can shoot bow and arrow. No can teach you."

"I will just take along my gun and try my best. Surely, other men have gone away from the event without bagging a pig."

"Potawatomi men call you woman," Bunny said, describing what would happen if this scenario ever unfolded at one of her tribe's hunting expeditions.

"They will not say it, but that's what the men will think of me here, too."

From this moment forward I seriously dreaded the upcoming hunt. Putting aside my poor shooting skills, I still was not convinced that if the opportunity arose, I could shoot a gun at a pig with the intention of killing it. What if I only wounded it, and it squealed in agony until someone, probably not me, shot it again to put it out of its misery? In the modern world, where meat arrives in your home already butchered, weighed, and wrapped in plastic, these images seemed positively grotesque.

Also, I felt pressure emanating from Bunny, whom I did not want to disappoint. She had formulated grand plans of serving a traditional Indian meal to Mr. Gallatin and me, with roast pig, a delicacy for her people, as the centerpiece. In her reasoning, I personally had to shoot the pig, because otherwise she would have to pitch in and prepare the feast for the polity, according to a recipe on which a majority of the cooks agreed. She required her very own pig to fulfill her vision, and I was appointed to supply it. Relating the opinions of the men in her tribe earlier, she meant to shame me into shooting better, which, in turn, would award her her prize.

To ready herself for the big event, Bunny prevailed upon me to take her to a cutlery store and purchase a set of steel white men's knives. In Fulton Street, among waves of meatpackers hauling sides of beef and skinned pigs to-and-fro, we found such a store run by a man wearing a top hat and bloody apron — a gentleman butcher. From his impressive stock Bunny selected four carving knives of various sizes, a meat cleaver, and a sharpening stone.

As he wrapped her purchases in a scrap of burlap and tied the bundle with a length of twine, our gentleman butcher quipped, "I trust you're not planning to use these knives to scalp your enemies! Ha ha ha!"

"Just getting ready for the annual pig shoot on Saturday," I said. I glanced over at Bunny, who scowled at the man as if he were the only person in the world she meant to scalp. Bunny prided herself on being a civilized Indian, not only since traveling east away from the frontier with me, but long before we met, as the member of a settled, stationary tribe of farmers and woodsmen that had inhabited their land for generations. She distinguished her tribe's situation from the restless, acquisitive Huron to the east and the nomadic, slovenly Sioux to the west. She considered neither bunch particularly civilized.

To encourage her improved behavior under Mr. Gallatin's influence, I praised Bunny for not punching the gentleman butcher, or worse. She seemed pleased that I had recognized her restraint, and she promised to act like a civilized lady in all of her dealings. For the remainder of the week we looked forward, with varying degrees of relish, to the big pig hunt.

I was unprepared for the massive exodus from the city, which began at dawn and lasted the better part of Saturday morning. Omnibuses, freight wagons, and private coaches carted passengers heavily armed with guns, forks, and knives up the city's three main thoroughfares, Broadway, Bowery, and Greenwich Street. A festive atmosphere reigned as hunters and hangers-on leaned out the windows of their conveyances, clutching pewter mugs filled with rum or beer and singing patriotic songs accompanied by fiddlers, banjo players, or accordionists. I heard lyrics slurred in no fewer than four languages, including English, Gaelic, Dutch, and German.

Bunny and I rode in a private coach that I had hired for the occasion. Closed within the passenger compartment we were happily insulated from the insults, rocks, vegetables, and spittle hurled between wagons hauling rival ethnic groups or gangs like the Bowery Boys and Plug Uglies. Clearly, more than just the Three Hundred attended this event; they may have received the official invitations, but the rest of the city was crashing the party.

Around eleven o'clock, after crawling up Broadway for about three hours, we reached Hamilton Hill, the meeting place for the hunting party. But for the masses of people and acres of parked buses, buggies, and coaches, Hamilton Hill presented the visitor with a bucolic setting, consisting of farm fields, orchards, pastures, cows, creeks, and ponds. A tent beside a flagpole flying an oversized American flag with twenty-four stars indicated the site from which we would embark on our hunt for runaway swine. Already, I heard gunshots in the distance. If you were unaware of today's event, you would think that a war had started.

Mr. Gallatin stood in the center of the tent, dressed much less formally than I was accustomed to seeing him, in hunting breeches, boots, and a deerskin jacket. He carried a rifle under his arm while he assigned newly arrived hunters to parties of four and instructed them to fan out in varying directions. Winking at Bunny, he pointed her in the direction of the womenfolk, who assembled in back of the tent around tripods of beans, potatoes, and biscuit dough heating over wood fires. I was placed in a group of three other men, one of whom had a peg leg. His name was Hebediah Barron. He introduced me to the man next to him, his business partner and good friend, Ezra Fripphouse. Both men carried primitive-looking blunderbusses that I associated with the Pilgrims of Plymouth. The fourth member of our party was a young student named Sam Tilden. Like me, he carried the latest model of hunting rifle.

As we traipsed westward along a creek toward the Hudson River, our quartet got acquainted. Barron and Fripphouse owned a business that imported English china, French crystal, and Chinese porcelain to the United States. Their success at marketing these goods to the Three Hundred had enabled them eventually to join the exclusive group. Having just turned twenty, Tilden stated that he was presently reading law at the firm of Bigelow, Strunk & Cushman. He expected to be admitted to the bar in another two or three years when his apprenticeship was through. He was attending today's festivities in place of Mr. Bigelow, who had stayed home in his Park Row mansion, being sick with gout.

After we had gone perhaps a half-mile, Barron requested that our party pause to rest. I understood his need perfectly, for it must have taken a lot of energy to limp this far on one good leg. Moreover, Barron was grossly overweight and this caused him to lose his breath easily. Just as men in the twenty-first century sat on their sofas and watched television all day and got fat, without the excuse of missing a leg, so too had inactivity led Barron to grow quite rotund.

We sat on fallen logs and passed around a flask of whiskey to quench our mounting thirst. "You're wondering how I got this peg leg, aren't you?" Barron asked, looking my way.

His remark embarrassed me, because in fact I was trying my hardest to ignore his artificial leg, but, fascinated, my eyes kept roving back to it. "Yes, I suppose I am," I answered.

"The story is really quite humorous if you can look past its tragic dimension."

Tilden and I sat forward with our ears pricked.

"It was 1828 or '29, was it not?" asked Barron of his friend.

"1829," said Fripphouse uninterestedly.

"At this self-same event in 1829, I had an accident which required the surgeons to amputate my leg below my knee."

"That's horrible!" I said. "What happened?"

"Do you wish to answer, Mr. Fripphouse?"

"No, you tell the story," replied Fripphouse, resigned to being the butt of his partner's oft-told joke on yet another occasion.

"We were blundering (needless to say we were drunk) through a patch of ground like this one, along a babbling brook lined with birch trees. Suddenly, a young pig bolted across our path. Startled by our presence it froze in its tracks, not five feet from my left foot. Would you estimate around five feet, Mr. Fripphouse?"

"Three feet," said Fripphouse, who had memorized his straight man's lines in Barron's well-rehearsed routine.

"'Hold still,' Mr. Fripphouse whispered to me. I held still while my trusted friend shot at the pig. Unfortunately, his bullet missed wide, precisely three feet wide, and blasted my foot instead."

"Yikes!" I said.

"Ouch!" exclaimed Tilden.

"Did the doctors at least try to save your foot?" I asked.

"Save my foot? Tell them what my foot looked like, Mr. Fripphouse."

Fripphouse looked annoyed now that he was being forced to relive the incident, over which he must have felt immense guilt and shame. "Nothing. I told you it looked like nothing."

"To reassure me, Mr. Fripphouse informed me that the injury to my foot looked like nothing. That's because it was completely gone! There was *nothing* where my left foot used to be!"

"It must have been a large-diameter ball to cause that kind of damage," said Tilden.

"A densely packed ball of grapeshot spat from the mouth of the very weapon you see there," he said, pointing at his partner's blunderbuss.

"What happened next?" asked Tilden.

"What do you think happened? I tipped over and lay prone suffering from blood loss. Mr. Fripphouse sat with me until a surgeon could be found. In one of my more lucid moments..."

"Delirious moments," interjected Fripphouse.

"Lucid moments!" responded Barron.

"Delirious!"

"Lucid!"

"Delirious!"

"In one of my more LUCID moments, I raised my head off the sod and promised Mr. Fripphouse that I would repay him for blowing off my foot — someday, somewhere, when he least expected it. It might take me months or even years, but I would return the favor. 'An eye for an eye, a foot for a foot' would become my motto."

"Then what happened?" asked Tilden.

"I fainted. When I awoke later in my bed, my leg ended in a stump just below my knee, and the oaken apparatus you see here had been installed in lieu of my shin, ankle, and foot."

From about fifty yards to our northeast, a series of gunshots, numbering about six, rang out. We all ducked instinctively.

"Someone must have run across a bunch of pigs over there," I said.

"Either that, or there is one pig that has six bullet holes in his arse!" jested Tilden.

Our party stood and cautiously crept toward the source of the shots.

"You did not finish your story, Mr. Barron," said Fripphouse.

"Pray, finish it," said Tilden.

As we trod across a rocky trail, Barron continued at a lower volume. "Well, my fine young man, ever since the accident, Mr. Fripphouse has lived in dread that I will blow off his foot. I might, for example, sneak up on him one night as he sleeps in his bedroom. Or I might greet him one morning at our offices with paperwork to sign in one hand and a gun aimed at his foot in the other. Or I might elect to have my revenge one of these years at this pig hunt, on the anniversary of my maiming. He does not know from one day till the next when I will pounce."

"Five years have passed, proving your words are idle boasting. I have nothing to fear from you anymore," said Fripphouse.

"Unless I select a time five years hence to seek my revenge!"

"Bah!" grunted Fripphouse.

"Why are you still business partners if you hate Mr. Fripphouse so much for doing this to you?" I asked.

"Hate Mr. Fripphouse? I don't hate the man. I love him like a brother. We have been through thick and thin together. We have survived boom-and-bust economic conditions. We have weathered the sinking of ships containing thousands in inventory! It's not too much of an exaggeration to say that we are like an old married couple, as comfortable together as a pair of old wool socks."

At this moment, four or five pigs darted out of the brush in front of us. All but one scampered away before any of us could take aim and shoot. The last pig lingered, evaluating which direction offered the best escape route. Hot in pursuit were two groups of huffing and puffing men, with whom our party united in surrounding the creature. A couple of men raised their weapons, intending to shoot.

"Halt! Gentlemen, hold your fire!" shouted a man from one of the other foursomes. "We are in a circle right now, and if we open fire, we will cut each other down like a Hessian firing squad."

"Yes, it is better that we form a ring, which slowly contracts until we are able to capture him by hand," said one of his companions.

At this man's signal we all took a step forward, then another, then another, as the noose tightened. The pig responded by running this way and that, attempting to pierce our defenses, but finding himself foiled at each turn as we scrambled to close gaps he tried to exploit. Yet, he was a fleet little bugger and nimbly evaded our efforts to grab him by the leg or tail. After a few minutes we ceased our exertions, finding ourselves in a frustrating standoff between twelve grown men and one diminutive pig.

"What can we do?" Tilden asked. "We can't shoot him. We're unable to catch him. Are we supposed to just let him go?"

"NO!" responded a chorus of eleven voices.

"I have an idea," I said. It was a risky plan, for if I failed I would look like a complete fool, and word of my folly would spread as gossip from the day was exchanged at the feast later. I decided to proceed despite the risk to my reputation. I uncoiled my whip, twirled it above my head a few times to gain velocity, and, with a tremendous crack, lashed the dirt only inches away from the surprised animal. I wound up and cracked my whip again, and this time I succeeded in striking the pig and knocking him off his feet.

As the pig lay still at the center of our circle, we closed in to investigate the damage my whip had wrought. "Did I kill him?" I asked, suddenly feeling nauseous at the thought.

"No, you only stunned him," answered Tilden, who knelt over the animal. "He's still breathing and his legs are twitching."

"Shoot him, for God's sake, before he wakes up!" Barron urged.

"As you wish," said Tilden. He stood, aimed his rifle, and with a single shot dispatched the pig to swine heaven. In my queasy state, I was extremely glad that I had not been called upon to perform this act. He stuffed the body into a leather quarry bag, which he walked over and presented to me, saying, "There's only a small hole in the neck, a very clean kill. Had these other gentlemen with their antique guns done the deed, we would be having pork hash for supper."

I slung the bag over my shoulder, and the other men came over one by one to congratulate me for my resourcefulness. Pride swelled in my chest, replacing the nausea that had churned my stomach. After sharing a celebratory sip from Barron's whiskey flask, our groups parted company and returned to the hunt. Only one other man in our party, Fripphouse, succeeded in taking down a pig that afternoon. As Tilden had predicted, the grapeshot from his blunderbuss shredded the poor animal, and we judged its corpse too damaged to eat.

As the sun sank closer and closer to the treetops, we headed back to Hamilton Hill to merge with the hungry, exhausted rabble. Already, pigs were everywhere roasting in pits and turning on spits, and their organs stewed in large kettles stirred by Negroes. I said goodbye to my fellow hunters and searched for Bunny, whom I found assisting a crowd of butchers with skinning and gutting, and I laid the bag at her feet. More excited than I had ever seen her, she ripped open the bag and yanked out my catch.

"White and black pig taste good," she said. "Better than pink."

I rather doubted that one color of pig tasted better than another, just as men from the white, black, or yellow races probably tasted exactly the same to a cannibal. Still, I was relieved that Bunny had found this attribute to praise, and she refrained from making fun of the animal's size, which was smallish, actually closer to a suckling pig than a fully mature one.

Faster than I could undress a woman in the heat of sexual attraction, Bunny peeled off the pig's skin and threw the rubbery inside-out likeness away. With a

"Ching-ching-ching-ching-ching" of her cleaver she chopped off its feet and tail. With a quick twist of her knife and a wet "schlupp!" sound she gutted it. As I watched the pig's entrails pour out onto the ground, I felt woozy and had to walk around for a few minutes, praying that I would not vomit.

When I returned, the pig, including snout and head, was arranged in a smoking pit along with whole potatoes, yams, squash, carrots, leaks, and turnips. Bunny stood over the pit and sprinkled from a deerskin pouch a mixture of crushed leaves, nuts, berries, seeds, and twigs over the pit. "Special Potawatomi spice," she explained. Next, she covered the pit and its contents with a layer of rocks, I presumed to seal in the juices and lock in the flavor. "Pig cook one hour," she announced, whereupon we joined Mr. Gallatin at his table and drank fine French wine from his wine cellar while we waited for dinner to cook. Bunny got tipsy after one goblet, and she tittered at her mentor's flirtations, which he delivered in Potawatomi. I am not precisely sure what he had said, but I could tell that Bunny was hugely charmed by his words. After an hour's time, Bunny excused herself to apply the finishing touches to the food she was preparing.

A few minutes later, Mr. Gallatin's butler, a distinguished-looking, white-haired Negro named Archibald, rolled a serving cart across the grass to our table. First, he set our places with silverware and china so fine that I would hesitate to take them out of their drawers and cabinets, much less out of doors. Next, he poured us soup from a mirror-polished silver tureen. "Dat Indian squall of yours, she don't know *nothin'* 'bout servin' no soup course," he complained. "Ol' Archibald, he cook de soup and bake de pie you be havin' fo' dessert."

Mr. Gallatin excused Archibald, and we supped our soup in the civilized circumstances of a handful of other attendees dotting the hill — under a yellow tent, at a table covered with a checkerboard tablecloth, lit by candelabra. Beyond the invisible walls of our tent, bawdiness and drunkenness generally prevailed, while the picnicking masses shouted, laughed, swore, bragged, argued, cried, mocked, snored, teased, threatened, and sang as they devoured the day's kill.

Bunny and Archibald returned as Mr. Gallatin and I were finishing our soup, a bland beef broth with barley that I did not believe tasted so special. Archibald had donned an apron, and he carved us steaming slices of roast pork, which he gently laid next to vegetables that Bunny had artfully arranged on plates. Such presentation made the food look marvelously appetizing, and I nearly forgot about the serving pan containing remnants of what could still be recognized as a pig.

My hunger outfought my scruples, however, and I promptly tore into some of the most delicious pork I have ever tasted. The seasonings that Bunny had incorporated into the dish pleased all four taste buds simultaneously. Each bite imparted a slightly different flavor, sometimes salty or sweet, sometimes bitter or sour, and sometimes a mixture of two flavors, as in bittersweet or sweet and sour. I suspected that, in addition to specially harvested seasonings, she had included in her recipe a certain amount of magic, what her people called "medicine," to combine such a remarkable range of subtle flavors into a single dish.

"You like?" she asked Mr. Gallatin. His mouth was full, so he could not answer, but he enthusiastically nodded. "You like?" she asked me second, which hurt my feelings somewhat, because I was her employer and protector, although I realized that Mr. Gallatin was the dominant figure in her life at present.

"Very much," I said, motioning to Archibald to serve me a second helping of meat.

"Yes," said Mr. Gallatin, pausing to pat his lips with a napkin. "A most extraordinary recipe. You must help me write it down, so I may include it with the other materials we have collected."

Bunny fairly beamed at all of the compliments she was receiving for her cooking skill. This made me realize — to my shame, because I had been ignoring this yearning to flex her hands and mind — that she longed for her own sphere, a well-appointed kitchen or a shallow barbecue pit, where she could practice the domestic arts that she had studied since childhood. Thus far in our travels, such an outlet for self-expression had been largely unavailable to her, and she needed it as much as her daily conversations in Potawatomi with Mr. Gallatin. Living in hotels, she had watched as hired women cooked our food and cleaned our rooms, leaving her feeling as if she were engaged in forced hibernation. I resolved to press the developer to expedite the construction of my new home, where I would install Bunny as queen of our household.

Archibald cleared our dishes when we were through eating (his apple pie was much more agreeable than his beef barley soup), and we drank the last dregs of wine. During dessert, Bunny busied herself with burying all of the bones and waste from our meal, and she spread dirt over her barbecue pit to extinguish any trace of flame. Looking from atop Hamilton Hill, I saw that the crowd below had thinned considerably; when Bunny rejoined us, we asked to be excused from Mr. Gallatin's table, and we strode arm-in-arm down the hill to our waiting coach. As we walked I congratulated Bunny out loud and myself silently for triumphing so handily in our first foray into New York society.

We waited awhile beside our coach for traffic back into the city to thin out. Periodically, men I had never met before stopped and asked to shake my hand; evidently, they had heard stories from Barron, Fripphouse, or Tilden, or a combination of all three, of how I had subdued a pig with my whip. They held my exploit in greater awe than even the most amazing shots delivered by marksmen. In their minds, I was like an expert swordsman; we both used primitive weapons that demanded a higher degree of skill and fortitude than a gun fired at a target from a cowardly forty yards away. It was supremely ironic: here I was attending an event where a man is measured by his skill at shooting, and yet I had never fired a single shot. I had received the highest praise from my peers for successfully wielding a weapon that I had recently taken up as a lark.

Among the men who emerged from the darkness to pay their respects was Sam Tilden, whose wagon driver was likewise waiting for the main arteries into the city to unclog. "You had an agreeable supper, I trust," he said. "I ate a delicious pulled-pork sandwich and three ears of sweet corn."

"My servant, Bunny, cooked roast pork Indian-style for Mr. Gallatin and me."

"Gallatin? You certainly are making friends in high places!" He peered at me with a curious expression, similar to moments earlier that afternoon, as if determining whether we had met before.

"Let me introduce you to Bunny," I said. "She's sitting inside the coach." I raised one of the leather curtains covering the window and asked Bunny to come outside, because there was somebody who wanted to meet her.

Bunny alighted from the coach. She quickly straightened her dress and combed her hair with her fingers, desiring to make a good impression.

"Mr. Sam Tilden, this is Listening Rabbit, whom I call 'Bunny' for short."

"Pleased to meet you," said Tilden, gallantly taking Bunny's hand and kissing it.

"Bunny, meet Sam Tilden, who accompanied me today on the hunt. He actually killed the pig we ate tonight."

"But not before Mr. Connor astonished our company with his bullwhip wizardry!"

Bunny said nothing by way of greeting; instead, she laid her hands on Tilden's face and felt his nose, cheeks, and eyes. Then she took his hands into hers and examined them under the light shining from a lantern hanging off the side of our coach.

"Bunny! Stop that! You're embarrassing Mr. Tilden. Please say something, or else he will think you're rude."

"You come from future time, like Connor," she finally said.

My heart came close to exploding when I heard this. "BUNNY! Get back into the coach this instant!" I ordered. Bunny's eyes welled up, unsure of what she had done wrong to provoke my wrath. "NOW!" I emphasized, and she hastily clambered back inside our vehicle.

"Being an Indian, Bunny believes in all kinds of hocus pocus," I explained to Tilden, hoping that he would not interpret her statement as anything other than evidence of an overactive imagination. "I'm sorry if she offended you."

"Why should I be offended?" he asked. "Her words are true. I AM from the future. 2063 to be exact."

"I beg your pardon?" It seemed that Tilden's imagination was working overtime, too.

"I'm a time pilot. Like you."

"You must have me confused with somebody else," I said, but I saw that I was the confused party in holding my belief that Bilson, Rachel, and I possessed some monopoly on time travel. After our initial voyages, it stood to reason that others would follow in our footsteps.

"No, you're a time pilot all right, a rather celebrated one in fact. I recognized you today when you walked into the registration tent, and I maneuvered myself into your foursome so I could meet you. Let me see if I remember your story correctly: Bruce Bilson, an early pioneer of time travel technology, ran off with your wife, Rachel, to the past. You followed hard on their heels by persuading Bilson's assistant to send you back in time also. Right now you're in the process of tracking down your wife and Bilson. Does any of this sound familiar?"

I confessed that it did. "Can you ride back to town with Bunny and me?" I asked.

"I'd be honored."

"But what about your driver and wagon?"

"I was one of several people in the wagon. It will be no big deal if I don't return with them. The driver is planning to leave at nine o'clock regardless of who is or is not present."

Chapter Nine

For the remainder of our ride back into the city from the annual pig hunt, and afterward late into the night, young Sam Tilden described to me the facts of his origins. He had an ocean of time to fill, because the coach in which we rode was facing the worst traffic jam I had ever experienced, counting modern Chicago's Kennedy Expressway in rush hour during spring road construction season (Here, I refer to a busy turnpike leading from Chicago's suburbs to the city's core that always lay in disrepair somewhere along its length).

Sam was a child prodigy who had grown up during the Information Age launched in my own childhood that, by the time of his birth, had penetrated every inch of the globe and invaded every area of life. To a born information sponge such as Sam, the spirit of the age had provided a breathless education. He had written poems at age three and whole essays by five, and he had memorized *Ulysses*, a long, difficult novel written by a modern Irishman named James Joyce, by the age of thirteen. He had graduated from high school at the tender age of fifteen, whereupon the Department of Homeland Security, a secret organization that pulled the strings of government, like the trust power in the nineteenth century, had recruited him into its fold.

America during that era — really no different than at any other point in its history — was in a dangerously chaotic state. Charged with protecting the nation's citizens, the Department had conceived of numerous plans to battle anarchy and social disorder, including sending time pilots into the past in an attempt to rewrite history. The theory was that current problems could be altered through changing the historical conditions from which they arose.

"My mission began in Rochester, New York," he explained. "The early time travel missions, such as yours, were immensely popular and successful. You have a leading place in history, my friend, at least in the time thread from which I hail."

Hearing this made me wonder what kinds of things were said about me. Was I a romantic antihero outside of the typical military or sports figure mold? Or was I a pitiful cuckold who went back in time to confront his wife and do ... what? Give her a piece of my mind? Beg her to return to me? That did not sound like a very appealing way to be inscribed in the historical record.

Sam continued, "The Rochester Institute of Technology became one of several regional sites that received the technology necessary for time travel. Each site had different emphases: MIT did engineering, Johns Hopkins medicine, Cal Tech transportation, and so forth. Rochester specialized in politics and diplomacy. My training involved altering political events and foreign policy to reshape the modern world."

"I can't believe that the government took over time travel technology to that extent. When I did it, they were still talking in terms of scientific curiosity, service to humanity, those sorts of things. Nobody spoke of pursuing selfish national ends."

"Revenge was the motive for your voyage, was it not? That seems pretty selfish to me."

"Point taken. They turned atomic research into atom bombs, after all." (Here I alluded to the most fearsome weapon of the modern world, which was capable of destroying an entire city with a single explosion.)

"Precisely. America already meddled in world affairs — the Middle East, Colombia, the Sino-Japanese alliance — so our leaders decided, 'Why not tamper with the past, too?' Thus, they sent me back in time to grow up to become President of the United States."

"You're joking!"

"Only a little. Rochester prepared me for a career on the nineteenth-century political stage. My ultimate goal is the presidency, but if I can become an influential senator or governor, that will do also. The Department determined that, of all their candidates, I had the greatest chance of succeeding. They obtained my parents' permission, and I received their blessing, to attempt this feat. One fall day in Rochester, I left my parents behind to go away to college. Only I planned to attend Yale University circa 1830, not 2063."

"It sounds like your parents had more preparation than my father had, which was basically none at all. I often worry that I left him with the biggest shock of his life. I hope he was able to make peace with my departure like your parents evidently did."

"My parents, in particular my father, who was descended from a series of decorated military heroes in his family tree, interpreted my decision as a desire to serve my country. They grieved over the loss of their eldest son, as if I had died on the battlefield. But they took comfort in the fact that I hadn't died in actuality.

Rather, it was like I had been transferred to another war theater beyond the reach of communications."

"And how was Yale? Different, I bet, from the party atmosphere of twenty-first-century colleges."

"I graduated first in my class. How could I not, with a storehouse of modern knowledge that was unknown to my classmates? After graduation last spring, I moved down to New York City from New Haven to clerk at Bigelow, Strunk & Cushman, the first rung on my ladder to the presidency."

By this point in our conversation, we had arrived back at the City Hotel. It was after midnight, but Sam had much more to tell me. So he might finish his story, I invited him upstairs to my suite for a nightcap. I shook the sleeping Bunny awake (for she did not comprehend much of our talk and quickly grew bored and slept the whole trip, emitting a light feminine snore), and I instructed her to go to the hotel's bar to retrieve us a bottle of whiskey and two glasses, three if she cared to join us.

While I changed out of my hunting outfit, which smelled strongly of barbecue smoke, Sam settled into one of the matching velvet chairs by the window, which afforded a view towards City Hall and the northern half of the city. I sat in the other velvet chair, and we awaited Bunny, who entered moments later carrying a tray with a bottle and two glasses.

"Bunny tired," she announced. "Must go to bed." She curtsied to Sam and me, something new she had been doing lately that was probably learned from Mr. Gallatin, and she retired to her room. The tray was decoupaged with a bald eagle clutching American flags in its talons. Practically everything I touched in those days, from dinner plates to coffee mugs to water pitchers, was decorated with patriotic themes — if not eagles, flags, or shields covered with stars and stripes, then the faces of historic personages, especially George Washington and Commodore Perry, the navy captain who had won the battle of Lake Erie during the War of 1812. Even butter pats came molded in the shapes of eagles or shields at the City Hotel. Such trappings, as commercial as they were patriotic, perfectly accented Sam's story.

"If I may be so bold as to enquire, what aspect of history are you intending to change if you become president?" I asked, getting back to our conversation.

"The Civil War. Either prevent it or ameliorate its effects."

"Whoa! That's a tall order!"

"Yes, well, it's no secret that the war and its principal cause, slavery, had caused untold amounts of problems in our country. In 2063, we were celebrating the two-hundredth anniversary of the Emancipation Proclamation, but the festivities felt hollow to everybody, because the white and black races were as alienated as ever. In fact, a civil war between the two races was a serious possibility."

"WHAT?!?" I had a difficult time believing this, for in my youth race relations in the U.S. had been at their apex. The civil rights battles of the twentieth century that we learned about in high school seemed finished and won in the distant past. In 2008, the country had even elected a Negro (more accurately, a Mulatto) to become President.

"It's true. A movement to force the federal government to pay reparations to the descendents of slaves took hold among the African-American population. Like the anti-slavery movement of the 1800s, it had taken decades to gain momentum before it had any effect on most people's lives. But when it finally hit — POW!"

"What do you mean by 'Pow?'"

"Their arguments had started to resonate with the American population, and a majority came to believe that the government should be held accountable for its role in advancing slavery. Advocates for the position lobbied extensively for the measure, and in 2062, on the eve of the anniversary of Lincoln's Proclamation, the Supreme Court ruled that the U.S. Government was liable for its support of slavery. Accepting the estimates for the total losses suffered by the African-American community in lost wages and property, the Court ordered the government to pay fourteen-trillion dollars in reparations to those who could prove that they had descended from slaves.

"Fourteen trillion dollars," I repeated. "That's a lot of money."

"It was more money than existed in the entire country."

"Jesus! How could the U.S. be expected to pay more money than existed?"

"In a typical politician's move, the answer lay in saying one thing and doing another. In public, the president, Bim Nguyen, declared that the country would honor its commitment by digging deep into its resources and eventually making good on its promise to repay African-Americans for their ancestors' toil and injury. In private, he feared that the Court's decision would rapidly bankrupt the nation and radically reduce Americans' living standards, at least of the non-black population, to those of Somalia."

"I can't believe the Supreme Court would do such a thing. My ancestors came to this country after the Civil War ended and had nothing to do with slavery whatsoever."

"You raise the primary objection of many opponents to the decision. Nobody could agree on who the recipients of the award should be. Many African-Americans had come to these shores from Africa or the Caribbean after the Civil War, or they were descended from free blacks in the North who had never experienced the deprivations of slavery. The moral imperative had cast aside any of the practical considerations."

"Like they meant well, but they tackled the problem in the completely wrong way."

"Precisely. Amid the mess of administering the Court's decision, President Nguyen secretly explored ways to undermine it. It took him very little time to seize upon time-travel technology as a way to turn back the historical tide that had led to the disastrous decision. No slavery, no Civil War. No Civil War, no Reconstruction. No Reconstruction, no ruinous reparations."

"What makes you so sure that your plan will succeed? I was warned not to interfere too much in events for fear of making the historical outcome worse."

"I confess I don't know. Nobody really knows. In regard to influencing the future, there are two theoretical possibilities, neither of which has been definitively proven. You may find it impossible to change the future at all due to the 'Granny Paradox.' This states that it's logically (and physically) impossible to go back in time and kill your grandmother before your father or mother was born, because he or she would remain unborn, as would you.

"The other possibility, which seems more likely, is that you enter another time thread separate from the one from which you started. A wholly new chain of cause and effect is started from the point you enter your new time. It's as though you are proceeding down a second branch of the same tree that's identical in most respects to the first branch. Whether these branches eventually meet again at a later date, or continue proceeding in parallel directions, is subject to intense debate. The agency that sent me on my mission is wagering that the second possibility is the correct one and that I will have some palpable influence on the future."

Maybe it was the lateness of the hour or the effects of the whiskey, but I was having trouble bending my mind around these abstract concepts. I requested that Sam personalize these theories to address my individual interests and purposes. "You know about me from history. Do you know if I ever find Rachel and live happily ever after?"

"Unfortunately, no, I don't know, and this fact supplies evidence in favor of the second possibility."

"How so?"

"Once Bilson, you, and your wife left the twenty-first century, your leave-taking was copiously documented. However, nobody has found evidence in the historical record of any of your exploits undertaken in the nineteenth century. We know of your intentions when you left, and we can hypothesize about your activities, but we don't know how you fared. This could be due to your never having accomplished anything of note if you remained in the same time thread that you left. Or it could mean that you accomplished a great deal that was written up everywhere, only it occurred in a parallel time thread."

"I've done all right so far. Bilson, though, burned down an entire town in western New York. Since then, he and Rachel have been missing in action."

"I wish I had some clue about their whereabouts. You will have to find them without the benefit of historical hindsight, using plain old nineteenth-century methods."

"I think they may be in New York City somewhere, lying low. You seem to have a fix on things. If you ever happen to hear anything..."

"My employers have their fingers in every pie in town. Should these two particular plums pop up, I'll let you know right away."

"Thanks in advance for whatever you can do."

"We time pilots have to stick together. Besides, sometime, somewhere, there might be something that you can do for me. As you might have guessed, I wasn't the only time pilot who was sent back to this era. A handful of others are out in the bush as we speak tonight, working on various plots to undermine slavery. Two are paramilitary experts assigned to organize slave insurrections. As you may know, there were only two before the Civil War — Nat Turner's rampage in Virginia and John Brown's attack on Harper's Ferry. Twenty-first-century military strategists believed that more frequent slave revolts would weaken the resolve of slaveholders and inspire them to free their slaves for fear of revolution striking their plantations."

"Much as I sympathize, I'm not getting involved in any slave revolts, I can tell you that right now."

"Me, neither. I only mentioned other time pilots to suggest the range of missions going on at present. My mission is here in New York City, which is where I foresee you being helpful. If you're not an established presence quite yet, you nevertheless have more access to the inner circles of power than a poor law student does. I hope you'll brief me from time to time about your interactions with important politicians and businessmen. Or sometimes let me tag along to your meetings."

I agreed to render Sam any assistance that I could.

The grandfather clock in my sitting room chimed four times. I told Sam that my eyes were bleary from sleepiness and drink, and I had to go to bed. I escorted him to the door, shook his hand, and promised to stay in touch. After a physically and emotionally exhausting day, I undressed and fell onto the bed. As soon as my head crashed into my pillow I was fast asleep.

It took a while before I heard from Sam Tilden again. A few months after his startling revelations, he called on me one afternoon at the City Hotel while I was poring over railroad stock prospectuses that Mr. Gallatin had forwarded to me. Before investing, I had to predict which company would prove the most successful: the Baltimore & Washington, the New York & Harlem, or the Pennsylvania. I had some memory of the third road, which dated back to my life in the modern world, so I was leaning toward selecting that one.

"As you may know, it's election season," he began. "There's a meeting in a few nights at Tammany Hall, where the city's Democrats are planning to choose their slate of candidates for next month's election. I'm attempting to redirect the Democratic Party from the corrupt Tammany faction to the reformist faction called The Friends of Equality."

Here, Sam inserted a brief history of the political war being waged in New York City at the time. Tammany Hall was the center of the city's political machine. Although Tammany did some good things — it favored extending political rights to workingmen, endorsed most of President Jackson's fiscal reforms, and integrated untold numbers of German and Irish immigrants into the community — it also did some bad things. Despite its anti-monopolist rhetoric, the Tammany machine continued electing officials to the state legislature, which then awarded exclusive charters to wealthy bankers, shippers, and merchants, who obtained them through undisguised bribery. These charters essentially created legal monopolies that erected barriers to business competition and free enterprise. The Restraining Act, which Mr. Gallatin railed against, sounded like a prime example of this type of anti-democratic thinking.

Sam urged me to lend my support to the reformers' cause. Initially, I was cool to the idea. I had never followed politics much beyond voting, and I had skipped even this activity during several election cycles. Also, I did not fully trust Sam Tilden. Given our origins, we should have been natural allies, but I was also aware of the all-consuming, unprincipled ambition of those who seek the presidency, and I detected this unattractive trait already in the young man. Besides, I had traveled to the past motivated by my own private business; I never signed on to take part in any secret mission to cover up centuries of mistakes committed by the United States government.

On the other hand, I always considered myself a progressive sort of fellow who disapproved of powerful, arrogant men, beginning with Phil Levy, Rachel's lawyer father, and her two lawyer brothers, who, in my opinion, had always found themselves on the wrong side of every controversy, standing up for the strong instead of the weak. The possessor of a vast fortune, which always makes men pay attention, I might finally have the opportunity to influence the political process with my opinions, which tended to be liberal. I began to think in terms of it being my patriotic duty to help with Sam's liberalizing efforts.

"What would I have to do if I were to join up with your friends?" I asked.

"Attend our caucuses. Vote for our platform at the party's convention. Maybe donate a little money to the cause."

"And you believe that this will eventually reverse slavery and prevent the Civil War?"

"My plan is a sound one, I think. Work my way up through the Democratic Party's ranks. Effect reform within the party structure. Turn the party away from supporting slavery."

"When do I start?" I asked.

"Tomorrow night at Tammany Hall."

"Fine. I shall meet you there. May I bring Bunny?"

"No, politics in the nineteenth century is solely a men's club. Remember, women don't have the vote yet. Technically, I shouldn't even attend. I'm not twenty-one yet. But I can easily pass for twenty-five, because my modern education makes me appear wise and mature in everyone's eyes."

I withheld from Sam my thoroughly mixed feelings about The Friends of Equality. On one hand, I stood to profit from the sort of internal improvements and exclusive franchises to which they objected. In their prospectuses, the railroads I was researching boasted of their exclusive rights of way through key sections of the country. Indeed, maintaining a monopoly over these routes was an integral part of their continued success. As a purely rational and economic animal, I should be expected to oppose any reform.

On the other hand, I was not a solely economic animal, to the great disappointment of my father, Rachel, and Rachel's family. I have noticed the bowed legs, gnarled hands, stooped shoulders, and battered faces of New York City's workingmen, and I realized that if I had been born in 1800, instead of 1986, I likely would have been stuck in one of their abused bodies, smelting iron, slaughtering pigs, digging canals, or felling trees. Neither my father nor my mother was especially gifted, socially connected, or highly educated. Transported back to the nineteenth century, their modest accomplishments would probably have yielded a son who grew up to perform backbreaking work.

As it was, I felt like a member of the working class from my experiences as a network specialist in my former life. We in network engineering, systems administration, and computer operations comprised a separate caste from the computer programmers and analysts, who were the information industry's elite and, therefore, respected more and paid more than we. Also, many of us had accents — Spanish, Russian, East Indian, South-Side Chicago — that our corporate betters generally did not. Few of us had earned university degrees; I was the only one in my department, and mine came from a third-rate institution. I may have dressed in expensive suits and shoes that made me look to the entire world like a gentleman of leisure, but I was closer in type to The Friends of Equality than I cared to admit.

To guide my actions, I decided to apply the "Which side would you be on?" test. As in, which side of the barricades would I have been on during the Paris Revolt of 1825? Which side of a union picket line would I find myself marching on? Where did I stand on the topic of slavery? Preferring to align myself with the underdogs in all three cases, I decided I would follow through on my promise to Sam Tilden and attend the Tammany Hall vote.

The plan called for The Friends of Equality to arrive two hours earlier than the scheduled start time of the nominating meeting, grab all of the chairs, and deny Tammany Democrats entrance into the meeting hall. Politics being a more bruising sport in the 1830s than in the modern world, the leader of The Friends of Equality, William Leggett, placed the brawniest men at the front of the mob; they served as our vanguard force in slugging our way into the building. A large, lusty man cast from the same die as Shakespeare's Falstaff, Leggett looked as though he enjoyed his vices — wine, women, cigars, and lots and lots of rich food.

Taken by surprise, the handful of Tammany Democrats inside the building could do little but watch sullenly as enemy forces invaded and occupied their citadel. Soon, the crowd was chanting, "Bring on the nominating committee!" and "What time is it? Time to vote!" in a call-and-response pattern between those seated on the right side and left side of the center aisle.

When the start of the meeting approached, I could hear a mob of outsmarted and displaced Tammany Democrats clamoring outside in the street. The strongest men on The Friends of Equality side were engaged with the strongest men on the Tammany side in a tug of war involving the door. Someone threw a stink bomb through a window. It released a horrible sulfur-egg-privy stench that caused me to cover my nose and mouth with my handkerchief and breathe shallowly until the foul smell dissipated. However, despite assaults from every quarter, The Friends of Equality held their ground and with increased urgency demanded that the voting begin.

Unable to delay the meeting any longer, five or six dejected Tammany bosses took their places at a long table on the stage. To their left stood a tall wooden ballot box. One of the men rose, cleared his throat to obtain the audience's attention, and commenced speaking.

"Let us begin our session with a prayer. Heavenly Father..."

"NO PRAYERS! WE'RE HERE TO VOTE!" exclaimed the audience.

"But we always begin with a prayer," argued the man from the stage.

"NO TIME FOR PRAYERS! TIME TO VOTE!" the crowd responded. The man grew pale and sat down.

Another man rose and attempted to lead us in song. "To honor the sacred duty we are about to fulfill, and to commemorate the founding fathers' wisdom and vision in architecting the liberties that we enjoy, please join me in singing "My Country Tis of Thee."

"GET OFF THE STAGE! QUIT STALLING! THE TIME HAS COME TO VOTE!"

This second man sat down ignominiously.

At this moment the gas lamps in the hall dimmed for a few seconds, and then they went out completely, plunging the hall into total blackness.

Apparently, Tammany loyalists outside had cut off the gas feeding the lamps. Confronting this new and unexpected development, the shouted demands rose in vehemence. "TURN BACK ON THE LIGHTS! NO FAIR! FRAUDS! CHEATS!"

Things looked dark for The Friends of Equality, both in color and prospects. "Without light," stated one of the voices from the stage, "it will be impossible to complete our ballots and count the results. We must postpone this meeting until tomorrow night or until such time as gas service is restored to this building."

"BOO! HISS! UNFAIR!" The audience began clapping hands and stomping feet in a demonstration of their extreme displeasure. They continued this activity for several minutes, indicating their unwillingness to leave and abandon the tactical advantage of filling the hall with their partisans. I sensed that the aborted meeting could grow violent.

Wondering why I had not thought of it earlier, I reached into my pants pocket and drew out a box of Locofoco-brand matches, which I usually carried to light pipes of chekagou or, at night, to read address numbers above doors in a city mostly unlit by streetlights. I announced, "Wait a minute! I have a box of matches. They should provide just about enough light to carry on with the vote." I stood and passed handfuls to the men behind me and to each side.

Matches were a relatively new invention when these events occurred. Most men started fires by scraping together a penknife and piece of a flint that they carried around in their pockets. Matches were not expensive, but they had not really caught on everywhere or with everyone just yet.

"Don't light your Locofocos until ballots are passed out. We must properly husband this precious resource," said William Leggett's voice, coming from somewhere near the stage. "Mr. Mayor? Have your men pass out ballots. We're going to vote now."

"This is totally irregular and illegal. It's an outrage!" said a voice from the stage, which I guessed was the mayor's.

"What is illegal, Mr. Mayor, is cutting off the lights and abridging this assembly's constitutional right to vote for our preferred representatives," replied Leggett.

"You'll never get away with this!" warned the mayor.

"I already have," said Leggett, who thereupon heaved his impressive bulk onto the stage (I heard him gasp at the effort), nudged aside the mayor and his deputies, and took charge of the meeting. Then he called out the numbers of the city's wards, one through twelve. After each number, Leggett paused as match lights flared around the hall while men marked their ballots with pens or pencils and then passed them toward the front. I marked my choices when the Third Ward was called. Sam Tilden bent down from the stage to collect the ballots and deposited them into the ballot box, lighting a match as he did so, so all present could see that no tricks were being played with their votes.

The scene was a rousing one. With each lighted match, another vote was cast for the good guys — The Friends of Equality. You felt hopeful, even patriotic, as though for the first time light shone on a process usually conducted in proverbial darkness.

When every man had cast his vote, Leggett proceeded to run a tally. By this time, a candlestick maker from the Fifth Ward had come forward with a couple of candles, which lighted the table where the portly gentleman jollily fingered through splayed ballots. The Tammany bunch gritted their teeth and observed in silence, unable to argue that any shenanigans had occurred, at least in regards to the physical ballots. As for the shenanigans pulled earlier when The Friends of Equality had snatched their meeting place out from under them, they probably were thinking of ways to invalidate the expected result.

To nobody's surprise, The Friends of Equality's slate won by a ten-to-one margin. I was not even aware of the candidate's names to be very honest, but I assumed they were preferable to the Tammany choices, based on the scattered information that I had received from Tilden and from the portions of Leggett's speech of the previous night when I was not asleep.

From that point forward, The Friends of Equality were known as "Locofocos," in honor of the matches that had provided just enough light to oust the corrupt Tammany candidates and replace them with honest, hardworking fellows who reflected the people's will rather than the machine's. In the general election, Locofocos achieved mixed results against the Whigs, winning some elections and losing others. For a time, they split from the Democrats and formed their own party, which managed to send a couple of representatives to the State Assembly in Albany during its brief life. Seeing its popular support erode, the Democrats co-opted most of the Locofoco platform, and William Leggett and his followers rejoined the party a few years after voting by match light on that spring night. The Locofoco exercise is credited with opening up the political process to a wider population, though still not to Ladies, Chinamen, or Negroes. That would come later.

However, a beast as big as Tammany Hall, with tentacles reaching into every New York neighborhood, plus north to the state capital and south to Washington, D.C., was nearly impossible to slay. In later years, Sam Tilden, by then a grizzled veteran of many political battles, renewed his war against the institution, and in his position as City Prosecutor he succeeded in smashing it for good.

I had every reason to feel proud of my participation, however slight, in the Locofoco Party. I built upon the reputation I had earned at the Pig Shoot as a shrewd problem solver, no matter that I had shrewdly dealt with a cornered pig and had solved a simple problem of darkness by striking a match. Even better, I had pleased Mr. Gallatin, who worried that I might become an apolitical, amoral wastrel, sitting on my fortune and contributing nothing to the community. No matter what stocks and bonds I ended up investing in, he thought my investment in the Locofocos was wise, judicious, and sure to reap me many rewards. Just as my bank account grew through the miracle of compound interest, my social capital grew as word of my exploits compounded.

Chapter Ten

June 10, 1835

New York City in 1835 isn't the New York City of 2015, that's for sure. It's a filthy stinking seaport that probably has more in common with Shakespeare's London than the city I used to visit with my parents when I was growing up.

Though I have to confess I remember New York being pretty dirty in the 21st century, too. What I visualize most are buildings plastered with graffiti and garbage bags piled high on the sidewalks.

I found it pretty ridiculous that out front of every restaurant, even the 4-star ones my parents took me to, there were these bulging green bags leaking God knows what into the gutter and smelling to high heaven. As if people had never heard of garbage dumpsters or back alleys to park them in!

By the time Bruce and I arrived in New York, I was accustomed to stepping in mud and manure everywhere. But I had hoped for more from the biggest, most sophisticated city in the country. Call me naive, but I was expecting paved or at least graveled streets, not manure-strewn horse paths.

But that's what greets my feet every morning when I leave our house on Barrow Street to shop at the wharves for bread or fish or produce. On rainy days, the streets are open running sewers. On dry days, powdered shit blows up your nose and rims your eyes.

Starting when I was a teenager, I dreamed of living in Greenwich Village. I fancied myself an intellectual who had escaped the stultifying suburbs to wine and dine with poets and artists in the bars and cafes up and down Bleecker Street.

I got my wish. Only it was granted a hundred and seventy-five years too soon, before all those bars and cafes were built.

The Village in 1834 is a sleepy suburb full of rustic cottages on tree-lined streets. Suburban conformity is the norm, which is ironic given the neighborhood's legendary reputation for nonconformity.

It's definitely a good place to lie low. Stuck in the northernmost corner of the city, we live far from the hustle and bustle further downtown.

Bruce says, and I'm inclined to agree, that we need to stay under the law enforcement radar for a while. We don't know with any certainty whether we're wanted criminals. But we're not taking any chances. Bruce spends most of his time inside the house, contemplating his next move.

My next move will not be to leave Bruce and strike out on my own, at least not right now. Bruce might be a loser, but he's the only loser I've got. Until I meet a few people and figure out what I'm going to do with myself, I'm going to stick with the loser I know as opposed to the winner I don't know.

Anyway, I don't feel as much pressure to stay out of sight as Bruce does. The Niagara Falls incident was completely his fault. The danger lies in the police tracing him through me. When I venture outside I don't call attention to myself. I get my shopping done, and then I head back indoors.

We have a modest but comfortable house. I paid the previous owner $600, and he forked over the deed thinking he had gotten the better end of the deal. He may well have, but by paying in gold I was able to avoid every legal entanglement except one: filing the deed with the city, which I did under the name Rachel Lewis. I hoped this would keep the sheriff off our tails.

We have four whole rooms, two more than our last place. Unusual for the neighborhood, we don't rent out rooms to boarders. Bruce has his bedroom, and I have mine. I've ordered chairs, tables, sofas and beds that ought to create a much homier atmosphere when they're finally delivered.

Needless to say, the furniture I ordered looks like museum pieces or something out of my Grandma Feinstein's living room (minus the plastic slip covers) — purple velvet cushions, big clubfoot legs and ornately carved eagles, American flags and other patriotic doodads top to bottom.

To someone like me, who was raised in a thoroughly modern split-level house surrounded by sleek ultramodern furniture, it's all totally gross to look at. Nobody in 1834 has heard the phrase "Form follows function."

I've told countless cabinetmakers to lose all the decoration, because their stuff would be cheaper to make. They're really resistant to the idea. In their minds, all those stupid curlicue inlays and carvings are a value-added service that they expect to be handsomely paid for.

I also ordered new carpets that I'm told are on a boat somewhere between Persia and here. A man named Mr. Barron sold them to me. I'm remarking on this only because he's the first person I've ever met with a peg leg. Poor man! His partner, Mr. Fripphouse, whispered to me that he lost his leg in a hunting accident.

The rugs are necessary to cover the counterfeit carpet painted on the floor. No fooling — the previous owner painted a bunch of flowers and squiggly vines on the floorboards in a cheap imitation of a room-size oriental rug.

The rooms we rented in Niagara Falls also had floors painted to look like carpet. (And I was appalled by that, too.) It must be the current fashion among the poorer classes.

I've splurged and hired a maid for a couple of hours every day. Mainly to help out with the cooking. I've given up doing it myself. It's too goddamn difficult. I had a hard enough time with a microwave and electric range in the 21st century. But to cook inside a fireplace with big iron kettles, fucking forget it!

Maggie's a sweet thing, a 16-year-old Irish girl fresh off the boat. She can work wonders cooking with a single pot. She makes delicious roast meats and about twelve different kinds of stew. I'm working with her to prepare more vegetable and fruit dishes. Meals in the 1800s are extremely heavy on meat and starch. I'm seriously craving lighter fare.

What I really miss from my former life is angel-hair pasta with marinara sauce. I used to have it delivered at least once a week from Leona's back in Chicago. I can't get Maggie to cook with tomatoes, though. She thinks they're poisonous and refuses to have anything to do with them.

Maggie's a good barometer of Bruce's frame of mind. She steers way clear of him. This might be traditional deference to men, especially from servants to their social betters.

More likely, Bruce's silent self-absorption makes her nervous. Every time he opens his mouth, her freckles just about leap off her skin.

To give Bruce his due, he seems on the verge of a breakthrough with his future plans. He's decided to get into the patent medicine business.

He's like, "With modern knowledge of biochemistry, I can produce medicines that actually work, instead of the snake oil you hear all kinds of preposterous claims about."

I'm like, "We've heard it all before. How you're going to apply modern knowledge to 19th-century problems. Then some disaster happens, and our lives are turned upside-down. I don't think I can go through another Fredonia or Niagara Falls."

"If it's done right, virtually nothing can go wrong. People will be thanking me instead of wanting to tar and feather me."

Specifically, he's going to manufacture plain ordinary aspirin. (Leading up to his decision I was secretly hoping he'd pick cocaine. No such luck!) When he rattles off his reasons, his plan makes sense:

- Cheap, plentiful raw materials
- Easy to reproduce formula

- Effective pain relief
- Distinguishable from other drugs in the marketplace, all of which contain either alcohol or opium (Show me where I can get my hands on those!)

Bruce remembers the process from a college chemistry class. The main raw material is common willow tree bark. The bark contains salacin, which is the active ingredient in aspirin.

Our lot has about six weeping willows, and there are close to a hundred more on our street alone. Last Tuesday, Bruce went on an all-night tree-trimming expedition. By morning he had gathered a giant stack of willow branches and twigs, which took up our whole living room floor.

Since then Bruce has carefully peeled away the bark and scraped off the green part into wooden buckets. After two or three weeks of this unbelievably boring activity, he's finally harvested enough green stuff to whip up a small batch of pure salacin.

I won't let him cook it up in the house, though, and that's been an ongoing argument. Back in the 21st century I heard too many stories about meth labs blowing up and taking houses along with them. So he's built a crude shed in our back yard where he's put together his lab.

It's scary how in recent months Bruce resembles less and less a hugely successful astrophysics theorist and more and more a mad scientist. I'm concerned that the neighbors might agree with me. The novel *Frankenstein* by Mary Shelley is a best seller right now.

What if they suspect Bruce is a budding Dr. Frankenstein? Greenwich Village could use a nonconformist or two, but that doesn't mean I want to be the first one.

Then I look around at the other backyards on my block, and I see the 19th-century version of men potschkying around with cars in their garages.

This one's trying to invent a better horse bridle, that one's boiling wax for candle-making, the other one's raising rabbits, an important dietary source — YUCK! — hereabouts. Bruce ought to fit right in.

Like Frankenstein's assistant, I'm sent on discreet errands at night. Only instead of body parts I bring home glass tubing or beakers or whatever. It's only two blocks to the scientific supply store, but I always walk with Maggie because it's unsafe for a man to walk by himself in New York City after dark, let alone a woman.

Maggie always slips a carving knife into her skirts before we leave the house. She lives in a tough neighborhood called Five Points, and she apparently knows how to sling a blade.

Thankfully, now that Bruce has a project to occupy him, his swagger is slowly coming back. I confess the sight of him no longer revolts me. But I'm a lot less susceptible to his charms than I used to be.

I'm also a lot less dependent on him for emotional or physical security. When we were traipsing through the wilderness, sure, I needed him to protect me from Indians and wild animals (and poison ivy and sprained ankles).

Now the only thing he's trying to protect is his bruised and battered ego. The variables r, a, c, h, e and l have been left out of his equations.

No longer a bright, shining star, Bruce is a brown dwarf. I learned about brown dwarves when I worked at the U of C physics department. It's what you get when a star uses up all its fuel and flames out.

Brown dwarves, I should also mention, have a much weaker gravitational field than full-fledged stars. Similarly, I'm decreasingly attracted to Bruce and increasingly drawn to other interests.

Problem is, I'm unable to indulge them; I'm stuck in the house all day. Herein lies one of the bitter ironies of my life at present. I'm well educated and reasonably good-looking (one night soon after our affair began Bruce just about made me cream when he whispered into my ear, "Your face is so pretty, it's hard for me not to stare at you.")

I also happen to throw a kick-ass party, even if I don't cook all the appetizers or mix all the cocktails by myself. That's why God invented caterers, as my mother used to say.

But I can't go out into society and exercise my attributes. This is the very same dilemma Lydia Maria Child lectured about when I saw her last year. What makes my situation doubly tragic is I'm not an ignorant farm wife or illiterate housemaid. I have a lot more untapped potential.

It's funny, I swore I'd never sacrifice my interests for any man. I could have easily married a wealthy, if nebbish, Jewish doctor and settled in Glencoe or Highland Park. There I could've overseen a huge house and raised a brood of three or four kids.

More than a little interest was expressed in me back in the day. But I wasn't into that scene. For a while I succeeded in living as an independent woman, first with the footloose freewheeling Dan Connor and then with the sober industrious Bruce Bilson.

Yet here I am, living in a century where a woman is considered a second-class citizen. This thought pattern seems to be wearing off on my "husband." Lately, I feel this pressure from Bruce to stand aside and let him work on his project. Last week he's like, "Don't worry your pretty little head. I'll handle everything."

I'm afraid a stronger will than mine drives Lydia Maria Child to completely reject such conventional thinking.

Then I remember I have a damn good track record of handling men. I've put Dan, who always drew out the worst in me, in his proper place: a hundred-plus years and a trillion miles away. I sometimes wonder if he's gotten a divorce from me yet? Or if he's met anybody? (God, I'm such a schmuck!)

I hooked up with the renowned Bruce Bilson, too, didn't I? And I successfully schmoozed all of those dorkwad scientists at the U of C. Even if my posterior hasn't been handed the most comfortable seat at present, at least my name and exploits will be handed down to posterity.

Who's to say I couldn't have the same effect on 19th-century men, a less sophisticated bunch than their latter-day counterparts? I've also proven I can manage women effectively. The secret is to act all helpless and entice their help. My new mantra? "Help me out here."

In light of these facts I should reconsider my situation vis-à-vis Lydia Maria Child. What I lack in will I more than make up for in intelligence. Who's to say an old women's studies minor like me isn't as smart and savvy as a famous feminist from history? After all, a 21st-century nurse is probably more knowledgeable about medicine than a 19th-century doctor.

Why couldn't I do something similar? You know, speak in public about what everybody is doing wrong to women.

Wait! Wait! Even better: a *talk show* where I dish about women's issues with guests like Lydia Maria Child. *Help me out here....*

I spent millions of hours when I was a kid watching TV talk shows like Oprah Winfrey and Jerry Springer. I'm intimately acquainted with the medium. Given the simple folk I'm dealing with here, I think I could pull it off, no matter that my only public appearance ever was spring play during my junior year of high school.

But NO-O-O-o-o-o!

I'm sentenced to house arrest due to my boyfriend's dopey actions upstate.

Screw that!

I'm breaking out of jail. The way I figure it, if the authorities discover who I am, I've got plenty of money to hire the best lawyers to defend myself. What's the purpose behind having a small fortune if you can't make it work for you?

I'm rich enough to hire the best producers and rent the classiest performance spaces. I think I've got what it takes to make this happen. Check it out — it's 1835 and I'm going to host my own talk show. I'm genuinely excited about something for the first time since 2015.

Chapter Eleven

In December 1834, Joseph Pemberton, the private detective whom I had hired several months before to locate Rachel, paid me a call at the City Hotel. Upon entering my suite he tracked slush onto my carpet, having failed to wipe his boots at any juncture after entering the hotel — neither in the lobby, nor on the stairs, nor in the hall. However, his sheer physical size and bold disposition prevented me from protesting.

"I've news of your wife and her lover," he announced.

My heart began to knock wildly against my breastbone. "Where is she?" I demanded to know. "Please, tell me everything!"

"I cannot claim to know where precisely she *is* at the moment. But I can tell you most assuredly where she *was*."

"Is she here, in New York City?" I asked, wondering why I had to keep interjecting. Obviously, I was anxious for any shred of information, and he was dragging out the telling, seemingly for maximum dramatic effect.

His eyes roved my sitting room until they lighted on a spittoon filled with flowers I had set on a bureau, having no compelling need for the fixture's original purpose. He walked over to the bureau, glared at me for my foolish re-imagining of this nineteenth-century necessity, reached out and brushed the flowers aside, and spat out a gargantuan plug of tobacco, which made a tremendous plop when it hit the water. Next, he helped himself to a glass of whiskey from the decanter on the bureau, and he sat down in an armchair. Sitting in the armchair opposite, I reconciled myself to the fact that he intended on sharing his news at his own leisurely pace.

"Your Mr. Bilson is a wanted man," he finally stated.

"Yes, I know. He burned down a town near Buffalo. Tell me something I don't know." I had to remind myself to watch my tongue, or else Pemberton was liable to rise up and strike me.

"He is wanted for something else entirely. Murder."

"WHAT?" I almost swooned as my mind leaped to the worst possible conclusion, based on his use of the past tense before. Rachel *was*. "My wife's not...."

"No, no, no. She's alive as far as is known. The victims did not include her."

Victims? Bilson was a snake and a rat, but I would never have envisioned him as a mass murderer.

Pemberton proceeded to tell me the tale. Bilson's murder victims turned out to be ten mechanics in western New York, who were electrocuted at his hands.

"I assure you, Mr. Connor, that this is no laughing matter!" scolded Pemberton. "Ten men lay dead and the culprit is still at large."

"I'm sorry, Mr. Pemberton," I said between paroxysms. "It's just that I find Bilson's spectacular failures so funny. He's a famous scientist where I come from."

"Where is that again?"

"Um, Switzerland."

"Ah, yes. I forgot."

"Of course, it's a tragedy of epic proportions," I soberly observed, scowling outside but grinning inside.

"Indeed."

"So ... if Bilson is wanted, then that must mean he escaped."

"Bilson and your wife disappeared the night before the discovery of the mechanics' corpses. Noticing that their carriage and horses were missing, the local sheriff and his deputies fanned out along every road leading from Niagara Falls and consulted with every ferryman along the Niagara River to determine if they had crossed over into Canada (they had not). A few days later the sheriff learned that the couple sold their wagon and horses to a farmer in Albany, which leads him to believe that they caught a boat downriver, perhaps as far as New York City."

"You're telling me that they could be less than a mile or two away from where we sit?"

"I am currently investigating that possibility, yes. I have arranged a tit-for-tat with the sheriff. He agreed to make me privy to any developments from upstate, and I agreed to take Bilson into custody should our paths ever cross here in the city."

Desiring to be as helpful as I could in sharing insights into Bilson's character, I offered the following observation: "I don't get the impression that Bilson is a murderer. The mechanics' deaths must have been the result of an accident."

"You probably are correct. The grand jury summoned to investigate the case will likely downgrade the charges once the facts are presented. Still, Bilson must appear as a witness for them to make this determination."

I was ecstatic at Pemberton's news. It sounded as though the couple had stumbled into my lair without suspecting that I lurked waiting to pounce. I joyfully anticipated that I would be reunited with my wife in a matter of days.

I paid Pemberton his weekly retainer, plus a ten-dollar bonus for bringing me this information. Then I dismissed him after exacting a promise to call on me immediately, day or night, if he heard anything further concerning Rachel or Bilson. After Pemberton had departed, Bunny busied herself with scrubbing his boot prints off the rug and replacing the flower water in the spittoon *cum* vase. Normally, I would have asked housekeeping to take care of these duties, but the perpetually bored Bunny insisted. To the rug she administered a mixture of salt and urine retrieved from the chamber pot underneath her bed. Incredibly, her improvised cleaning solution completely washed away the boot prints and left no lingering smell.

When several days and nights had passed since Pemberton's visit, during which time he brought me no news about my wife, it became clear that my belief that she would soon be found was naïve and unrealistic. If they were smart — and they were about one-hundred seventy-five years smarter than everybody else, despite their recent setbacks — then Bilson and Rachel would have gone into hiding and divorced themselves from normal everyday social interaction. In fact, I had no evidence whatsoever that they had landed in New York City. They could have just as easily settled upriver, for example, or continued their journey by transferring to a ship headed for Boston or Charleston. London even. Rather than a mile or two away, they could have been one or two *thousand* miles away.

Such ruminations did not prevent me from joining the search effort. The chances of finding Rachel may have been slim, but actively looking for her was a more palatable prospect than sitting in my parlor idly waiting for visits from Pemberton. I began to travel in an ever-growing radius beginning at the City Hotel in the hope of bumping into my wife. No matter how hotly they were pursued, Bilson and Rachel had periodically to emerge from their hiding place, if only to buy bread or use the privy.

Why should I have believed that Rachel would have me back if I found her? For reasons, naturally, of profound and persisting animal magnetism (a popular if dubious 1830s lyceum topic). More importantly, my recent investing triumphs and community victories had transformed me, at least in my sight, into a promising mate with bright prospects. Certainly, I could boast of many more successes in the nineteenth century than Bilson could.

I started by checking the hotel register. The City Hotel would have been a magnet to someone of Rachel's refined tastes. (Unless Bilson had bankrupted her with his failed schemes.) The hotel covered enough acreage and comprised enough floors that she plausibly could be a guest and I would never have encountered her. The hotel manager, Mr. Beckham, gladly accommodated me by allowing access to his records. However, neither Rachel nor Bilson had registered under their names, nor under the name of William Bruce, and I didn't recognize Rachel's tiny, crimped handwriting.

Next, I turned my attention to the surrounding neighborhood, the city's main commercial district straddling Broadway. I walked past dressmakers' shops, food emporiums, furniture makers' workshops, and sundry other stores that sold every imaginable trinket and gewgaw. In their display windows I saw stylishly dressed mannequins, skinned rabbits and sausages hanging from strings, cherry-wood cabinets emblazoned with flags and eagles, silk scarves and stockings, gold rings and pocket watches, silver and tin cutlery, china plates and crystal goblets, linens for bed and table, wooden animal pull toys, pipes and cigars, spectacles, and, everywhere, false teeth carved from wood or ivory.

Such fashionable streets and avenues would have served as a magnet to Rachel. A staunch materialist, she could not long resist their attractions, I theorized, and they would sooner or later draw her out, exerting a stronger pull than even hunger. Just as fish had to swim and birds fly, Rachel had to shop; it defined her.

As I roamed farther afield, the streets became less commercial, less residential, and more rundown. The people dressed less nattily, had fewer teeth inside their mouths, and had a higher percentage of missing appendages than those in the vicinity of my hotel. Pigs, perhaps cousins of the unfortunate one I had hunted earlier, rooted through garbage piles unceremoniously dumped on every street corner. I began to notice starkly contrasting red stains on the snow, sometimes three to the block. On closer examination I determined that these were composed of congealed blood.

When I commented to a shopkeeper on the cruel fate befalling our urban swine — butchered in the streets where they stood — I was counseled not to be alarmed for their sake. Because, like as not, the blood was human, the result of robberies in which someone had been punched in the nose, bonked on the head, stabbed in the gut, or worse. That this blood appeared so frequently underscored the danger of walking in the city alone. Henceforth, I would have Bunny accompany me, plus I would always carry my bullwhip concealed on my person. If any potential assailant chose to attack us, he would receive more in return than he had bargained for, given Bunny's strength and ferocity and my standing in the community as a whip expert.

Soon thereafter, a knavish pair foolishly set upon Bunny and me one evening outside of Fraunces Tavern, an historical landmark where George Washington himself had supped, after we had stepped inside to wet our whistles. We probably looked like easy prey — a tipsy gentleman slipping and sliding in the snow while escorting his drunken lady friend.

"Yer money or yer lives!" growled the first assailant, who, in filthy shirtsleeves, evidently needed my money to purchase a winter coat. He had perhaps the worst complexion I had ever seen: mountainous pimples and whiteheads and blackheads on top of small-pox pits.

"Ya best obey if ya wanna live!" seconded the other as he displayed a knife. He wore a frayed wool coat that perhaps he traded off wearing with his partner. Absent the knife, he could have killed with his pungent odor.

Bunny took one look at the knife and burst out laughing. Emboldened by alcohol, I, too, laughed, for the robber wielded a dagger not much larger than a common penknife. With all of the belligerence he could muster, he waved it threateningly in front of our faces, his awful smell wafting behind the figure eights he drew in the air.

"You'll find this funny, awright!" he said upon lunging at my midsection. The other robber stood by, roguishly smiling, savoring how his partner was about to teach us a lesson in response to our insolence.

Before I could react and dodge the blow, Bunny parried the move by grabbing my attacker's wrist, bending his arm back, and forcing him down onto his knees. "Help! Help!" the robber cried to his partner, who froze, dumbstruck, unable or unwilling to come to his friend's aid. I also was awestruck by Bunny's maneuver, and I stood aside to let her manage the perilous situation after her own fashion.

While holding the robber's other flailing arm at bay, Bunny wrenched his hand, which still clutched the knife, against the side of his head. With a quick flick of his wrist she caused him to slice off his own ear.

"YOU BLOODY RED-SKINNED BITCH!" he screamed, dropping the knife and frantically patting the snow in search of his severed ear. After finding it beside his left knee, he raised it to his head and attempted in vain to place it back where it belonged. Because he lacked the means, like needle and thread, to re-attach it, it fell once again onto the street. He repeated this action a couple more times before finally scooping up the pulpy mess and running after his partner, who had meanwhile disappeared up the street. On this occasion, at least, the blood staining the street belonged to the robber and not the robbed.

"Who he calling bloody redskin?" Bunny asked me. "Him the one with bloody red skin." Then she let out a blood-curdling war whoop that drew curious faces out of every window up and down Pearl Street. Our state of affairs dismissed by the neighborhood as an ordinary street altercation, heads popped back inside again, windows were lowered, and shutters were slammed. Bunny picked up the knife and slipped it into her handbag; she has kept it to this very day as a keepsake of the one instance in her life when she played the role of brave instead of squaw.

Everyone who lived in New York during those days remembers the moment when a grotesque silhouette of the city's anarchy was branded upon his mind. This was mine — a thwarted mugging. That such encounters were nearly universal among New Yorkers demonstrated that some manner of help was needed to ameliorate the antisocial behavior of our fellow citizens. Presented was the classic problem of what to do with your poorer cousins writ citywide.

Attuned to twenty-first-century theories on crime fighting, I held the view that better employment prospects and housing opportunities would prevent the criminal classes from attacking the general citizenry. I considered civic and political reform as the surest path to improving the lot of the criminal classes.

This belief set me at odds with most of my contemporaries, whose blather was deeply tinged with evangelism. In God's eyes — so these fill-ins for God proclaimed — to refrain from alcohol, fighting, and fornicating put one's soul closer to God's knee. A thoroughly modern man agnostic in his judgments, I didn't cotton to the idea of kneeling at some supernatural creature's knee. In fact, I regarded alcohol and fornication as two of the few things available to comfort humans while they were under the steady assault of death, disease, loneliness, and taxes.

I had never subscribed to the cult of self-improvement that was so prevalent in the modern world. If, for example, you chose not to refrain from drink in the twenty-first century, you were judged a reprobate by your peers, or you were considered to be "in denial" about your "disease." You were socially ostracized until you completed a twelve-step program of prayer, confession, meetings, and apologies to those you had injured. All this added up to a significant number of sober, self-righteous alcoholics who proclaimed that they were powerless over their addiction, and they attempted generally to spoil the fun of everyone around them.

Thus, I turned down all invitations to engagements involving reformers, and I especially avoided revival or "tent" meetings held outside the city as if they were small-pox epidemics or cholera outbreaks. I had read several eyewitness accounts of these events published in the *New York World*. Typically, a minister possessed of a sensuous nature whipped up a church congregation into a sexually charged religious frenzy. The "saved" were said to have a personal relationship with Jesus to whom it was said men and women were wed, including all that implied in the *boudoir* — that was how much joy and pleasure could be derived from being one with God.

Yet, despite my efforts, I stumbled upon a mob demanding reform of some dastardly thing or another fairly often, especially during the 1830s and 40s. Mobs gathered around reformer leaders like flies orbiting horse manure, particularly those with controversial views like Sylvester Graham, who zealously promoted the health benefits of celibacy, or, at the opposite end of the continuum, John Humphrey Noyes, who enthusiastically preached in favor of free love.

One blustery night in March 1835, Bunny and I had the misfortune of running into a raucous assembly outside of the Downtown Lyceum before a talk by the aforementioned Sylvester Graham, hyperbolic bishop of radical vegetarianism.

The dour Graham dressed like an undertaker who headed a shabby, down-on-its-luck mortuary. It was here that I recognized a common attribute among reformers (and also professors): each displayed the same inattention to dress. On their backs were the same mismatched threadbare clothes. In seasons when wide suit-coat lapels were in fashion, they wore narrow lapels. In years when narrow lapels were the norm, they wore wide lapels. Their cheap leather shoes were scuffed beyond repair and stank up whatever room they strode into. And the beards clotted with scrambled eggs after breakfast that I could count? Innumerable!

Graham could plead guilty to most of the above. Still, it could be argued that he had a hardy look about him from his devotion to a clean-living regimen — removal of everything that crept or swam or flied from the diet; vigorous outdoor exercise consisting of hiking, skiing, climbing, and shooting; daily bathing using lots of cool, room-temperature water; and complete and total abstinence from all sexual relations, including heterosexual, homosexual, oral, anal, bestial, and onanistic.

In stereoscopic fashion the scene unfolded in all of its fury: on one side butchers were throwing entrails at Graham. Flying through the air were brains, livers, and intestines, which alternated with waves of stale breadstuffs flung by the city's bakers, whom Graham also singled out for criticism. Graham shook off each strike and continued to harangue the crowd regarding the benefits of cleansing the colon of meat remnants.

On Graham's other side, about three-quarters of New York City's thirty thousand Irish-Catholics were shouting, gesturing, crying, and fainting at the thought of interrupting procreation, and, moreover, not engaging in copulation, an end in and of itself among these drunken, pleasure-seeking people. "Ice packed around the organs of reproduction will cool the most enflamed passions!" Graham yelled under a rain of offal. "Preserving the body's secretions is fundamental to retaining a youthful visage!"

A third contingent of appalled, but fascinated, Fifth Avenuers, standing in line on the nearby wooden-plank sidewalk waiting to be admitted to the auditorium, watched the goings on. A fourth group that contained yours truly either stumbled onto the scene or was drawn to it by the commotion echoing up and down the streets and lanes. Many of the newly arrived joined forces with one faction or the other, adding reinforcements to the riot-in-the-making.

Graham soon was forced to retreat indoors. Behind him slammed the Lyceum's front door. A flurry of animal parts and hard rolls drummed the closed door. Rent organs and moldy bread rebounded onto the finely dressed folks at the head of the line who stood adjacent. Several ladies and gentlemen, perhaps fearing that the dual mobs might attack them, dropped out of line and hastily departed, leaving no doubt as to their reason for being there, which was less of a commitment to vegetarianism and more of a thirst for popular entertainment.

After the door re-opened awhile later, those that had stayed and braved riotous conditions for a date with the celebrated Sylvester Graham began to file into the auditorium. When it appeared that the butchers and bakers were holding their fire for the time being, no doubt encouraged by the ring of policemen that had suddenly formed around us, Bunny and I followed the audience inside; I was exceedingly curious as to why this man stirred such volatile emotions.

After taking our seats, I immediately regretted the decision to attend the event, for we ended up seated next to a most tedious and talkative woman. Ignoring and perhaps even a little frightened of Bunny, she cornered me in my seat and narrated her life's story.

"Which are you?" she asked.

"I beg your pardon?" I responded, having no clue what language she was speaking.

"Which reform are you? I'll bet you're temperance. No wait. Abolitionism?"

"None of the above. I'm here purely as a spectator."

"Translation: you're a *dilettante*." She patted the knee of the man sitting next to her. "Hiram hates it when I use French vocabulary. He says it sounds like I'm putting on airs."

Hiram barely registered my presence. He was a man who managed to be haughty and colorless at the same time. I guessed by his demeanor that he was a lawyer. I had seen the same detachment and disinterest a thousand times before, in both the nineteenth and twenty-first centuries.

"Which are you?" I asked, pretending that my interest in her was reciprocated.

"I subscribe to the whole sisterhood of reforms," she replied. "It started with temperance. Then it proceeded to African colonization. Then I caught the female suffrage bug. Then I graduated to vegetarianism. Lately, I've looked into the practice of phrenology." She eyed my head, adding, "I should like sometime to examine the top of your skull. My reading would be purely amateur, of course. For a true reading of your character, you would require a trained doctor of phrenology. I could introduce you to a very good one if you wish..."

"No offense, but the bumps on my head are my private business. Though I thank you for the offer." I looked around at Bunny, who sat on the other side of me, to see if she could take over and save me by becoming a sociological experiment to occupy this lady's over-welling of bourgeois sympathy. But Bunny was not sitting in her seat; rather, she now sat on the other side of Hiram. She poked and prodded him and made silly bird and animal sounds in an unsuccessful quest to bring a smile to the pursed lips of this severe and humorless man. I was on my own.

"I'll bet you're wondering how a respectable lady such as myself, a veritable matron of domesticity, reached her arms beyond hearth and home to embrace the world's miserable and downtrodden."

I wasn't, but that fact would never have occurred to her.

"I do not like having to admit it, but my husband's brother is a total sot. After enduring numerous drunken episodes of his — vomiting on the Christmas goose, burning down our privy, touching me inappropriately when we danced —

I desperately sought answers to the problems he brought into our lives. Beg your pardon, but are you yawning because I'm boring you?"

"No, not at all! The room is crowded and there's a shortage of breathable air."

"I'll finish my story then. I read an advertisement for the New York Temperance Association in the newspaper and went to one of their lectures — at this very venue, as it happens. What overcame me afterward was nothing short of a revelation. I discovered that the devil had given my brother-in-law strong drink to occupy his idle hands. I urged my husband's beloved brother to pray for his redemption from alcohol. As well, I pray every night for his deliverance."

"How's that working for you?" I asked, unable to resist.

"So far he has yet to see the light. I am not discouraged, however. God takes no direction from humans like you and me. He works in his own mysterious way and according to his own schedule. I am sure that when God determines it is the proper time He will make my brother-in-law stop drinking. I only hope it happens before my annual Fourth-of-July barbecue in a few months."

"Maybe prayer isn't the best method of treating alcoholism. Did you ever pause to consider that it might be a disease that needs a doctor, not a minister?"

"Certainly not. It is a sin that those of a morally weak constitution indulge in."

"Maybe a strong thirst for drink is inherited. Like hair color or big ears."

"The ability to consume copious amounts of ale is no more inherited than the ability to become president or play the violin."

"Are we forgetting about John Adams and his son, John Quincy Adams?"

"Pure coincidence. I am sorry, but there is nothing you can say that will convince me that my opinion is unsound."

Actually, there was a great deal more I could say on the subject; from my former life I knew a fair amount about addiction. Numerous medical studies would bear me out. Problem was, the scientific research I relied upon would not be conducted for at least another hundred years, so I had no authority on which to rely in arguing my case with this woman. Yet again, I had to throw out everything I knew from the twenty-first century, howsoever specious its claims, because it simply did not apply in the nineteenth. I elected to change the subject.

"So tell me about this business of African colonization. What's that entail?"

"I'm glad you asked. The organization I joined, the American Colonization Society, pursues the goal of repatriating all Negro slaves in Africa."

"All? Are there not millions of slaves?"

"Some four million, yes."

"Isn't shipping that many people across the Atlantic impractical? Not to mention expensive?"

"It is imperative that the political will and financial resources be found to accomplish this project. Legislators need persuading and slave owners recompensing. For, much as we sympathize with the Negro's plight, he is not on the same intellectual or physical level as whites are. Colonization would be for his own good as much as ours. Would you want to stay in a country where you are hated?"

"Yet ponder the Irish of our very own city," I responded. "They're hated, but they're all too glad to reside here. Life, for the most part, is better here than in County Derry or County Cork."

Although this was an adequate argument, one of "analogy" if I remember correctly from college logic, I would have loved to proffer examples of African-Americans' contributions to American culture. However, no white American would acknowledge the genius of a black man. Only Nat Turner, whose murderous rampage through Virginia still clung heavily to people's memories three years later, might possibly have been considered a genius — albeit an evil genius, not the prototypical Benjamin Franklin type of genius. Having this conversation caused me to see the folly of Sam Tilden's enterprise in high relief. The "Negro Problem" was, and always had been, too complicated to be remedied by quick fixes. Or slow ones for that matter.

I did not share these ruminations with the lady; rather, I surrendered and confessed that she might have a point. After what she said next, I could have shod my feet and kicked myself hard in the rear end.

"Then you must enlist in our cause! I am empowered to collect subscriptions on the American Colonization Society's behalf. What size donation may I put you down for? Five dollars? Ten dollars? Even smaller amounts are welcome, because it all adds up." She retrieved from her handbag a pocket-size ledger book filled with the signatures of others whom this woman had entrapped, plus the amounts they had pledged.

It certainly would not have bankrupted me to slip her five silver dollars. But I resisted out of principal. I had recently read in the *New York Tribune* about a competing group, the New York Antislavery Society. The article profiled their leader, Louis Tappan, a rich merchant counted among the city's Three Hundred. A mob had recently broken into his home, where an Antislavery Society meeting was being held, had thrown him and his associates out, and then had burned his home down. "Slavery is the worm at the root of the Tree of Liberty," he had declared in reaction, vowing to continue his fight for immediate universal emancipation of slaves. Despite having a one-hundred-thousand-dollar bounty placed on his head by slave-owning Southerners, the only personal protection he allowed himself was a copy of the New Testament in his breast pocket. I frankly respected his courage and knew (with the benefit of historical hindsight) that emancipation would eventually carry the day, and not colonization. I informed the woman that my donations to the antislavery cause would be going to Tappan's organization.

She went from affability to mockery upon learning this. "Hiram! This gentleman believes that the radical abolitionist cause deserves his charity. As if slave owners would voluntarily forfeit their slaves without remuneration! As if primitive Negroes could be trusted to live among civilized society!"

I peeked around to see Hiram's reaction. Unexpectedly, he looked as though he was having the time of his life — he was smiling and bantering with Bunny and looking generally much less constipated than before. Such was Bunny's effect on men. I wondered if he knew what she was concealing beneath her dress. It was no tomahawk!

Fortunately, Sylvester Graham was introduced at around this time, finally putting an end to this tiresome dialogue. At the emcee's signal a pack of boys swarmed through the auditorium and snuffed out the lights, and everyone directed his attention to the stage.

Looking significantly cleaned up, but no less shoddily dressed, Sylvester Graham commenced his lecture. "I have long and publicly taught the doctrine that, as a general proposition, man causes his own sickness and suffering — that in almost all cases, he is to blame for being sick, and that he as truly owes society an apology for being sick as he does for being drunk."

Already, the audience signaled its approval, nodding heads and murmuring agreement.

"New Yorkers have an unprecedented array of foods to choose from, new methods of procurement and preparation, and an unparalleled number of dining establishments to frequent. The farmers of Brooklyn and New Jersey supply them with an abundance of healthful foods.

"Yet what is it that most New York residents put into their mouths? Commercially prepared foods that cause everyone, even those in polite society such as yourselves, to suffer from difficulty of digestion or fermentation in the stomach or guts. The casual visitor to this fair city notices immediately that practically every New Yorker strolls about the streets moaning and clutching at his belly. Sad to say, few are so happy as to pass through a life of ordinary duration without undergoing a protracted struggle with digestive maladies."

Confronted with and scolded for their poor eating habits, everyone in the audience sat in sullen silence, like naughty children.

"You buy bread from commercial bakers that use refined flour stripped of husks and oleaginous germ and whitened with chemical agents, because it bakes more quickly and allows them to sell more bread loaves at a rapider pace. What is the result? An almost crustless loaf virtually devoid of proper granular texture or nutritional value. Simply put, these bakers place their personal profit above the health of the metropolis."

A few spectators grumbled their disapproval of the city's bakers, while Graham paused to allow these vocal individuals to assist him in persuading the rest of the audience of the truth of his words. Then he continued.

"Your babes drink marketplace milk, much of which is drawn from cows fed on leftover distillery mash, with the anemic, liquor-inflected liquid made presentable only by the addition of chalk, plaster of Paris, and other adulterants. Children raised on such impure milk are fatally weakened in their ability to resist disease epidemics. I ask everyone here to recall the cholera epidemic of 1831. Who were its first victims, swept away on a river of diarrhea? The smallest among us, made even more helpless against illness by profiteering dairy interests selling an unhealthful product."

A collective gasp, which consisted of one-half nausea on behalf of the city's children and one-half guilt for unwittingly letting them consume a tainted drink, erupted in the auditorium.

"What, then, is the solution to this disturbing state of affairs?" he asked, glowering from one side of the audience to the other. Then: "One only has to examine the physiology of a species that closely resembles mankind — the orang-utan."

Louder gasps could be heard as the audience considered what Graham was saying: that they were comparable to monkeys.

"Explorers and zoologists that have visited Borneo have observed these orange apes in their jungle abodes and noted their predilection for eating leaves, roots, nuts, berries, and bamboo. No animal matter, either quick or dead, ever passes their lips. Not even insects or grubs — only the native flora that God, in his great beneficence, has bestowed in abundance.

"One could ascribe this very healthful preference to simple instinct instilled by Nature. But taking into account scientists' claims that orang-utans are among the most intelligent members of the animal kingdom, is it unreasonable to assume that they smartly *choose* a vegetarian diet? And if it is possible for them to choose thusly, how is it that a much more intelligent creature such as man chooses his diet so poorly?"

Properly chastened, we in the audience listened silently and obediently to Graham's diet prescriptions. For the next hour-and-a-half he railed against meat (especially pork), sausage, white bread, distilled spirits, wine, beer, hard cider, tobacco, opium, coffee, tea, sugar, pepper, mustard, and, curiously, asparagus. After ruling out ninety percent of foods and beverages, and one hundred percent of those things that were fun to eat, drink, and smoke, he made the following recommendation: "Food should be taken in the natural and simple state, plainly prepared, or cooked with no other seasoning than a very little salt, and eaten in moderate quantities, at regular periods, and well masticated."

As the lamps were re-lit and light again suffused the auditorium, the lady next to me asked, "What do you think so far? Isn't Mr. Graham wonderfully wise, a true visionary?"

"Ahead of his time," I said. The woman could not have known this, of course, but from the vantage of the twenty-first century, Graham's dietary notions had by and large been proven correct — although I disagreed that a beefsteak was as injurious to the colon as he or latter-day vegetarians argued.

Wishing to escape this woman's clutches, at least during intermission, I turned to Bunny to encourage her to take a walk with me and stretch our legs. She was asleep, however, mouth agape with her head resting on husband Hiram's shoulder. I reminded myself to get her fitted with false teeth next week and have the gap through which she softly whistled each time she exhaled filled. She awoke with a start, excused herself to Hiram, who stood up and bowed, and followed me to the lobby. A number of men there furiously puffed on cigars, too self-conscious, I supposed, to indulge their habit in front of Graham and his health-conscious audience. (Strange as it may seem to my nineteenth-century friends and colleagues, nobody smoked in public in the modern world. It had gradually been made unlawful in the public places of nearly every city, creating the pitiful sight of smokers congregating outside doorways in rain or snow to engage in their favorite pastime.)

Meantime, in the lobby and up and down the auditorium's aisles, Graham's associates were selling spring water and crackers made from Graham (unrefined) flour. I tasted a Graham cracker, but I found it bland and unappetizing, for it lacked the honey or brown sugar associated with the twenty-first-century version.

I sent Bunny home, for she had complained that she was bored. I told her not to worry about my safety; I planned to hire a hack to drive me home. (I didn't worry on her account. Even though she was never trained in Indian-fighting techniques, she had observed them throughout her life and could competently apply them against five, six, or more assailants.) I wondered why I did not accompany her; I agreed with most of what Graham was saying and hardly found him as controversial as his reputation warranted. Indeed, I found him to be rather long-winded. He already had presented an exhaustive (and exhausting) survey of the dietary landscape. And now he had the whole second portion of his performance to complete. Much as I tried, I could not guess how he was planning to fill the allotted time. In the final analysis, I stayed because I was curious.

The tedious woman and her husband returned to their seats just as Graham bounded back onto the stage, where a loud ovation greeted him. "Hiram and I signed a pledge in the lobby to commit our stomachs and our selves to Mr. Graham's program," she shouted over the din. "We are now certified Grahamites."

Hiram paid no attention to his wife, but rather twisted his head every which way in search of, I presumed, Bunny.

"Sorry, I sent Bunny home," I informed him.

"Drat," was all he said, and his face lapsed back into its naturally grim and snooty expression."As we observed before the intermission, proper diet and free peristaltic action of the bowels are keys to a healthy, happy life. Yet these are but two of three essential ingredients that lead to this desirable result. In every condition of the human race, the physical, as well as the moral, state of the people is of the highest consideration, but more especially in a country like ours, where the aggregate of individual character and individual will constitutes the foundation and efficiency of all our civil and political institutions.

"All kinds of stimulating substances; highly seasoned food; rich dishes; the free use of flesh; and even the excess of aliment; all, more or less — and some to a very great degree — increase the concupiscent excitability and sensibility of the genital organs.

"Beyond all question, an immeasurable amount of evil results to the human family from sexual excess within the precincts of wedlock. Languor, lassitude, muscular relaxation, general debility and heaviness, depression of spirits, loss of appetite, indigestion, faintness, and sinking at the pit of the stomach, increased susceptibilities of the skin and lungs to all the atmospheric changes, feebleness of circulation, chilliness, headache, melancholy, hypochondria, hysterics, feebleness of all the senses, impaired vision, loss of sight, weakness of the lungs, nervous cough, pulmonary consumption, disorders of the liver and kidneys, urinary difficulties, disorders of the genitals..."

This last phrase got the audience stirring uncomfortably and whispering.

"... weakness of the brain, loss of memory, epilepsy, insanity, apoplexy — and extreme feebleness and early death of offspring — are among the all too common evils which are caused by sexual excesses between husband and wife."

I, surely like my fellow audience members, was questioning if I understood Graham correctly: that intimate relations within the institution of marriage caused severe, and even life-threatening, health conditions. This was a totally foreign and bizarre concept to me. Usually the devout among us railed against the sins of fornication and adultery, but they withheld their criticism of married couples. The rustling and stirring became more insistent and the murmuring grew louder.

Graham continued, oblivious. "The mental and moral faculties of the brain are fully involved in these general and special injuries. And the mental powers and manifestations are proportionably impaired. The mind becomes exceedingly carnal, and inclined to dwell on sensual subjects, and cherish sensual images. Its energies and elasticity gradually decline, and by imperceptible degrees it becomes weak and fickle."

As if to prove Graham's point, a sense of collective hysteria was slowly building in the room. Women were fanning themselves with handkerchiefs or bonnets, and men shifted in their seats and tugged the fabric of their trousers. I recognized this behavior from my own experience: they were adjusting their clothes and genitals to disguise the erections growing in their pants. I nearly laughed out loud while I considered the scene. People were reacting as if they were viewing a pornographic film, a common, if illicit, twenty-first-century experience, instead of listening to a quasi-medical lecture consisting of fairly clinical language.

Graham had yet to summon his most extraordinary powers to shock. He submitted to us a graphic illustration of what were, in his opinion, the debilitating effects of the most extreme type of sexual activity, "self-pollution."

"One need only observe the skin blemishes that plague our young men and, alarmingly, an increasing number of our young ladies, which publicly incriminate them for pursuing this unnatural practice in private. In the most severe cases, ulcerous sores break out upon the head, breast, back and thighs, and these sometimes enlarge into permanent fistulas of a cancerous character and continue, perhaps for years, to discharge great quantities of fetid, loathsome pus, and not infrequently terminate in death."

At this, chaos broke out in the auditorium as dozens of women fainted outright. Many others, including the woman who sat next to me, battled loss of consciousness by vigorously flapping handkerchiefs or scarves in an effort to direct oxygen to their faces. One poor woman a couple of rows ahead of me bled profusely from where her head struck a seat back. Seeing how Graham's words affected their womenfolk, enraged husbands leaped up and shouted deprecations at Graham, while others demanded that he cease his lecture immediately. A few men, who had smuggled in eggs and tomatoes for just such an emergency, flung them at the figure on the stage. One man charged the stage in defense of his wife's honor. A stout policeman who stood by to protect Graham in this eventuality caught the man and hurled him back up the aisle.

Meantime, Graham stubbornly stood his ground and continued speaking, as the occasional rotten vegetable or fruit hit its mark. Amidst the pandemonium, his speech was largely unintelligible, but snippets reached my ears. "All irritations or excitements such as hunger or sexual desire exhaust our organs." And the most memorable yet ridiculous idea of the night: that, to preserve their life force, married couples should have sexual relations no more often than twelve times a year!

It was then that I noticed through sidelong glances that a number of men had retained their state of excitement. In the time it took for one to snap his fingers these men's organs metamorphosed from centers of pleasure and procreation to sources of vengeance and violence. I recalled a phrase from the modern world, which went like this: "So-and-so *has a hard-on for* such-and-such." Meaning so-and-so was eager to exact his revenge on his opponent for a real or perceived slight. For the first time I saw demonstrated how male rage, and not simply unbridled lust, led to the crime of rape.

Several policemen finally fought a path through the melee and ascended the stage, where they flanked Graham. The most senior looking of the brigade announced, "Show's over, folks. The quack has the right to speak. But he loses that right if he causes a riot."

"Sir, I object!" said Graham. "I am no quack. I am a doctor of health and..."

"Shaddup! On account of you and your hooey, I had to leave a poker game where I was up by almost four bucks."

Except for a few isolated pockets, the audience quieted down almost as quickly as it had exploded into bedlam. To those remaining few who wouldn't heed the policeman's warnings, he announced, "If you don't shut yer holes I'll be forced to shut 'em for ya — with a billy on yer noggins! I don't care if ya do live on Park Row." The crowd immediately fell silent; not normally the types to be intimidated by their social inferiors, they listened when an inferior threatened them with socially sanctioned violence.

As the audience slowly exited the auditorium, my tormentor for the evening and her spouse pulled alongside me. "That man is horrible! Obscene!" she exclaimed. "I could no sooner join his organization than I could put myself in thrall to a lecherous slave owner!"

"Buttercup, what do you say we go to the Cock and Bull and share a nice, juicy steak?" asked Hiram, changing the subject.

"That sounds perfect, darling!" answered "Buttercup," who then turned to me and asked if I cared to join them.

"NO!" I shouted, whereupon I realized that I had declined her invitation a little too strenuously. Softening my tone I added, "I mean, I should return home and check after Bunny."

Disappointed, but not all that disappointed, she nodded and clutched her husband's arm as we three passed through the door and entered the crisp, cold night. Happily, the rioting bakers and butchers had gone home, so we were able to leave the aborted lecture unmolested. My companions hired a carriage, and even offered me a ride, but I declined their invitation — a little less vociferously this time — and told them I planned to walk home.

"I never caught your name!" the woman called out as their coach pulled away.

"I didn't tell it to you!" I responded, a conscious decision, because I did not want her and her meddlesome friends beseeching me for donations of money or time to their crackpot social causes. Phrenology indeed!

As I walked back to the City Hotel, never straying from the gas-lit main streets — although even this was not a one-hundred-percent guarantee of my personal safety, nor even eighty or ninety-percent — I marveled at the contradictions in Sylvester Graham's character. How could the man be so right when it came to food and diet but so wrong about sexual matters? Whatever the answer was to this question, I did not really care to learn how Graham had come by his beliefs, and I resolved to put the matter behind me. Likewise, I promised myself never to attend another lyceum lecture.

I arrived back at my rooms without a scratch. After looking in on the soundly sleeping Bunny, I retired myself. In bed I spent many hours lying awake while I pondered the immutable foolishness of men. For the first time since I had landed in a new century it occurred to me that my goal of finding Rachel, let alone winning her back, might be the most foolish quest of all.

Chapter Twelve

Midway through the year 1835, I moved finally into my Gramercy Park residence. It cost me ten-thousand dollars, plus I had access rights in perpetuity to the private park adjacent. When I took over the property, the developer, Mr. Samuel Ruggles, presented me with a gold entry key to the park gate. No one but holders of a gold key, limited to nearby residents, could enter the park. Civilization was rapidly creeping uptown; my home, on East Twentieth Street, stood on New York City's northernmost fringe, yet the city's fathers already were platting streets numbered in the thirties and forties. I felt fortunate to have a green space I could call my own, even if it was only one square block.

My home was a veritable mansion, a three-story townhouse, plus an attic comprising the servant's quarters. Bunny set up camp in there, but she did not seem to mind the cramped situation. With its bare rafters, it reminded her of sleeping in the log house, she claimed. My bedroom, dressing room, and bath (with running water!) were on the third floor. On advice of a neighbor, who cautioned me to sleep with a floor or two barrier between myself and criminals prowling the city's streets, I settled here. Below me on the second floor were guest bedrooms and my library, which for many years appeared rather sad and empty, as I was never an avid collector of books. Still, I hosted many business meetings in the room, and I eventually stripped out the shelves and filled the space with artwork —Hudson River landscapes and dramatic sea battles, mostly. My taste in art, as coached along by Rachel, tended more to the abstract side, but no one painted in that fashion in those days.

The first floor contained a palatial living room and large dining room, really more a dining hall, which led to a kitchen in a separate wing jutting out into the back yard. A fireplace the size of a modern-day garage door was the living room's focal point. In winter, Bunny stacked logs in a pile taller than she and lighted bonfires that on more than one occasion threatened carpets and drapes. Always good for entertainment at parties, Bunny tossed crushed-up leaves and twigs into the fire. Depending on what plants she had foraged that day, the fire would flicker with a blue, green, or magenta hue. It became apparent that, far from serving a decorative purpose, these occasions were religious in nature. After throwing a handful of magical powder at the flame, Bunny discerned shapes and patterns in the colorful display that addressed her questions about life, love, death, and what to serve for supper. Like magi of old, who regularly consulted oracles seeking hints about the future, Bunny performed this ritual before my fireplace at least once per week.

As for the rest of the living room décor, every piece of furniture, accessory, and knick-knack was emblazoned with patriotic imagery. Eagles, snare drums, shields, flags, crossed muskets, and the Liberty Tree were carved, inlaid, sewn, or painted on tables, chairs, sofas, hassocks, rugs, cabinets, lampshades, glassware, trays, cigar boxes, and the piano. It was as though the calendar read "Fourth of July" every day of the year. When I complained to my contractor about the excessive Americana polluting my living space, he retorted, "Perhaps you would like to hire an unlettered farmer in Brooklyn or the Bronx to cut you a chair with his ax. That is, if you do not mind sitting on what looks like a log cabin with armrests."

"Do you have any such farmers you can recommend?" I asked sarcastically. Thus and so, I was burdened with unwanted furniture fireworks.

Bunny quickly rose to the rank of Mistress of the House, and, in terms of her responsibilities, she became almost a co-owner of the property. Her work was essential in the home's upkeep. After a few months spent in coming to know its personality and rhythms, she increasingly farmed out work to apprentice servants. She favored one particular fourteen-year-old Irish girl named Lizzie, whom she was grooming as her protégée. Soon after Lizzie joined Bunny's staff, the duo could regularly be found in the kitchen singing Indian songs and wiggling their posteriors in a most provocative manner. Lizzie reciprocated Bunny's support and guidance by advising her in matters of white culture unfamiliar to her, for example, the proper way to lay out silverware and the limits of polite society's palate.

Bunny never tired in her attempts to serve wild game at the supper table. She constantly boasted of how opossum, squirrel, and rabbit could not be surpassed for their bold flavor. Though these and plenty of other nontraditional dishes like roast dog and fricasseed cat were sold at the city's markets, Bunny insisted on trapping the animals herself out in Gramercy Park. The sight of a dark-skinned woman on her knees in a grass-stained *au courant* dress setting traps in the shrubbery prompted one of my more elegant neighbors to remark, "You can take the Indian out of the frontier, but you cannot take the frontier out of the Indian."

It became an ongoing game with Bunny to try to trick me into eating her exotic recipes. I was never fooled; I knew what cooking beef, pork, and chicken smelled like, and I rejected any plate served to me when the odors emanating from the kitchen departed from this familiar set of smells. Bunny continued her ruse, saying of the pile of unrecognizable carcasses and limbs, "Beef" or "Pork" or "Tastes like chicken," while she smiled her checkered smile and patted her stomach.

On the rare occasion when her game recipes escaped my detection, camouflaged by a robust gravy, for instance, Lizzie alerted me with hand signals behind Bunny's back, whereupon I returned the food to the kitchen prior to ever taking a bite, foiling her plot yet another time. Next, I sought my supper at one of the myriad dining establishments downtown, where steak and a bottle, costing twenty-five cents, was considered a meal fit for a king. Bunny, meanwhile, stayed at home and ate her serving of wild game and mine, too, a gastronomic windfall, and she later jested and traded housekeeping hints with Lizzie until bedtime.

Under Mr. Gallatin's tutelage, Bunny had grown pleasantly civilized since our arrival in New York. She had metamorphosed into a real lady, who, on her best days, was able to hold her own alongside any member of the city's Three Hundred. None of our acquaintances appeared to care about her race. Indians had long ago left the region either voluntarily or at musket-point, so they no longer posed an imminent threat like in Chicago, a startup metropolis close to the forest's edge. Likewise, everyone left Bunny alone regarding her sexual proclivities. Granted, she garnered strange looks from people we passed on the street, but these always fell into the curious rather than the hostile category. Overall, old New York was a reasonably tolerant place, more so than most modern American cities.

The only thing not tolerated was lack of money. For this, people were severely discriminated against. New York exemplified the Great Chain of Being in how people lorded over their poorer neighbors. Native-born Americans discriminated against the English, who in turn discriminated against the Dutch, who discriminated against the Germans, and so on down the hierarchy, from the Swedish, to the French, Spanish, Irish, and, at the very bottom of the economic order, Negroes. New Yorkers could not give a hoot about the color of your skin or the presence of a royal title. But if you commanded financial resources, or at least acted like you did, people practically threw themselves at your feet in adoration, no matter what your color. Witness how famously Bunny and Lizzie, who was part of the recently arrived Irish rabble, got along. Lizzie's friends and cousins were usually seen heaving rocks or hurling racist epithets at the city's darker skinned inhabitants, who by chance may have wandered onto their territory.

Bunny proved time and again to be a capital house servant, agreeable roommate, and peerless confidant. However, after a few months of co-residency, there appeared this one exception: she acquired the habit of meeting men while about the city, inviting them up to her room for a nightcap, and, while involved with them in sexual congress, making rude, loud noises similar to those of a quarrelsome pig. I never saw Bunny's paramours, for they departed via the back stairs after they had had their pleasure. "Men stay all night people call Bunny whore," she said in defense of her practice of evacuating her boyfriends from her bed before dawn.

Though my eyes never lighted on Bunny's conquests, my ears certainly registered their rooting and grunting presence, as my bed was situated directly below hers. Moving my bed across the hall to the suite's other sleeping room neatly solved the problem. Despite my loss of sleep during those early months, I never raised a complaint; I felt it was none of my business to condemn Bunny. On the contrary, her attractiveness to men fed her self-esteem, and I believed this to be a healthy trait. While we were drinking one night at Delmonico's Restaurant, she boasted that men found her irresistible. They liked her exotic looks, and they loved her inability to conceive. Really, what business was it of mine to stand in the way of the unions occurring above my head?

Disturbed sleep was not the only remnant of Bunny's midnight liaisons. I was reminded of the contrast between her exciting life and my own pitiful, lonely existence.

Mr. Pemberton, my private detective, had picked up no scent of either Rachel or Bilson. "There is no news from any of my contacts in Boston, Norfolk, or Charleston. It is very likely that they slipped through the net we cast," Pemberton informed me when he paid me a visit one night. Un-intimidated by the big man, Bunny demanded upon his passing through our front door that he remove his boots before stepping onto the gleaming marble tile of my foyer. She glared menacingly at him, determined never again to mop up muck left behind in his wake, as she had upon earlier occasions. Perhaps feeling outnumbered (in a fight, I would take a single Bunny over three Pembertons), he complied, gingerly entering my sitting room and sitting in his chair almost delicately. He continued: "I now believe that they could have gone as far afield as New Orleans or even, perhaps, Texas. It makes sense that they would want to put the greatest possible distance between themselves and New York."

Upon hearing these words, I had a quick daydream that Bilson had volunteered for the Texas militia in an attempt to turn back the clock on the impending massacre at the Alamo, a battle where I would continue to bet heavily on the Mexicans if Bilson were involved any way.

After this imaginative flight, in which my anger was mostly subsumed, my heart sank, for I started to abandon hope that I would ever see my wife again. I remembered from previous meetings that Pemberton liked his whiskey; I produced a bottle from my stock and poured us both a stiff drink. "Do you have any colleagues in the Southwest that might be in a position to learn of their whereabouts?" I asked, gulping down my whiskey in an attempt to anesthetize my aching heart.

"I'm well-acquainted with a soldier-adventurer whom I believe to be living in Texas at present. We served together under General Jackson during the Creek

War. I can make some inquiries as to where he is stationed and try to get a letter out to him."

"Anything you can do."

"Sir, as long as you continue to pay my bill, you have my deepest devotion. Together, we shall bring closure to your unenviable plight." I was surprised that a note of sympathy had penetrated Pemberton's ordinarily gruff exterior. Acting like he had a brass bottom apparently disguised tender feelings residing in his breast. Although disappointed that Rachel hadn't yet been found, I felt confident that Pemberton was doing everything in his power to find her.

If my heart weren't so targeted toward one woman, New York offered a gigantic array of romantic options. Nearly as numerous as the pigs and dogs that roamed the island were the so-called "ladies of the evening," although time of day never seemed to affect their commerce. These notorious women paraded singly, in pairs, or in packs of four or five up and down the city's streets, most especially along a decrepit stretch of Bowery Road near The Tombs, the newly constructed metropolitan prison. They accosted and pawed every passing man, both to titillate and to pickpocket the inattentive. These were the true streetwalkers, the women that serviced the city's working class teamsters, porters, bricklayers, blacksmiths, and carpenters. Hard physical labor resulted in a clientele possessing rough hands and stooped posture, whereas a different sort of physically taxing work created a class of ladies one saw all across the city with rough faces and sagging busts.

Should it come to it, I could afford to lie with a much better example of the genus *woman* than a pick-up from the street — safer, too, in regard to venereal disease, a real concern in an era before infection-fighting medicines were invented.

One night at a gentlemen's smoker in the City Hotel's lobby, I overheard a conversation about Mrs. Doolittle, proprietress of the city's most stylish and expensive brothel on Leonard Street, between, fittingly, Church and Chapel Streets. As the overseer of such an exalted institution, patronized by the cream of male society, she was in a position to employ only the handsomest women with the most pronounced carnal appetites. Moreover, all of her staff had received advanced educations in music, poetry, French, and spinning from renowned ladies' finishing schools. Thus, they were prepared both to screw lustily and to discourse intelligently on the merits of a tariff on British steel or President Jackson's efforts to shut down the Bank of the United States.

After a few weeks of pondering the existence of Mrs. Doolittle's "boarding house" — for that was its official designation on the property tax rolls — I decided to glimpse this shrine to sensual pleasure in person. Minus Bunny one night I took a stroll past the establishment: a typical three-story brownstone with tightly shuttered windows and an oversized scarlet door at the top of a short flight of stairs. On subsequent forays down that block of Leonard, I never saw anything amiss, neither women shouting lewd propositions to potential customers nor drunken men stumbling about with trousers around their ankles. Rather, the street out front seemed unnaturally quiet and peaceful.

Likewise, a lovely, tranquil environment greeted the visitor inside, as I learned the first night I entered Mrs. Doolittle's foyer and assessed my surroundings. After I stepped a few feet into the parlor, a team of ladies wearing only petticoats removed my top hat, suit coat, and shoes, and I was beckoned to sit on a fluffy sofa while rum was served. I was promised that a selection of "fair maidens" — whose maidenheads I challenge any doctor to locate — would be at my command in a few minutes.

The first thing I noticed upon looking around was the complete absence of patriotic tributes on the furniture and walls. Instead, libidinous themes held sway. Dominating the room was a large oil painting whose subject was the birth of Venus. On a rocky beach a nude woman of generous proportions emerged from a scallop shell with a frothy, wind-tossed sea in the foreground and, in the background, craggy peaks obscured by purple clouds lit by orange sunbeams. The picture frankly depicted the sexual awakening of women and reminded the viewer that, with regard to animal instincts at least, humans are not so very far removed from life's aquatic origins. We are one part swirling sea and one part bubbling swamp.

Encouraged in no small part by chekagou, which Bunny had planted in her vegetable patch in Gramercy Park, I pondered the picture's symbolic content for a few moments. My reverie was broken when a young, bucktoothed Negro girl handed me three finger's worth of rum and started massaging my shoulders. Realizing that this activity was all still prelude, I began to wonder how much this evening was going to cost me. Then, under the influence of rum and the steady pressure of the girl's palms and thumbs, I felt increasingly warm and loose and didn't give a jot anymore.

Around this time, seven beautiful women, four brunettes, two blondes, and one redhead, wearing silk sleeping gowns, high-heeled slippers, and little else, entered the room. I suddenly became aware that I was supposed to select one of them as my consort for the evening. Each was equally gorgeous, so my decision was extremely difficult. After some embarrassed hemming and hawing, for I was not wholly certain I even wished to take the drastic step of cheating on my wife (who, it should be remembered, had spurned me), I ended up following advice I had received during a secret game I used to play in early adolescence when abusing myself. In my fantasy I was a young king, and I had to decide which of a passel of slave girls would pleasure me. "Pick the one with the biggest boobs," my most trusted counselor had always advised.

This turned out to be one of the blondes, who introduced herself as Miss Constance Periwinkle. A tall, statuesque, leggy woman with sparkling green eyes and highly developed upper arms (a trait she shared with other bosomy women I have observed), she looked as though she were descended from a race of Amazons. The other candidates took their rejection in stride, and they filed out of the room.

Miss Constance, for that was her preferred appellation, this being a genteel house, clasped my hand and led me upstairs. It occurred to me as we ascended the winding staircase that Miss Constance was the anti-Rachel — a short, frizzy-headed brunette with sly brown eyes and a build that was nowhere near as gracefully proportioned as the woman then ushering me into her *boudoir*: Rachel was smaller through the chest and wider through the pelvis.

Without a doubt, Miss Constance was the closest thing to physical perfection I had ever had the privilege (or dumb luck) of lying next to. After slipping off her nightgown, Miss Constance, fully nude, reclined beside me on the feather bed. "Lord!" I gasped involuntarily when my eyes took in the tantalizing creature. I hastily stood up and shooed myself and my growing member to the far corner of the room, where I stood slightly hunched and protective of my unmentionables, with my back to the woman.

"Oh. I see that you're a shy man. Apologies, sir. We shall make love gradually in steps." I heard the rustle of her gown, which she hastily put back on.

"I think that's the best strategy," I said, my voice quavering.

"We have all night. Don't we?"

"Um, yes," I answered, realizing that I had just signed on for what the modern world called the "deluxe treatment."

"We can start by having a pleasant conversation."

"That sounds nice." I remained where I stood, staring at wallpaper depicting a woodland scene where naked nymphs and naiads romped around trees and over brooks.

"What do you wish to talk about?"

I looked around my immediate surroundings and saw to my left on the dresser an astonishing vase. Glorified stick figures with enormous erections that extended above their heads paraded around its circumference. "How about we discuss that vase," I said, thinking an arty yet suggestive topic might perchance help my anxiety to dissipate.

"It's a Golden Age amphora from fifth-century Athens," she said, effortlessly shifting from stacked seductress to prim pedagogue. "The drawings depict some sort of fertility rite, probably in homage to the god Dionysus."

"You mean to say it's genuine?"

"Very much so. I hear it is quite rare and valuable. A descendant of Lord Byron, who regularly patronized the house a few years ago, gave it to Mrs. Doolittle in appreciation of her unmatched hospitality. I understand it was rescued from destruction by the poet himself during the Greek Civil War."

"Fascinating," I said, turning around and approaching the chaise where Miss Constance now reclined. I clumsily sat down.

A few minutes of awkward silence followed. Miss Constance smiled patiently and benignly at me. Under her gaze I felt a nervous wreck — I looked at her, I smiled back, looked away, loosened my collar, coughed into my fist, scratched my backside, took out my handkerchief and blew my nose, &c. Then she suggested, with the concerned and instructive tone of a medical nurse, "Perhaps if you put your willy into my mouth. That has a tendency to make the most stubborn and resistant organ come to life."

I felt my cheeks burn crimson. "I, um, I, uh, ah...."

Miss Constance looked concerned that she had overstepped a boundary that did not exist with most of her other clients. "A thousand apologies, sir! Boldness is my personal curse."

I somewhat regained my composure. "What I meant to say before is this: What if we just merely slept together? Lay close to one another. Maybe work up to a kiss...."

"That's a lovely idea! You have a romantic streak in you, Mr. Connor — unlike the hurried, pawing bunch that normally passes through our doors."

Miss Constance climbed under the feather quilt and motioned for me to join her in bed. I stripped to my long underwear, flipped up my half of the quilt, and quickly crawled alongside her. The heat her body gave off was irresistible to me, and I sidled closer. She turned facing away from me, reached behind herself and pulled me closer. I embraced her from behind and felt my body conform to hers. We fell asleep in this attitude while we discussed topics such as the city's pestiferous water supply and the various measures being taken to improve its quality.

We also spoke of our hometowns. Miss Constance hailed from Jay, New York, in the Adirondack Mountains. She had left to avoid the harsh winters and harsher outlooks of the town's residents. I described what I remembered of frontier Chicago, instead of the southwest suburbs of the modern-day metropolis where in reality I was raised. All told, we enjoyed a very informative and chaste time together, excepting the moment when I cupped her breast in my hand. Miss Constance may have been sleeping, but her nipple was wide-awake, judging by how it nudged my palm in response. I forgave myself for sneaking this cheap feel; one hour before, it had taken every ounce of will power not to pursue a host of lewd activities with her. Besides, even if I had forestalled sexual relations with her, at least I got to touch a prime part of a sublime female.

Come morning I was glad I had successfully fought off Miss Constance's temptations. Along with my abundant financial capital, I had successfully stored a goodly amount of moral capital in the bank for when the moment came to confront my perfidious wife. Nevertheless, when it came, in the form of a perfumed note delivered to my home by a street waif in rags, I readily accepted Miss Constance's cordial invitation to the theatre.

"My Dear Sir," the note began,

Allow me to say "dear," for I assure you that you are so to me. I think of nothing but you. You alone of all the creatures of your sex by whom I am surrounded have evinced the most sympathy for my feelings and intellect. Think, then, how anxious I must be for your society. If you have the least spark of compassion for me, then please join me for an evening at the Park Theatre Sunday next. Let me behold the light of your countenance once more. *Adieu jusqu' aux moments delicieux.*

—Constance

I was not so naïve as to believe that Miss Constance's note amounted to anything more than an advertising circular, albeit one precisely and skillfully targeted to my particular circumstances. Still, the prospect of setting aside thoughts of my wife for a night to enjoy the company of such a fair creature as Miss Constance, and all that that could potentially entail, remained attractive.

So, one Sunday hence, after leaving Bunny in charge at home, I caught a hansom to the Park Theatre, on Park Row near City Hall. The latter structure always made me snigger when I passed it. Facing front, Corinthian columns buttressed a rather handsome white marble Greek Revival *cum* Early Federal edifice topped with a cupola. Facing the viewer from the rear were two utterly blank and featureless walls. The city fathers who had planned the building never expected the city to expand farther north than this point, and they had figured, really, why bother decorating the back? Urchins and lovers had decorated the back for them with graffiti.

Outside among the crowd waiting to get into the theatre stood Miss Constance. She wore a low-cut, green silk dress decorated with a wide black belt around her waist and orange lace trimming her cuffs and throat. Her hair was tied up in back and tucked under a gaudy gray hat ringed with miniature red roses and baby's breath. The surrounding area smelled distinctly of roses, which commanded the attention of a number of men smoking and milling about. As I approached I saw her shake her head in response to three different individuals who approached her and offered to escort her inside. She smiled when I came into view; I waved in return, and I walked over to her. After giving me a quick peck on the cheek (discreetly hidden behind a raised handkerchief), Miss Constance hooked her arm through mine and we stepped up to the box office.

After buying two tickets to a play called *Metamora*, we entered the lobby and were confronted by a brutish ex-boxer-type, who, before taking our tickets, grabbed Miss Constance's left hand and inspected her ring finger. Then he grabbed our tickets, examined them closely, and said, "These are orchestra tickets."

"Yes, I like sitting on the main floor," I said. "Is there a problem?"

"Ladies without benefit of matrimonials have to sit either in the third balcony or in a private box. It's back to the ticket seller with youse two."

Embarrassed, Miss Constance led me back to the box office where I paid an additional fifty cents, not an insignificant sum, to obtain a box for us. In response to my confusion, she explained, "In many theatres, if you cannot show a wedding ring when seeking admission, you are consigned to sit in the upper balcony with all of the unescorted ladies, Irish men, and Negroes. I thank you for your generosity."

Twenty boxes or thereabouts, distributed evenly along the right and left walls, overlooked the action on the stage. To attain access to the boxes, Miss Constance and I passed through a second checkpoint manned by another tough customer. With the correct tickets now, we swiftly passed and climbed a series of stairs in search of our box. Others doing the same hauled picnic baskets or arms full of liquor bottles. Already, I could see the logic behind the theatre's box seats and its policy towards unattached ladies. Emanating from more than a few boxes we passed were kissing, moaning, and other telltale sounds of what in the modern world was known as the "perfect make-out spot." Shortly before the curtain was raised, we found our box near the top of the stack almost fifty feet above stage left.

Witnessing the action from overhead, rather than from the front as the director intended, proved to be a hindrance. We could discern neither facial expressions nor hand gestures. We had difficulty hearing the dialogue. And, whenever an actor veered onto the left half of the stage, our view of him was obscured. Yet no one but I appeared to be bothered by these distractions. For they were otherwise occupied in a number of activities: talking, eating, drinking, heckling, snoring, card playing, and lovemaking. Virtually nobody's eyes but mine were trained on the actors' machinations onstage. Joining the inattentive ranks, Miss Constance leaned into me, and within a short time, she pulled my arm up from my seat's armrest and placed it over her shoulders. She closed her eyes and purred softly into my armpit.

Starring Edwin Forrest, who would later become a Gramercy Park neighbor of mine, in a role he originated and reprised over the years, *Metamora* told the story of an Indian chief who attained great notoriety during King Philip's War. In a classic swashbuckler role, Forrest spent most of the first act prancing around the stage, emitting war whoops, swinging on ropes, and removing the scalps from the heads of other actors with his toy tomahawk. By the first intermission, the stage was littered with the bodies of massacred frontiersmen and women whose wigs he wore around his belt. I thought that Forrest had done an adequate job portraying an Indian chief, with the exception of his war dances, which lacked the improvised character of Bunny's authentic Indian repertoire.

At the first intermission, an organ grinder strolled up and down the aisles blatting out a series of patriotic tunes, including "Yankee Doodle," "When Johnny Comes Marching Home," and "My Country Tis of Thee." Next, a quartet of acrobats bounded onto the stage and started jumping, leaping, vaulting, and tumbling. After a few minutes of these activities, two of the acrobats separated from the group and juggled and tossed bowling pins back and forth. The other two marked time by leapfrogging across the stage; then, when it was their turn, these two hurriedly set up a target and backdrop. One stood before the target while the other threw knives in rapid succession, just missing his partner's knees, elbows, shoulders, neck, and head. When the man stepped away from the target, it was seen that the dozen or so thrown knives delineated his shape. Meanwhile, the first two acrobats smiled ingratiatingly and jogged in place off to the left of the action. The audience expressed its strong approval through clapping, whistling, and raining pennies and halfpennies onto the performers, who scooped up the coins in between stunts.

Next, the first pair twirled plates atop sticks while the second pair somersaulted across the stage. One acrobat had set three plates spinning on sticks balanced on his palms and chin; the other attempted to replicate his partner's feat, but when he batted one of his plates to speed up its revolutions, it flew off the stick and shattered on the stage floor. As quickly as they had obtained the audience's support, the performers lost it, as everyone either laughed meanly or shouted some depredation. The two acrobats hastily ended their plate twirling routine, while the other two stepped center stage and began juggling butcher knives. The audience immediately forgot its displeasure and rousingly cheered the daring feat being performed onstage.

I have since learned that the chance of drawing blood provokes endless fascination in theatre audiences. It was more than the skill involved and the physical threat imposed; it seemed symbolic of overcoming mortality itself, if only during the few minutes that the arcanely skilled young men diddled around onstage. Also, that nobody was hurt amidst very real danger attested to the existence of perfection, which New York theatre audiences both demanded and reveled in. Thus, a few moments later, when a juggler lost control of a butcher knife, and it fell flat on the floor, the night's pursuit of perfection had failed, causing the audience to turn against the acrobats for good. Its members started booing, catcalling, and flinging eggs, fruits, vegetables, and other contents of their picnic baskets at the performers. In addition to their fascination with danger, audiences lived for the times when they were called upon to throw rotten objects at the performers.

Fortunately, before all hell broke loose, the curtain dropped, signaling that Act Two of the play was about to begin, and the audience settled down. Miss Constance took this opportunity to place her hand in my lap and massage me through my pants. I politely removed her hand just as the curtain rose again. Chief Metamora (Forrest) was back at the Indian village, boasting to the other characters of his bravery in attacking the settlers. While relating the story of his victory, he began to notice forlorn white-faced children surrounding him, the only survivors of the massacre, now held in captivity. (These were not real children but actors who were short in stature.) Moved by their pitiful visages, he underwent a sudden change of heart toward the white race, and he adopted the children as his own and attempted to raise them in the Indian fashion. With varying degrees of success, he taught them to hunt, fish, plant, fight, and worship the Great Spirit. The children exhibited a decided lack of success in pursuing these tasks. Simply put, they were not Indian material.

Instead, they demonstrated talents and proficiencies unimaginable to their Indian captors, like reading, writing, and ciphering, the sophistication of which Metamora recognized as far outstripping that of his people. Moreover, their stubborn faith in a Christian god and utter rejection of Indian gods suggested that theirs was a deity who dealt in stronger medicine than his. As the second act came to a close, Metamora questioned in a long soliloquy whether he and his fellow tribesmen could long resist the onslaught of white civilization. Upon the conclusion of his speech, the curtain dropped, the gas lamps were turned up, and the second intermission commenced.

Fabulously entertained by the repartee between the performers and audience during the last intermission, my eyes were trained on the stage, lest I miss some onstage provocation and the audience members' response. Miss Constance showed signs of irritation that I was paying her little attention of the sort to which she was accustomed. She boldly climbed onto my lap and started kissing my hands, neck, and cheeks in an attempt to incite lustful urges. I pretended that I needed to stand and stretch, and I asked her to remove herself. She jumped off with an exasperated sigh and announced that she wished to buy a drink. I gave her a couple of bits to cover the cost and gladly excused her. I did not know whether she planned to return, but I honestly did not care, because I wanted to watch the *entre-act*, consisting, according to my program, of a Mr. T.D. Rice singing the song "Zip Coon."

To the accompaniment of fiddle, banjo, "bones," and tambourine, a Negro dressed in rags shuffled onto the stage and danced an awkward jig while he sang these words to the tune of "Turkey in the Straw":

O ole Zip Coon he is a larned skoler.
O ole Zip Coon he is a larned skoler.
O ole Zip Coon he is a larned skoler.
Possum up a gum tree an coony in a holler.

Possum up a gum tree, coony on a stump.
Possum up a gum tree, coony on a stump.
Possum up a gum tree, coony on a stump.
Den over dubble trubble, Zip Coon will jump.

O zip a duden duden duden zip a duden day.

O zip a duden duden duden zip a duden day.
O zip a duden duden duden zip a duden day.
Zip a duden duden duden zip a duden day.

Waves of laughter erupted in the theatre as this poor man flopped around the stage on a gimpy leg. I could not determine which I found more offensive: laughing in response to his deformity or his poverty, the latter evident from his battered straw hat, coarse threadbare shirt, filthy white gloves missing fingers, and calico patches covering the seat of his breeches. Despite all, he bravely carried on under the cascade of coins tossed his way:

I tell you what will happin den, now bery soon,
De Nited States Bank will be blone to de moon;
Dare General Jackson, will him lampoon,
And de bery nex president will be Zip Coon.

An wen Zip Coon our President shall be,
He make all de little Coons sing possum up a tree;
O how de little Coons will dance an sing,
Wen he tie dare tails togedder, cross de lim dey swing.

These lines resulted in fervent cheering, as Mr. Jackson's controversial attempt to shutter the Bank and stifle any dissent from Congress figured heavily in the news of the day.

I turned to Miss Constance, who had meantime returned to our box, and said, "The world is truly a cruel place to allow such humiliation of a penniless, limping Negro. Everybody in this theatre ought to be ashamed of himself."

"That is no Negro," she responded. "Tis a white man made up and dressed like a Negro. There are no actors among the Negro population. At least none that performs onstage in a respectable house such as this. You are watching Thomas Dartmouth Rice, today's preeminent interpreter of Negro music and dance."

I had thought that laughing at a poor, crippled Negro was rude enough. But this insight troubled me more deeply. In the modern world, one could hardly think of a thing more offensive than a white man in blackface ridiculing Negroes. Taking as my model the audience behavior of before, I stood up and began loudly to shout my disapproval. "Get off the stage, you racist bastard!" I screamed. "Making fun of Negroes sucks eggs!" I added. "Go fuck yourself, T.D. Rice!" I hollered through my hands.

Sorry to say, my words had little impact on the performance; Mr. Rice continued jollily to engage in his hurtful rendition of Negro habits.

"What are you doing?" Miss Constance asked. "You are embarrassing me!"

"Are you not embarrassed by this so-called performer and his egregious subject matter?" I retorted.

"No, I am not. In fact, I was finding it rather amusing."

"I'll show you amusing," I said. I do not know what mischievous sprite had entered our box to inspire such a response, for I next reacted in a manner much removed from my usual conduct, even when I was a champion imbiber of alcohol. I calmly unbuttoned my trousers and urinated over the railing and onto Mr. Rice's *faux* nappy head. After a moment of not knowing what had hit him, he broke off his song and dodged the forceful yellow stream that effectively chased him off the stage.

Miss Constance may have been a prostitute, but she was a prostitute with impeccable manners. She screamed in horror at my vulgarity and ducked down so none of her clients, existing or potential, could connect her with the uncouth ass pissing onto the stage from above. Either that, or she anticipated the barrage of tomatoes and wormy apples that were lofted our way and exploded like mortar shells on the floor of our box. Meanwhile, taunts of "Abolitionist!" and "Nigger Lover!" bruised my ears.

While I hastily buttoned up my unmentionables and backed away from the railing, tomato pulp splattered my hair, but I otherwise escaped unscathed. Miss Constance was not quite so lucky; a hard green apple struck her in the face and blackened her eye. "You ... you're mad!" she exclaimed, and then she swept the curtains aside and raced down the stairs at a full gallop.

Was I mad? I most likely was in that moment. Certainly, I was angry — mainly with Thomas Dartmouth Rice and the Park Theatre audience that had found his act so uproariously funny. And I was also angry with Miss Constance, who, though refined and educated, could not easily shed her era's false, ridiculous beliefs on race.

I was not crazy, however — as proven by the acute sense of self-preservation that flooded my every capillary from head to toe. With the crowd's anger growing ever stronger, and each fusillade of fruits and vegetables arriving closer to their mark, I decided to follow Miss Constance's lead and hightail it to safety. I charged down the stairs two at a time, skated across the marble-floored lobby, and burst out the doors onto the darkened street. Unfortunately, I missed the last act of *Metamora*, so I did not find out how the story ended until a decade later, when I saw the play a second time. Sadly, Metamora's change of heart toward the country's white inhabitants arrives too late. In the play's climax a great battle occurs, and the chief is killed and his scalp taken by white settlers bent on revenge. In a landmark instance of overacting, Mr. Forrest takes about twenty minutes of stage time to die, while he alternately groans in pain and soliloquizes about the inevitability of the white race supplanting the red in America.

When I arrived on the street, I saw neither hide nor hair of Miss Constance; she had disappeared into the darkness of the dimly lit city. I wished to speak with her further about what had just transpired in our box and offer her some justification or explanation for my outburst. Alas, this desire would not be fulfilled. Then, as I rode home in a cab, I chided myself for acting as though I owed her this, that my relationship with Miss Constance amounted to something more than an arm's length commercial transaction, like, for example, renting a horse for a Sunday afternoon pleasure ride.

As the week proceeded my mind wandered to other subjects, and my manly urges had largely subsided. Actually, I had tried my psychic best to bury my impulses and tamp them down with a stout spade. When Rachel was found, they could always be dug up again, or so I hoped. Any guilt engendered from my aborted interlude with Miss Constance quickly passed. That is, until the same rag-tag boy who delivered her first letter appeared on my doorstep offering up her second. On the chance that he might apply them to the purchase of new clothes, I paid him a couple of pennies; as he walked away, I noticed that he bit into each coin to ascertain its authenticity. Expecting a scolding inside the envelope, I put off opening it for several hours. Then, around dinnertime, when I considered the possibility of it containing a message of forgiveness and pending reconciliation, I elected to open it. My first guess proved to be the correct one:

Mr. Connor:

Although you may have yielded to a temporary insanity at the theatre Sunday last, you should be made aware of a proper sense of what is due to your companion. I am very sure I had not merited such treatment.

I pictured you as an image all-divine. In you I found high, generous, noble, independent feelings, such as I had never before met with. I would have found much pleasure in attempting anything that may have been productive of happiness to you.

But your refusal on certain matters convinced me that I reigned in your heart with no very deep-seated preference. It spoke volumes in favor of your feelings for your wife, but very little for your partiality for me. If you could read my heart, you would pity me, and yet I would not have your pity; it seems so very much like contempt.

I hope you accede to my wish that you should never again call on me. Do not think I will endure this or future mortification. Your correspondent with cracked heart,

—Miss Constance Periwinkle

P.S. Please remit five silver dollars to Mrs. Doolittle's care. Even if no services were rendered during our recent interview, the time we "enjoyed" together must be accounted for in her ledger.

P.P.S. I had a little private chat with the manager of a certain theatre since your tirade, which I explained and obtained entire absolution for. However, I am most positive that you shall not be allowed to return to the scene of your indiscretion.

I gladly granted Miss Constance's request and never paid another visit to Mrs. Doolittle's house, nor to any other house of ill repute. I was firm in my decision to save my love for its proper object, my wife. Problem was, the likelihood of finding her looked increasingly remote. I had no great aversion to going to the Texas Territory if Rachel and I should be reunited. Such a trip required an ocean voyage to the port at New Orleans, which I would have found most agreeable — I have always loved a good boat ride, dating back to when my father acquired his cabin cruiser after my mother died. However, I refused to spend the time and money unless I had solid evidence in hand of Rachel residing there. Mr. Pemberton could not say with authority that Texas was where she could be found.

For the first time since I had arrived in the nineteenth century, I looked down the proverbial wishing well and glimpsed a murky future. I suddenly faced the prospect of being forced by circumstances to abandon my quest and the necessity of seeking a new life companion. If that came to pass, I surely would not look in a brothel, where the women charged money for their affections; a tavern, where the women were beholden to the bottle; or a theatre, where unmarried women were not even allowed to mingle with unmarried men.

Already in my life, I had defied the second of these rules and, to boot, ignored the sound advice of my father. When I graduated from college, and I was finally eligible to claim a wife, according to my father's thinking, he sat me down and advised me, "Never marry a girl you meet in a bar. Fool around with them all you want, but don't marry them." As it happened, Rachel and I had met in a bar. My question for my father was this: what can one do when fooling around evolves into full-fledged love, and the next logical step is to marry? As circumstances turned out, my father was right in his position and I, evidently, was wrong.

To hedge my bet with myself that eventually I would locate Rachel, I contemplated joining a church or some social club where available ladies were as plentiful as hens on a poultry farm. I took issue with the literal-mindedness of most devout assemblies, but I reasoned that a higher percentage of the women were decent-hearted, compared to the general population. I resolved to seek Mr. Gallatin's counsel regarding a good Presbyterian church or progressive — but undogmatic — club to which I could devote my time and energy in hopes of having my good deeds rewarded with a dose of femininity.

Chapter Thirteen

November 8, 1835

I have to confess that things are going pretty damn well right now. Sure, I'd like for somebody to hurry up and invent tampons. (That's what Bruce should spend his time on, not stupid aspirin.)

And I could really use an indoor toilet, too, especially now that the weather is turning colder. And I'd absolutely love a big plate of pasta drowned in marinara sauce with a little side of *broccoli rabe*.

But I really have little room to complain these days. For yours truly has become a bona fide celebrity. Everything's happened so suddenly that I haven't had time, diary, to fill you in.

What started the snowball rolling was a letter I mailed to Lydia Maria Child. First, I buttered her up by telling her that I thought she was the greatest speaker in the world. She was smart, witty and dedicated to women's causes.

I told her that I, too, held strong pro-woman beliefs and wanted to try a career in public speaking. I didn't share with her my precise plan, because I didn't want her stealing my idea for a talk show. Not that she would, but you never know.

Then I popped the question: would she be able to take time from her busy schedule and share a little career advice with a novice like me?

I assured her that this wasn't some passing fancy. I was willing to risk everything to make this dream of mine come true — money, ridicule, even personal safety.

Surprisingly, she sent me a letter in return that contained all kinds of helpful hints, as well as a sincere-sounding wish that I succeed in my mission.

With her letter she included the names of a couple of New York lyceum managers, although she confessed she didn't know whether either would agree to let me put on a show in their spaces.

Just as she'd predicted, both managers refused to listen to my proposal. They couldn't get their minds around the interview format that I envisioned. "What need do I have of you, when there is a William Lloyd Garrison or a Sylvester Graham in the house?" asked one.

When the other pretty much asked the same question in slightly different words, all I could come up with was, "I'd translate for the audience what the guest is saying."

Realizing this sounded hopelessly lame, I added, "I'd be like a mediator. Put the guests' opinions in proper perspective. Approach them with a healthy skepticism. Show how this or that person's thoughts relate to the audience."

Needless to say, the man remained singularly unimpressed.

However, when he learned that I planned on funding the show by tapping into my own personal fortune, he became a lot more interested. And why not? It was I alone that would assume the risk of paying for every empty seat in the house in case nobody showed up.

He ended up giving me a date in September, a Monday night. I wasn't too crazy about doing it on a Monday. People were still worn out by their marathon church sermons on Sunday. They probably wouldn't be receptive to an edifying talk come Monday.

I had almost a month to locate my first guest. I knew my choice could make or break my little enterprise, so I had to pick a big name. Maria Child was the obvious choice. Unfortunately, she was lecturing in Cincinnati on that day, and I had to think of somebody else.

Meanwhile, I worked out the show's format in my head.

First, there would be a short lecture — emphasis on "short" — by the guest. Then I'd spend some time deconstructing the guest's opinions. Next, I'd go into the audience and allow a few audience members to ask questions.

While I obsessed over the plans for my upcoming show, Bruce perfected his aspirin formula. Once he was satisfied it did what it was supposed to do — making my headache or menstrual cramps go away — he began marketing it.

I'm not sure what made me agree to be his guinea pig. His track record left something to be desired. Maybe I was eager for him to succeed and wanted to help expedite the process. Maybe I was desperate to get him the hell out of the house.

Whatever, the stuff works. You dissolve a teaspoon in water, and your aches and pains go away.

Sometimes your stomach might be upset, though. Maybe the water is to blame. You always take your chances drinking it.

Or maybe the aspirin-induced churning in your stomach takes your mind off the pain in your temples, fooling you into thinking your headache is gone.

Regardless, without any interference from the Food and Drug Administration, which doesn't exist yet, Bruce put on a fake beard that I scored for him at a costume supply house to disguise himself, and he called on every apothecary shop in town to see if the owner wanted to carry his formula.

Some did, and some didn't. Typical of those pharmacists that didn't was one who runs a shop on Broadway between Duane and Reade Streets.

When told that Bruce's pain-killing formula contains neither alcohol nor opium, the incredulous shopkeeper said, "If this be true, then you are a bigger miracle worker than Christ himself, who could turn water into wine."

The owners of about half of the city's approximately seventy apothecaries weren't as skeptical (or religious) as this man and cut Bruce a break. Thirty-two stores stocked it its first week out in the marketplace.

I could tell that the whole experience was deeply humiliating to Bruce. Look how far he'd been reduced: from directing a huge staff making scientific history to begging glorified witch doctors to accept his magic powder into their shops.

We weren't around, of course, to witness the global celebrations of Bruce's exploits that must have occurred after we left in 2015. We could only imagine how thrilled the world was when the news broke.

I'm sure these thoughts enters Bruce's head a thousand times a day as he glumly sits in our living room, day after day, whittling bark off willow branches and scraping the green stuff into buckets.

Suffice it to say, in his former life he'd have had an army of lowly grad assistants available to do such grunt work.

Just as I expected, getting his name back into the newspaper perked him right up. During the time I knew him leading up to our trip to the past, he was quoted in the newspaper at least once a week.

Sometimes it was something simple like responding to a new scientific discovery by one of his colleagues: "Judging by my observations of background radiation, I'd put the age of the universe at 45 billion years, not 50."

For a few months his face could be seen in a series of magazine ads for TIAA-CREF, an investment fund for academic types. He was always photographed without his glasses on, standing all studly in front of the atom smasher at Fermilab.

The ad we placed in the *New York Tribune* was a lot lower key:

Bill & Son Aspirin
Patented Formula Developed Exclusively
By Dr. Ezekiel Bill
Cures Headaches, Muscle Pain & Female Cramps
Lowers Fevers
Helps Prevent Heart Attacks & Strokes
No better arthritis or rheumatism relief available
All without Alcohol or Poppy Ingredients
Request it by name at your neighborhood druggist

Or order by mail from Bill & Son, No. 24 Barrow St.
Accept No Substitutes!

We judged that we were far enough away from western New York that Bruce could reclaim his name (sort of) and surface somewhat from his life underground. And, anyway, nobody knew his real name at Niagara Falls.

"Bill & Son" was my idea. Bruce chose the first name "Ezekiel" in honor of his great-great grandfather, who had that very 19th-century-sounding name.

Of course, Bruce had two PhD's, so he could honestly be called "Doctor," even if he wasn't exactly a medical doctor.

Based on a timely recommendation from Maria Child, I scored my first guest. First *two* guests, actually: the Grimke sisters, Sarah and Angelina. Maria described them as "abolitionists and suffragists of the first rank."

Sounded good to me — enlightened and progressive and bound to be controversial. They were exactly what were needed for my first outing to attract maximum press attention, which would lead to asses in the seats.

In what has become a habit with me, I spent the days and weeks before the show reading up on the impending guests. With all of the sisters' pamphlets for sale across the city, it was easy.

The Grimkes originally hailed from South Carolina. They were the daughters of a slaveholding father, but when they grew up they renounced the plantation lifestyle, emigrated north and became bitter enemies of slavery.

They lectured all over the North and published scathing articles about the institution. Because they grew up in the South, they were intimately familiar with slavery's many evils, and their words sounded that much more credible.

I'm not a full-blown abolitionist, although I obviously strongly disapprove of slavery.

But you really don't speak about the topic in 1835. Never around the dinner table, for example, which can result in hurt feelings from a too-heated discussion, someone abruptly excusing themselves and pushing in their chair violently, or even knife or gunplay, if the penny papers can be believed.

Slavery is a subject best left to professionals who know every argument, front and back. Somebody who can handily dispatch seasoned debaters and unruly hecklers both, while I sit beside them and bask in their reflected righteousness.

After I got the sisters' letter accepting my invitation, I set a show date. A few days after that, the Downtown Lyceum posted a sign in its front window that read:

Rachel Lewis presents
in conjunction with
the Downtown Lyceum
The Grimke Sisters:

"Miss Sarah Grimke
Miss Angelina Grimke
Discourse on Slavery,
Women's Rights, and
the Bank Question"
Mon., Sept. the 6th
Tickets 5 Cts
at the Box Office
No children, dogs,
or chickens allowed

I'm not sure what the reference to dogs and chickens was about. Maybe it was okay to bring cats and goats. I don't know. Maybe offended dog and chicken lovers were the reason advance ticket sales were slow, making me a nervous wreck in the days leading up to the show.

Slow sales also worried George Parkinson, the lyceum manager. "Are you certain you do not have something to peddle? If you have not published a book, then is there something else you can sell?"

I confessed that the only thing I had to sell was myself.

"How about selling umbrellas or ladies' hats? I know a man in Brooklyn, a real sharp cock, who could sell them to you in bulk. He would probably charge you only a half-penny more per piece to stencil your name on them."

"No thank you. I'll bear the losses."

"Attempting to soften the blow of an empty house is all, Mrs. Lewis."

After this conversation on the way home, I found myself agreeing that my show needed a hedge against an empty house. Where would Oprah Winfrey be without laundry detergent? Where would Jerry Springer be without truck-driving schools?

Then it hit me: Dr. Ezekiel Bill should be my show's sponsor. The marketing opportunities seemed perfect: a medicine that cured the aches and pains of the sex most prone to them, which happened to be my target audience.

Mr. Parkinson immediately liked the idea. Bruce, unfortunately, took longer to win over, especially when he learned that he would have to pitch his miracle drug to the audience in between guests.

"You're the best at sounding all persuasive and authoritative," I said. "It's how you lived or died in the 21st century funding your physics projects."

"Making pitches to Air Force generals or Cabinet undersecretaries is a lot different than recommending aspirin to a bunch of women to treat their menstrual cramps. Besides, what if somebody from upstate recognizes me?"

"We'll dig out your fake beard. Dress you up in a white lab coat."

"Inadvisable."

I wasn't standing for any more of Bruce's static. "You're going to do this for me," I informed him, staring into his eyes so intensely that he had to look away or else his eyeballs would melt.

Then, leaving zero room for argument, I calmly put on my shawl, walked out the front door and went around the corner to the dress maker's shop to check on a couple of stage outfits I'd ordered the week before.

I couldn't believe I was behaving toward Bruce like this. We always did what Bruce said — remember, I'm the ditzy secretary and he's the once-a-century genius. But here was the deal:

Bruce and I had moved beyond his gift to me of an all-expenses-paid trip to the past. No matter how unbelievably cool that was, after a year's worth of almost Biblical trials and tribulations, I had stopped owing him and he had started owing me.

To prepare myself for my public debut, I rehearsed in front of a mirror. I perfected some signature facial expressions, like shaking my head disapprovingly, pursing my lips quizzically, and pulling the ties of my bonnet to look like I'm strangling myself out of exasperation.

Trouble reared its ugly head the very same minute the Grimke sisters arrived at the Downtown Lyceum in the hours before the show. The older sister, Sarah, not realizing we were planning for a co-ed audience, freaked out.

"Sister, when will you get over your aversion to everything modern?" asked Angelina, Sarah's younger sister.

"At about the same time that everything modern conducts itself with more modesty," said Sarah.

"Please excuse my older sister," Angelina said to me. "On all questions except slavery she bids us return to the Middle Ages."

Angelina had a point. Sarah looked about twenty years older than Angelina and dressed in clothes from another century. The word "spinster" came to mind when you looked at her.

By contrast, Angelina was very pretty in that pasty china-doll way. She had an ethereal quality that translated well on stage. People just instantly liked her, whereas her sister took some getting used to.

"The audience will be overwhelmingly female," I said. "Can't you concentrate on the women and ignore the smattering of men?"

"Oh, no, I cannot, no, no," said Sarah. "Scripture dictates that men and women should remain separate in the public sphere."

I felt the impulse to strangle her. Maria Child hadn't prepared me for this crap.

"Dear Sister," said Angelina, "as I have tried to explain on many a frustrating occasion, that proscription is from the Old Testament. The lamb has washed away our sin. The New Testament supersedes the Old."

"If Sarah doesn't want to speak," I said, "then maybe Angelina could do a solo performance just this once."

"Oh, that is rich," said Sarah. "Angelina is a veritable compendium of facts and figures. She will tell you so herself. Go ahead, sister."

Angelina responded to Sarah's sarcasm by meekly agreeing and not, as you'd expect, hauling off and smacking her in her pinched, uptight mouth. "Sarah is correct; I cannot shoulder the burden alone."

"Why the hell not? How many dozens of lectures have you given? You should have it all memorized by now." I was practically yelling.

"Let me simply confess that ever since childhood I have suffered from certain mental debilities that prevent me from remembering any of the facts or arguments that we use to defend our cause."

"Angelina is as dumb as a fencepost," Sarah interjected.

"Hush, sister! You know full well that I am as intelligent as you. My intellectual deficiencies have always involved lapses in memory and never any inability to reason. You dried-up old prune."

"There it is. Always, it boils down to the image of us that everybody holds in his mind, dating back to Mother and Father. You are the pretty, charming one, and I am the ugly, smart one."

"You said it, sister, not I."

"HUSSY! Why, I'll..."

"Can't we think of some solution here?" I pleaded, ready to knock their damn heads together.

"Springfield, Massachusetts," Angelina said cryptically.

"Huh?" I said.

"My dear sister is offering a compromise based upon an earlier occasion when we experienced this self-same dilemma," said Sarah.

Angelina painted the picture for me: "I appear in person before the audience, for I have no prejudices concerning its composition, while my dear sister speaks from behind a curtain."

"A curtain?" I asked.

"To protect her modesty."

I looked at Sarah, who was blushing fiercely. I didn't get this hang-up about modesty. It's not like her outfit revealed any skin. Black wool covered her from neck to ankle, and every bit of her hair was stuffed under her bonnet. Only her face showed, and it wasn't too handsome.

I couldn't imagine what had gotten her so agitated. To me, she looked like a weather-beaten middle-aged woman with a taste for funereal clothing. I honestly wondered what sorts of looks she could possibly be expecting from men.

"It has to be a thin curtain so she can be heard," said Angelina.

"Muslin is the perfect fabric for this purpose," said Sarah.

"I'll see what can be rigged up," I said, turning to go search for Mr. Parkinson and get his input. Leaving Sarah to putz around the stage, Angelina accompanied me.

"In my sister's eyes, I am a harlot," she said. "That is all right. I consider her a hypocrite. She professes to advance the rights of women, but she cannot assert herself in the presence of a man."

"She's definitely a prima donna," I agreed, as we climbed the sloped seating area on the way to the lobby and box office, where I expected to find Mr. Parkinson.

In a positive development for my shattered nerves, the sisters patched up their spat (which I'm guessing is ongoing and heads into remission maybe once a month) long enough to appear on stage with me. We put on a decent, though far from flawless, show.

Angelina and I sat in plain wooden chairs center-stage. To our left sat Sarah behind a bunch of white bed sheets sewn together and strung up to the rafters. Mr. Parkinson had the scenery director place a lamp behind Sarah that flashed her silhouette onto the fabric.

What followed was totally surreal. I felt so fucking nervous that my numbing mechanism took over and made me feel like I was having an out-of-body experience.

Essentially, the audience saw a shadow puppet show, exactly like the one I saw performed once in Park Row based on "The Legend of Sleepy Hollow," right down to Sarah's herky-jerky mannerisms.

The sisters had their act down pat. They carried on this Socratic dialog in which Angelina pitted a question about slavery to Sarah, who responded like some ancient soothsayer from behind the curtain.

Angelina remembered things better than advertised. As the asker of questions, she fulfilled her role admirably. Sarah brought her admittedly sharp mind to bear on the subject of slavery, slicing and dicing until only the empty moral core of her opponents' arguments were left.

During one exchange, I forget what it was about, the dynamics of their relationship became clear to me:

Angelina was limited to asking questions, and Sarah to answering them. Angelina tried hard to question authority while Sarah staunchly clung to her authoritative airs. One supplied the spark; the other supplied the fuel.

Separately, they couldn't argue their way out of a wet paper bag. Together, they were lethal to anyone who dared to disagree.

As for *my* performance, it didn't amount to much. I was reduced to the status of a street mime, reacting to the sisters' points with shocked, amused and perplexed facial expressions. All I did all night was introduce them. After that I couldn't get a word in edgewise.

Happily, Bruce rose to the occasion — the first time anything of his rose in a long time, if you catch my drift — saying his few perfunctory words about the magical properties of aspirin. He ended up selling twenty-four envelopes of the stuff. He made four bucks, enough to eat for a couple of weeks, but nothing great.

We nearly filled the house, pleasing Mr. Parkinson, along with my banker, Mr. Biddle, who didn't want to see my savings depleted. In fact, I made money. Sixteen dollars.

I've hosted a second, less noteworthy, but still good, show with the Reverend Charles Finney. With him, I was able to engage in a real question-and-answer session, as a Presbyterian minister tried to explain what a religious revival was to a Jewish princess whose idea of a revival was the umpteenth go-around of *Fiddler on the Roof*.

Meantime, I'm psyched about the next couple of shows, on December 1st and 12th, when I host radical feminist Fanny Wright, followed by super abolitionist William Lloyd Garrison. Those two ought to cause quite a stir.

Chapter Fourteen

December 16, 1835, was an auspicious date for me as well as every other New Yorker then living. The city experienced a massive fire that devastated the downtown financial district, killed a dozen people, and cost millions of dollars in lost real estate and financial instruments.

The month began rather routinely for me: I helped pack short barrels of sugar, flour, seed corn, and rice that were destined for the homes of needy families living in the city's decrepit precincts. Three months before, I had volunteered to work on the first weekend of every month at the collection point, a dingy waterfront warehouse on South Street. City residents of average or above-average means generously donated foodstuffs to a largely appreciative constituency — though I often wondered what anyone could do with apple cores, coffee grounds, and moldy bread, which were charitably, if misguidedly, dropped off on occasion.

I settled upon volunteering for a food disbursement organization when I found the prohibitions on personal behavior at churches too cumbersome. Drinking, cigar smoking, card playing, and cursing headed the list of forbidden activities, quickly followed by freethinking and fornicating. Let other men believe in whatever god they will, but I personally could not see what use religious fellowship among women would be without the potential for fornication.

At the food pantry, none of these prohibitions was present — volunteers smoked, drank rum and whiskey, and told filthy stories. Unfortunately, there were no women present at these gatherings, not counting Frankie, the mannish woman who wore men's trousers, cropped her hair short, and spoke in a deep, husky voice. Bunny, who, in her mind, had become too much of a lady to perform such manual labors anymore, stayed at home.

Still, the male fellowship proved agreeable, and the cause was a good one, so I stayed with the process, which continued monthly up until a few years ago, when I retired from it. We men built fast bonds during our marathon packing sessions.

This proved no truer than when Sam Tilden joined our bunch. Ever the political operator, Sam connected us to a system of shared favors among gentlemen. For example, for the German butcher, Adolph, he obtained citizenship with the aid of Judge Grady, who received a weekly "subscription" of choice meats. For me, he arranged a deal wherein a grand-nephew of John Jacob Astor received exclusive rights to transfer to his family's shipping fleet cargo hauled by the rail line (a predecessor of the Pennsylvania Railroad) in which I held the controlling shares.

What did Sam get out of his machinations? Brokering my little deal launched a lucrative career of representing railroad interests. He also gained attention for the food pantry and for himself due to his association with it. Already, at the tender age of twenty, he showed a flair for publicity and self-promotion that all budding politicians display. Sam's efforts brought in a higher volume of donations to our pantry, and he cemented his reputation in the public mind as a civic goody-goody two-shoes.

Of course, as the former New York City prosecutor and the bane of Tammany Hall, Sam still possesses this do-gooder trait in the extreme, especially since his loss in the 1876 presidential election, which he blames on Southern congressmen sympathetic to his Tammany enemies. The two groups share much in common, he explains: each has an ironclad grip on a subject population, "freed" slaves in the former case and the urban proletariat in the latter. The agreement that they have struck on the backs of their constituents to push Tilden aside have to be resisted, or else relations between the races will remain forever strained.

I dwell on this part of Sam's character only to contrast it with a darker, seamier side of the 1876 presidential candidate. Sam's baser nature revealed itself for the first time during the first weekend in October 1835. While our contingent sawed apart cheese wheels with long copper wires, one of our number, I believe it might have been Governor Clinton's son, told an off-color joke involving two children who duck behind a barn to show each other their private parts.

"It's a miracle!" exclaims the boy after looking up the girl's dress.

Tickled by the boy's comment, the girl allows him another peek.

"It's truly a miracle!" the boy repeats.

Flattered, the girl asks, "Do you like my puss so very much?"

"No, that's ugly and wrinkled. It's a miracle your guts don't slide out!"

Sam laughed more loudly than anybody else at this silly joke, inappropriately so, I thought. His reaction appeared to be related to his activities for the remainder of the weekend, when he took each of us aside in turn and, *sotto voce*, informed us of the availability through his connections of some extremely frank drawings from France. I confess that I was intrigued by the proposition, and I requested to see a sample.

A few evenings later, Sam appeared at my townhome's service entrance. He slipped inside, clutching a satchel with uncommon possessiveness. We retired to my library and drank a glass of brandy from the crystal snifter. To accompany the brandy, I loaded a pipe of chekagou and smoked it with Sam while we talked.

Sam unsnapped his satchel and brought out a stack of postcard-sized drawings along with a few larger color lithographs. What was depicted in these materials stunned and amazed me: all manner of hand-drawn, machine-reproduced pornography. In every position imaginable, lecherous men were putting it to buxom young ladies who had eagerly shed their many layers of skirts and hoops and invitingly spread their legs.

"A most" ... gulp! ... "comprehensive collection," was all I managed to say, as I felt suddenly embarrassed to be looking at dirty pictures with Sam standing nearby. Viewing pornography should be a solitary pastime to enable the viewer to indulge his lustful fantasies without anyone's opprobrium.

"It's funny that there are virtually the same categories of porn as the world you and I are from — straight, gay, oral, anal, group, lesbian, interracial, bondage — it's all represented. You know what else? They use the same six sexual poses as modern-day porn — missionary, cowgirl facing front, cowgirl facing rear, doggie style, man seated in a chair, woman standing on her head."

"And just exactly how did you become such an expert on the subject?" I asked, both because I was curious and because I wanted to tease Sam.

"Holographic pornography. The perfect sexual partner for teenage boys," he answered, referring to a technology available in 2063 but not yet in 2015. "You know, holograms of beautiful women that you boot up to do your sexual bidding. And here I had always thought it was a lack of sufficient computer memory that accounted for so few positions, not a lack of imagination." (Primitive holograms, three-dimensional stereoscopic-like images projected into the air, existed in 2015, but not to the sophisticated degree that Sam was describing. Holograms were mere curiosities in my youth, years away from staple status in the pleasure industry, which, together with war, has always led the curve in underwriting and capitalizing on an era's inventions.)

—Next, Sam laid out several more lithographs. These catered to a more perverse taste — nude women bound and gagged and lorded over by masked men in chain mail wielding maces; or crouched in the hay of horse stalls fellating restless stallions; or stuffing sundry household items like candles and wine bottles into their gaping orifices.

He produced from his satchel one last drawing. "Given the current political winds, I don't dare show this one except to the most discriminating collector." The artist's subject was a Southern belle who enjoyed the amorous attentions of a gang of Negroes (depicted with ape faces and outsized manhoods), while her plantation-master husband sits off to the side and leers.

This intimate look inside Sam's personal business was disquieting. I suppose that our intimate talk indicated that I had finally let down my guard in relation to Sam Tilden. I had never quite trusted Sam until this moment. He was such a political animal ingratiating himself to everyone he met that one never knew which Sam was the genuine Sam. I speculated that, for however short an interval it promised to be, I was dealing with the real Sam that night in my library.

Or perhaps not. For Sam quickly chameleoned from personal confidant into impersonal dealer of smut after we had spent a few moments looking aslant at the explicit pictures while feigning indifference. "You won't come across quality erotic art like this until photography is popularized in another twenty-five years," he pitched. I conceded that Sam's collection exhibited a high degree of artistic skill, and I offered to buy a picture. For two dollars I selected an artfully drawn portrait of a nude, dirt-smeared, fear-stricken woman chained to a dungeon wall. Thinking back, I wonder if this particular picture appealed to me because I subconsciously wished that this punishment were meted out to my wayward wife.

Sam gathered up the remaining pictures and replaced them in his satchel. He departed soon thereafter, and I was left to contemplate his odd personality, a pastime to which I periodically return, up to and including the present day. Single-mindedly, Sam Tilden strived to elevate his station in life and establish his political bona fides. That I know of, he neither courted any woman nor married; there was simply no time to spend on such frivolity. To illustrate how unusual his situation was, had he been elected president in 1876, he would have been just the second bachelor president, after James Buchanan. From all outward appearances, he lived a life of Spartan discipline *apropos* his secret twenty-first-century mission to alter the course of political and military history.

Yet with us today is the selfsame old bachelor who parlayed his early hobby of peddling erotic images into what is now recognized by society's whispering classes as the largest collection of pornography on the Eastern Seaboard. Well into his sixties, Sam continues to host invitation-only erotic art and photography exhibitions at Greystone, his hilltop mansion in Yonkers. For years, Sam has used these secret events to curry favor with Manhattan's and Albany's movers and shakers. Some politicians ply their constituents with money or barrels of liquor; in Sam Tilden's case, he proffers naughty pictures.

Only two weeks later the unsold drawings, which he kept in his room at his boarding house, burned up in the Great Fire, along with the rest of his belongings. This placed him so far in debt to his distributors, the actual owners of the erotic art, which paid Sam a percentage of each sale, that he had to win a couple of quick law cases to repay them or else have his legs broken. Happily, he paid his associates on time, retained the use of his legs, and slowly rebuilt his illicit business while plucking the juiciest images for his own personal collection.

It is strange to remember Sam's loss so clearly, when others lost so much more in the fire, for example, Thaddeus, my favorite concierge at the City Hotel, who all but managed my social calendar while I lived there. As he fled the fire engulfing his downtown home, he lost his life, tragically, when creeping through a cellar that firefighters, unaware of his presence, had flooded with water in their attempt to douse the flames upstairs, accidentally drowning him.

A few people even managed to gain something amid all of the loss and destruction.

The people that made out best were the handful of insurers among the many clustered around Hanover Square, who had the foresight to purchase newly introduced fireproof safes. This allowed them to retain copies of their clients' policies, plus the cash to pay out claims. One would think that the insurers whose policy documents had gone up in smoke made out better, since in many instances clients could not prove that they were covered by any policy. Yet this situation led to protracted lawsuits that had cost the insurers more money in the long run than simply paying their claimants and closing the matter.

Benefiting almost as much were the city's ministers. To them, the disaster literally was a godsend — they believed that God had handed them a calamity they could use to crucify the city for its immoral ways. In the weeks following the fire, Sunday sermonizers blamed an assortment of evils for drawing God's fire and brimstone down upon our town. One holy representative blamed the armies of prostitutes that plagued the city, birthing orphans weaned by the state, weakening workingmen with syphilis, and corrupting the bonds between husband and wife. Another respected reverend argued that the public's excessive consumption of alcohol in the city's two hundred taverns had provoked God's wrath. He noted that fleeing the rapidly advancing fire sobered up even the most besotted individual, bringing him closer to God.

The number one cause that ministers cited for the disaster was slavery. Even though New York State had outlawed slavery eight years before, in 1827, a number of individuals continued to benefit from the institution, including merchants who profited from commercial intercourse with the South, politicians who courted Southern votes, and editors of newspapers who sought Southern subscribers. Yet, these same ministers were unable to explain why the severe judgment of heaven was inflicted on our metropolis instead of a southern city like New Orleans, which profited directly from slave labor and frequent slave auctions.

Other New Yorkers gained in more modest, less tangible ways. Bunny, for instance, discovered through the disaster her true calling in life and became a counselor to married couples. As a berdache she had a natural propensity to be a spiritual adviser, and she had received training from her tribe's medicine man on spiritual topics. However, when she left her old life behind by following me eastward, this training was interrupted. The events of December 16 inspired her once again to take up where she had left off, albeit in the white man's tradition rather than her own.

The city's countless self-improvement lectures had already begun to pique her interest in matters of mind and spirit in the months before the fire. She learned of these by reading the newspaper. Impressed by her intelligence and thirst for knowledge, Mr. Gallatin hired her to assist with working on his latest tome, which recorded his observations and comments on the subject of aboriginal languages. She proved invaluable in advising him about grammar and pronunciation, particularly of the Algonkian languages prevalent east of the Mississippi River. During this process, she learned much about the structure of languages, particularly English, and in a short time she learned how to read. As with anyone learning a new language, she read it better than spoke it, although she demonstrated increased oral proficiency the longer I knew her.

Her favorite lecture topics involved phrenology, mesmerism, and spirit rapping, which should not surprise one given how she was raised and by whom. Feeling the bumps and indentations on a person's head to predict his future or communicating with the dead via knocks on a séance table would, despite their quackish quality, naturally attract one raised in a culture that danced to make it rain or shook rattles over the sick to heal them.

It gladdened me that Bunny had acquired an interest outside the home, and I encouraged her to attend these events whenever she wished. They served double duty, by flexing her mind and contributing to her manners. The only prohibition I placed on this activity was that I refused to escort her, because I could not abide sitting through dull talks by pseudo-scientists.

Nevertheless, through a steady campaign of nagging and needling, Bunny prevailed upon me to join her on December 16 at the Downtown Lyceum to see a woman whom the newspapers had stated was turning the traditional lecture format on its head. Rather than standing before the audience and droning on about the latest English poetry or some heretical religious belief, she sat down with the well-known and highborn and spoke with them one-on-one. Her skeptical and common-sense approach, plus her brave choices of co-conversationalists, had won her many accolades from the press and public.

I admitted that this method of presentation sounded promising. If nothing else, two speakers that spoke at different tempos with voices of varying pitch and timbre would be an improvement over the monotony of a single voice and its solitary perspective. So I gave in to Bunny's entreaties, and on the appointed night we took a coach to the venerable lecture hall. It was a bitterly cold night. The wind swooped down on the city from the northwest, as if ten pairs of lips on the chubby faces of old, gray-bearded men symbolizing prevailing winds on ancient maps blew all at once. The only benefit of such weather was that the human sewage and animal waste in the streets had frozen solid and locked their foul smells inside the ice.

The evening's nasty meteorological events did not prevent an angry mob from assembling outside the Downtown Lyceum, as we saw when our coach pulled up. People had braved the cold temperatures to denounce vigorously that night's interviewee, Mr. James G. Birney, who was slated to discuss abolitionism. Mr. Birney, I understood, had started life as a cotton plantation owner in Alabama. He had owned hundreds of slaves and was not known as a particularly enlightened master.

But in 1833 Mr. Birney had undergone a conversion experience of the sort commonly experienced by many in that era through which God or the holy ghost or maybe Birney's conscience had instructed him to turn his back on his sinful, if lucrative, livelihood. He heeded the advice, sold his lands, freed his slaves, moved to New York, and donated many of the proceeds to the American Anti-Slavery Society, of which he became vice-president. Since that time he lectured tirelessly in promoting immediate manumission of the nation's slave population. For this, he was subjected to abuse from pro-slavery forces in both the South and the North.

The mob heaped insults on everybody who attempted to enter the venue, which made me happy that Bunny stood at my side. It mattered not, for the mob blocked us from approaching the building as effectively as a moat filled with crocodiles. We lingered down the street and watched the spectacle in relative safety, hoping that the mob would soon run out of steam and disperse. Unfortunately for our purposes, the mob grew louder, angrier, and more threatening as the minutes passed, and several fist fights and shoving matches ensued. I wondered where the police were and why none had appeared to restore some semblance of order.

Bunny, despite her *haute couture* wardrobe, was aching to throw off her ankle-length fur coat and dive into the fray. Between her blood-curdling war whoops and her Indian-fighting techniques, I fully expected her to pummel a few faces, gouge some eyes, and kick some crotches, wresting control of the situation from troublemakers on all sides. We shall never know how she would have fared, however, for soon a couple of barefoot boys of about ten years old rounded the corner and ran past us yelling, "FIRE! FIRE! Run for yer lives!"

No one, including Bunny and I, took the alarum seriously at first. The mob continued to verbally assault Mr. Birney and his sponsors and physically assault one another. I stood agog at the sight of my fellow countrymen, ever vigilant about preserving their own liberties, demonstrating against an entire class of Americans who demanded the same consideration.

It quickly became apparent that the boys were not pulling a prank. The smell of burning wood, ever-present in a city where thousands of chimneys bellowed smoke from heating and cooking fires, became more pronounced. Ominously, an orange glow to our southeast grew brighter, and it appeared to be edging closer to us. When a great gust of wind shot flames onto a nearby roof, which quickly became engulfed, the mob quit its quarreling and hastened to disperse. Bunny and I thought it prudent to exit also, and we sped away, attempting to maintain our lead over the stampeding horde behind us.

Once we had run several blocks we paused on Beaver Street to catch our breath and survey the scene. The light of the fire, spreading far and wide over the red sky, illuminated the whole city. The harbor was brilliantly lit, the water a sea of blood. Every ship mast and spar was distinctly visible. Smoke clouds, like dark mountains suddenly rising into the air, were succeeded by towering tongues of flame. I read later that the fire could be seen in Philadelphia from the Independence Hall bell tower. Indeed, crews from that city's fire department ran with their wagons a good distance into the suburbs in search of the fire. Unable to find it, they returned, supposing it raged in some very distant place, never guessing that it could be as far away as New York.

The cacophony attacking my ears frightened me more than the actual fire: the loud and incessant ringing of the city jail's bell at the commencement of the fire; the rattling and clanging of all the city's and suburbs' fire wagons; the terrible roaring of the flames that leaped out of the windows of burning buildings; shards of shattered glass jingling onto the street; the heavy tumbling of the rafters as they successively gave way; the blazing roofs sending up their sheets of fire, then sinking with a frightful crash.

The fearfulness of the night was intensified by the depth of the snow, the tempestuousness of the winds, and the extreme bitterness of the cold. The firefighters' main sources of water to put out the fire, hydrants and rivers, were frozen. Firemen poured boiling water over hydrants to unfreeze them. Gangs of other firemen chopped holes in the river ice and inserted hoses into them. Water to fight the fire was suctioned out of still-functioning hydrants by still other firemen who furiously pumped the levers on their fire wagons. The streams of water instantly became ice particles. Strong gales blew the water back onto the firemen, whose helmets and scarves were no defense against the icicles forming on their eyebrows and beards.

After a quick discussion — "People needum help!" argued Bunny — we decided to return to the fire's rapidly advancing front lines and offer our assistance to firefighters, the general public, and the city's merchants, who stood to lose millions in burned merchandise. In order to do so we had to wade through a thousand spectators, their gaping eyeballs looking pink in the red glare around them. Many gazed in disbelief as the whole of their property burned before their eyes with a rapidity that nothing seemed able to check. So intense was the heat that metal roofs melted and oozed into gutters.

Our first mission of mercy saw us joining a frantic group of merchants and clerks who carried a great quantity of valuable goods into the Old Dutch Church near the Stock Exchange. Bunny and I carried loads of china, linens, and stationery from a dry goods establishment down the block and deposited them among the aisles and pews. It was believed that the church, built of heavy stone, would be impervious to the flames. But the church caught fire, and the whole interior was consumed, including all of the merchandise we had just hauled inside. Once aflame, somebody, I know not whom, climbed the stairs to the organ loft and played Mozart's "Requiem," the last notes that would ever emanate from that instrument so soon to be reduced to ashes.

Seeing our work foiled, we redoubled our efforts in an attempt to save *something*. Upon hearing panicky voices shouting that the Merchants' Exchange was threatened, we rushed to offer our aid. As we ran, we saw that block after block of stately edifices had been consumed and reduced to smoldering ruins. Scenting the air were various burning articles: wood, of course; flesh, unfortunately; and scorched coffee, memorably. Unfortunately, we reached our destination too late and witnessed the Merchants' Exchange, Wall Street's greatest ornament, in its last moment of life as its walls collapsed inward, opening a view all the way to the East River, where flames were busily destroying wharves and ships above the ballast line.

Next, we turned our attention to the Tontine Building, whose roof had caught fire. The Tontine, home of the city's Commodities Exchange, was on the north side of Wall Street; had the flames taken this building, nothing would have saved the upper part of the city, including, conceivably, my own house all the way up in Gramercy Park. Two solitary fire engines, numbers 13 and 46, squirted their feeble streams at the flaming stores opposite with what little water they had managed to obtain. I called their attention to the burning cornice of the Tontine, and I promised to donate one thousand dollars to the Firemen's Fund if they extinguished the blaze. After the Old Dutch Church fiasco, I had decided to contribute money to the cause instead of my arm, leg, and back muscles.

Captaining No. 13 Engine Company was a man who introduced himself as Captain Zophar Mills. Seeing the danger and knowing that the hose would not convey water to the top of the Tontine, Captain Mills directed his men to drag a display case out of a store from across the street and set upon it a rack that ordinarily held liquor barrels, which niftily supported the hose and nozzle in such a way that water could reach the building's shingles. The use of this contraption kept the fire under control, and the upper portion of the city was saved.

Subsequently, a controversy broke out as to what fire company was entitled to my reward for extinguishing the Tontine's blazing roof. While the stores across the street continued to burn, firemen surrounded my person on all sides and tugged at my coattails and sleeves, entreating me to award the money to their firehouses. Bunny, on guard nearby, had seen me jostled long enough and let out a horrific scream, which immediately stopped everyone in his tracks. To the interlopers she pointed and ordered, "Move butts and fight fire." The men obeyed, deploying their spray once again on the stores where it belonged.

I explained to Captain Mills and the other lingering captain that it was true: firemen from both companies had come to assist. But it was Captain Mills' company that had improvised a solution which, in my estimation, was mostly, if not entirely, responsible for extinguishing the fire. Moreover, because the check would be written to the general Fire Department fund, which company received credit was not of much consequence. My listeners seemed satisfied by this explanation, especially Captain Mills, whose company retained boasting rights about the feat.

In addition to the Fire Department's efforts — or perhaps in spite of them — many clerks and their employers had succeeded in requisitioning all of the city's drays and carts and even hackney coaches to convey their goods away from stores and warehouses in danger from the fire. Much merchandise was saved by the incredible exertions going on all around us. We determined that the situation was as under control as it could be, and we opted to walk the mile and a half home. While proceeding up Broadway, we spotted ahead of us near City Hall a woman, obviously of some refined taste, in stylish matching fur hat and coat, whose body quaked from sobbing. We dashed toward her, and I called out, "Miss! May we be of some assistance?"

"My husband is missing! I'm afraid he's lost in the fire," she called back, turning to face us.

O, reader, you can hardly imagine the complex mélange of love, anger, hate, jealousy, lust, exhilaration, relief, and sheer damned joy surging through my breast when I recognized the woman as none other than Rachel, my long lost wife!

"Your husband isn't lost," I declared. "He's right here."

Rachel squinted through the smoky air to make out who had made this bold claim. "Dan? What the shit?!" she exclaimed. Then she fainted dead away, collapsing into a heap on the street.

Bunny and I raced to her side to revive her. I had honestly never seen anybody faint before; I had always believed it was a storybook device authors used to dramatize shock in their characters. So I did not really know how to make her regain consciousness. I took her hand and patted it, like I had seen in plays and motion pictures, while Bunny sprinkled snowflakes onto her face. A face, I noticed, that was more lined than I remembered, due either to the ravages of nineteenth-century life or to the lack of cosmetics beyond a little white powder to disguise her facial imperfections. Still, she looked as though she were sleeping peacefully with a little half smile on her face which I believed, probably vainly, was a response to my presence. In truth, I thought she looked beautiful.

After a few moments, Rachel awoke and stared at Bunny and me with a look of complete and total confusion. "Dan? How is it possible you're here? Is the fire part of some long extended nightmare?" she asked. "Ra-chelll! Wake u-uppp!" she yelled.

"No, you're not dreaming (and thank you for thinking I belong in a nightmare of yours). I persuaded Barry Stompke to send me back in time, too, the day after you and Bilson left. I've been following only a few steps behind you for over a year. But the trail went cold, and I believed you were far away from New York. I'd just about given up on ever finding you."

"Is this, um, your girlfriend?" she groggily asked, referring to Bunny.

"No no no, nothing like that. Let me introduce you to Listening Rabbit. She's my servant. How we joined up is a long story."

"Evidently."

"Call me Bunny," commanded Bunny, taking Rachel's hand into hers and shaking it. Bunny next clasped Rachel's forearm and gently helped her to her feet. Rachel looked off at the fire in the distance, extremely forlorn.

"Bruce and I got separated in the fire. He could be trapped. He could be dead!"

"If only," I whispered under my breath.

"We have to find him!" she admonished.

While the fire continued to burn out of control and claim buildings at a disturbing rate, it seemed that most people had fortunately been able to escape its fury. "I'm sure Bilson will turn up," I reassured Rachel. "The best policy right now is to get inside from the cold and search through the ruins tomorrow. Wouldn't you agree, Bunny?"

Bunny nodded. Before we three began to head in the direction of my town home, we paused for a time to stare at the conflagration, amazed by its sublimity. It was then that I noted one of the Great Fire's many unforgettable sights: the regular and unconscious motion of a church clock ticking steadily onward and striking the hour of two, even as the flames ascended the steeple. I interpreted this as a positive omen that my marriage to Rachel would similarly soldier on despite having suffered the worst possible tests.

As we trudged home, Rachel recounted her recent history. It turns out that she was the selfsame performer that Bunny and I had gone downtown to see earlier in the evening, which completely astonished me.

"You remember Oprah?" she asked. "Well, I stole her formula and put it to work in nineteenth-century New York. It's not exaggerating to say I'm famous these days. I'm surprised you haven't read about me in the newspapers."

"I don't follow the lyceum circuit too closely," I replied. "I came out this evening at Bunny's insistence."

We arrived at my home about forty-five minutes later. I opened my front door and waited for Rachel's reaction to my not-very-humble abode, which rivaled her parents' suburban Chicago showplace in size and opulent decor.

"Goddamn, Dan, you've come up in the world," she said, agog at the luxurious furniture and tasteful appointments.

"I'm glad you appreciate what I've put together here. With a smattering of knowledge about investing in stock funds and 401Ks, plus the advantage of knowing what technologies would survive and thrive in the nineteenth century, I've parlayed a small stake into a modest fortune."

"You've done better in the 1800s than Bruce has done, that's for sure." At this, her eyes welled up with tears; she clutched my arm, buried her face into my shoulder, and sobbed. Between wails she sputtered out a confession for her misdeeds and begged forgiveness.

"Oh, Dan, I was such an idiot! If I had known before I left what I know now, I wouldn't have ever left!" She recounted her travails in great detail, concluding that it would have been safer, securer and altogether more convenient if she had stayed in the twenty-first century. As an afterthought she acknowledged that she had grievously injured me and sorrowfully deprived her parents of her company.

"Even if you knew that everything would turn out uniformly positive, you still shouldn't have left," I scolded. I was fully prepared to accept Rachel back as my wife — the whole point of this time travel exercise was to reclaim her from Bilson, after all — yet I did not wish to appear too eager to reconcile, and, indeed, I wanted her to realize the extent of my anger that her actions had provoked.

She sniffled loudly. Bunny, who looked on with much concern, offered her a perfumed handkerchief. "I'm sorry, I'm sorry. God, I'm such a fuck-up!"

"Now, if you had divorced me first, that would've been a totally different story. I wouldn't have ever followed you. But when you left you were still my wife. You remain my wife today, if truth be told."

"I'm an adulterous asshole!" she cried.

"Yes, you are. I realize it's very late, and we're all exhausted, but can I at least ask why you left? Did you intend to hurt my feelings and injure my pride? Or was that a by-product, and you never considered how I would react? Short answer, please, because we can easily continue this conversation tomorrow."

"The short answer? I thought my life was in a rut, and I wanted something exciting and glamorous to happen. I didn't want to hurt you, but I didn't feel obligated to spare your feelings, either. Our marriage was hurtling toward failure, if you'll recall. At least that's the way I saw it. Becoming a time pilot was my ticket out."

"Fair enough," I responded, wounded by the fact that Rachel had considered my feelings even less before her departure than I had supposed. "Bunny will escort you to the guestroom. She'll find you bedclothes and build you a fire. Goodnight."

"Goodnight, Dan. Again, I'm incredibly sorry. I'm glad we ran into each other tonight so I could finally say that." She followed Bunny up the winding staircase; as she climbed the stairs, she shed her hat and coat. I noticed that she had slimmed down, and, without the benefit of a perm (a hairdresser's technique used in the modern world to curl hair chemically), her hair had changed from frizzy to absolutely straight, as if someone had ironed it. The same feelings I had felt toward her when we originally met were rekindled, warming me from my heart to my unmentionables. While the metaphorical torch I carried for her burned brighter and hotter, firemen continued to battle the literal fire downtown.

Keeping me awake, in addition to jangling nerves caused by the night's excitement, were the sounds of distant explosions, like the discharges of heavy artillery. I later learned that the source of these sounds was New York Militia troops blowing up several buildings which stood directly in the fire's path, leaving it nothing to feed upon. At last, firemen and guardsmen succeeded in stifling the blaze around noon on December 17. The toll on the city was enormous: the fire swept away six-hundred seventy-four buildings, covering seventeen square blocks. It destroyed the district containing most banks, the Stock Exchange, the Post Office, many insurance companies, two churches, several dry goods warehouses, and some of the finest, most ornate buildings in the city. Even as late as the following spring, when workers were clearing away rubble to begin rebuilding, they discovered that many cellars still smoldered.

Who was at fault? Firemen were quoted as blaming the weather. Wells, hoses, hydrants, even the East River had frozen solid. But many city residents blamed the volunteer fire companies. They were unprofessional and disorganized, though full of pride in representing their neighborhoods and aspiring to do their part to save the city. Some fire companies were little better than street gangs; during chance encounters, rival companies would fight each other rather than the flames. The controversy outside of the Tontine Building had indicated first-hand how ill-prepared and incompetent New York City's fire fighters were at managing such a calamity. And yet, to give credit where deserved, many self-sacrificing firemen did their duty — did it, too, under the most adverse circumstances.

Next morning, Rachel and I dined in my sunroom, which normally overlooked Gramercy Park, but the view on this morning was blocked by frosted-over windows. Both of us smelled prominently of smoke, and in her morning ablutions Rachel had overlooked some soot streaking her left cheek. Bunny and Lizzie served us bacon, eggs and toast. Never one to obey her religion's dietary laws, Rachel gobbled down the bacon and asked for a second helping. While Lizzie retrieved more bacon, Bunny whispered in my ear that she had sprinkled a special ingredient on our eggs that promoted affectionate feelings. As Rachel shoveled eggs into her mouth, Bunny stood beside the breakfast table, her face beaming. Knowing that Rachel ate with a singular intensity when feeling anxious, I worried that her anxiety would trump the effects of any magic potion that Bunny had mixed.

After some small talk about my home's décor, the weather, our food, &c, I led our conversation in a more serious direction. "I've gone to a lot of trouble and not insignificant expense to track you down. But, surprisingly, I never prepared a speech to deliver once I found you."

"Well, I never expected you to show up, so I definitely don't know what to say," said Rachel, whose normally frank gaze lowered from my face to her lap.

"Suffice it to say I still love you, despite all, and I hope you'll join our little household here as my once and future wife."

"Dan, I..."

"Back in the twenty-first century, Bilson was a rousing success. He was internationally known for his scientific knowledge, and he left behind a hero's reputation. However, through my travels I've learned he's fallen on hard times. He's been a failure at everything he's tried."

"He's got a pretty successful business making aspirin right now..."

"I realize my status in the century we left was lowly. I could never compete with Bilson in terms of talents or brio."

"Dan, don't..."

"As you've observed, I've 'come up in the world.' I've survived a number of travails..."

"Me, too!"

"...yet I've found through all of them I possess a unique combination of traits enabling me to thrive in the century where we presently find ourselves. Education at a mediocre college and employment at a middling-level job aren't enough to excel in the twenty-first century, but they're a perfect fit for the nineteenth."

"Dan, please..."

"Your Bilson, with all his academic degrees and honors, is just too damn smart for 1835. His intelligence has bred arrogance, which is only one step away from recklessness."

"I agree completely. I came to that same conclusion six or eight months ago..."

"Then, perhaps, there's a slim chance you'll consider returning to me and becoming my wife once again, since your mind has changed about Bilson and his prospects?"

"Whoa, Nelly! We just ran into each other for the first time in over a year. (Or is it a hundred and sixty-five years?) Twenty-four hours ago I never expected you to show up in a million years. A billion years."

"You should know by now that nothing's outside the realm of possibility," I said. "Look at you, leaving the house without your hair permed."

Rachel chuckled at my joke. Even during the worst moments in our former life together, when she stared icily at me, enraged by my injurious remarks, she always warmed to my use of humor. "Look, I'll think about it. Give me some time to sort things out in my head. Your appearance out of nowhere has been a huge shock to me."

"That's all I can ask, that you give my proposal serious thought. Now, let's escort you home."

"What about Bruce?" she asked.

"Unless he's out searching for you, I'm guessing we'll find him at your house, waiting for you to come home."

"Given all the crap I went through last night, he'd *better* be out searching for me. Or else it's *definitely* over between us."

I was quite pleased to hear this, for it sounded like I had gained a leg up on Bilson. I crossed my fingers that we would find him at home, fiddling in his lab while the city yet burned, disregarding Rachel's fate, and undermining his cause still further.

Chapter Fifteen

January 28, 1836

Diary, you won't believe what's happened during the last month-and-a-half. I know, I know, I've started virtually every entry in this diary with a "Can you believe it?" tone. But this tops everything.

My husband, the real one, Dan, showed up out of nowhere! What's more, he arrived as my rescuer from the big-ass fire last month!

While running from the fire with a thousand other panicky people, I lost track of Bruce. Or should I say he lost track of me? Whatever, I was totally lost without him. Then, suddenly, the smoke from the fire divided like curtains, and Dan emerged like some gallant knight ready to scoop me up onto his horse.

Unable to handle the stress of the fire and the shock of seeing Dan, my brain shut down. For the very first time in my life, I fainted. When I came to, he was still there hovering over me, and it began to sink in that I wasn't dreaming.

I ended up staying over at Dan's awesome townhouse (in a separate bed — I'm not that shameless, diary). Considering the city was up for grabs, we figured this was the safest option.

Needless to say, I couldn't sleep all night, despite the roaring fire and cozy feather down comforter. I spent all night going over in my head the triumphs and setbacks that had led me to this particular point in space-time, Dan's spare bedroom.

The next morning Dan and his servant, a transvestite Indian named Bunny, escorted me home. Smoke still rose from the ruins downtown, but, thankfully, the fire stopped far short of my neighborhood.

I had plenty to mull as we walked. During breakfast in his informal dining room (his house featured a formal dining room, too), Dan made it known that he wanted us to get back together. His new station in life made the prospect very tempting.

And it's true: I was plenty sick of Bruce by then. Every step he had taken since 1833 was another step in deep shit. But I wasn't sure if I was ready to dump him just yet. We had weathered number of crises together, after all.

I didn't know what to expect when I arrived home. I didn't even truly know if Bruce was alive or dead. All I knew was that we had gotten separated during the fire, and it didn't appear that he had doubled back to find me.

When we approached my front door, we heard a commotion coming from the backyard. Dan and Bunny took off around the house, and I followed. Another typical Bruce scenario was playing out: two massive dockworker types were beating him up.

"You two!" shouted Dan. "Unhand that man!"

"Fuck off!" yelled one, continuing to punch Bruce's face.

"This don't concern you, mister," yelled the other, who was busy kicking Bruce's midsection.

"Him said stop!" shouted Bunny.

"Butt out. Or you'll be next, you Indian cunt!" said the first attacker.

Bunny was about to jump into the fray. But Dan grabbed his/her shoulder and calmly said, "Allow me." Then he pulled out a whip from under his cloak, which he twirled above his head a few times and then let fly, knocking the first attacker clean off his feet.

While he writhed around on the ground in pain, cussing out Dan something fierce, Dan took aim at the second attacker, and with another whip-crack knocked him over, too. Seeing Dan get ready to mete out more punishment, both men hastily picked themselves up and stumbled off, clutching their stinging asses.

I couldn't believe what I had just seen. Dan had somehow become an expert with a whip. "Whoa!" I said, genuinely impressed. "Where did you pick that up?"

"I had to figure out some activity to kill time without radio or television. My whip has come in handy on several occasions now."

"I'll bet."

Meantime, Bruce struggled to his feet. Both of his eyes were blackened, and he had a fat lip. He was covered in snow and rocks and straw. He looked horrible. He did a double and then a triple take when he noticed who his rescuer was.

"My god," he said. "Dan Connor. Let me guess. Barry Stompke put you up to this."

"I decided on my own to track you two down. Stompke was just the ferryman."

"I suppose you're — oof! — here — ouch! — to get your revenge and make our lives miserable." Potentially broken ribs made speaking difficult for Bruce.

"From what I've learned in the past year, you've done plenty all by yourself to accomplish that objective. You don't need help from me."

"What can I say? The people and the environment in this stupid century haven't cooperated."

There it was: the statement that pushed old Rachel into the Dan column permanently. It showed me that Bruce, despite all of his intelligence and education, would never learn his lesson.

Bunny helped Bruce to his bed inside, where he lay down and would spend a week recovering. "Why were those guys waling on you anyway?" I asked while serving him a cup of tea containing a big dose of his aspirin powder.

"They claimed my formula — groan! — nearly caused their brother to die from stomach bleeding. I guess — ow! — I'll have to work on its — yowch! — buffering properties."

A few days later I broke the news to Bruce that I was moving back in with Dan. As a sort of consolation prize, I offered to let him stay in my house rent-free until he could earn a solid living from his aspirin business.

Although I've cast my lot with Dan, we have lots of issues to work through. He doesn't trust me to remain true to him, and I'm afraid he'll prey on my feelings of guilt to take advantage of me.

The fact that we haven't made love since being reunited is symptomatic of our mutual wariness. We're like two animals crossing paths in a forest, sniffing out each other's intentions from a distance.

I expect the sex issue to eventually resolve itself, along with all of our other marital issues. We had a fantastic sex life before we became alienated, and I can't wait to resume it. I'm optimistic, most especially, because living under our very roof is a talented marriage counselor!

Bunny grew up under the tutelage of a medicine man, Thunder Wind, who, before she met Dan, was molding her into a kind of tribal arbitration expert.

It seems that berdaches, the Indian name for transvestites, are tapped to settle interpersonal differences among their fellow tribe members. They see right through problems and come up with sensible solutions.

Sometimes we sit down with her in formal sessions. In these she reinforces our belief that we belong together. She sees the same color glow surrounding each of us, which means we're thoroughly compatible.

She doesn't call it that, but apparently there's an aura around every individual. It varies in color from person to person, ranging from white to purple.

"What about black?" I asked one time.

"Black mean dead," Bunny answered.

Dan's and my glow is blue. It works best when you have the same color glow as your spouse. Also, there are several workable combinations and a bunch of unworkable ones. Bunny's glow is yellow, she said, which also goes well with blue.

While our appointments go a long way in supporting the general underpinnings of our marriage, they don't solve our day-to-day conflicts. For these we run downstairs to the kitchen to plead our cases before Bunny like baseball players arguing with an umpire about an out.

The subject of Bruce is a sticking point with us. I'm keeping him on, at least for now, as a commercial sponsor of my shows. Dan always objects when Bruce and I meet to hash out some business point. He wonders if our lunches and coffees will lead to a resumption of our affair.

I'm always complaining about Dan's pot smoking. He and Bunny, who grows it out in Gramercy Park, along with corn and beans, smoke it pretty often. I know it's reasonably harmless, but watching them partake stirs up my appetite for coke.

We'll make it over these hurdles, I'm sure, with Bunny's help and the passage of time.

The other big news in my life: I'm the toast of the town! And I'm making money at a rate that my father and brothers, who always thought of me as a fuck-up, would envy the shit out of.

My regular venue, the Downtown Lyceum, burned down in the fire. Now I'm appearing once a week at the Bowery Theatre. It's a much larger auditorium that attracts a bigger, more diverse audience base.

The newspapers have sung my praises after each of my nineteen outings thus far. And the audience has grown every time. They're numbering in the high hundreds now. In the 19th century people actually read newspapers, unlike in the 21st. When the press plugs my show, people buy tickets.

It obviously helps that I choose my guests carefully. Yes, I invite controversial guests, but they're knowledgeable, credible people saying things about feminism or abolitionism or medicine that should be heard.

I scour the penny papers hunting for potential invitees. This is the most tedious part of the process. The newspapers publish these incredibly long articles that have to be read word-for-word to ensure the subject knows their stuff.

Usually what happens is after reading, like, 12,000 words, I'll discover they're full of crap. Next!!!

Then there are those people who come out of the woodwork with the kookiest notions you've ever heard. Mesmerists and spiritualists (frauds), phrenologists and water curers (idiots) and, my least favorite group, religious revivalists (hypocrites).

I was so impressed with Bunny's relationship expertise that I booked her on my show. Bunny's date was last Monday.

After I introduced her and described her Potawatomi upbringing back in Illinois, I focused particularly on this aura business. Our exchange went something like this:

"Bunny. You've told my husband Dan and me that you sense a glow surrounding everyone. Tell the audience more about this."

"All people born with spirit glow," she said. "Baby in papoose glow."

"And the glow you see can vary in color?"

"Whole set of colors. Pink, red, orange, yellow, green, blue, purple. Whole rainbow."

"Do the colors mean anything? I mean, you've told me that my glow is blue. What does that say about me?"

"You strong woman. Believe in yourself. Maybe like whiskey too much."

"You've sure got me nailed! What about you? I understand that your glow is yellow. What does that signify?"

"Strong arms and back. Feel things deep. Learn medicine easy."

"You've also told me that certain colors go better with some colors than others. Can you tell the audience more about that?"

"Blue and yellow go good. White and purple go good. Green and orange go good."

"What about colors that don't go so well together?"

"Red and pink go bad. Yellow and orange go bad. Blue and purple go real bad."

"How is it that you can see the glow around people? I mean, I'm looking straight at you, and I don't see any glow."

"Not look hard enough."

I stared exaggeratedly at Bunny for the audience's benefit. "I still don't see anything," I said finally. A few people snickered.

"Not look hard enough."

"How can you see a person's glow? Did your training with Thunder Wind, the medicine man, teach you?"

"Thunder Wind make me look hard."

Bunny went on to explain that when we choose our friends and lovers, we all sense their glows, even if we don't perceive them visually. We process this information one of two ways.

Either we do the healthy thing and pick someone with an aura that is the same as ours or contrasts with ours. This bodes well for a successful relationship.

Or we do the unhealthy thing and pick someone whose aura color is bad for us. We may be attracted to them precisely *because* they're bad. They're charismatic alcoholics or womanizers or swindlers.

A third possibility: we may want to do the healthy thing, but we're fooled into doing the unhealthy thing, because we're somehow comfortable with it. Hence, my relationship with Bruce, who has the same unattractive egomaniacal qualities as my father.

Bruce's glow is purple, according to Bunny.

My conversation with Bunny ended on a properly uplifting note. I'm glad, because my audience, which is made up of about ninety percent women, generally has a rough time of it and needs an optimistic message to get through a day that usually involves hard work, screaming kids and obtuse husbands.

After the show, audience members mobbed Bunny, seeking information about their glow and how their personal situation is affected by it.

Overwhelmed by the response, Bunny had them write down their names and streets and promised to call on each and every one and hold a personal interview. I dare say Bunny has a lucrative career ahead of her.

My calendar is booked solid for the next six months. Upcoming guests include my hero Maria Child (March) and a young freethinker named John Humphrey Noyes (July).

I'm really looking forward to the latter. He's a young seminarian who's obviously been reading scripture differently than the rest of us. He's going to talk about some of his unorthodox ideas regarding property and marriage.

In addition to pushing the benefits of a communistic, egalitarian society, he preaches the doctrine of "complex marriage" — in other words free love. Everybody can have sex with everybody else without guilt or consequences (other than pregnancy).

But pregnancy is okay. Couples have no direct responsibility for the output of their input, because children should be raised in common. He argues that this is the best way to free women from the marriage trap.

John really ought to shake up all the respectable middle-class and upper-class ladies that make up the bulk of my audience. They'll be peeing in their seats from shock. But it'll be good for them to hear this stuff, I have no doubt.

When we read *The Great Gatsby* in modern lit class in college, we studied the life and times of F. Scott Fitzgerald to gain a little perspective on the novel. Fitzgerald was a total boozehound stuck in a dysfunctional marriage, sort of like me before I left the 21st century.

One of his famous quotes that we had to write a midterm exam on goes like this: "There are no second acts in American lives." I remember defending this statement, mainly because that's what the professor wanted.

In my little blue exam booklet I dutifully wrote about the American emphasis on youth and climbing the socioeconomic ladder and succeeding early in life.

Maybe I was too young and callow, but at the time I ignored the sad part of this quote that implies you're a failure if your life doesn't follow this pattern. At 19 or 20 I had every expectation of being successful.

Unfortunately, that didn't happen for me, or Dan either, during the first act of our lives. It's happening in the second act, however. We're living proof that Fitzgerald didn't know what he was talking about. Just because *he* flamed out early doesn't mean we *all* have to.

I'm so proud of Dan and me, and Bunny, too. We emerged from the fire together, and we're thriving.

Epilogue

Rachel, Bunny, and I have happily spent the remainder of our lives together. We have outlived the Panic of 1837, the Mexican War, Bleeding Kansas, the War Between the States, Lincoln's Assassination, Radical Republicanism, Southern Reconstruction, Grant's Corruption, and the Hayes-Tilden Compromise of 1876. (Much as he tried, Sam Tilden could not alter the march of history.) Now, in 1882, we are living in an era of excess that the best-selling author Samuel Clemens has jokingly labeled "The Great Barbecue." I suppose that Rachel and I are guilty of contributing to the orgy of consumption occurring at present. After the war we moved from New York City to a mansion overlooking the Hudson River near Tarrytown, New York. Built in the prevailing Victorian style, our home contains eighteen rooms, including a crystal-chandelier-swagged ballroom, a glass-enclosed arboretum, and a fully equipped telegraph office.

Bunny, who still reigns over our household staff, lives on the property in a separate structure built to resemble a log house remembered from her Potawatomi youth. It is one of the few vestiges of her days living as a squaw on the Illinois prairie. These days, she is an extremely feisty old lady who is enjoying her retirement after having single-handedly invented the psychotherapy industry. She has traveled throughout most of the United States and Europe instructing aspiring therapists in the ancient ways of her medicine man, Thunder Wind.

Rachel, likewise, has traveled the globe to present her "talk show" to an audience numbering in the hundreds of thousands. During her career she has interviewed literary lights Emerson, Dickens, and Longfellow; educators Bronson Alcott and Margaret Fuller; military generals Zachary Taylor and William Tecumseh Sherman; ladies' suffragists Elizabeth Cady Stanton and Susan B. Anthony; former slaves Frederick Douglass and Sojourner Truth; and more European dukes, duchesses, barons, and baronesses than one can possibly count. She, too, is retired and tends the arboretum's exotic trees and flowers as a hobby.

During Bunny and Rachel's forays abroad, I usually stayed home, oversaw my investments, and visited old friends like Sam Tilden. Alas, my dear friend and mentor, Albert Gallatin, passed away over thirty years ago. He is buried in lower Manhattan near the school he founded, New York University, where Bunny continues on the faculty as a professor emerita. We lost track of Bruce Bilson during the 1850s, when he sailed off to San Francisco, California. He had become a reasonably successful purveyor of patent medicines, but he decided to abandon this business and seek new opportunities in the West.

I generally enjoy the life of a country squire. Even at the age of seventy-three, I walk approximately five miles per day through the hills and woodlands of the Lower Hudson Valley. Also, Rachel and I, and sometimes Bunny, ride the train into Manhattan to eat a meal at Delmonico's and afterward see a play or listen to symphonic music. We simply walk down the gravel path to the train tracks along the river bank and catch a train that stops when I prearrange it via telegraph with the rail line's dispatcher in Poughkeepsie. Such is the benefit of being a major stockholder in railroads.

Our neighbors are for the most part agreeable. To the south, descendants of Washington Irving live on his old Sunnyside Estate. They are friendly people, full of conviviality. The neighbor to the north is another story. Not long ago the robber-baron Jay Gould acquired the Lyndhurst Estate as his summer home. Such an architectural monstrosity — a sprawling, thoroughly obnoxious Gothic Revival castle straight out of Mary Shelley's *Frankenstein* — comprises appropriate living quarters for a monster such as Gould. His quiet, unassuming nature betrays the heartless, ruthless, cutthroat manner in which he does business.

Crossing both our properties is the Croton Aqueduct, which yearly carries millions of gallons of drinking water into New York City from Croton Lake. Similar to his notorious plot to corner the gold market in 1869, Gould attempted to hold the water for ransom a few months ago. Out walking one day, I ran across a team of engineers and workers digging up the wide underground pipe behind his home. When I queried the foreman about their purpose, he explained that they intended to install a shutoff valve at Gould's direction. I gleaned immediately what this meant for the city below us and demanded that they cease. The foreman ignored me, and his men closed in on me menacingly, with shovels cocked.

Knowing that Gould's army of lawyers eats even substantial men like me for breakfast, I decided a legal assault would not be prudent. Instead, I asked Bunny to take matters into her worthy hands. One night, using the techniques of stalking prey that she had observed as a child, she sneaked past Gould's bodyguards and entered his bedroom, where she threatened to kick his arse all the way to the Pacific Ocean if he continued to tamper with the city's water supply. The next day the workmen had vanished, and the hole they had dug was covered up. Bunny always tries talking sense to people first, but, even now in her golden years, she is capable of applying a good licking when the situation calls for it. She still occasionally smacks me on the forehead to make me stop ranting about this or that sin Rachel has committed.

Although I believe this account of my life should stand alone as an instructive example to others, I am aware that readers will wish me to offer some concluding advice. There are two things I should mention. First, I agree with Rachel when she states in the previous chapter that people should never accept that Fate has locked them into a single path in life. I advise people to believe that they have the power to alter the course of their lives. Yes, it may be argued that it is easy to succeed when one is advantaged with twenty-first-century knowledge in the nineteenth century. Yet, I would argue that all Americans have the capacity to reinvent themselves. Witness the large numbers of ordinary individuals who have pulled up stakes in the East and migrated westward. Or consider the many thousands who have left behind the shores of Europe to seek their fortunes in the New World.

Second, I advise all of the world's leaders to keep a tight rein on German ambitions. Germans will attempt to wreak serious political havoc twice in the twentieth century. If unchecked, this will lead to widespread death and destruction. When a minor archduke is assassinated in Sarajevo in 1914, let diplomacy solve the crisis that will arise. And when a formerly undistinguished Austrian corporal with a silly little moustache attains power in the 1930s, fight his territorial annexations tooth and nail.

Books Available from Gival Press

Fiction and Nonfiction

Boys, Lost & Found: Stories by Charles Casillo

ISBN 13: 978-1-928589-33-4, $20.00

Finalist for the 2007 ForeWord Magazine's Book Award for Gay/ Lesbian Fiction / Runner up for the 2006 DIY Book Festival Award for Compilations/Anthologies

"...fascinating, often funny...a safari through the perils and joys of gay life."

—Edward Field

The Canninbal of Guadalajara by David Winner

ISBN 13: 978-1-928389-50-1, $20.00

Winner of the Gival Press Novel Award

"...a devilishly delicious and disorienting novel. Food, sex, ghastly travel experiences, tantrums, Cannibal has it all, along with one of the most peculiar versions of the family triad in literary years."

—Joy Williams, a Pulitzer finalist, received the Strauss Living Award from the American Academy of Arts and Letters

A Change of Heart by David Garrett Izzo

ISBN 13: 978-1-928589-18-1, $20.00

A historical novel about Aldous Huxley and his circle

"astonishingly alive and accurate."

—Roger Lathbury, George Mason University

Dead Time / Tiempo muerto by Carlos Rubio

ISBN 13: 979-1-928589-17-4, $21.00

Winner of the 2003 Silver Award for Translation, ForeWord Magazine's Book of the Year ~ A bilingual (English/ Spanish) novel that captures a tale of love and hate, passion and revenge.

Dreams and Other Ailments / Sueños y otros achaques

by Teresa Bevin

ISBN 13: 978-1-92-8589-13-6, $21.00

Winner of the 2001 Bronze Award for Translation, ForeWord Magazine's Book of the Year — A bilingual (English/ Spanish) account of the Latino experience in the USA, filled with humor and hope.

The Gay Herman Melville Reader edited by Ken Schellenberg

ISBN 13: 978-1-928589-19-8, $16.00

A superb selection of Melville's homoerotic work, with short commentary.

An Interdisciplinary Introduction to Women's Studies edited by Brianne Friel & Robert L. Giron

ISBN 13: 978-1-928589-29-7, $25.00

Winner of the 2005 DIY Book Festival Award for Compilations/ Anthologies. A succinct collection of articles for the college student on a variety of topics.

The Last Day of Paradise by Kiki Denis

ISBN 13: 978-1-928589-32-7, $20.00

Winner of the 2005 Gival Press Novel Award / Honorary Mention at the 2007 Hollywood Book Festival — This debut novel "...is a slippery in-your-face accelerated rush of sex, hokum, and Greek family life."

—Richard Peabody, editor of *Mondo Barbie*

Literatures of the African Diaspora by Yemi D. Ogunyemi

ISBN 13: 978-1-928589-22-8, $20.00

An important study of the influences in literatures of the world.

Lockjaw: Collected Appalachian Stories by Holly Farris

ISBN 13: 978-1-928589-38-9, $20.00

Finalist for the 2008 Eric Hoffler Award for Culture / Finalist for the 2007 Lambda Literary Award for Lesbian Debut Fiction

"*Lockjaw* sings with all the power of Appalachian storytelling—inventive language, unforgettable voices, narratives that take surprise hairpin turns—without ever romanticizing the region or leaning on stereotypes. Refreshing and passionate, these are stories of unexpected gestures, some brutal, some full of grace, and almost all acts of secret love. A strong and moving collection!"

—Ann Pancake, author of *Given Ground*

Maximus in Catland by David Garrett Izzo

ISBN 13: 978-1-92-8589-34-1, $20.00

"...*Maximus in Catland* has all the necessary ingredients for a successful fairy tale: good and evil, unrequited love and loving loyalty, heroism and ancient wisdom...."

—Jenny Ivor, author of *Rambles*

Middlebrow Annoyances: American Drama in the 21st Century
by Myles Weber

ISBN 13: 978-1-928589-20-4, $20.00

Current essays on the American theatre scene.

Second Acts by Tim W. Brown

ISBN 13: 978-1-928589-51-8, $20.00

"Really clicking, *Second Acts*, is a picaresque, sci-fi/western, such as Verne or Welles might have penned it, but with tongue planted firmly in cheek. Tim W. Brown's tale of a husband's search for his fugitive wife takes readers on a whirlwind tour of America, circa 1830. In subverting history Brown's tale celebrates it, with a scholar's eye for authentic details and at a pacing so swift the pages give off a nice breeze."
—Peter Selgin, author of *Life Goes to the Movies*

Secret Memories / Recuerdos secretos by Carlos Rubio

ISBN 13: 978-1-928589-27-3, $21.00

Finalist for the 2005 ForeWord Magazine's Book of the Year Award for Translations. This bilingual (English/Spanish) novel adeptly pulls the reader into the world of the narrator who is vulnerable.

The Smoke Week: Sept. 11-21, 2001 by Ellis Avery

ISBN 13: 978-1-928589-24-2, $15.00

2004 Writer's Notes Magazine Book Award—Notable for Culture / Winner of the Ohionana Library Walter Rumsey Marvin Award. "Here is Witness. Here is Testimony."
—Maxine Hong Kingston, author of *The Fifth Book of Peace*

The Spanish Teacher by Barbara de la Cuesta

ISBN 13: 978-1-92858937-2, $20.00

Winner of the 2006 Gival Press Novel Award / Finalist for the 2007 ForeWord Magazine's Book of the Year / Award for Fiction-General / Honorable Mention for the 2007 London Book Festival. "…De la Cuesta's novel maintains an accumulating power which holds onto a reader's attention not only through the forceful figure of Ordóñez, but by demonstrating acutely how ordinary lives are impacted by the underlying social and political landscape. Compelling reading."
—Tom Tolnay, publisher, Birch Brook Press and author of *Selling America* and *This is the Forest Primeval*

That Demon Life
by Lowell Mick White
ISBN 13: 978-1-928589-47-1, $21.00
Winner of the 2008 Gival Press Novel Award & Finalist for the 2009 National / Best Book Award for Fiction
"That Demon Life is a hoot, a virtuoso tale by a master story teller."
—Larry Heinermann, author of Paco's Story, winner of the National Book Award

Tina Springs into Summer / Tina se lanza al verano
by Teresa Bevin
ISBN 13: 978-1-928589-28-0, $21.00
2006 Writer's Notes Magazine Book Award—Notable for Young Adult Literature. A bilingual (English/Spanish) compelling story of a youngster from a multi-cultural urban setting and her urgency to fit in.

A Tomb on the Periphery by John Domini
ISBN 13: 978-1-928589-40-2, $20.00
Finalist for the Gival Press Novel Award. This novel a mix of crime, ghost story and portrait of the protagonist continues Domini's tales in contemporary Southern Italy, in the manner of his last novel *Earthquake I.D.*

Twelve Rivers of the Body by Elizabeth Oness
ISBN 13: 978-1-928589-44-0, $20.00
Winner of the 2007 Gival Press Novel Award
"*Twelve Rivers of the Body* lyrically evokes downtown Washington, DC in the 1980s, before the real estate boom, before gentrification, as the city limped from one crisis to another—crack addiction, AIDS, a crumbling infrastructure. This beautifully evoked novel traces Elena's imperfect struggle, like her adopted city's, to find wholeness and healing."
—Kim Roberts, author of *The Kimnama*

For a complete list of titles, visit: *www.givalpress.com*.
Books available via Ingram, the Internet, and other outlets.
Or Write:
Gival Press, LLC
PO Box 3812
Arlington, VA 22203
703.351.0079

Made in the USA
Charleston, SC
16 September 2010